Praise for the Novels of Rosalind Noonan

IN A HEARTBEAT

"Complex, intriguing characters and an intensely emotional plot make *In a Heartbeat* compelling." —*RT Book Reviews*

ONE SEPTEMBER MORNING

"Written with great insight into military families and the constant struggle between supporting the troops but not the war, Noonan delivers a fast-paced, character-driven tale with a touch of mystery." —*Publishers Weekly*

"Noonan creates a unique thriller that is anti–Iraq War and pro-solider, a novel that focuses on the toll war takes on returning soldiers and civilians whose loved ones won't be coming home." —*Booklist*

"Reminiscent of Jodi Picoult's kind of tale . . . it's a keeper!"
—Lisa Jackson, *New York Times* bestselling author

"Gripping and emotional, the story could not be more timely."
—*RT Book Reviews*

"Carefully plotted, well-paced, and taut, this novel builds to a stunning conclusion." —*The Romance Readers Connection*

"This is an intense and emotional story that readers are sure to enjoy. Grab a hankie; you will need one for *One September Morning*." —*Romance Reviews Today*

Books by Rosalind Noonan

ONE SEPTEMBER MORNING

IN A HEARTBEAT

THE DAUGHTER SHE USED TO BE

ALL SHE EVER WANTED

Published by Kensington Publishing Corporation

ALL
SHE EVER
WANTED

ROSALIND
NOONAN

KENSINGTON BOOKS
www.kensingtonbooks.com

KENSINGTON BOOKS are published by

Kensington Publishing Corp.
119 West 40th Street
New York, NY 10018

All Kensington titles, imprints, and distributed lines are available at special quantity discounts for bulk purchases for sales promotion, premiums, fund-raising, and educational or institutional use.

Special book excerpts or customized printings can also be created to fit specific needs. For details, write or phone the office of the Kensington Special Sales Manager: Kensington Publishing Corp., 119 West 40th Street, New York, NY 10018. Attn. Special Sales Department. Phone: 1-800-221-2647.

Kensington and the K logo Reg. U.S. Pat. & TM Off.

ISBN-13: 978-0-7582-7498-4
ISBN-10: 0-7582-7498-X

First Kensington Trade Paperback Printing: January 2013
10 9 8 7 6 5 4 3 2

Printed in the United States of America

For my sisters.

You share your gifts
and work your magic
to make things right for everyone else.
I'm so happy you're my sisters.

PART 1

Chapter 1

The first time Chelsea Maynard saved a person's life, she was seven years old. The sunny day marked her extended family's Easter celebration, an occasion for all the cousins to gather, nibble on chocolate bunnies, and hunt for Easter eggs over and over again. Chelsea prided herself on being a good finder of lost things. She was a lot better at it than her male cousins, who were always whining for Mom to help them. The boys had decided to stage the next egg hunt down by the creek on her grandparents' property, and Chelsea had gone along with the idea until it had all dwindled into a hunt for toads and lizards and water snakes. Boy stuff.

She jiggled her stash of candy eggs in her basket as she climbed back up to the house. There was no way she would eat them, but they were a sign of status nonetheless.

She was humming a song about a rabbit when a cry peeled from up the hill. A car was coming down the driveway, rolling faster and faster down the straight lane.

With the glare on the windows, she couldn't see who was driving, but she started running like the wind. She had to get to the turnaround first.

That driver wasn't going to see the little cousins riding their Big Wheels around and around on the flat part of the driveway.

Chelsea dropped her basket and ran.

When she looked back on that day, she remembered a pulse pounding in her ears and a weird energy that made her feel like she was zooming over the land. She made it to the little ones, snatched Katie from her pink tricycle where she sat probing the pavement with a stick, and yelled at Max to get over in the trees.

Just as they dove into the ferns under the tall pines, the car swooshed down to the turnaround. Like a beast, it groaned and sparked as it bottomed out on the pavement and lurched forward, crunching over Katie's bicycle.

Such a sickening sound.

After the car had rolled to a stop with two wheels hanging over the pavement and buried in dirt, there was a moment of quiet. As if the earth has stopped spinning.

Chelsea looked down at Kate and Max, all safe, and hugged them close. She didn't know why she was shaking and she couldn't get that horrible crunching sound out of her head.

"Let me go!" Max complained. "You're squeezing the stuffing out of me."

Afterward, Easter dinner had been punctuated by tears and grateful prayer, laughter and endless recollections of who saw what from where. Dad and the uncles had spent an hour hoisting the car out of the dirt, using Grandpa's riding mower to give it a good pull. Uncle Steve was now parked at the bottom of the hill, and he planned to get his brakes checked first thing tomorrow.

"I am really sorry," he kept saying, but no matter how much he apologized, Aunt Paige was still mad at him.

"Everyone is fine," Mom pointed out. "All safe."

Chelsea had known Mom would say that.

"You're a hero, Chelsea." Dad beamed as he handed her an extra-big piece of Grandma's Easter cake with coconut dyed green to make a nest for the candy eggs.

She had giggled, the image of that smashed tricycle pushed from her mind by all the fuss. So much attention for something anyone would have done. Batman was a hero; she was just a girl glad to have extra cake.

* * *

A decade later, it happened again, with far less drama and a smaller audience. Chelsea had come home after school to find her mother handing out snacks to her kids. Judith Maynard ran a home day care center at their house, which Chelsea secretly enjoyed. As the youngest child, she had hated watching her older sisters leave the house for college and jobs and life. The day care meant having lots of kids around—always.

While her mother took one of the kids to the sink to wash off some yogurt, Chelsea circled their little table, hoping to grab some snacks for herself. One of the kids started to get up from the table, looking confused.

"You're supposed to stay in your seat, Jason," a little girl at the table told him.

The boy seemed confused. He bumped into the table, and then swung toward Chelsea.

"Are you okay?" she asked.

When he didn't answer, she scanned the food on the table. Crackers and mini-carrots.

"Are you choking?"

When she saw the faint blue tint around his panicked lips, she quickly knelt behind him and placed her fist to his belly— just above the navel.

Two pushes, and it was out—a nubby piece of carrot.

By that time, Judith had rushed over from the sink. She sank down in front of the kid to touch his face and smooth back his hair.

"Oh, dear Lord! Jason, are you all right?"

"It hurt my throat," he whimpered. "The carrot did it."

"I'll bet. You poor thing." Mom hugged him close. "You'll be fine. You just need to chew your food before you swallow."

Patting Jason's back, Mom looked up at Chelsea and mouthed, "Thank you!"

"Sure," she said, still stunned. No longer hungry, and definitely not in the mood for carrots.

* * *

Today, Chelsea was going for save number three, and she wasn't thinking about her high school softball career.

Today, she needed to save herself.

All through the morning, hope had pulled her ahead, a warm orange light beckoning her across this valley of endless winter. Chelsea had kept her eye on the prize from the minute she slid from her warm bed that morning to begin the mind-numbing routine of motherhood. The predawn alarm of Annabelle's whimper. The cold wood floor underfoot. The soggy diaper. The clang of the radiator in the bathroom. The holding pattern of exhaustion as she sat with the baby in her arms, waiting for Annabelle to finish nursing.

Hurry up and wait. Hurry up and wait.

Each day she couldn't wait for the relief of sundown. Each night a sour gloom convinced her that the sun would never rise, and when it did she dragged herself from bed wondering how she was going to survive another maddening day of servitude to the schedule. "Baby jail," as her older sister called it. Melanie always said it with a smile, but Chelsea thought it was dead-on, except that jail implied that there were other inmates to commiserate with. Here, in the house that Chelsea had once considered her dream home, she spent most days alone with her baby, alone with her dark thoughts.

Solitary confinement.

But today, she was going to peel away the gloom and lift herself from the bed of clouds. Today, she was being proactive, facing her problem . . . going for it.

She was going to get help from her doctor.

Annabelle had dozed off, much to Chelsea's relief. The only good baby was a sleeping baby. She shifted the weight of the baby in her arms, pulled her shirt closed, and nestled into the corner of the sofa as the gentle voices from the television washed over her. The movement jostled Annie's little pink mouth open, sending milk dribbling from the crescent of her lips. Chelsea caught it with a soft diaper and dabbed it away. Got to ward off the stains for her appointment with Dr. Volmer. This wasn't one of those sweatpants-and-nightgown sort of days.

Today she had showered and dressed with time to spare.

Annie sucked at the air, and then dozed off again.

Such a sweet baby. Her downy hair clung to the flannel receiving blanket, a halo around her little head. Her hair was so transparent, it was almost invisible. In stark light Annabelle still resembled a cute little old man. "Lady Baldy," as Leo sometimes called her. Then he would soften the insult by nudging her belly and teasing that his hair was starting to thin, too. Leo had a way of talking to their baby that made it seem as if they had a dialogue going.

Not me.

Chelsea had no words for Annabelle.

Somewhere in her logical mind, Chelsea knew she had a good baby. But since the day Annabelle was born, she couldn't avoid the feeling that her heart was being squeezed in a fist. A fierce, relentless grip.

It wasn't something she wanted to talk about; she tried to ignore it, thinking it would go away. But Leo seemed to be on it from day one, watching her with an odd curiosity, and Leo wasn't one to mince words.

"What the hell's going on, hon?" he'd been asking her lately. "This is not you. What's the deal?"

She closed her eyes, not wanting to think about how many times she had dodged that question. How many times she had lied to her sisters, insisting that everything was fine. Here in the little house she had begun to rebuild with her own hands, she and Leo finally had their angel baby. This was all she'd ever wanted.

The perfect life.

So what did she have to complain about? Nothing. Nothing at all.

The actress on television bit her lips to keep from crying as she looked at the plastic stick of the pregnancy test kit. She gasped and her big round eyes flooded with tears.

"Negative?" her actor husband said. "I'm so sorry."

"No, no! It's positive!" The woman's voice squeaked with

emotion as she looked up at her husband. "Plus is positive! It's a yes. We're going to have a baby!"

Tears stung Chelsea's eyes as the couple embraced. That was her story. That was exactly the way it had been with Leo and her! They had yearned for this baby. Not so long ago they both knew that their lives would not be complete until they had a family of their own. Whenever Chelsea's sister Melanie visited with her four kids, they had come alive. Leo got down on the floor to push a truck behind Sam and help him build a bridge, while Chelsea enjoyed seven-year-old Nora's help in the kitchen. "You can't flip the pancake until there are bubbles around the edge," Nora would say, holding the spatula over the griddle from her place on the step stool.

Like pixie dust, the magic of Melanie's kids had always made this house sparkle. Chelsea and Leo would talk about the kids for days after Melanie and her crew headed back to their home in central New Jersey. Anecdotes about the kids' cuteness kept popping up. How Lucy threw better than her twin brother Max. The way Sam said, "More juice, pweeze." The way Nora tried to mother them all.

"I love you, Aunt Chelsea," Nora always said as she folded herself into Chelsea's arms to say good-bye. Holding her close, Chelsea would close her eyes and wish for a daughter like Nora.

She had always known she would have a baby girl.

When she tossed a coin into a fountain or wished upon a star, the wish was always the same—a baby girl with thoughtful eyes and downy hair.

Annabelle.

Their baby was supposed to be a dream come true, but reality had smacked her awake. She spent most of her time denying it. When Leo or Emma asked, she claimed to be tired. And though she was exhausted, sometimes she couldn't sleep for the dense, dark pressure behind her eyes. The fear that gripped her was overwhelming and contradictory; both dull and sharp, painful and numbing, frantic and deadly calm.

On the television screen the man whirled the woman

around in his arms, then paused tentatively, worried that he would make the baby dizzy.

The joke was worn and corny, but Chelsea snickered, swiping one hand over her wet eyes as the tender scene continued. How many times had she heard that joke? But she still laughed. The movie had been one of her favorites for years. She and Leo could have written that script; they had lived it.

Minus the happy ending.

She sniffed. Well, that was going to change, starting today. Dr. Volmer was going to give her some happy pills to chase the blues away. Her sister Emma had researched the whole thing and learned that there were medications Chelsea could take while breast-feeding.

It sounded so simple; she didn't know why she hadn't turned to him sooner.

"Silly pride," she said, looking down at her sleeping baby. "Mommy has silly pride." There . . . she could talk to her baby. Or did it count when she was talking about herself? Had she even said the words aloud?

Chelsea bit her lips, hoping that her failure as a mother hadn't affected Annabelle too much. She wanted to do everything right. Perfect. Her chief weakness was her perfectionism. Listing it as a fault had always worked well on job applications, but in real life, the need to be perfect could be a bitch.

Well, not anymore.

With a sigh, she summoned the energy to push off the couch and place Annabelle in her carrier. Time to find her way back to happiness.

Chapter 2

Chelsea had never liked Dr. Volmer. The dour man with the threadbare home office had always frightened her a little. His slick comb-over and tired eyes made her think of a failing executive scraping together yesterday's crumbs—and that was not the sort of doctor a girl wanted to entrust her most vulnerable parts to. At least she'd had an affinity for Dr. Hurley, who'd delivered her baby.

Her former gynecologist had been in a newer office building with plenty of parking. But she'd had to give up that health insurance when she left her job at the magazine. Under Sounder Health Care, choices were limited. Volmer was the only ob-gyn in their new insurance plan with an office that was reasonably close to their house in New Rochelle. One doctor had spoken with a thick accent that had been too hard to decipher. One wasn't taking new clients, and the specialists in the Bronx came with another set of city problems like parking and traffic.

In the end, Chelsea had gritted her teeth and chosen to suffer through Dr. Second-Rate.

"You brought the baby?" The woman in the crisp blouse at the reception desk craned her neck to look over the counter at the stroller behind Chelsea. What was her name? Despite the visits during the past three months, Chelsea couldn't remember. "Dr. Volmer doesn't allow that. Didn't you read the instructions?"

Chelsea swallowed. "What instructions?"

"On the Web site? When you made the appointment." The stripe in her blouse brought out the teal in her eyes. Cold but sophisticated, it was the sort of color you'd find in a south Florida mansion. All the times she'd been here, she had never paid much attention to the receptionist before. "Didn't you see the red warning about no babies in the office?"

"I didn't know. My husband made the appointment for me. My sister usually watches her, but she's back at work now."

"Mm-mm-mm." Translation: You're in trouble. When the woman rose and emerged from the reception cubicle, Chelsea stepped back.

Was she going to chase them out?

Instead, the woman cut around her and leaned over the stroller to coo for Annabelle. Light flashed on the silver name-plate on her shirt, making it look like a piece of jewelry.

Val . . . Chelsea's senses swam with the gentle scent of her perfume, a delicious mix that reminded her of baby powder and flowers. Without the cover of the desk, Val's teal blouse no longer concealed her shape, the soft, doughy body of a Care Bear.

She wished Val would take care of her. A big, soft, plush hug would be so nice right now. Chelsea bit her bottom lip, missing her mother.

"You'll have to take her in," Val said without looking up from Annie. "But he's not going to like it."

"Okay. Sorry." Chelsea adjusted her oversized sweater, which tended to bunch at her puffy waist. How did other over-weight people like Val manage to look so together—so sharp? In that moment she would have given anything to have Val's life. A pretty blouse that matched her eyes. A quiet cubby to spend the day in. Lunch with friends. She probably had time to read books and soak in the tub with those amazing scents.

"Oh, look at you!" Val fussed. "Such a beautiful baby, and you know it, too! Yes, you do."

Chelsea didn't think Annabelle was so beautiful, with her

flaky cradle cap and chubby jowls. Why did people always say that?

"And with your pink little booties I can tell you're a girl. What's her name?"

"Annabelle."

"A name almost as pretty as you."

Annabelle's eyes opened wide in response to Val.

"Oh, aren't you yummy?" Val shot Chelsea a look. "Do you mind if I hold her? It's been so long since I had a little one."

Chelsea nodded and stood back as the woman lifted her baby in her capable arms. Sometimes it reassured her to see other people give her baby the love she couldn't find in her own heart. She imagined Annabelle's senses coming alive to the sweet perfume, her fears and muscles easing in the nest of warm, capable arms.

"You are cute as a button," Val cooed. "But you don't belong in this big doctor's office. Mommy needs to get a sitter."

"But it's just an office visit," Chelsea said. "A consultation. I'm not due for an exam."

Val shrugged. "He doesn't want the babies in here. Next time, you really need to leave her with a sitter."

One more expense that wasn't in their budget. Since Chelsea had left her job at the magazine, they were living on one salary and there was no room for any extras now.

"Who's the cutest baby here?" Val cajoled. "Who is? Who is?"

Annabelle's eyes lit with interest as she pressed a little fist to a chubby cheek. They seemed to like each other, Annabelle and Val. And Chelsea was the outsider, watching them through binoculars. Why was she a million miles away from her own baby?

The door behind them opened and a nurse appeared, chart in hand. "Chelsea Maynard?"

"That's me." Chelsea's back ached as she took Annabelle from the woman and leaned down to place her in the stroller.

"Don't forget to buckle her in," Val said. "We don't want any mishaps."

Like the baby slipping out, her head thumping as it hit the floor.

No, that wouldn't happen . . . but she might bump it on the wheel.

Or if she fell out in the parking lot, the impact on the concrete might draw blood.

Chelsea closed her eyes against the horrible images that flooded her mind. Why did she let herself go there? Such sick, horrifying scenarios of the terrible things that could happen.

"Let me help." The nurse reached down and clicked the clasp on Annie's seat belt. More a means of moving Chelsea along than an act of kindness, but Chelsea nodded gratefully, then pushed the stroller inside.

The office was a tired room that aspired to be a paneled library in an English manor house. Only here, the paneling was the prefab kind and the built-in shelving was no more than kitchen cabinets with a walnut stain. Chelsea assessed the quickest and cheapest way to make the room over as Dr. Volmer went over her chart, grunting out a few questions now and then.

A coat of paint could open this room up and give it a more modern look. A buttery yellow, or a more neutral pearl gray. Silver mist. Were there decent walls under the paneling? Chelsea's fingers itched to pry one loose and take a peek. If necessary, the paneling could be painted. . . .

She hadn't expected that she would miss her job at the magazine, but it was hard to back away from an occupation when you knew you were so damned good at it. Granted, she had plenty of projects of her own waiting back at the house, and the managing editor was hoping she would freelance for the magazine, either by editing or turning one of her projects into a "how to" feature. But that wasn't like basking in the social glow at the office each day. She missed the adult conversation and the design challenge. There was a certain adrenaline rush in taking on a new space, triaging the worst elements, and making it better in less time than some people took to decide on vacation plans.

"Your weight could be a little lower," the doctor said, jarring her from her reverie. "Are you getting exercise?"

"I do some walking. Not enough."

"You need exercise."

"I know, but the weather's been crummy, and the C-section really knocked me off my feet for a while." The surgery had been complicated, traumatic, with some repair necessary to her uterus. The ordeal had sucked all the joy out of Annabelle's birth. For hours Chelsea had been splayed open on the table, shivering in alarm as the surgeons had worked behind the drape. She still hated thinking about it.

"Get yourself moving," he ordered. From his gray complexion and slight paunch, she doubted that he was pumping iron at the gym, but she didn't argue. "It will help you feel better."

"I'll get walking again." She would go with Emma, whose doctor had been on her about exercise, too. She was pregnant with her first baby.

Dr. Volmer closed the chart and started cleaning his glasses with a tissue. "Then I'm satisfied with your progress. You're good to go."

Her confidence slid down to the floor. "Wait . . ." How had she lost control of the appointment? "I came in because I'm having some problems. Didn't the nurse tell you?"

"Mmm." He put his glasses back on and opened the folder. "So tell me why you're here."

"I need an antidepressant." She noticed his scowl as she said the words. "I—I just feel really bad all the time."

"You came for drugs?" His magnified eyes were huge behind the wall of his glasses. "I'm not one of those doctors who will send you home with a handful of prescriptions when all you really need is rest and fresh air." His annoyance was abrasive; he didn't even pretend to be patient.

She wanted to ask him how she was supposed to get rest when she had to feed Annabelle every three hours. How did other mothers do it? She wanted to ask them, to shout a question out to the new mothers of the world, a plea for them to share their answers, reveal their secrets. Other mothers were competent. They managed to feed their babies, to coo and snuggle with them. Chelsea so desperately wanted that for herself, and for Annabelle.

"What about a blood test?" she asked. "Isn't there some kind of screening you can do?"

"To tell me that your hormones are off balance? We already know that. You've just got a case of the baby blues," Dr. Volmer said. "That's normal."

"But it's more than that. There's something really wrong with me. I'm not happy about anything anymore, and I feel so . . . I go from being numb inside to feeling broken."

"The baby blues," he repeated.

No, no, it's so much more than that. Can't you hear what I'm saying? I'm slipping into a dark hole. I don't feel anything for my baby. I can't remember the woman I used to be.

And I'm so worried that something is going to happen to Annie . . . if I drop her, if she flies out of the car in a crash. If I drop her down the stairs . . .

She closed her eyes against the rhythmic thumping of her baby down the stairs—the rolling, falling bundle of skin and bones. All in her head, of course, and she couldn't tell Dr. Volmer about that. She couldn't let him see that she was a terrible person inside.

She could handle this. She would handle this. On her own.

"The hormones will even out eventually. I could give you an antidepressant, but you know anything you take will go through to the baby while you're nursing."

She nodded, not wanting to face him because that would make her cry. Everything made her cry these days. "I don't want to do anything to hurt my baby." Her voice was tight, her throat dry and scratchy. "But isn't there something? My sister said there are some medications that can be prescribed to nursing mothers."

"Your sister . . . is she a doctor?"

She opened her eyes. "No."

He grunted. "Diagnosing you over the Internet, I take it?"

It was true, but why did he make her feel bad for asking? "I came here because I can't take this anymore. I can't go on feeling this way." She brought her burning eyes to his hateful face. "I need your help."

"Well." He frowned, and she looked down as a tear ran down her cheek. "If it's that bad I'll write you a prescription for something that won't harm the baby. But it takes a while to work. You probably won't notice it taking effect for a week or so." He took a pad out of a drawer and scribbled something on it. "There. Is that what you wanted?"

Chelsea clutched the prescription as if it were a lifeline. "What about therapy?" Emma had told her to ask about it.

"That's only in the worst cases, and I don't think it's warranted here. The baby blues go away on their own. . . ." The doctor's voice was fuzzy, as if coming from the other side of a wall.

A massive wall.

Chelsea was walled in. Imprisoned with her baby. And talking about things changing in a few weeks or a few years was like the promise of a parole hearing in thirty years. It was too far away to be real.

"Of course, if it's really bad, I can recommend a therapist." He flipped through her file and rubbed his jaw. "I can't tell if your insurance would cover that. You'd have to call and find out. Chances are you'd have to pay out of pocket."

Their health care insurance was another issue. It wasn't long after Chelsea's discharge from the hospital that unresolved claims from Sounder Health Care had begun flooding in—all of them with a series of complicated footnotes implying problems.

No . . . she couldn't face trying to get one more approval from Sounder Health Care and they certainly couldn't afford to pay out of pocket.

She would tough it out without therapy.

I can do this, she told herself.

"Honey, with your determination, I believe you can do any-thing." That was what Mom used to tell her. When Chelsea announced that she was going to run for class president, find a job as an editor, or restore their little house one tile at a time, her mother always gave her the green light. *"If anyone can do it, it's you."*

Mom would have understood. She would have driven up from Florida, parked her suitcase in the guest room, and sent Dad grocery shopping while she fussed over Annabelle and cooked up a storm. Chelsea had seen Mom take over at her older sister's house every time Melanie had a new baby. For Mom, it had been a labor of love, and people were always happy to submit to Judith Maynard's loving authority.

Mom should be here . . . but she wasn't. They had lost her just days before Annabelle was born . . . so close to Chelsea's due date that she hadn't been allowed to fly to Florida to attend her own mother's funeral. Sometimes anger flared when Chelsea thought about it. Resentment that she couldn't be there to say good-bye and fury with her mother for refusing treatment. They could have had more time together. Mom could have met her granddaughter. . . .

As if on cue, Annabelle let out a little squeak.

Chelsea saw the baby's lips moving. It would be time to feed her soon. The poor little thing. Did she sense that she was the source of so much pain and contention? A baby needed to feel love and comfort. She needed smiles and happy words . . . not the quavering voice of the person who was supposed to care for her and shape her world.

"Okay, then." Dr. Volmer closed the file and took off his glasses again in what she now recognized as his "wrap it up" gesture. "I'll have Val give you a list of therapists in case you want to go that route." He rose, and Chelsea had no choice but to get to her feet and leave.

He cleared his throat as he seemed to notice Annabelle for the first time. "You got a good baby there. Most of them would be screaming by now."

Annabelle's hat was off, and the white flakes of her cradle cap were visible on her scalp. The pediatrician had told them to rub mineral oil into her scalp, but it left her skin flaky and her scalp slick. "A butterball head," Leo had called her. Her face was turning red as she squirmed. A storm warning. Any minute, the hunger cries would come.

As soon as Volmer opened the door, Chelsea wheeled her good baby out to the reception area, where she searched the faces of the women there, searched for someone to take her baby. Maybe Val could take her home. Maybe some other lactating woman sitting in the waiting room could take her into the bathroom and sit on the toilet to breast-feed her. Surely there was a woman here with the confidence to nurse right out in the open, sitting grandly in a chair, while Chelsea scrambled to her car and drove south on the Interstate . . . south toward Florida and warmer weather.

Annabelle was a good baby, but right now Chelsea wished she could hand her off to someone else while she went off with her happy pills. And she hated herself for it.

All hope of a quick exit faded when Annabelle let loose with her hunger cry. Chelsea paused, panic burning a path up her throat. There was no way she could make it home with a hungry baby screaming in the backseat of the car, but she wasn't able to breast-feed in public. Neither the waiting room nor the car would work.

The dinky little bathroom would have to do.

Chelsea put the toilet cover down and huddled on the seat with Annie heavy in her arms. The sweet stink of deodorizer reminded her of orange Creamsicles, in a sickening way.

"Why are we here?" she asked.

Annabelle's whimpers dissolved as she started nursing. Her baby didn't care that they were trapped in an airless bathroom with cloud wallpaper from the eighties. Annie could find contentment with food and a nap.

Unlike her mother.

Looking down on her baby, Chelsea tried to swallow back

the keening wail of loneliness deep in her throat. Annabelle was physically attached to her and comforted by it, but Chelsea felt no comfort in being a provider. She was tapped out, exhausted, and the baby at her breast was draining her of her last ounce of energy.

She reached over to turn on the water.

Maybe that would drown out her sobs.

The ride home loomed before Chelsea. Weariness dimmed her vision as she navigated the parkway, watching the pillars of the guardrail whip past. Her hands gripped the wheel, but the car was hard to steer. The guardrail tugged at the car like a powerful magnet.

One turn of the wheel, and she'd plow into it. She imagined a pillar tearing into the car. Cutting it in half.

Or would the car hit head-on and spin around, slamming into other vehicles swimming along behind it? She saw it all, as if caught in slow motion. Cars pressing into each other, collapsing, wrapping and twirling together like lovers on a dance floor.

The bold confidence rising inside her was the most solid emotion she had felt in weeks.

She was going to do it.

One slight turn of the wheel would end her pain.

"I'm losing it." As she reached for her cell phone in her bag, she realized she was fishing through the diaper bag—the only purse she carried these days. The sweet baby smell reminded her that Annabelle was sleeping in her car seat in the back. If she crashed, something terrible could happen to her baby.

She jerked the wheel in the opposite direction, overcompensating, making the car wobble on the road.

How could I even think of crashing? But as the thought escaped, the barrier seemed to beckon from the side of the road, promising a way out, luring her to finally do something.

Do something.

Stop sitting around and take action.

Her hands shook as she called her sister on speed dial. The bleating ring stretched before her like the broken white line at the center of the highway. When Emma's message came on, she was about to hang up, but something kept her pressing the phone to her ear. As soon as the beep ended, desperate words spilled out.

"I need help. . . ."

Chapter 3

Emma Wyatt walked away from the lockers, casually paused in front of the mirror, and opened the towel just enough to reveal the swell of her belly. Even in the harsh light of the locker room, the slight curve of her pale stomach was a beautiful sight, like a Michelangelo figure sculpted in marble.

She was really pregnant.

After all the mornings in bed with the basal thermometer, the embarrassing doctors' appointments for her and for Jake, the trip to the clinic with a little vial of Jake's swimmers tucked between her breasts to keep it warm . . . now, at last, she could press a hand to her abdomen and make contact with the life growing in the cradle of her hips.

She stepped away from the mirror before one of the other women began to think she was stuck on herself. Though right now, the sense of well-being that cloaked her made her feel immune to anyone's disapproval. This prenatal swim class was the perfect way to end a busy week, though she did have to rush here as soon as the last parent picked up their kid each Friday afternoon. The forty-five minutes of pool exercise made Emma feel loose and invigorated. For the first time in days, her feet and toes were warm. Life was good and full of promise.

Holding the towel to her breasts, she leaned into the open locker and noticed that her phone was buzzing from a message.

Three messages, actually. All from her sister.

Poor Chelsea was struggling through a bad patch, and Emma wasn't sure how to help her. Her normally articulate sister had grown quiet and sullen. It was as if the thoughts and feelings that had once bubbled forth couldn't even find their way to the surface anymore. Emma had cajoled and prodded, but Chelsea didn't want to talk about it. In fact, Chelsea didn't want to talk at all. These days she seemed grateful to hand off little Annabelle so that she could frown into the shadows of the room or doze off.

Having suffered through depression, Emma recognized the symptoms. Difficulty concentrating. Fatigue. And the guilt. More than once Chelsea had worried aloud that she was a terrible mother, and though Emma had reassured her, it was a worry. Chelsea was so hard on herself, but there was something to her concern. Surely Annabelle could sense the sadness around her.

Chelsea didn't want to admit that anything was really wrong, but Emma was pretty sure she was suffering from postpartum depression. She had searched online and talked with Chelsea and Leo—more than once. For a while, neither of them could fathom that Chelsea could be depressed about the thing she'd wanted most—a beautiful little baby.

"But this isn't about whether or not you love Annabelle," Emma kept telling her sister. "You're reacting to all the physical and emotional changes that your body is going through. After delivery, hormones can be all out of whack. Estrogen and progesterone levels drop and prolactin and oxytocin shoot up." She had reminded Chelsea that her body was still healing from a difficult C-section. The traumatic surgery was one risk factor for postpartum depression. Losing Mom within a week of Annabelle's birth was number two, although that was something Chelsea didn't want to talk about. And then there was the transition from being managing editor at a successful magazine like *Home Handyman* to being a stay-at-home mom. On top of everything else, the loss of status and social support had isolated Chelsea, leaving her alone at home for most of the day. Of course, that was the way she and Leo had planned it;

no one could have foreseen the depression that would over-whelm Chelsea after the birth.

But there was no disputing the reality: Chelsea was de-pressed. She needed help, starting with her doctor.

Emma leaned into the locker to check the phone for text messages. Maybe this was good news. Today was Chelsea's ap-pointment with her ob-gyn, right?

But there were no texts. Emma was tempted to take the messages now, but cell phone use wasn't allowed in the locker room, and Emma understood why. She'd heard the story of the group of teenage girls who had inadvertently snapped a photo of a nude woman while they were posing in front of the big mirrored wall. One of the many "exposures" of the elec-tronic age.

Emma dressed quickly, pulled her hair back with a clip, and then made her way out to the lobby, a phone-safe zone.

"I need help." Chelsea's voice was tight and strained. "I'm driving home from the doctor and I . . . I think I'm going to slam into the barrier."

Emma's heartbeat began to pulse in her ears as her sister's frantic words played on. Where was Chelsea now? Had she pulled over? Did she make it home? Emma slid into her jacket as she forced herself to listen to the rest of the desperate mes-sage.

Unable to wait, she cut off the message and dialed her sis-ter's number.

No answer . . .

Shouldering the gym door open, she plunged out into the cold as her finger hit the redial button again and again. "Come on, Chelsea. Answer the damn phone."

She thought about calling 911. This was an emergency, but what could the police do? Telling them that her sister was driving around somewhere with suicidal thoughts wouldn't give them enough to go on.

She needed more information. She needed Chelsea to pick up the damned phone.

The third time it went to voice mail, Emma was already behind the wheel, tearing down the street.

Chelsea's house . . . she would meet her sister there, praying that Chelsea made it that far. Yes, Chelsea would be there . . . with Annabelle. Oh, dear Lord, was Annie in the back of the car? Of course she was. Chelsea had realized she would have to bring the baby when she found out Emma couldn't sit for her. Emma set her teeth and punched the gas pedal, angry with herself for not intervening sooner.

At the amber glow of a traffic light she had to force herself to press the brake, slow it down to a safe pace. *You have to make the right choices, too,* she reminded herself. It was up to her to take care of herself and her unborn child.

Stay calm.

Which was hard for her. Emma had always been excitable, sensitive, and nurturing; it was the reason she'd been drawn to nursing. She was sure she had been put on earth to take care of others. Chelsea was the one who was calm and in control. A superwoman.

She drummed her fingers on the steering wheel as she waited for the light to change. But she blasted through the intersection as soon as the light turned green.

This couldn't be happening. If Mom were here, she'd know how to fix things. How to snap Chelsea out of this funk and bring her back.

One of her last conversations with Mom came back to her. Emma had hopped a plane to Florida when the doctors warned that the end was near. Sitting by Mom's hospital bed, she had sobbed into her hands. Silent but without shame, she had cried for Mom.

How she'd longed for the days of her childhood when Mom was healthy. She saw Mom doling out treats to the girls and the neighborhood kids, their feet bare in the lawn, cool and dark with clover. There were the "Surprise City Days" Mom had sprung on them once or twice a year when they were in grade school: Emma remembered trading her Keds and jeans for a baby-doll dress with lacy biker shorts to take the train into the city and see a Broadway show or visit a museum. Mom had not worried that they were missing school, and the girls had put aside their usual bickering to enjoy the day in the city with their mother.

Lost in thought, she hadn't noticed Mom stirring in bed. "Emma?" Despite the brutal rounds of chemo and radiation, Judith Maynard's voice still held the smooth dignity that had always reassured Emma.

"I'm here, Mom." Emma sniffed. "Crying, as usual." It was a family joke; the sight of a lost puppy or a sentimental coffee commercial could bring Emma to tears.

"You always were the crier, but it's not a bad quality. I never had to worry about you bottling things up inside. But Chelsea . . ." Judith lifted the arm that didn't have an IV line attached and pushed hair off her forehead. "You need to watch out for Chelsea."

"She's the strongest of all of us. Nothing ever gets her down."

"Everyone has a weak spot. Some are better hidden than others."

"I guess. But if you look at Chelsea, she's led a charmed life. The perfect job. A wonderful husband. A charming house and a baby on the way."

"Everyone has problems, sweetie."

"I know that." She had thought it didn't apply to Chelsea to the same degree as the rest of the world. Nothing ever seemed to bother Chelsea. When Emma got up to pour Mom more water, Judith's eyes were clear and shiny as dark stones in a riverbed.

"Promise me you'll watch out for Chelsea," Mom had said. "She doesn't have the tools you have."

"Oh, Chelsea has plenty of tools. How do you think she and Leo rebuilt the downstairs of their house?"

But Mom didn't go for her joke. "Promise me. She's going to need your help. I know she comes on like a bear sometimes. But she hasn't learned about the middle ground in life. She hasn't learned to see the gray areas yet."

"It seems to be working for her."

"The problem with thinking like that is that you're crushed when you don't achieve perfection, and this is not a perfect world."

Although Emma didn't really get what Mom was saying about Chelsea, the conversation had stuck with her. Of course, Emma had agreed, though the promise wasn't necessary. The Maynard girls supported each other in any way they could.

When her thoughts snapped back to the present, she was exiting the parkway and turning into the little neighborhood where Chelsea and Leo had bought a house last year. Her pulse pounded in her ears as she made the turns she knew by heart.

Please, God, let them be there. Let them be safe. . . .

Chapter 4

When the sobs had drained out of her, Chelsea lifted her head from the steering wheel and took in the charming little Cape Cod–style house with its dormered windows, gray siding, and bright white trim.

Home.

How had she gotten here?

The stir of cloth nearby startled her. She turned to see Annie strapped into her car seat, kicking against the flannel blanket tucked around her legs.

Did I strap her in?

Did I drive us here?

Of course you did.

Part of her knew that. But there was that dark side, the gaping holes just behind her eyes that sucked in conscious thought and tormented her.

Torment.

Why was everything so difficult? Why was she so miserable?

The house staring back at her had become more of a prison than a home, and she longed for the days when she had reveled in every nook and cranny, seeing opportunity for color and light. Those days when she had imagined the loving moments that would take place under this roof.

Great potential . . . that was what Leo had said when they'd first seen this house a year ago. House hunting with Leo had been fun, but she'd been anxious to find the right match. After looking at dozens of homes, some that were disaster zones and others that they could not afford, she had known this house was the one.

The beveled glass windows winked at her in the winter light. Those windows had taken her breath away when she and Leo had first pulled up. They whispered of the house's charm and grace, its history.

"The trim needs painting," Leo had said that first day as he parked in the driveway.

"Paint is cheap," she'd answered cheerfully as she'd popped open the car door, eager to get a closer look.

After weeks of traipsing through sad little houses that left her feeling cold, she could barely believe the charm of the little New Rochelle house. The log burning in the fireplace drew her close. The mantel was made of tacky fake brick, but she could remove that. It would be a project.

The wood floors were worn, but they could be refinished, and she loved the warmth of hardwoods throughout the first floor. The kitchen could use updating, but for now it was functional. Of course, it would require some fixes. Paint and windows. Yard work. Someone had painted over the wallpaper upstairs, and the garage door was hanging by a thread. There was evidence of a mouse in one of the closets. None of that frightened her.

Leo ran his hand down the wood banister, testing it for strength. "Sturdy. I like the looks of it."

"It has good bones." Chelsea had noticed a few settling cracks in the plaster, but no signs of water damage or structural defects. "And a good heart. You get the feeling that wonderful things have happened here."

Although Leo usually didn't like it when Chelsea waxed metaphysical, this time he didn't argue. "I like it," he said. Three simple words, but coming from him, it was a rave review. "But you're the expert. Managing editor of *Home Handyman* magazine. What say you? Like it, Love it, or Gotta Have It?"

"I love you," she said, "but this house? I Gotta Have It."

He nodded. "I knew that. I could tell."

She scooted up to him, slipping into his arms. "I can see us being very happy here." Despite some obvious mistakes of the previous homeowners, Chelsea knew this was the right house for them. It was easy to imagine living here a very long time with Leo and their little ones.

Children . . . Walking through this house, it was so easy to see herself as a mother. If a house marked the beginning of their fiscal responsibility, children were the ultimate prize. Chelsea wanted to be a mother one day, and she had always felt fortunate to have found Leo in a sea of Manhattan single men who placed "having kids" as a low priority on their list of life goals.

Leo had chosen to begin their house hunting in New Rochelle, an area not too far from the city that was ranked as one of the best places in the country to raise children. Despite his penchant for making light of things, he was serious when it came to planning for the future. Maybe it was because of his childhood, a reaction to the feeling that no one was fending for him when he was a kid.

"We need to make an offer," she said.

"You're sure?" he asked her. "I know you like the way things are now. The apartment. Living in Manhattan. It's the center of the universe."

At the start of their search, she had been reluctant to give up their sublet in the city. They had it good. But now that she'd seen this house . . . well, she could say good-bye to Manhattan Island and never look back if she lived in a house like this.

She pressed her cheek to his chest and sighed as her eyes swept up the old wooden staircase. "Wherever you are—that's the center of my universe."

"And that is the right answer, for fifty points. Care to move to the bonus round?"

She shook her head. "I just want to move in here."

Right then and there, Chelsea and Leo made an offer on the house.

While the Realtor went off to do her thing, they decided to explore "downtown" New Rochelle. The burgers at AJ's were delicious, the price suited their budget, and the place reminded Chelsea of a burger joint in the town where she'd spent her childhood in Maryland.

They talked budget and career plans. Leo's sales job was going well, and Chelsea had just completed her third freelance article to supplement her meager income at the magazine.

This is real life, Chelsea thought as she filched a french fry from her husband's plate. Not jobs, but careers. Not a lease, but a mortgage.

A house and a yard.

Leo talked fast through the meal, devouring his burger with his usual speed. She loved seeing him that way, that spark of excitement in his brown eyes. Animated.

And she felt a sure sense of destiny, strong as the pull of the undertow at Jones Beach. This was nothing like the uncertainty she had waded through when it was time to apply to colleges or choose a major.

This decision felt right.

Leo was signaling for the check when they got the call from the Realtor.

Their offer had been accepted.

She high-fived Leo, and worked out some details with the Realtor. Their online mortgage application was complete and they were preapproved, but there would be an inspection and they needed to decide when to lock in the interest rate. "Big-time decisions," Chelsea said.

"Really. If we don't watch out, we'll turn into grown-ups," Leo said.

Chelsea couldn't wait to tell Emma they would be living in New Rochelle, too, and it wasn't too late to call Mom and Dad in Florida to let them know.

She would never forget that day, driving home, wanting him so much. Van Morrison was playing in the car—"Into the Mystic"—as Leo drove them into the dusk, into their future. A light snow had begun to fall while they were eating, and it was sticking to tree branches and traffic signs, covering everything in a sugary white coating.

The snow accumulated quickly, slowing traffic. As they approached their neighborhood, they commiserated about the time it would take to find a parking spot.

But as they turned the corner onto Riverside, there it was— a wide-open, legal expanse on the street.

"Grab it!" she said, and a second later Leo swung the car in.

"In New Rochelle, we'll have our own garage with a driveway," he said giddily.

"Luxurious." Neither of them had wanted a car in Manhattan, but Leo needed it for his job.

The snow was crisp and squeaky underfoot. Chelsea hooked her arm onto Leo's and they stood still as mannequins on the quiet street.

"I love snow in the city," she said. "It makes everything clean and white, and it puts a hush over all the noise."

He stepped away from her and bent down to grab a handful of snow.

"What are you doing?" She backed away as he packed it into a ball. "Think twice about that. I was the best pitcher on St. Philip Neri's softball team."

"Yeah. And we all know what a powerhouse they were in the late nineties."

Laughing, she turned and raced down the street, sliding as she cut around a bus shelter where snow was sticking in a jagged pattern that covered half of the billboard for *Wicked*. Shielding herself with the Plexiglas siding, she squatted to gather some snow to fire back at him. She peeked around the shelter, and a snowball whizzed by, clipping her shoulder.

"Whoa! That was close. Remember, you need me to pay half of that mortgage!"

He tossed the snowball from one hand to another. "Now you're getting personal?"

"Absolutely." She took advantage of his hesitation and launched a snowball at his chest. He turned, and it struck him squarely in the back.

"Hey!" he called after her as she took off running through the snow.

"You won't get off that easy."

She was a decent runner, but she was giddy from the chase, slowed by laughter and the soft bed of snow underfoot. Leo caught up to her easily, and they both slowed as they caught sight of the footbridge, where the snow encased the pillars and covered the lamps built into them. A warm light of orange and gold and lemony yellow suffused the entire footpath.

"Look at that." He squinted, snowflakes catching in his lashes.

It was all so beautiful . . . the wonder on his face, the snow-flakes lingering in the air, seemingly suspended under the light of the streetlamp, the glowing bridge ahead of them.

"It's magical." So warm and bright, a sign of good things to come.

She linked her arm through his and leaned close to Leo. They seemed suspended in time, on a floating island of snow, as they walked down the crystal lane, flanked by trees lifting white arms to the sky.

We could be walking through a poem . . . the center line in a haiku.

It was a poetic, magical beginning to their life together.

"This house is going to be great for us," Leo said. "After the apartment, it'll be a freakin' castle for the two of us."

"Maybe three soon."

His lips stretched wide in that smile that always softened the rough edges of a situation. "You know, maybe we'd better get started on that," he'd said. "Don't want to waste any time."

"I was just thinking the same thing."

In the back of her mind there was the worry that she might have the same problems conceiving that her sister Emma had endured. But then Emma had always suffered from cramps; she'd always had female issues. Chelsea had a feeling that their journey would be different. They had always made a good team, but they were moving into new territory now, buying a house, leaving the city, starting a family.

As they headed back to the apartment, she leaned into Leo, thinking that snow had never looked so beautiful.

Snow with iridescent city lights pooling upon it, like a water-color tray.

Ice crystals that sparkled silver on the bare trees.

Snowflakes filling the air, whispering excitement . . .

Not like the snow fading on their front lawn.

She lifted her head from the steering wheel long enough to glom onto the gray patch melting by the edge of driveway.

This was not the snow she had wanted to share with her daughter. It was faded like everything else, its brilliance tainted by the shadows that seeped from her dark soul. It just wasn't pretty anymore.

Chapter 5

As soon as she turned onto Chelsea's street, Emma saw the familiar green Subaru parked in the driveway.

Thank you, God.

As she parked on the street, she noticed a figure in the driver's seat behind windows that were opaque with steam. Chelsea was still in the car. For how long?

Through the misty window she could see the baby carrier in the back. Annabelle squirmed, probably eager to get out.

Chelsea was a mound in the driver's seat, hunched over the steering wheel.

Emma rapped on the window, the glass cold against her knuckles.

Her sister didn't move.

Emma knocked again. "Chelsea, honey, it's me. Are you asleep?"

Again, no response.

If it's locked, I'm calling the police, she thought. She didn't know how to handle this. Chelsea needed real help, not her ditzy sister who had barely made it through Psych 101.

Her fingers closed around the door handle, and it popped open. From this close, she could see her sister's shoulders trembling. Strands of hair fell over Chelsea's face, and the scrunchie was slipping loose from her ponytail.

"Oh, honey . . . am I glad to see you." She pressed her hand between Chelsea's shoulder blades and gave her a little rub intended to sooth her. "You had me so scared."

"I'm going crazy," Chelsea sobbed into the sleeves of her jacket.

Such a thin blazer, and it was freezing out here. In the twenties. How could Chelsea stand to be out in this cold without her coat?

"I wanted to smash into the barrier. I almost turned the wheel and crashed the car with . . . with my *baby* in the back. I'm losing it. I've lost my mind."

"You're not crazy." Emma banged into the steering wheel as she hugged her sister, wishing she could transmit feelings of love and security and hope with her touch. "But you're going through a scary time. Promise me you won't do anything to hurt yourself or Annabelle."

"What's the point? I'm crazy." Chelsea's shoulders shook as a sob tore through her.

"Chelsea, you are the most honorable person I know. So if you make this promise, I know you'll keep it."

"I don't know what I'm doing anymore."

"Just promise me," Emma said, trying to rationalize her sister to a place where everyone could be safe for now. "Promise me."

Chelsea sniffed. "I promise."

"Okay then." Emma stroked a hand over her sister's smooth, shiny hair. She noticed a slip of paper on the passenger's seat. A prescription. "Can you walk? Let's get you and Annie inside, where it's warm. I'm freezing my petooty off out here."

Although Chelsea didn't laugh, she did push away from the steering wheel and slide out of the car. Emma balanced her sister on one arm, struggling as she reached in to extract the keys. Chelsea was dead weight. She was falling apart and it was up to Emma to help her out of this. Mom had warned her that Chelsea would need help.

She guided her sister to the side door, managed to unlock the door with the key on her set, and ushered Chelsea in to the small kitchen. The place wasn't looking its best, with dirty dishes and stacks of mail here and there. Clearly it wasn't up to Chelsea's high standards, which Emma suspected made Chelsea's outlook even darker.

While Chelsea settled into her favorite corner of the sofa, Emma hurried back to the car for Annabelle. It worried her to leave the baby even for a minute, even with the car locked. Such precious cargo!

But Annie was fine, squirming and chirping those sharp little squeaks that probably were a sign of hunger. From her observations, nearly every one of Annie's little disturbances seemed to boil down to cries for her mother's milk.

Emma unstrapped her and lifted her out of the infant seat. "You're getting heavy."

Annabelle's stern eyes found hers and her face puckered.

"Oh, don't take it personally. You're supposed to be gaining weight. Just like your aunt Emma." She slammed the car door and moved up the driveway, stepping carefully. By the time they reached the door, Annie's whimpers had accelerated to a crying session.

"Music to my ears," Emma whispered, holding her close. She was so relieved that Annie and Chelsea were okay.

"It's okay, little one," Emma cooed as she carried the baby into the living room and placed her gently on the changing table that had been set up behind the couch. Although she couldn't seem to reach Chelsea, this was something she could do . . . loving Annie. She leaned in to one of the baby girl's chubby, sweet cheeks and planted rapid-fire kisses.

"What's the matter, Annie-bananee?" Emma ignored the baby's bleating cries as she stripped off her little terrycloth outfit. "I think you need a diaper change."

Annabelle raged in response, her face red, her arms shaking.

"Oh, I know, my hands are cold," Emma said. "Sorry, sweetie."

Loving the infant squirming on the table, Emma set to changing her diaper. The changing table was chic, a cabinet that blended into the living room décor when the doors were closed. Chelsea had driven out to Long Island to find just the right table. Décor had been important before Annie was born; not so much afterward. Today the cabinet doors were open, with a balled-up diaper and a stray wipe on the floor by Emma's feet. Before Annabelle was born, Chelsea had worked out every little detail of this room so that its design was interlaced with function. Eventually, Chelsea would care about things like design again . . . just not today.

Annabelle had soaked through her onesie, so Emma quickly replaced it with a pink romper with covered feet. "This is such a cute outfit. I love the little baby footie pajamas. I need to get some for these cold winter nights."

Emma lifted her head to check on Chelsea, nestled into the couch. "So what do you think this cry means? You think she's hungry?"

"She just ate at the doctor's office. How could she be hungry again?" Chelsea pressed her fingertips to her temples and let out a breath. "She never follows the schedule. Whoever thought a baby would pay attention to a feeding schedule? It's all so ludicrous."

"What do you think?" Emma scooped Annie up and rocked her in a dancing rhythm. "Should I try to put her down for a nap?"

"I don't know. I'll feed her again. Just give her to me."

She sat beside Chelsea and held the baby toward her. "Here you go, Mom."

Chelsea turned toward her, her blue eyes flashing with anger and annoyance. Was it because she'd said the word *Mom*, reminding them both of their own mother? Frowning, Chelsea took the baby, resting her on her lap while she unbuttoned her shirt.

Brushing the awkwardness aside, Emma offered Chelsea water or tea, or maybe a snack.

"Some cheese and crackers?"

It seemed inappropriate, offering a snack to someone who'd just been to the edge of hell and back, but Chelsea seemed unfazed. "No."

Emma bit her lip, studying her sister. Should she press Chelsea to talk about her panic attack? She wanted answers, but she didn't want to batter her poor sister with questions.

"Chels, do you want to talk about it? What happened on the parkway?"

Tears flooded Chelsea's eyes. "There's nothing to talk about. I freaked out. Crashing into the wall suddenly seemed like the right thing to do. I know it sounds crazy." She swiped at her cheeks with her free hand. "I guess that's it. I'm losing my mind."

"But you're not." Emma sat down again, wishing she could hug her sister, spin her around. All the tricks that used to work to calm Chelsea when they were kids were now useless. "Honey, you're upset because you care so much. I know you love Annie, and you're not going to hurt yourself, right? You promised."

Chelsea nodded.

"So just remember that, for starters. And when your medication starts to take effect, I'm sure you'll start feeling better."

A red flush suffused Chelsea's cheeks as she collapsed into a sob. "The medication. Yeah, I have to get that filled, but it will take a week, at least. And I'm not allowed to see a therapist. And there was no blood test or screening."

Emma squinted at her. "What do you mean?"

"Dr. Volmer says it's just the baby blues and I should tough it out. And the insurance won't pay for it."

"Are you kidding me? There's no toughing it out in your situation. I can't believe that guy."

Chelsea stared down at the floor. "Dr. Volmer doesn't even like to prescribe medication."

"Well, I don't like to eat my vegetables, but it doesn't keep me from digging into the broccoli." Emma was so furious with Dr. Volmer, she wanted to march into his office and demand that he treat her sister properly. "Did you tell him everything that's been happening? That this isn't just a bad mood?"

"I told him enough." Chelsea's mouth twisted as she tried to hold back tears. "He said stuff like this happens to every new mother. He thinks I'm just a complainer."

"Which couldn't be farther from the truth." What kind of a doctor treated a depressed woman this way? "You're one of the strongest people I know. You've been dealing with this practically on your own since Annabelle was born, but honestly, sometimes the most difficult part of any illness is asking for help. You reached out for help, and he turned you away. What kind of a moron doctor can't diagnose postpartum depression?"

"*If* that's what I have," Chelsea said, her voice hollow and thin. "We don't know for sure."

"I know for sure. Honey, you've got all the symptoms, and some of the key risk factors, too. Any decent doctor would see you're suffering from postpartum depression."

"That's just a guess, Emma. You're not a doctor. You're not even a nurse."

The comment stung, but Emma tried not to show it. Though a few years had passed, she was still sensitive about dropping out of nursing school. Nursing had been a dream of hers, but six months into the intensive program she had realized she didn't have the math tools to make it through the meds and chemistry classes.

"I'm not a nurse," she said quietly, "but I know how to research a topic, and I've been all over the Internet on this one." She had combed through some books from the library, too—books she'd passed on to Chelsea—but she didn't want to bicker right now. It wasn't about winning the argument; the important thing was to get Chelsea some help. "This thing that's knocked you over, there's a cure for it. There's a treatment that goes beyond a prescription. And, honey, you need the cure. It's time to do an end run around this Dr. Volmer and get you to a specialist."

Chelsea shook her head slowly, lowering the baby who had dropped off to sleep.

"Do you want me to take her?" Emma offered.

"Please, take her." Chelsea handed Annabelle to her, pulled her shirt closed, and curled into the couch. "Take her away.

Take her home with you so I don't hurt her. I can't be a good mother to her, but I know you'll take care of her. You'll keep her safe."

"Oh, honey, don't say that."

But Chelsea closed her eyes and withdrew into herself, leaving Emma sitting there with the baby in her arms and a terrible feeling of inadequacy.

Chelsea needed help. She had almost run her car off the side of the expressway, and Emma couldn't get her to talk about it. Her arms full of life and beauty, Emma leaned down to kiss the baby's forehead.

Sweet Annabelle . . .

Someday, your mother will be back to normal, and you'll know how much she loves you. Someday, you'll bask in her love.

Hold on, little one. Better days will come.

She let Chelsea doze off while she took Annabelle to her crib and settled her on the mattress. "Sweet dreams."

Back in the living room, Emma picked up two pillows that had fallen to the floor and sat beside her sister. Nestled in the couch, Chelsea rubbed the cuticle of one thumb as if scraping off paint. There was such turmoil in her demeanor, so much raw pain behind her stormy blue eyes.

Emma's heart ached for her.

"About the doctor," Emma began, trying not to badger. "I think it would be better if you saw someone else . . . a specialist."

Chelsea shook her head. "Dr. Volmer is my assigned ob-gyn now. And we can't afford to go out of plan. I promised Leo we could make his health insurance work."

That was so typical of Chelsea: buck up and stick with the plan, even if it was killing you.

"Honey, I'm not going to let you suffer with this just because your lame insurance provider doesn't want to shell out the money. We'll put a little pressure on them and make them pay."

"But they don't listen. I struggle with them every day . . . all the time." Chelsea chewed her thumb as she looked over at the disheveled stack of letters on the desk. "Sounder Health Care does not cave with pressure. They're ruthless. They're still refusing to pay for my C-section. The excuse is that the procedure wasn't preauthorized, which was true. So I keep calling and telling them it was emergency surgery. And they keep saying my doctor has to submit some extra form, which they'll send to me. P.S. Three months later, I still haven't received the form. Instead I've got a mountain of bills they won't pay."

Chelsea wasn't exaggerating; the bills were about to spill off the desk. "But we know they'll pay eventually," Emma pointed out. "Not to diminish your frustration, but a lot of insurers drag their heels. I think they just hope that people like you will give up and pay it themselves."

Chelsea's lower lip jutted out. "We can't afford to pay it."

"I know, honey. I just used you as an example."

Tears flooded Chelsea's eyes. "You don't understand. Every day I call them. Every day they say they'll fix things, but they don't. They haven't paid any of Annabelle's bills either. They say she's not on the plan until they scan her birth certificate. I've sent them five copies. Five. And still they don't have it on record. They say things like 'lost in the mail' or 'it takes time to scan in.' "

"Monsters . . ." Emma felt a rush of sympathy. Normally, her sister would tear into unscrupulous business practices like this, but right now Chelsea didn't have the stamina or strength to fight this battle. "I'll help you straighten it out. Jake, too. We'll get him to sue their ass. But for now, we've got to take care of you. I'm going to call my doctor, Virginia Chin. She's a real woman's advocate and a lot better informed than your Dr. Volmer."

"But we can't afford it," she said. "We're already drowning in insurance bills."

"Don't worry about the money right now. If we can get you in to see Dr. Chin, it will be my gift to you. Mine and Jake's." Emma realized that this would probably cost hundreds of dollars, but at this point she would pay thousands to get help for her sister. She reached into her purse for her cell phone. "I'm going to call her office right now. Maybe she'll get you started on a prescription over the phone."

"Would a doctor really do that?"

"Maybe. It doesn't hurt to ask." Emma rose and paced into the kitchen. The yogurt and berries she'd had for breakfast were a distant memory, and she didn't want to deprive her baby of nutrients. The stack of dirty dishes, with something dark swirling in the water, put a dent in her appetite. She grabbed two slices of cheddar cheese from the fridge, then stepped out into the cold to make her call.

Sucking on the tart cheese while she waited on hold, she circled the little bench in the side yard, an old castoff that Chelsea had turned into a piece of art. Covered with mosaic tiles, it glimmered in the waning light of the pearl-gray winter sky.

The bench was a reminder of Chelsea's vision and resourcefulness. In her work for the magazine she had brought old houses back to life, turning them into beautiful, functional spaces.

Emma wanted her sister back. Healthy and happy . . .

Dr. Chin was not available, but the nurse practitioner came on the line, and Emma quickly explained Chelsea's situation.

Donna agreed that it sounded like Chelsea was suffering from PPD, but the doctor wouldn't prescribe medication without an exam. "Dr. Chin will want to see her."

"But she's in a very dark place," Emma said, stepping into the light streaming out through the kitchen storm door. "She needs help now, and I know Dr. Chin is booked six weeks out."

"Let me check her calendar, but I promise you, we'll squeeze her in sometime in the next week or so. Dr. Chin will stay late if she has to."

Emma's shoulders sank in relief. "Thank you. I'll hold." Shaking off the cold, she stepped into the kitchen with a new sense of hope. It would only take a few minutes to clear those dishes from the sink. She could get this place in order. With Dr. Chin on the case, Chelsea's life would be back on track in no time.

When Donna came back on the line, she apologized about the delay in the doctor's schedule. "I keep forgetting she's away next week at a conference. The best I can do is the following Wednesday." Emma snatched it. Between the appointment with Dr. Chin and the medication, things were looking up for Chelsea.

"Good news!" she chirped, heading into the living room.

Chelsea didn't answer. She was asleep on the couch, her face pressed into the cushion, her back rhythmically rising and falling.

Watching her for a moment, Emma felt a new sense of peace. At last, help was on the way.

It only took fifteen minutes to fill Chelsea's prescription for Nebula at the corner pharmacy. When Emma returned and found both Chelsea and Annie still asleep, she got to work straightening up.

This had been the routine since Annabelle had been born. Chelsea, once the Queen of OCD, could barely lift her head from the couch these days, and Leo sometimes worked long hours. So Emma usually straightened up when she visited. She took care of the dirty diapers and the dishes in the sink. She swept and Swiffered the kitchen floor. She ran a dust cloth over Emma's pride and joy—the beautiful blue-and-white fireplace with precious tiles from the Dutch city of Delft. Painstakingly preserved by Emma and Leo, the fireplace was once the center of their home, the gathering place for family dinners and parties. They had painted all the trim in the room white for a clean look. The walls below the wainscoting were a creamy vanilla, with a cornflower blue on top to pick up the color in the tiles. "Straight out of one of your magazine spreads," Emma had commented when she'd seen the finished room.

"It's a peaceful haven, perfect for the baby," Chelsea had said. Back then, the baby had been the focal point of all her plans and renovations.

Not so much anymore. These days, the fireplace was always dark and cold, though there was a stack of wood piled beside the garage out back. Most likely the chore of fetching wood and building a fire was too much for Chelsea to handle these days. Even the most basic task such as loading the dishwasher or making a sandwich overwhelmed her.

With the woodwork and tiles of the fireplace gleaming, Emma turned to the antique desk in the corner covered by bills from the notorious Sounder Health Care. She didn't dare mess with the paperwork. Poor Chelsea had been fighting with the insurance provider since Annabelle's birth. Emma had come to hate Sounder, but Leo had explained that they had to stick with the plan; it was the only health care coverage his employer provided.

A wooden frame stuck out from under the fold of an invoice. Sighing, Emma slid it out and frowned at the empty shadow box, one of Chelsea's projects. Just before Annabelle was born, Chelsea had talked a mile a minute about creating an archive of her baby's birth mementoes. The knit skullcap from the hospital, a copy of her birth certificate, her footprint and baby booties—these souvenirs would be arranged in the box and decorated with bows that had been saved from Chelsea's baby shower.

Of course, the box was still empty. Gathering dust.

Emma wiped it off and set it on the kitchen table. She was going to take it home, along with the knickknacks and the footprint they'd made with pink paint last week. When she returned next week, she would give it to Chelsea all assembled. Maybe that would help cheer up her sister.

In the kitchen she noticed the calendar hanging on the cork board. There were two notations under today's date: the appointment with Dr. Volmer and "date night."

Earlier in the week Chelsea had mentioned her plans to have dinner with Leo, their first date in weeks. She had asked

Emma to babysit, but Emma and Jake had plans: dinner with one of the partners at Jake's firm. She checked the wall clock.

It would be good for Chelsea to get out. And after Chelsea's episode this afternoon, Emma would feel better knowing Leo would be by her side throughout the evening.

"Hey, sleepyhead. Are you still on for your date with Leo tonight?"

"What?" Slowly, Chelsea's eyes slid open. "Is it Friday?"

"It is. Do you want to start getting ready? I'll listen for Annabelle if you want to take a shower."

Dazed, Chelsea sat up on the couch, pushed off the fleece throw blanket, and raked her hair back. "I forgot about the date. I'm not really in the mood. The black holes are back."

"Well, maybe this will help." Emma took a pink pill from the new container and handed it to her sister. "I got your prescription filled while you were napping."

Chelsea stared off into the distance. "Thanks. I need a shower."

Emma knew that a shower was one of Chelsea's only relaxations. "Indulge yourself."

"Okay." Chelsea rose, letting the blanket drop onto the floor.

Watching her head upstairs without picking it up or straightening the pillows on the couch, Emma found it hard to measure just how far Chelsea's life had wavered off course.

Later, as she styled her sister's long auburn hair with a blow dryer, Emma told her about the appointment with Dr. Chin. "The soonest I could get was a week from Wednesday."

In the mirror, she saw Chelsea's glum expression, the strain of her lips as she mulled it over.

"Is that date okay for you? You didn't have anything on your calendar."

"I guess," Chelsea said, staring down at the floor. "But by that time I'll be all cured from my little pink pills."

"That would be nice, but I'm trying to be realistic. I know you get sick of hearing me be your cheerleader, but these bad times will pass. This is temporary. Dr. Chin is going to help you, and you're going to start feeling better soon. You'll be your old self again, ripping down walls and building window seats. You'll start to enjoy being a mother. And in six months, my baby will be here, and the cousins can grow together and bond like siblings."

She brushed Chelsea's hair away from her eyes. "They'll be close like us. Two nuts stuck together like peanut brittle." It was an old family expression coined by their uncle John one summer vacation when Chelsea and Emma had spent endless hours together on the lake.

Chelsea nodded, still a million miles away.

"And then I'm going to need your help. You're going to be the one with the experience, while I'll just be learning how to be a mother. You'll help me out, right?"

But Chelsea didn't answer. She just kept staring at the floor, her blue eyes icy and vacant.

Chapter 6

One hand on the steering wheel, Leo Green sang along under his breath with the radio, allowing himself to feel a little happy. It was the end of the week, his last meeting had gone well, and he and Chelsea had their first dinner date in a long time.

Man, he needed a night out. They both did.

The past few months had been hell for Chelsea, he knew that, but he also knew things would get better soon. Well, he hoped so.

Chelsea had gotten a double whammy, losing her mom and then going through a difficult C-section just days later. And because of the baby coming, Chelsea wasn't allowed to fly down to Florida for the funeral. The timing had been terrible.

Judith's death had cast a shadow over their baby's birth—at least for Chelsea. From the outside looking in, Leo could see that without being swept away by the feelings that had overcome his wife. Emotional grief from losing her mother and physical shock and pain from the surgery. If depression was a churning river, Chelsea had slipped in around the time of their baby's birth and she was still struggling against the current.

And here I am, kneeling at the edge of the river, clutching her hand to keep her from being swept away.

He wouldn't give up. He kept trying to pull her out. But honestly, he had thought they would have made some progress by now. Three whole months. People lost their parents, and time healed those wounds, right? And the doctor said her body was fully recovered from the C-section. But still, whenever Leo was around, she sat in the corner of the couch, curled in a ball. Tuned out, checked out . . . sometimes emotionally vacant. When she cried, she couldn't tell him what had set her off.

This was not the girl he had married. He had fallen in love with a capable, fast-talking dynamo of energy. Full of life and ideas and dreams and hopes . . . that was the thing. Chelsea's beautiful blue eyes had lost that glimmer of hope.

Sometimes, when he talked about news from the office or possible renovations to their house, she perked up. She would lift her head from the sofa and speak and even fire back ideas at him. Traces of the old Chelsea made him wonder if it had been a mistake to let her give up her job at the magazine to be a full-time mom, but when Chelsea made that decision there'd been no arguing with her. "A baby needs full-time care the first year of its life," she had told Leo, "and I'm not going to let someone else step in and do that for us. I'm the DIY Girl, right? I'm going to be home for our baby."

Her decision had appealed to the part of him that loved old traditions. His mom had been at home for him and his siblings, and though he'd resented her meddling at times, in the long run he knew that her watchful eye and guidance had kept them all on the right path.

He wanted the same for his daughter . . . but somehow it wasn't working out that way. Right now, Chelsea wasn't there for anyone. Not for him or for Annabee. Her aloofness had pressed him to spend more time cuddling and cajoling little Lady Baldy. He and the baby had bonded in a way that surprised him, but he hated seeing Chelsea watching them from the outside. It tore him up to see her crying, and it really annoyed him when she said there was nothing wrong.

But he was past annoyance now.

He had moved into action phase, pressing her to reach out for help, and finally, Chelsea was there, too.

She had made an appointment with her doctor. Today was

the day, and from talking with Emma he was pretty sure his wife would be starting on antidepressants. "Postpartum depression," Emma had called it. He didn't know much about women's things, but he was glad it had a name and a cure. Medication and maybe some counseling. Once Chelsea figured it out, she would be all over it, driving across town to therapy and setting her phone alarm to remember her medication.

Or at least that was the way Chelsea used to be, before the baby.

He couldn't wait for the day when he came home from work and found his old Chelsea back, turning the attic shutters into a coffee table or coming up with a design to turn an unused closet into a powder room. For Leo, there was no turn-on like a woman who knew how to use a miter box and wield a hammer.

The glare of the setting sun made him squint, and he reached for his sunglasses. Driving had always been therapeutic for him, and it was even better to be driving on a Friday after kicking butt in a meeting. Things were looking up.

His cell phone rang, and a local number he didn't recognize came up on the screen. Probably someone calling from Olney Inc. After the presentation he'd just made, they had to be ready to sign on. "This is Leo."

"Did you miss me?"

The sultry tone of the woman's voice made him sure that this wasn't one of the client's reps in the meeting. "Who's this?"

The laugh that cascaded through his car chilled him.

Jennifer.

What was his ex-wife doing, calling on a local line? "I didn't recognize the number."

"Or what? You wouldn't have answered? I know you've been ignoring my calls. I hate that."

Leo wanted to cut the line right then, but he knew that would only rile her into doing something obnoxious. "Why are you calling me, Jen? Remember our talk about moving on? Living our own lives?" After the divorce, he'd tried to be a friend to her, but it didn't work out that way. Whenever they had talked, she had felt compelled to tell him every little detail of her wayward love life. He had suspected that she'd been trying to make him jealous so that he'd come running back to her, but it wasn't going to happen. He had broken up because he couldn't stand being smothered by her. Well, that and she was a little too crazy for him. The good crazy, the "let's do it in the fitting room at the mall" hadn't aged well for Leo. Once it was over, he had never looked back.

"You didn't tell me you had a baby," she said flatly.

His teeth locked painfully. Damn! The more she knew about his personal life, the worse things would be. "There are a lot of things I don't tell you. What did you do, hack the files at Social Security?"

Her laugh sounded forced, a witch's cackle. "Silly. I drove by your house and saw wifey with the stroller."

"What are you doing in New Rochelle?"

"If you'd answered my messages, you'd know I'm back."

Whenever Leo saw that he had a message from Jennifer, he deleted it right away. Life was too short to listen to messages from your ex-wife.

"You would know that things didn't work out with the job in Philly," she went on. "Or the boyfriend. So I'm back in New Rochelle. They gave me my old job back at Sparklet."

Leo winced. Jen, living in New Rochelle? This was not going to be good.

"Hello? Are you still there?"

"Yeah, I'm here." He rubbed his knuckles against the bristles on his chin.

"We must have a bad connection because I didn't hear you jumping for joy. This is the part where you say, 'Welcome back, Jen. I missed you.' And I say, 'Thanks, Leo. I missed you, too.'"

"Honestly, Jennifer? I've moved on."

"Everyone moves on. But I'm sure you can still find some time to see your old friend."

"I'm busy. Between work and the baby, there's no time . . ."

And if Chelsea hears you're back in town, it will put her over the edge. Chelsea knew all about his ex-wife's borderline personality. She'd been dating Leo when Jen was still stalking him, leaving notes on his car and sneaking into his apartment until he changed the locks. Chelsea had always been cool about it, knowing that Jennifer was a part of his past that preceded her. She also knew that he'd never given Jennifer any play since the divorce, but that didn't make it easier to deal with the psycho ex.

"Your stroller is adorable, with those little green elephants on it," Jennifer cooed, as if she were talking to a newborn. "Chelsea isn't looking so good, but she never was big on fashion. It got me thinking, though. I'm sorry we never had a baby."

Leo winced. Thank God that never happened.

"It would have been a little bit of both of us." Her voice was low and seductive now. "A little bit of you for me to hold on to forever."

A way for you to tighten the noose around my neck.

"It wasn't meant to be," he said. "We weren't a good couple, Jen."

"But don't you ever think about what would have happened if I didn't lose that baby?"

His hands gripped the wheel, white-knuckled. Jennifer had gotten pregnant once, but she had miscarried in the first few weeks. Thank God. A kid between them would have made it even harder to extract her from his life, and they wouldn't have done the kid any service, being split up and fighting whenever they saw each other.

"You've got to live in the here and now," he said. "And I've got to go."

"Okay, but I'll see you around. Now that I'm back in town we just might run into each other."

He heard the threat in her singsong voice. "Don't plan anything, Jen. I'm counting on you to give us some space."

"It could be a coincidence!"

"Good-bye, Jen."

"See you around."

Leo cut the connection, vowing not to let Jennifer ruin his good mood and the evening ahead. He was going on a date with his wife and best friend, and Jen wasn't going to spoil their evening together. He would worry about her tomorrow or next week . . . or some random day when she leaped out in front of him at the hardware store with a slightly mad gleam in her eyes.

Jennifer was a problem he could handle later.

Chapter 7

It was all so random.

The day had dawned full of hope, then plunged so low she felt sure it would be the last day of her life. Then, hours later, the skies had opened up and served Chelsea a slice of blue heaven. In the purple light of dusk she found herself dining with her husband, surrounded by soft music and laughter and the smell of warm bread.

Seated beside Leo in a booth with a view of the dancing flames in the restaurant's gas fireplace, Chelsea allowed herself to fantasize that they were vacationing at a mountain lodge—just the two of them. He looked so handsome—like a clean-cut lumberjack in a flannel shirt—and she actually felt like a woman again in a royal-blue V-neck sweater that brought out the color of her eyes.

While they'd waited for a table, she caught a glimpse of an elegant woman in the window with shiny dark hair and sumptuous curves that couldn't be masked by a black jacket. When she turned her head and the woman turned at the same time, she realized it was her.

So she didn't look as bad as she felt. She had nodded at her reflection—a small nudge of encouragement.

They had left Annie in the care of a professional baby nurse, whom Leo had found through an agency two months ago.

Helen Rosekind was crazy expensive, but capable and tidy. "She seems to like Annabelle," Leo had said as they drove off.

"Baby nurses have to act that way," Chelsea had countered.

"Well, Annie likes her," he had said.

Annie likes everyone, except her own mother, Chelsea had thought, but she let it drop. The farther their car had traveled from the house and the baby, the lighter she had begun to feel.

The spell was lifting. The short break was giving her room to breathe.

The waiter arrived with their appetizers—roasted-pepper tapas and crab cakes—and the cloak of doom lifted as they turned their attention to the food. Chelsea loved the tapas—sweet and just a hint of hot.

"I wish we could make roasted peppers at home." She spooned a dollop of minced peppers onto a small disk of bread. "But you really need a gas stove to do it right."

"I wonder what it would cost to bring in a gas line."

"Mmm . . . and we could bring it over to the fireplace, so we'd have a fire at the touch of a button. Better for the environment, too."

Leo swallowed, studying her. "Uh-oh. The wheels are turning."

"Did someone say kitchen renovation?"

Leo swiped a napkin over his mouth. "We don't have the money for that right now."

"But if we could bring the gas line in cheaply . . . I wonder how much of that I could do myself? I mean, of course I wouldn't mess around without a plumber on the big stuff. But I could patch the walls, inside and out. There's a lot I could do. And it would increase the value of the house. . . ."

Chelsea saw herself standing at a gas stove in their kitchen, holding a pepper over the burner until its skin bubbled brown as the aroma suffused the air. Gas was the only way to cook.

"It would be good for me to have a project. Something I could write up for the magazine." She craved her old life. She would do anything just to get a piece of it back.

When she'd left her job, she planned to write in her spare

time—while the baby was napping. So far, there hadn't been any spare time. Well, not really. When Annabelle took the rare nap, Chelsea fell into bed, too exhausted to think straight.

But it didn't have to be that way. Tomorrow, when Annie dozed off, she would open her laptop and start researching the cost of a gas line.

"It would be great if we could swing it," Leo said. "I just don't want to give you any more pressure than you already have."

"But that would be a fun job." And she definitely felt up to it. Tonight she felt pretty and independent again.

Alive.

Later, while they were eating their entrees, Leo reached his fork over to give her a taste of the lobster with vodka sauce, and a drop of creamy sauce fell to her chest. It missed her sweater, plopping on bare skin just above her cleavage.

Seeing that no one was looking, Leo wiggled his eyebrows mischievously, stuck out his tongue, and swooped down to lick it off.

The gesture was more comic than sensual, and they both shook with suppressed laughter.

"Tasty," Leo said triumphantly. "Let's see the chef try to top that one."

"I guess I'm one of today's specials," she teased, noticing how broad his shoulders looked in his flannel shirt. Such a soft flannel. If she pressed her face to it, she might never again lift her head.

Chelsea took a leisurely breath, relaxed by the warm air and red wine she'd sipped from a beautiful round glass. Sitting here, caught by his smoky brown eyes, she remembered why she had fallen in love with him. Silly and serious, proud and humble, Leo possessed the contradictions that fascinated her every day. She smiled.

"Now that's the Chelsea I know. When was the last time I saw that smile?"

"When there was just the two of us and I could sleep through the night."

"Ah, sleep. Such a beautiful thing." He swirled the red wine in the fat glass. "You haven't been getting enough. I'm sorry, honey."

She shook her head. "Sleep is just one part of it. I miss our old life. The quiet. The freedom to do what we wanted whenever we wanted. Even the stupid things, like the luxury of a quick shower and then flying out the door without a diaper bag or a million instructions to the sitter."

"Yeah. You really get the brunt of it, having Annie all the time."

"I never thought I'd say this, but I miss work. I miss having a cubicle to go to. The whole office scene with people to talk to. I want to commiserate with the other staff about the bad coffee and the weather. Chat about kids and in-laws and movies and TV shows. Buy bad candy bars for fundraisers and take people to lunch for their birthdays."

"Please . . . I had to buy two chocolate bars last week for Mitch's kid. They're still sitting in my desk drawer." He scratched the center of his forehead, where the creases formed when he worried. Annie had those creases, too, though Chelsea wondered what she could be worrying about. "But it will get better," Leo promised.

"I don't want better. I want my old life back."

Without Annie.

She couldn't say it, but the unspeakable words buzzed in her subconscious.

Without Annie.

She longed for her life before the baby. She wanted to turn back time and get a major do over.

"Wow." Leo looked down at the table. "I can't imagine life without Annabelle anymore. The house would feel weird without her. You don't think about it before you have a kid, but they just fill every minute. When you're not doing something for them, you're watching the stuff they do or trying to interpret their squeaks."

As Leo described the things Annabelle did that fascinated

him, she ran her thumb over her water glass and tried to find the same enthusiasm in her soul. She wanted to love her baby. But when she searched inside . . . there was nothing but pain and resentment.

"But here's the thing. I know we're in different places right now." He took a sip of wine, swallowed, those worry lines creasing his forehead. "I talked to Emma while you were getting ready—just for a minute—and she told me that Volmer wasn't so helpful. She mentioned your breakdown on the ride home."

Chelsea winced. "Let's not ruin our night out."

"Just give me a minute and we'll get off it. I just have to say this." He covered her hand with his. "Honey, you're suffering. I see that. The depression and the visions . . ."

She pressed her fingertips to her temples, as if she could hold on to her composure as guilt blew over her. Of course, she had told Leo about the bad visions. . . .

He would have been an idiot not to notice when she hid away the kitchen knives because she imagined them flipping through the air and landing on Annie, slicing clean through her body. And the stretch of days when she refused to use the oven because she kept imagining how Annie's little body would fit inside.

"What you're going through, it's more than anyone should have to bear."

Her throat was getting tight. She didn't want to do this here . . . not now. She didn't want to think of that growing mountain of insurance statements and doctors' bills in the corner of the living room.

"All I'm saying is, I think you should go to this appointment with Emma's doctor. Even if we have to pay, it's worth the money to get you better. Screw the insurance. We'll dip into our savings if we need to. Okay?"

"Our savings?" Her hands dropped away as she faced him. "You would use our savings on a doctor?"

"Of course. Whatever it takes . . . whatever you need, honey."

His compassion made Chelsea want to cry. He was so sweet. She had married a good guy.

"What if Dr. Volmer's little pink pills help?" she asked.

"He's not really addressing the problem. He wouldn't even order a blood screening."

She swallowed back the knot in her throat, taking a swig of wine for good measure. "I'll try Emma's doctor. I hate to blow our savings, but Emma said she would help."

"We'll figure it out."

With Leo beside her, promising his help, hope seemed as real and solid as his hand on hers. Maybe he was right.

As their entrees were served, she dreamed of mornings spent on the kitchen project and afternoons spent writing about it. She could imagine the momentary buzz of success when she stood beside a plumber, turning a switch to spark the flame of a new gas stove. She could see better times and happiness ahead.

The only problem was that she could not see Annabelle in that picture.

Their magical night ended all too soon. A trip to the ladies' room revealed that the pads in the cups of Chelsea's bra were damp; she would have to either feed the baby or pump soon. Disappointment was a bitter taste on the back of her tongue. She didn't have an ounce of freedom.

"No dessert for us," she told Leo when she returned to the table.

"No problem. I'll get the check." He was good-natured about things. Sometimes she wished he would join in her anger at the futility of trying to have a life of her own.

But not Leo. He talked about Annabelle's cute habits as they drove home. He was worried about missing her when he went away on his business trip next week.

"Maybe you should cancel your trip," she said as dark anxiety came seeping back into her thoughts. "I don't know how I'm going to handle nights without you." Sometimes the only break in her day was handing off the baby to him when he got home from work.

"I can't. This is the convention that gives us our biggest sales boost."

"This is the Boston trip?" She knew it was huge for him, but it worried her to be alone with the baby right now.

"Let's see if Mrs. Rosekind is available to come over a few nights," he suggested. "She would be a big help to you, right?"

"We can't afford her."

"We're dipping into our savings."

"Not for a sitter." Especially at forty bucks an hour. She had balked the first time the woman at the agency had mentioned the price on the phone. "We represent licensed nurses with experience caring for infants and children," the woman had told her. "Sometimes you have to pay extra for peace of mind." And after they'd come home from a dinner and found their teenage sitter making out on the couch with a goth boy introduced as "Krispy," Leo had decided they needed to pay for peace of mind.

"The trip is more than a week away," Leo said as he pulled into the driveway. "Your medicine should kick in by then. Maybe you'll feel ready to handle Annie-bananee when the time comes."

Chelsea's hand squeezed the armrest. Better to pinch the hell out of the car than lash out at her husband. "We'll see."

Their little house looked quaint, the yellow squares of light from its windows shining cheerfully against the indigo sky. It was a cute house. So why did dread tug at Chelsea as she plodded up the steps? Her breasts ached and she suspected that milk had soaked through to her sweater. She had to get inside and pump or feed the baby, but every step was difficult.

Inside, the kitchen smelled of bleach and the fixtures over the sink gleamed.

"I think she scrubbed the floor." Leo nodded, impressed.

Chelsea wanted to point out that the woman was here to watch their baby, but it seemed like a lame argument when she'd left the house sparkling.

The living room smelled of lemon wax. The sofa cushions were plumped. The magazines were fanned out on the coffee table, like in a doctor's office. Mrs. Rosekind sat in the Scandinavian rocker that Chelsea had restored. The lamplight turned her hair to pale gold. For a woman in her forties, Mrs. Rosekind had young skin, but the washed-out shade of her hair always reminded Chelsea of a schoolmarm. She was a little thick through the middle, but she wore it well, with strong cheekbones and cheerful animal-print scrubs, the kind that pediatric nurses wore. The nurse was reading a copy of *Parents Magazine,* which Chelsea hadn't been able to focus on since before the baby was born.

She glanced up, the line of her bifocals evident in the light. "How was your dinner?"

"Nice," Chelsea and Leo said in unison.

Chelsea wanted to escape upstairs and pump, but she didn't want to seem rude.

"Did she cry?" Leo asked.

"For a little bit." She rose and smoothed down her smock.

"I was hoping she wouldn't give you a hard time," Leo said.

"All babies cry, Mr. Green. But she took the bottle right away, and after some fussing she went to sleep."

"She really fights sleep at night," Chelsea said.

Mrs. Rosekind nodded sympathetically. "Little Annabelle might have a touch of colic."

"That's what I was thinking," Leo said. "Sometimes when she cries at night, it sounds like she's in dire pain."

"I hope she wasn't that bad for you. I know a baby like Annabelle must be more challenging than a good baby."

The nurse turned a stoic face to Chelsea. "Oh, they're *all* good babies, Ms. Maynard. Some of them just need more care than others."

"Well, sure." Chelsea fiddled with the button of her jacket, feeling awkward. *Of course Annabelle was a good baby. She was just stuck with a bad mother.*

Leo paid the nurse, asking her if she could help out the following week when he would be out of town for business.

"Oh, no. I have a full-time job Monday to Friday, and my weekends get booked up weeks in advance. My husband would divorce me if I start working a second job during the week. But I do enjoy the little ones, and Annabelle is precious. She reminds me of my daughter when she was a baby."

Leo beamed. "Underneath all that fussing, Annie does have a great little personality."

"She's a sweet little thing," Mrs. Rosekind said. "And don't worry. I never mind the crying."

I hate the crying, Chelsea thought as she escaped up the stairs. She wished that she could say that in front of the nurse. *I hate it all . . . the whole mother thing. And you're so good at it. You'd be a better mother for my baby. Why don't you take her home for a few days . . . weeks . . . months?*

Just take her.

Chapter 8

"**Y**ou put dee lime in dee coconut, drink it all up," Leo chanted as Annie looked up at him with those amazing blue eyes that had won his heart from the moment she was born.

The delivery room docs had insisted that she couldn't see him because of those drops they always put into babies' eyes, but from the way she stared up at him, stern as a lawyer cross-examining a suspect on the stand, he knew the doctors were wrong. Annie could see him, and she wanted some answers. She wanted to know who the hell he was, what the hell she was doing here in this brightly lit room that seriously lacked décor—her mother's daughter—and why was everyone fussing over the lady on the other side of the curtain?

"You got a lot of questions for a little bundle with a button nose," he'd told her. The surgical nurses had put him in a chair at the side of the room and told him to stay put with her. So, seeing all the questions in those eyes, he'd rattled off the answers.

"I'm your dad, Leo Green. You're in an operating room. Sorry, kid, but with a C-section you didn't score the birthing suite. And all those people in blue scrubs and hats and booties and masks are working on your mom. You'll get to meet her soon, and I'm pretty sure you're gonna love her. I know I do."

Leo had talked with his daughter from the start. He gave a play-by-play on each diaper change. He asked her what she wanted to wear. Whenever he gave her a bottle, he sang to her. And though she didn't talk back yet, the look in her eyes was enough of an answer. She liked his rap.

This particular Saturday morning, it was the coconut song.

"Put a little burp in the coconut, then you'll feel better," he sang as he flipped her little body to burp her on his knee. He'd seen the position in one of Chelsea's baby books and Annie seemed to dig it.

A belch popped out, and he turned her upright in his arms. "That was a good one, Lady Baldy. Care for some more elixir of life?" He turned on the British accent as he offered her the bottle once again.

She started sucking again, less enthusiastically but that was okay, since she was almost done. This time he sang "Born to Run," singing to fill in the guitar licks. Thank God Annie-bananee was a good eater. With everything that was going on with Chelsea, he didn't know how he'd manage a picky baby.

And to Chelsea's credit, she had stayed on top of the feeding thing. Even though she was exhausted she had kept breast-feeding because she knew it was healthier for Annie and cheaper for them. She pumped milk a few times during the day so that he could do the nighttime feedings by bottle. And weekend feedings like this.

Yeah, Chelsea was trying, but after a week on the medication, he didn't see any signs that she was getting better. Granted, she hadn't had another crisis in the car, but she still wasn't the old Chelsea. She was listless and teary and lacking in energy. And with the Boston convention starting Monday, he worried about leaving Annabee alone with her.

The crisis in the car still worried him. In the past, Chelsea's freak-outs had involved harmless fantasies, like imagining Annie flying into the wall or thinking how her little body would fit into the oven. Sick ideas, yeah, but she had never thought to act on any of those visions.

Until last week in the car.

And the car—that was like a soaring rocket. A serious threat to his wife and daughter.

Annie had dozed off. He took the bottle away, and her lips still smacked at the air. Her eyes were closed, but her pale brows lifted in a hopeful expression, and then relaxed as she settled into a deeper sleep. Nothing else in his day gave him the same contentment as taking care of her. But now he felt like he was letting her down, going off to Boston and leaving her alone with Chelsea. And Chelsea didn't seem to trust herself. Last night she had begged him to bag out of the convention.

He had half a mind to call his boss and cancel the trip, but in the long run it would hurt his commissions and his chance for promotion. Boston was the plum conference. If he bowed out, he'd be cutting into his income. His family's income.

But he couldn't take the chance of Chelsea having another crisis . . . the chance of either his wife or baby being injured or worse.

He wasn't sure what to do.

With Annie napping in her bucket seat on the kitchen counter, he started making breakfast. Most meal preps started with a search for the kitchen knives from wherever Chelsea had hidden them. Today he checked the cabinet where they kept the pots, the high cabinet over the fridge, and the coat closet, where he located the butcher block of knives in the back with a scarf wrapped around the handles. The knife hunt was always a pain in the neck, but he indulged her on it.

He chopped chives and ham to put in the scrambled eggs, and took bagels out of the freezer. His boss, Mark, wouldn't be too happy if he ducked out at the last minute. Shit. Well, it was worth a phone call to Mark's cell today, just to see how hard it would be to send someone else. He glanced at the clock and realized the call could wait. Nobody liked to do business before eight on a Saturday morning.

If he had to go, he needed some plan to keep Annie and Chelsea safe. Maybe Chelsea would agree not to drive the car while he was gone. He could hide the keys to her Subaru.

Yeah, but what if there was an emergency? His wife was a grown woman; he had to trust her with the car keys.

He just had to make sure everything was in order for her. He would clean the house today—thoroughly—and get everything under control so that Chelsea could focus on taking care of Annie while he was gone.

He scraped a block of cheddar against the grater. Yeah, take out your frustrations on a brick of cheese.

Major frustrations . . . and a fair share of anger that he kept tamped down way below the surface.

Leo considered himself to be a flexible guy. He could roll with the punches, but never in a million years had he expected this. To see his wife drained of life and enthusiasm. That she could become such a zombie that he wasn't sure if he could trust her with their baby. . . . That was sick.

With everything prepped for the scramble, he decided to flake a while and give Chelsea some more time to sleep. He switched on the television and paced over to the windows. A fine snow was falling, but it didn't look like anything that would stick. Across the fence, Louise Pickler's yard looked pristine—a bed of smooth white snow with a shiny melted glaze. Their neighbor was still at her winter place in South Carolina.

By contrast their backyard was a haphazard pattern of snow mounds and trampled areas where he had walked Annie around in the snow last weekend. A happy mess, framed by the fence that he and Chelsea had put in themselves. The memory of her boundless energy for the project made him smile. His beautiful wife had gotten right in there, mixing cement and fixing posts. In her baseball cap and overalls, she was a holy terror with a nail gun.

That was the sort of enthusiasm she brought to everything, before the baby.

He missed his wife.

His breath clouded the window and he turned away, looking at the clock and the foods chopped and ready to go. Suddenly, he didn't have the energy to pull it all together.

Besides, the whole world looked better after a nap. He'd crack this nut later.

He placed a receiving blanket over the sleeping Annabee. Stretching out on the couch, he pulled a fleece throw to his chin and closed his eyes.

Chapter 9

Leo's voice, so animated and full of love, pulled her from sleep. It wasn't a bad way to wake up. Her breasts were thick and sore as she stretched toward the clock.

After ten thirty?

Leo must have given Annie a bottle so that Chelsea could sleep in.

"Don't be a wiggle worm." Leo's voice came from the nursery next door. "If we get this diaper on, you get to eat." Leo actually seemed to enjoy changing Annie's diaper.

The floor was cold on her bare feet, prompting Chelsea to move faster. She put on a robe and fished through the cluttered closet floor for her slippers as her husband cajoled the baby. He was pleased that her diaper rash was better, and he touted the fact that they'd been using "good old-fashioned Vaseline."

With all the books she had studied before the baby was born, all the tips on baby care, she had never thought she'd be too alienated to use the information. But whenever he was here, Leo was the one caring for Annie. Leo did the shopping. Leo did the cooking. If Chelsea didn't produce milk, she could physically bow out of the family triangle. She could be free.

Well, almost. Guilt would follow her like a gray shadow.

Her lips puckered as she struggled to hold back a crying jag. She took a deep breath and pulled the brush through her dark hair. Despite last night's sleep, there were violet circles under her eyes and her face was puffy. This was not a good look for her; depression was sucking her soul away.

Brushing her hair back, Chelsea wondered if her mother had gone through this. If only she could ask her.

"Let's go wake up the *mamasita*," Leo told Annie.

"She's up," Chelsea called.

"Hey, sleepyhead. I'm getting Annie changed so that I can take her for a walk in the park when she finishes eating. I figure you could use some downtime."

"Sounds good."

"Don't worry," he told the baby. "We'll bundle you up. I'll zip you into that little pink puffy thing that makes you look like a Christmas goose."

She envied the easy conversation Leo had with the baby. He connected with her. He loved her.

"Don't you worry about Mommy," he said. "She gets to see you all the time, but I only get Annabee weekends and nights."

You would think he was talking to a real person.

Well, Annabelle was real. Just not close to possessing conversation skills yet.

She met them in the hall, where Leo held Annabelle so that she faced out, her little eyes shining as she stared at Chelsea. In Leo's arms, she looked cute and innocent.

"The milk truck has arrived," Chelsea said, reaching for her.

"I'll carry her down," Leo offered, turning toward the stairs. "If you want, I can scramble some eggs while you're feeding her. I've got it all ready to go. You hungry?"

"Famished."

In her usual spot on the couch, Chelsea pulled the baby to her breast. Annie latched on and seemed to snuggle against her.

The emotion that tugged at Chelsea was bittersweet. She didn't mind feeding the baby knowing she'd be taken away for the rest of the morning. Was that normal? Staring down into Annabelle's serious blue eyes, Chelsea knew she had strayed from normal three months ago.

Leo chatted as he cooked. The weather. Annabelle's new

Yoda smile. His upcoming trip. He was so darned happy; Chelsea hated to be the spoiler in his day.

"Hey, it's day eight, right?" He had been keeping track of her time on the Nebula. "How are you feeling? Notice any changes?"

"I do. They're not the happy pills I'd like them to be, but I'm thinking more clearly, and things don't seem to be as dark and overwhelming as they were a week ago."

"That's great!" Leo stabbed the spatula in the air as if it were a trophy. "You're doing great, Chels, and I know it will keep getting better and better."

Chelsea hoped he was right. She was worried about being on her own with Annie this coming week—a first for them.

When Annabelle finished nursing, Leo produced a plate of steaming eggs, a buttered English muffin, and orange wedges.

"Thanks." Chelsea didn't know what she would do without him. Leo was the only thing that kept her going.

"You're welcome." He checked the kitchen drawers, the hook by the stove . . . the drawers of the rolltop desk.

"What are you looking for?" she asked, holding a forkful of eggs in the air.

"Your car keys." He rolled open the desktop and whistled at the mound of bills. "Hon? These look like they're getting out of control," he said gently.

Her chest tightened. "I know."

"Are we behind on our bills?"

"It's all insurance stuff and doctors' bills. It's all their mistakes. They still haven't added Annabelle to our policy, so all her bills keep bouncing back."

"I see that." He leafed through the bills.

All this week, she hadn't made a single call to Sounder. "I've been waiting until I feel better, and you know, I think I can face it now. I'll get on it today."

"Do you want some help sorting this out?"

She put the plate on the coffee table. She would love help, but this was her job. She was supposed to take care of the bills so Leo could focus on work. Clients and commissions. "I can do it. I'll call them today, during their Saturday hours. I just think they secretly try not to pay, thinking that they're going to wear you down. I bet a lot of people just give up trying to get through on the line and pay the damned bills."

"Could be," he said absently. "But we need to get this stuff resolved. Some of these bills are two months overdue. We don't want to screw up our credit."

"You're right. I'll call Sounder today."

"Thanks, honey. And if you need a hand with it, I'm game. I've got the afternoon to set you up for the next week. I'm going to clean the house and stock up on groceries. You'll be good to go for the week."

After Leo carried Annie out the door, Chelsea went straight to the shower. The hot stream of water was her only waking escape, and she sighed as she stepped in and faced the faucet. Often she sat on the floor and cried, letting the hot water wash away her tears. But today, she didn't need to collapse on the floor.

Was that a sign that she was getting better? She hoped so.

Her hair was still drying when she opened her laptop. Last week, after she had come up with a mission, she had pushed herself to start researching the gas line installation. She wasn't ready to jump into the project, but she could start some research.

As she waited for her laptop to turn on, the ugly pile of bills caught her eye. Leo would be so pleased if she made a dent in it. With a decisive frown, she clicked on the Web site for Sounder Health Care. There had to be some way to reset her password.

She tried logging in under her usual password, but it was invalid. She requested a new password and it sent her a link, but when she tried to use it, she was knocked off the site.

"Grr. This is why I hate you so much!" Fired up, she snatched the phone and called the company's eight-hundred number.

"*Thank you for calling Sounder Health Care, where your*

health needs are our priority," said the man on the recorded message.

"I don't think so." She paced from kitchen to living room.

"Do you know you can pay a premium or settle a claim using our online service?" the recording asked.

"Actually, you can't, because the Web site won't let me in." She knew she sounded like a raving lunatic, but it felt good to argue with the dummy voice.

"Your call will be handled in the order that it is received. You are currently caller number seven."

"Lucky seven. You'd just better answer before you close shop." On Saturdays the "helpline" was only staffed until one p.m. She wondered if Janet, her "personal rep," would really be taking her call on a Saturday.

She sat down at the little desk and leafed through the invoices, trying to stack them in order.

One pile was for Annabelle. None of the bills from Annie's pediatrician had been paid because Sounder claimed to have no record of her birth. Chelsea had sent them the birth certificate five times. Five maddening trips to the grocery store to use the photocopy machine.

And then there were Chelsea's bills, rejected for a variety of reasons. Somehow she had been added to the policy as Chelsea Green—Leo's last name—though she had always been Chelsea Maynard. The company refused to pay for the C-section surgeon, saying the procedure wasn't preapproved, though it had been an emergency.

Chelsea nibbled on a cuticle as she waded through the bills. Eventually, the company would pay these; she knew that. The frustrating part was that she had to waste her time and energy taking them to task on every invoice.

After twenty minutes of waiting and pacing, her neck and shoulders ached and she fantasized about the scathing letter of complaint she would write to the president of Sounder.

After nearly thirty minutes, a female voice answered. "This is Janet. . . ."

My personal rep.

"How may I help you?"

"I have a mountain of medical bills that need to be straightened out because your company keeps rejecting all our claims," Chelsea said, trying to temper her anger. "There's so much paperwork here, I don't even know where to start."

"Let's start with your name and policy number," the woman said smoothly.

Chelsea paced impatiently as she recited reams of personal information. Insured's name. Policy numbers and Social Security numbers. Dates of birth and employers. Address, phone, and cell. "Do we really have to go over all this, when I have a stack of claims to straighten out?"

"We need to confirm that you are who you say you are, Mrs. Green."

"Well, for starters, I'm not Mrs. Green. My name is Chelsea Maynard."

"Mmm. I see some documentation about a name change here." A pause, and then Janet added, "I'm not sure who handled this before, but there's a note from the underwriters saying that you need to supply us with a copy of the court order changing your name to Chelsea Maynard."

"I have always been Chelsea Maynard."

"Is that your maiden name?"

Maiden name was such an archaic term. "You people were the ones who insisted on calling me Chelsea Green, just because Green is my husband's last name. It was your mistake and you need to fix it."

"Where I was raised, a woman changed her name when she got married." The Sounder representative sounded smug, judgmental. "Are you and Mr. Green legally married?"

Chelsea pressed a hand to her head, trying to keep her comments in check. Yelling at Janet would only slow down the process.

"Next claim . . ." Chelsea picked up the stack of claims for Annabelle and asked if she had been added to their policy yet.

"Annabelle's birth certificate was scanned in, but not processed yet," Janet said, as if she were proud to have found the information.

"What does that mean?"

"Processing takes two to four weeks."

"Another four weeks?" Chelsea tossed Annabelle's claims into the air. "She'll be four months old! The kid will be out of diapers by the time you pay a cent for her!"

"That's our procedure." Janet's voice was deathly calm. "We have to authenticate a document before adding a child to a policy."

"It's ludicrous!" Tears stung Chelsea's eyes. "Just as insane as refusing to pay for an emergency C-section!"

"If you are referring to a claim, you need to give me the claim number."

Through her tears, Chelsea read off the number on the printed form.

"It's the coding that's the problem," Janet explained. "This procedure wasn't coded as an emergency surgery, so we're not contractually obliged to pay for it. Elective surgery requires thirty days approval time."

Defeated, Chelsea collapsed on the sofa. "I was splayed open on the operating table like a filleted fish," she said, her voice low and hollow. "My uterus was outside my body. Inside out. And I was awake and shaking and sick when I should have been welcoming my baby into the world."

A sob rolled from her throat, and for a moment she forgot about the woman on the phone and cried for the woman who felt like she was dying while the object of her dreams, the baby she had carried inside and tried to nurture, was beyond her reach, experiencing the world away from her mother.

She cried for herself. She cried for the baby who had been taken from her womb and somehow had never reconnected with her.

Her thoughts were far distant when the voice on the phone brought her back.

"Listen to what I am saying." Janet spoke slowly, like a condescending first grade teacher. "The charges and procedure need to be properly coded and resubmitted."

"Why can't you change the code yourself? Just fix it, please."

"I don't have the authority to do that. Your doctor needs to sign off on it."

"Are you fucking kidding me? The doctors don't even sign these bills when they're submitted electronically."

"Let me remind you that I don't make the rules. I am an employee of Sounder Health Care."

"This is how the contract goes. I pay my premiums and you pay my medical expenses. You pay to take care of my baby and me when we have medical needs . . . and you can't withhold payment."

"We'll be happy to pay when the coding is corrected."

"Oh, it will be corrected. And then, then you'll pay through the nose. You'll be paying for my shrink, because I'm depressed and delusional." The fury frightened Chelsea, but she couldn't stop now. "That's right. Your company has driven me crazy! I keep seeing my baby die a hundred different ways, and I've considered ending my own life. I almost crashed my car into a concrete post. How would Sounder like that? Maybe I won't die and . . . and your company will have to pay to keep me suspended in a vegetative state. How about that? Or do you not have a code for brain-dead?"

After a pert silence, the rep continued. "I see here that you're on Nebula for postpartum depression. How is that working?"

"It's helping a little . . . I don't know. Are you a doctor?"

"Ms. Maynard . . . Chelsea . . . I understand that you're upset. You sound absolutely overwhelmed. Maybe your husband should handle these insurance matters. Can you put him on?"

"My husband has a full-time job and he's leaving town Monday and . . . I'm trying to handle this if you would just do your job and help me."

"I would like to help you, but I can only process what I've been given. You need to get your doctor to resubmit some of these invoices, and then there's the matter of your name change."

"I never changed my name!"

"I'm simply telling you what the procedure is to correct these issues."

Chelsea had two words for Janet from Sounder, but she didn't want to waste her breath. She took dark pleasure in cutting off the connection and tossing the phone onto the couch. Curled up in her familiar spot on the couch, she sobbed into her sleeve.

The disk had beckoned to her from the drawer when she was tucking away some paid bills, and now Chelsea sat mesmerized, hugging her knees to her chest, as she watched her old self and her handsome husband talking to their unborn child.

The woman on the screen glowed with happiness.

Her blue eyes sparkled like sapphires and her dark hair framed her heart-shaped face perfectly as she rubbed her belly and looked right into the lens of the video camera. She had worn her favorite maternity outfit for the video—the black-and-white houndstooth with a black velvet collar and buttons.

Leo sat tall beside her in a button-down black shirt, and she thought his broad shoulders and lean belly were such a nice complement to her round, very pregnant shape.

"I have always wanted to be a mother," the old Chelsea told the camera. "It's always been the number-one thing I knew I had to accomplish in life. Ever since I was a little girl playing with dolls."

Leo sat beside her, his goofy smile indicating he was about to spring a joke. "And I never really played with dolls," Leo said, "but I'm looking forward to playing with you."

"He means it," Chelsea added. "He's like an otter. If it's not fun, he won't do it."

"Don't tell her that." He nudged her. "She'll think her old man is a couch potato with no work ethic."

"Between the two of us, she's going to see plenty of work getting done." Chelsea smiled at the camera. "So we're in our eighth month, but we haven't decided on your name yet. I'm in love with Chloe."

"Isn't that the name of a perfume?"

"I also like Samantha."

"Sam." Leo rubbed his chin. "Perfect name if she's going to sell used cars."

She turned to him. "And what's wrong with selling cars?"

"Nothing at all. But wouldn't you rather she sold brand-new Mercedeses than used Plymouths?" Leo squinted, then snapped his fingers. "Wait! How about Mercedes? You can't argue with superior quality."

"You might as well call her Beamer or Porsche."

"Then we could have our own version of *Leave it to Beamer*."

Chelsea rolled her eyes. "As you can see, your father has name issues. But don't worry, sweet pea. I won't let him name you after a car. We'll work it all out before you get here."

The front door opened and Leo's greeting boomed through the downstairs just as Chelsea was watching the beautiful couple on the monitor wave good-bye.

"Whatcha watching?" he asked, depositing Annie's carrier on the coffee table. He tilted his head at the screen and brightened. "Hey! I know that couple! Play it again so that Annabelle can watch. I don't think she's seen it yet, has she?"

"She's three months old. She doesn't even tune in to *Baby Einstein*."

"But she might get something out of it. Play it again, hon. I haven't seen it in a long time."

His down jacket still on, he sat on the couch beside her and watched, his mouth slightly open in awe. Did he notice how beautiful she used to be? That glimmer in her eyes before her mind had become dead space?

"Look at us." He squeezed her thigh. "Are we a cute couple, or what? See, Annie? See how we talked to you even before you were born? Mommy and Daddy recorded a message, just for you."

"Back in the day when Mommy could string more than five words together in a coherent sentence," Chelsea muttered.

"What? What are you talking about? You've got a better vocabulary than anyone I know."

"But I don't need to use it anymore. I don't need to talk at all. When you leave for Boston, I could go for five whole days without talking to anyone at all."

"Not true. You gotta talk to Annie. And there's your sisters. And the man behind the deli counter."

"Titillating conversation, discussing the merits of turkey over ham."

"See that? Titillating. That's a word I would never come up with." He put his arm around Chelsea's waist and nuzzled her neck. "Just how much titillating conversation are you planning to have with that deli guy?"

She closed her eyes, wishing she could communicate how broken she was inside. "I love you," she said quietly. "But I'm so alone in this. So alone and scared."

He stopped teasing her neck and pulled away so that she could see the sadness in his smoky eyes. "I know that. You know I'm worried about you."

She nodded.

"You know I love you. But I don't know what more I can do to help besides getting you to that new doctor."

Stay home! Don't leave me here alone. . . .

She was so scared to let him go, even for a day . . . so scared of what she might do.

But Leo had a job to do. He was their sole provider.

And it was up to her to pull together and take care of Annie for a few days. This was the baby she had always wanted . . . hadn't that bright replica of herself just gushed about it in the video?

This was her dream come true.

But somehow, it had also become her personal nightmare.

* * *

All day Sunday Chelsea dreaded tomorrow when Leo had to leave for his business trip. Since Annie's birth he'd been away for a night here and there, but never for a full week.

While Leo was out doing errands with Annie, Chelsea pulled herself off the couch to fold the dry laundry. A week was so long, and this was a bad time. The twisted mass of socks and T-shirts was overwhelming, especially when she was blinded by tears. She needed help. She needed her mom.

If only Mom were here to help . . . to show Chelsea how to be a mother. But Mom was gone . . . and Chelsea still felt terrible about not having a chance to say good-bye or mourn her.

"It's probably better that you're not here," Melanie had told her when she called from Judith's bedside in those last days. "It would be really hard on you, and Mom is completely out of it. She doesn't recognize any of us."

But she would have known I was there. Chelsea was convinced that a person on the threshold to the next world could still sense the presence of loved ones around them. Torn between the desire to be with her mom in her last hours on earth and the doctor's orders to avoid air travel and stick close to the hospital, she had stayed. Of course, she had to take care of her unborn child. The light of her life!

But sometimes, it still felt wrong. The jumble of anger and loss and blame and regret that surrounded Mom's death was still a tight black lump in Chelsea's chest. People said that time healed all wounds, but this one—this dark stone of anguish— would never melt away.

Later, after Leo disappeared into the bedroom to pack, she knew she had to try one last time to stop him. She carried a pile of his clean T-shirts into the room, setting them on the bed beside his open duffel bag.

"I don't think I can be here alone." There was a tremble in her voice, and she hated herself for having to beg. "Can't you tell your boss that your wife and baby need you?"

"I don't think Mark will buy that anymore." He didn't look up as he stuffed balled-up pairs of socks into the bag.

"But it's true."

Leo shrugged. "I already asked him if someone could sub for me. He kind of laughed it off and told me to have a nice trip."

"That's mean."

"He's got a business to run. And really, he's doing me a favor by sending me to Boston. I made a lot of connections at this gig last year. Leads that turned into lucrative deals. I gotta go, hon."

He told her he'd been talking to Emma, who'd be coming around to help out. He'd worked out some sort of plan with her, but the details faded as Chelsea stared at the duffel bag he was packing.

How easy it would be to tuck Annie inside.

Her little body would fit in the canvas between the stack of boxers and the rolled T-shirts. If she stayed quiet Leo could stow her under the seat and no one would ever know. And if he checked her through with his suitcase . . . She imagined the cold, dark belly of the plane. It was no place for a baby.

I belong there, she thinks. *Cold and dark and airless. No more sorrow and guilt. No more.*

"Emma is going to stop in every day after work," he was saying when she tuned back in. "And don't forget, you've got that appointment with Dr. Chin on Wednesday. Maybe you should hire a sitter for that afternoon. Mrs. Rosekind is great."

"But she works during the week," she reminded him. "And I'm not going to call Eleni again."

"Eleni isn't a bad sitter," he argued. "I trust her, as long as the skateboard stoner boyfriend doesn't come along."

Chelsea shook her head. She couldn't leave Annie with that girl.

"Maybe Emma can get out of work that day," he said. "That would solve the problem."

Chelsea stretched out beside his duffel bag on the bed, wishing she could be as hopeful as Leo. When he saw solutions, she saw a mass of twisted socks and shirts with their sleeves tangled in a knot. She thought of the cold mornings ahead and the long, dark nights she would spend pacing with a crying baby in her arms. Right now a week was a lifetime. Leo might as well say he would return in seven years.

From this close she could smell his aftershave, already packed into the bag. She closed her eyes and imagined herself as a tiny speck of dust, billowing through the air and swirling, landing and attaching herself on Leo's undershirt.

She would hold on tight and never let go.

Chapter 10

Cheerios. Bread. Cheese. And two gallons of milk.

Chelsea went down the aisle of the supermarket Monday morning, hoping that Annabelle would stay asleep in the carrier that filled most of the shopping cart. When she'd opened the fridge that morning and found it lacking, she had cursed herself for begging Leo to watch the baby instead of letting him make a grocery run last night. She had imagined a quick daytime shopping trip this morning, and so far, Annabelle had napped under the fluorescent lights of the bread-and-cereal aisle. If she could grab some meat and fresh fruit, they could get home without a scene.

Maybe it was the cool mist in the produce section. As soon as Chelsea edged near the carrots, Annabelle snorted and started to cry.

"Don't do that here . . . please," Chelsea begged under her breath as she shoved a bunch of carrots in a bag and grabbed two onions.

Before she could reach the fruit, Annie's cries had accelerated to shrieks: that wretched wail that seemed to indicate terrible pain. Chelsea could feel other shoppers turning to stare at her.

A woman in a fat down jacket stopped picking out potatoes to give them her full attention. "Is everything all right?"

"Sorry. She cries like that sometimes." Chelsea pushed her cart away, but the woman followed.

"She sounds like she's in distress."

"She'll be okay." Chelsea ripped off a plastic bag for apples, trying to dodge the woman's disapproving stare.

"She's very cute," the woman said sadly, but Chelsea knew that translated to: *Shut that baby up!*

"Why don't you pick her up?" asked an elderly grandma in a jaunty cheetah-print cap. Her eyes were suspicious dark beads in her face.

"It won't make her stop crying," Chelsea explained, "and it's such an ordeal to unbuckle her and take her out. I just stopped in for a few things."

"But you can't let her cry like that," the older woman said.

I can't make her stop crying! Chelsea bit her lower lip to keep herself from snapping back at the woman. She knew it was annoying and disturbing and disruptive, but she had to listen to it all the time. Could these people just put up with her for ten minutes while Chelsea picked up her groceries?

A man with bushy eyebrows scowled as he blew by her with his cart like an angry motorist passing a car with a flat tire.

"Are you going to let the poor thing make herself sick?" Cheetah Woman asked. "Take care of her!"

"I'm trying." And what baby ever died from crying? Really . . . these people pretended to like babies, but in truth none of them had an ounce of compassion. Chelsea gave up and pushed the cart to the checkout counter. She would have to make do without the other items on her list.

The woman in front of her looked back in annoyance, as Chelsea lined her cart up beside the chewing gum display.

"Can you give that kid a pacifier or something?" the woman asked in a biting tone.

Annabelle never took to a pacifier, but Chelsea reached into the diaper bag, wanting to feel as if she were doing something. The shrieks were angry bleats now, seared by a scalding edge that made it sound as if Annie would lose her voice soon. A sour suspicion tugged at Chelsea as she dug through the diaper bag.

Where was her wallet?

In the car. She had tucked it into the console after she'd loaded Annie into her child safety seat.

Damn!

With Annie screeching, there was no way the clerk would work with her. And at this point she didn't have the energy to dump the groceries with the manager and carry Annie through the parking lot in her heavy seat.

It was all such an ordeal. . . .

She pulled out of line, pushed her cart to the side of the store, and transferred Annie to an empty one.

"Come on, cranky-pants," she muttered, wheeling Annabelle out of the store.

The drive-through at Taco Bell promised hot food and an opportunity for Annie to wail in the privacy of their car. The line wasn't moving, and while she waited Chelsea shot off a text to Leo about Annie's meltdown. She could never reach him during the day when he was at a convention; that hadn't bothered her before she was stranded with Annabelle. She ordered a burrito, then made it two, deciding to save one for later.

"Something to drink?"

"Do you have milk?"

She thought the muzzled answer was a yes. After she paid and peered in the bag, the small container of milk gave her an idea. She circled around the parking lot and went back to the drive-through to order again.

"Ten milks, please." At least that would tide her over until she made it to the grocery store.

When Chelsea pulled into the driveway, she was surprised to see her neighbor standing at the curb, unpacking a minivan loaded to the gills. Louise Pickler was back from South Carolina already?

Chelsea wasn't thrilled to see Louise, who savagely protected her dingy home from solicitors and stray baseballs. Louise had stick-thin legs and a belly that made her look slightly pregnant. She seemed to be in her sixties, though it was hard to tell under the makeup that could have been applied with a paint roller. Her long brown hair showed two inches of gray at the roots, and her lips always curved down in a grimace. This time of year, she always wore a black trench coat that made her resemble a fairytale witch.

The bad witch of the south—South Carolina—had returned.

Chelsea would have liked to duck straight into the house, but there was no avoiding Louise. She unloaded the stroller and popped it open. Fortunately, Annie stopped crying as soon as Chelsea removed her from the car. Did she sense that Louise was one of the most intolerant neighbors on the face of the earth and it wouldn't be wise to push her buttons, or was it just a response to the cold air? Taking a deep breath, Chelsea wheeled her over.

As she passed the van, Louise's little dog, ChiChi, bounced from the front seat to the dashboard, yapping incessantly.

"Louise, you're back early," Chelsea said. "The snow hasn't even melted yet."

Louise eyed her suspiciously. "I missed my home."

"Well, you're back now." Chelsea looked for the larger dog, known around the neighborhood as a biter. She didn't want her bounding up out of nowhere and attacking. "Where's Coco?"

Louise clutched the bright raspberry-colored scarf at her neck. "Gone to doggy heaven, may she rest in peace." She misted over. "I miss her so much."

Chelsea felt a flutter of sympathy for the woman. How sad to be all alone in the world, except for one or two scrappy dogs.

"Yes, I miss my little Coco." Louise's pout hardened to a frown as she pounced on Annabelle, leaning down to put her face frightfully close to the baby. "But I didn't miss hearing *you* cry."

Sympathy for the older woman drained away, and Chelsea rolled the stroller back, away from Louise's clutches. Louise had been living next door for the first two weeks of Annie's life, before she left for South Carolina, and though it was a dark blur in Chelsea's mind, she did remember Leo dealing with the older woman's complaints on the phone.

Louise straightened, still staring at Annabelle. "How's the colic?" she asked in her husky voice. "Tell me I'm not going to hear her crying outside my window again."

"Not as bad, but she still cries," Chelsea admitted, feeling assaulted by the woman.

"That's not what I want to hear. Why are you such a bad baby?" Louise asked Annabelle in a ridiculous baby voice.

That voice edged under Chelsea's skin. "She's not a bad baby." Her discomfort was galvanized by the yapping dog that had started rocking the van. "And we didn't miss ChiChi's barking."

"Dat's not a bark!" Louise responded in her clownish voice as she opened the door and let the dog out so that it could sniff and snap at Chelsea's ankles. "Dat's ChiChi talking to Mommy!"

This woman is crazier than I am, Chelsea thought. She turned the stroller around as Louise hunkered down to give little ChiChi hugs. She stopped at the car to grab her Taco Bell stash and tucked it into the stroller basket, not wanting the neighbor to see the evidence of her shame and failure. Then she whisked Annabelle into the house, locking the door behind her.

Since Annabelle seemed content in her stroller, Chelsea quickly stashed the milk and second burrito in the fridge and perused the shelves. Nothing but condiments and Leo's microbrew beers.

The cupboard was bare.

Besides the burrito in the fridge, there was nothing besides cereal and oatmeal to eat in the long, dark nights ahead.

Her cell phone buzzed, and she retrieved a message from Leo.

Sorry about the groceries. I should have stocked up.
My bad. Get someone to help you. Emma or Eleni?

Leo was right. She needed some help. Emma would stop by tonight, but Chelsea knew they would both be too tired to head out for groceries at that point of the evening. She needed a plan, and returning to the grocery store with Annabelle in tow was no solution.

She scrolled through her cell phone and found the number for Eleni Zika, the teenage sitter, and shot off a text:

Can you watch the baby right after school for an
hour or two?

It was the right thing to do—build a network of support. It would only be for two hours, and babysitting on Monday afternoon wouldn't give the girl the same temptations as a Saturday night. There would be no boyfriend on the scene; Chelsea would make sure of that.

The little squeaks from across the room reminded her that it was feeding time. Chelsea grabbed a half-pint of milk and sat down to nurse. A few minutes later, Eleni's message indicated that she could be at the house by three.

Okay. This was going to work. She would make it work. She had to patch meals and sleep together until Leo returned.

When Annabelle dozed off, Chelsea nestled the baby into her chair and hurried through a shower so that she'd be ready to go when the sitter arrived. She blew out the hair around her face with a round brush, then tried on a tweed jacket she'd loved pre-pregnancy.

The buttons didn't close comfortably, but the shoulders fit and the lines were flattering.

Just like the old days. She flipped her dark hair over one shoulder as she checked her profile in the mirror. She could see herself grabbing her keys and driving to the office, singing along with the radio on the way. Independence was so under-rated.

Downstairs, Annie was still asleep—a gift. She checked the mail, her stomach lurching at the sight of three more bills from the hospital.

You can do this. Call now, and it will ease your conscience.

She picked up the phone and called Sounder Insurance's eight-hundred number. Pacing with the bills in her hand, she waded through the choices on the menu. A recorded voice kept reminding her that she could "do it all" on the Web, but when she'd tried their Web site, it had only given her a list of the invoices that had been rejected.

After a few minutes, there was a click and a smooth, calm voice. "This is Janet Walker."

Janet . . . wasn't that the woman she'd yelled at on Saturday?

"How can I help you today?"

Determined to keep her cool, Chelsea gave her name, rolling her eyes as she answered the endless questions that verified her coverage. She told Janet that she was calling about a new set of bills for Annabelle, who was supposed to be covered under their policy. Yes, she would hold while Janet checked on it.

To her surprise, Janet came back on the line quickly. "Ms. Maynard? I have some good news for you. Your daughter, Annabelle, has been added to the policy, and we can begin to process claims for her."

Chelsea frowned. "What do you mean 'begin'?" Hope waned when Janet told her that she needed to resubmit each invoice for Annabelle's treatment.

"Are you kidding me? All that paperwork?"

"It *is* company policy," Janet said. "But maybe I can help you. Do you still have the original invoices?"

"There are three right in front of me." Chelsea glanced at the rolltop desk. "And I know I can dig out the rest."

The insurance rep asked Chelsea for the case number from the corner of an invoice. "Give me a minute and I'll try to resubmit these electronically." There were clicking noises as Janet input the data. "Looks like that one went through."

"Hallelujah."

"Do you have another invoice for Annabelle?" Janet asked.

Chelsea started reading off case numbers. She found a stack of invoices for Annie's treatment in the rolltop desk and fed those to Janet, too.

"It looks like they're all going through," Janet reported after she had processed every bill for Annabelle that Chelsea could find. "Yes. We'll be processing those invoices for payment sometime within the next thirty days. Is there something else I can help you with today?"

There was another stack of bills—folded paperwork with complicated billing codes that hadn't gone through—but Chelsea didn't have the time or energy to deal with that right now.

Take the small victory and run.

"That's all I can handle for now," Chelsea said.

"Ms. Maynard? Are you okay?"

"What?" Chelsea raked her bangs back from her eyes, not sure she'd heard correctly.

"When you called Saturday, I was concerned."

Chelsea closed the rolltop desk and turned away from the paperwork. Janet was concerned. Besides Emma and Leo, no one else in the world even noticed her these days.

"That's very nice of you."

"Your health and your baby's health are the number-one priority. That goes for Sounder Health Care, and it should go for you, too." Janet's voice dimmed. "When you said you thought about hurting your baby . . . well, that goes against all the things we stand for."

"I . . . I never hurt her . . . I don't want to hurt her. It's just that I get these visions. Bad images of how she could be hurt or killed. Things that I would never have believed I was capable of thinking, but somehow they pop in to my thoughts."

The silence on the line made Chelsea imagine the woman sitting back and shaking her head in judgment. But then came the steady click-click of Janet's fingers on the computer, and then her voice. "Therapy isn't usually covered under your plan," the woman said. "But if you get a referral from your ob-gyn, Sounder will pay for three sessions if it's related to postpartum depression."

It was a nice thought, but Dr. Volmer would never rally behind her.

"But you didn't hear it from me," Janet added.

"Thank you." Chelsea hoped that Emma's specialist would offer her a solution so that she would never have to go back to Dr. Volmer for anything. As she hung up, she took a deep breath, enjoying the quiet in the house, mindful of the burden lifted by having Annabelle on their policy at long last.

The baby lay on her stomach, pushing against the thick baby quilt, mewling to herself as if she had just found a voice, along with hands to support her heavy head. Watching her, Chelsea smiled.

Was this how hope felt? Light and orange and glimmering around the edges?

The doorbell chimed, and Chelsea hurried to answer, not wanting Eleni to give up and slip away.

Dressed in black with more than a hint of cleavage showing and dark hair down to her waist, Eleni had a goth look that gave Chelsea a queasy feeling.

She's not a black widow spider, Chelsea told herself. *This is how kids dress now.*

"Hi, Mrs. Maynard. Is she awake?" Eleni asked, dropping her backpack by the front door. "Oh, you are!" Eleni's most endearing quality was her ability to relate to an infant. She knelt at the edge of Annabelle's blanket, lifted her under the armpits, and put her face close to Annie's. "Hey, girl. Wassup?"

No matter how sweet the teenager's smile was, it seemed incongruous for hands with black glitter nail polish to be holding her baby.

Chelsea laid down the rules. "No friends over. Including Krispy." In her former life, Chelsea would have gotten a charge out of Eleni's boyfriend, Krispy, a longboarding, nose-pierced slacker who was obviously a stoner. But not anymore. It made her nervous to think of a dark star like that being around Annabelle.

"You're here to focus on the baby," Chelsea said, catching Eleni's dark eyes.

"Absolutely," Eleni agreed. "Don't worry about us, Mrs. Maynard. We'll be fine. Right, Annabelle? Do you want to wave good-bye to your mom?" And as the sitter lifted the baby's chubby arm in a waving motion, Annie actually seemed to smile in the girl's arms.

Just gas, Chelsea told herself as she let herself out, locking the door behind her.

Chapter 11

The vibration of the cell phone in his pocket was yet another jolt of guilt that Leo had to ignore. He felt bad about leaving Chelsea alone, and he missed the little mushmelon. It felt strange knowing that he'd be spending the night in a bland hotel room while Annabelle's eyes searched the room for his familiar face. Yeah, she was only three months, but she recognized him. He could tell by the way her face lit up when he came close to her.

The phone had been buzzing nonstop for the past hour, but the booth had been so slammed with prospective clients, Leo had only been able to answer one text from Chelsea. He wished he could be more responsive to her, but he couldn't turn away prospective customers like the man examining the display right now.

"So just what are you selling?" asked the tall man with snow-white hair.

"We've created an application that collects and sorts data. We can customize it to suit your business needs."

The man scratched his chin as he stared down at the video games set up in their display. "How does that work?"

"These display units are programmed to collect data," Leo explained. "Say a customer comes into your store and plays a video game. Our program records how long he or she plays, what games are played—even what the player scores."

"Nice," the man said. "But I run a chain of produce stores."

"And do you have an app to monitor your inventory and sales?"

"Not entirely. Shipments are on one program, sales on another. But there's no easy way to sort through the sales receipts to see just what people are buying."

Bingo.

This man was a perfect candidate for their services.

"That must be hard with produce. How do you monitor the pull dates for the fruits and vegetables?"

The man crossed his arms. "Let's say I have some excellent store managers."

"I'm sure you do." Leo turned a monitor toward him and quickly brought up an application his company had designed for the produce department of a grocery chain. As he showed the man some of the features, his cell phone buzzed again.

Damn.

What if there was an emergency, and he was spinning his wheels with clients.

The man seemed interested in the program, so Leo took a chance and gestured to the mouse and keyboard. "Go ahead. Plunk in some numbers or requests and see how it responds."

Frowning, the man clicked around the screen.

"That's it," Leo encouraged him, casually slipping his hand into the pocket of his trousers to retrieve his phone.

Eleven missed calls. His heart sank until he checked the number.

They weren't from Chelsea. It was Jennifer calling him. He had put her new number into his address book so he would know when she called and be sure not to answer.

"You've got a directory of fruits here?" The man laughed. "I hate to admit it, but that could come in handy. Lots of folks don't know a kumquat from a rutabaga."

"Exactly," Leo said as he slipped his phone back into his pocket. "That's why we thought employees should have the information at their fingertips."

The man handed Leo a business card. "I'm Dan Attolino,

owner of Apple Dan's. I'd appreciate meeting with someone from your outfit in the next few weeks so that we can talk pricing and time frame."

"Perfect." Leo handed Dan Attolino one of his cards and shook his hand. "I'll handle it myself, Mr. Attolino. I think you'll find we're competitively priced in this market."

"I hope so. This is the best program I've seen so far."

As Dan Attolino headed off, Leo noticed that his boss had been watching.

"When did you get back from your meeting?" Leo asked casually.

"I've been here long enough to see you working every angle possible," Mark said. "Apple Dan's would be a sweet account."

Leo nodded. "And while you were gone, I spoke with a CFO from a major rental car company. That would be a fun program to pull together."

"Really? I'm sorry I missed that. Why don't you take a few minutes? You've been going nonstop since the doors opened this morning."

The phone buzzing in Leo's pocket confirmed that he needed a break. "Okay. I'm going to wander around a bit. Back in a half hour or so."

"I got it covered. Take your time." Mark nodded, looking pleased as he sat on a stool in the booth and struck up a conversation with two passing women.

Leo had his cell phone out for one more look at the list of calls. Shit. All twelve of them were from Jennifer. What was wrong with that woman? He wasn't her husband anymore, and he wasn't going to be her "bestie" now that she'd moved back to New York. He walked past the line of booths, unable to focus on any of them as he tried to formulate a strategy to deal with Jennifer.

Apparently, ignoring her was not going to work. But he wasn't going to see her, and he hated even talking to her without letting Chelsea know what was going on. He didn't want her to think he was skulking around, but she'd been so messed up before he left that he couldn't bear to make her feel any worse with Jennifer's news.

He purchased a chicken wrap and downed it in a few bites. Chelsea always said he ate too quickly, but at times like this he saw food as nothing more than fuel. He was tossing the wrapper in a can when his phone buzzed again.

Jennifer.

Steeling himself for her inevitable attempt at manipulation, he answered it. "This is Leo."

"Why aren't you taking my calls? You're so mean to me."

"I figure that if it's important, you'll leave a message," he kept his tone low and level. "Or text me, like the rest of the world."

"I can't stand being back here and not seeing you. When can we get together?"

Try never, he wanted to say, but he knew her wrath was worse than her obsessiveness.

"It's not going to happen, Jennifer." He made his way down the aisle, looking for some privacy by a bank of windows. "I told you, I have a wife and baby now. And a job that I was trying to do when you called, like, a hundred times."

"Patience was never my thing. And as I remember it, you were always pretty quick to pull the trigger."

Before he could stop it his wretched mind went there. In bed with Jennifer, her naked body slithering over his, skin on skin . . .

He hadn't had sex for months. The doctor had asked them to wait six weeks after the baby was born, but even after that Chelsea hadn't been into it at all. He understood. He totally got it. But sometimes a man's body had a mind of its own.

He gritted his teeth, took a breath, and pulled himself together. "Did you have some reason for calling me, or can I get back to work?"

"I want to be your friend. I want to hang out with you. We had a lot of laughs together, right? We can do that again. And I'll even let you stay married."

"It's not going to happen, Jennifer. Find yourself another boyfriend."

"But I want you. I want to meet your kid . . . the girl version of Leo."

The thought of Jennifer going anywhere near Annie perked up his defenses. "Not going to happen, and I'd appreciate it if you stopped calling me. We made a clean break and it worked out pretty well. Let's keep it that way."

"Oh, now you're pissing me off."

"A necessary evil. You always test a person's limit, Jennifer."

"Honey, I haven't begun to fight. And don't think you're getting rid of me so easily. I know where you live. I've seen wifey and baby, more than once. And to be honest, the old girl looks like hell. I guess motherhood doesn't agree with her."

Fury flamed in his chest as he paced in front of the tinted glass windows. Jennifer couldn't have known that her comment touched a sensitive spot. He didn't want to give her the satisfaction of hearing his pain, but he wasn't going to let her tear down Chelsea.

"Leave my wife and baby alone," he snarled. "What you're doing is borderline stalking, Jennifer, and I'm not letting you near my wife and kid. Don't think I won't call the police."

"Leo, Leo, you were always so quick to jump to conclusions. I wouldn't dream of upsetting your applecart. But if wifey and baby were to just happen to be in the same grocery store or restaurant, well, nothing I can do about that."

"Stay away from them."

Her laugh was cold and forced. "Oops. Gotta go."

"Stay away!"

"Call you later, babe."

The line clicked off, leaving him to deal with an afternoon of indigestion and worry.

Chapter 12

On the way to the grocery store, Chelsea turned left at the stop sign and right at the traffic light. She passed the 7-Eleven, where she used to stop for coffee every morning on her way to work. Yes, this was the route to her office, as familiar and comfortable as her favorite slippers.

How she wished she were going there. She pretended that she had a meeting this afternoon. Meetings were great—one of the most social aspects of working on the magazine. And after the meeting, when others were turning off lights and computers and heading home, Chelsea would be settling in to work during the twilight hours when the office grew quiet and the only thing that mattered was the article taking shape—morphing and growing and finding its own voice.

On impulse, she stayed on the road and shot right past the Safeway. Her mind cheerfully ticked off the small landmarks along the way—the deli with the picture of a boar's head on the sign, the funeral home that was so well kept it resembled a movie set. She passed the row of stores where someone had once nicked her bumper while she was picking up clothes from the cleaners.

These were her old stomping grounds.

Her pulse was beating a little faster as she pulled into the parking lot of the six-story building. Her fingers automatically pressed the button for the fifth floor, and suddenly she was there, surrounded by the familiar noises and faces and smells of the magazine office.

Her gaze went right to the cubicle by the pillar—her work station. She'd been working here when she met Leo. The evening of their first date, she had slipped away from that desk to redo her makeup in the bathroom mirror. When she found out she was pregnant, she had sat there during her lunch hour, searching online for baby quilts and parenting advice. And sometimes she would stay late going over her lists of things to do, getting her ducks in a row. She had wanted everything to be perfect in the nursery and in the house when the baby arrived. Back then she had been in control—so happy and hopeful. . . .

"Chelsea?" Stan Dombrowski looked up from his desk. He didn't spare her a smile, but there was a warm inflection in his voice. "It's a blast from the past."

People greeted her warmly.

"How ya doing?" Marco paused on his way to the elevator, shifting his clipboard under one arm.

"Did you bring the baby?" Tansley asked. "I want to meet her."

Chelsea shook her head. "I wasn't really planning to stop by."

Across the room, Sasha Barton dropped a batch of proofs onto a table and threw her hands in the air. "What the hell are you doing here?"

Chelsea bit back a smile as her closest friend at the magazine rushed through the rows of cubicles—the ice cube tray, the employees called it.

Sasha threw her arms around Chelsea and danced her back and forth. "Why didn't you tell me you were coming?" she spoke quietly in Chelsea's ear.

"I didn't know myself."

"Mm-hmm?" Sensing that something was up, Sasha stopped rocking. Her bracelets jangled as she leaned back to assess Chelsea.

With shiny dark hair and mocha-colored skin, Sasha always complained that she was ordinary looking. But there was nothing ordinary about her startling green eyes and high cheek-bones. Add in the emerald stud in her nose and her penchant for jewelry, and she was positively exotic. "Well, we need to talk," Sasha said.

For the next few minutes Chelsea fielded questions about Annabelle and passed around her cell phone so that everyone could see pictures.

"What a beauty!" someone said.

"You've got it all now."

Tansley cooed over the baby, and everyone wished Chelsea well. "You must be over the moon with happiness."

"You're lucky to be out of here," Marco said. "Now that we're up for sale, every procedure is being micromanaged."

"You're up for sale?" Chelsea hadn't heard that news.

"Yeah, but who's going to buy a print magazine in this changing market?" Sasha pointed out.

"Do you think Annabelle looks more like you or like Leo?" Tansley asked.

"I don't know," Chelsea said, trying to tune into a question asked by Alexa Garcia, who'd just joined the group.

"Remember that Staten Island kitchen we're upgrading?" Alexa asked. "The couple has decided that they want to take out the center window and substitute a gas fireplace. Do you think that can be done within our budget?"

"I don't know." Sasha tilted her head to one side. "I haven't done a gas fireplace recently."

"Is there a gas line running to the kitchen already?" Chelsea asked.

Alexa nodded. "But no chimney."

"You don't need a chimney," Chelsea said confidently. "On an outside wall, you'll vent it right through the wall. It's actually not a bad idea if they want to replace the window."

"Great," Alexa said. "I'll call the home owner."

"How did you know that when you've been out of the biz for three months?" Tansley asked.

"I've been researching it for my own house." It felt good to be back in the office, in the thick of decisions and conversations.

Sasha and Marco exchanged a look. "I told you," Sasha said. "Chelsea is the Can-Do Girl. Once she starts researching something, this one never gives up."

"Come back to work, please!" Marco pleaded.

"Don't even say that," Tansley insisted. "Chelsea is living the dream, with a great husband, a house, and an angel-faced baby. Why would she come back?"

Because I feel alive when I'm here. Because I was happy here, and I need to find my way back to a safe, sane place.

Tansley wanted to hear more about the baby, but Chelsea longed to talk business. Conversation began to fizzle as phones beckoned, and one by one people returned to their desks.

"Let's talk in my office," Sasha said.

As Chelsea followed her friend, her fingers twitched, longing to pick up the layouts and get a preview of the articles the staff had been working on.

"Sit if you can find a free inch," Sasha said, gesturing to the chair and table piled with proofs.

The batch on the chair was old; corrections had already been made. But Chelsea felt an odd contentment just holding the pages in her hands, leafing through them. "I miss this."

"You're kidding, right?"

Chelsea shook her head. "Talking about the gas fireplace just now, I felt more alive than I have since Annie was born. I wish people didn't close me out. I feel like an outsider when they tell me how I'm so much better off out of here."

"They're just looking at the facts. Subscriptions are down, and the magazine doesn't translate well to e-trade. Management announced that there will be no raises this year, and we might have to cut staff. You really are lucky to be out."

"I don't feel lucky." Tears filled her eyes, but fortunately Sasha was digging through her desk drawer and didn't notice.

"As I remember it, you couldn't wait to get out of here and be home with Leo and the baby."

"That's what I thought, but I was wrong." A tear dripped down her face, and she swiped it away with the back of one hand. "I'm a terrible mother. I'm tired all the time. Every day is the same, chasing dirty diapers and a dirty house and bills. Feeding Annie every few hours. It never ends and there's no hope in sight."

"You sound bad." Sasha came around and perched on the edge of her desk. "I wish there was something I could do to help you. Have you talked to your doctor?"

"He says it will pass."

"Typical man. I'm no expert, but this sounds like depression."

Chelsea shook her head. It didn't matter what it was called . . . no name or label could change the dark void that waited for her back in that house.

"You know, my sister went through something like this." Although Sasha did not have children, her large family included a mix of white and African American women who had plenty of stories to tell. "She kept imagining terrible things happening to her baby . . . like slipping off a bridge. Stuff like that."

"Me, too. I get these . . . dark visions."

Sasha bit her lower lip and held out a box of tissues. "Tell me about it, honey."

She let it all spill out in no certain order. Sasha listened sympathetically, and Chelsea was grateful that her friend wasn't trying to judge her. When Chelsea was through, Sasha cleared off another chair and sat close to her.

"I've known you for years, and this is not you. You seem to be getting help, and that's good. There's a place inside you that holds peace and love. I know that. Right now, you're hurting bad, but you will find that peace again."

A new wave of tears overcame Chelsea. "I can't see that happening."

"It will. But get with your sister and that new doctor. Let them help you."

Chelsea pressed a handful of tissues to her eyes. "What happened to your sister?"

"She's fine now. But she left her baby with my mother. Just dropped her off one day and didn't come to pick her up for six months."

Chelsea wished she could drop Annie off somewhere and leave her for a few months. It would be such a relief to be free of the baby . . . free again.

Her own person.

But that would never happen. She was stuck, imprisoned in the very life she had longed for.

Chelsea felt like a shadow of her former self as she left the building, mourning the loss of her old life. After a quick stop at the grocery store she arrived home to find Annabelle napping and Eleni entertaining herself by texting.

"How did it go?" she asked, reassured that there were no signs of a visitor.

"Fine." The girl didn't even glance up from her cell phone screen. "She slept most of the time."

Of course she did. Chelsea wouldn't have been so lucky had she stayed home.

Their voices seemed to summon the baby from sleep. Annie twisted her lips and began to mouth her fist. Hungry, of course.

Chelsea got Eleni to help her put the perishables away, then paid her, arranging for her to return Wednesday so Chelsea could keep her appointment with Dr. Chin. With the groceries half unpacked, she washed her hands and sat down to feed the baby.

Down in the deep hole worn into the corner of the couch.

Her black hole.

Exhausted by the outing, she dozed off with Annie in her arms. When she opened her eyes, Annie was sleeping in her chair, though Chelsea didn't recall putting her there. The splattering down of raindrops seemed so near. Had she left a window open? She rubbed her eyes, thinking that it was too cold for rain. . . .

She turned and marveled at the fountain springing forth from the light on the kitchen ceiling. Water spewed out from the round fixture like a radiant sun. It struck her as beautiful until she realized it was splattering onto the floor and the electric range.

"Oh, my God." A pipe must have burst upstairs. She arose from the couch, then bolted to the stairs. The hallway was clear, but the bathroom floor was a pool of water an inch deep. It brimmed over the marble door saddle when she stepped into the cold lake to get a better look at the torrent gushing from behind the toilet.

Had the feed line snapped?

Squinting against the cold spray, she reached in to shut off the valve behind the toilet. It turned, but the jet of water didn't slow. The valve was shot.

Where was the next cutoff?

With a moan, she pulled away from the gushing water, trying to remember where the next cutoff was. She pictured valves on naked pipes . . . the utility closet beside the kitchen.

Blinded by panic she hurried down the stairs and fumbled in the small closet with the hot water heater. There it was . . . but there were two valves. She turned the top one, hoping for the best, then ran back upstairs, noting her wet footprints on the carpeting.

The bathroom was silent, a serene pool of water over white-and-black tile. The swollen white rug was an island of pale sand in the center of the calm lake.

It was a surreal dream . . . a nightmare.

A little whimper escaped her throat. Why was this happening to her?

She leaned against the doorway and sobbed. Where did you even begin to clean up something like this? And that damn valve behind the toilet . . . how could it just stop working?

Through her tears she saw the cool reflection of light on the surface of the water. It had to be draining through pinholes in the tile, down the kitchen ceiling. Would they have to redo the drywall downstairs?

Maybe. But right now, it was pouring out through the lowest point, the light fixture. She had to stop the water as quickly as possible.

With a gasp, she stepped in and waded through the cold water. She grabbed the bucket that held Annie's tub toys, tossed them into the sink, and started bailing. She grabbed another big cup and used two hands, dumping water into the tub as fast as she could. When the cups no longer filled, she got the mop. When she got down to dry tile, she went downstairs to assess the damage.

Annie slept peacefully against the backdrop of water dripping slowly from the kitchen. Chelsea wished she could slip onto the couch across from her and sleep it all away, too.

The step stool brought her close enough to take down the kitchen fixture. It was a struggle to maintain her balance and keep the globe full of water from sloshing over her chest, but she managed to hobble down and pour it into the sink.

The ceilings didn't look too bad, but there would always be the question of moisture and mold. Did they need one of those restoration teams in here, with those giant fans? She had done an article about them, but she knew they were pricey. Ka-ching. She dried her hands on the kitchen towel and called Leo.

"Hey, hon!" His voice was cheerful but he was shouting over the noise in the background. "You caught me at a meet-and-greet cocktail party. Can I call you back?"

"We have a problem here," she said, feeling herself shiver from the damp cold. She'd been working in bare feet, and as she explained about the broken valve, she went over to the thermostat and turned up the heat. There went the gas bill. Ka-ching.

"Are you serious?" Leo said. "What a nightmare!"

"Exactly."

"Are you okay? Is Emma there?"

"She's coming over after her doctor's appointment."

"Chelsea, I'm sorry. Who else can we get to help you?"

"The cleanup is almost done," she lied, realizing that Leo

didn't get it. She couldn't wait around for someone else to show up and take care of things.

They discussed calling in a restoration company and decided to wait until Leo got home. As they were talking, she followed a slurry of water to the closet and realized that everything on the floor there was soaked. "Oh, no, the closet! All the water got in."

"What was that? Sorry, but it's hard to hear."

"I gotta go finish it up. Call me later, when your party is over."

"I'm sorry you have to do this alone, hon."

She was sorry, too, but she kept silent, not wanting to ramp up Leo's guilt. "Call me later."

She put a plastic garbage bag on the table, then started lining up their wet boots and sneakers from the closet. There was the bin of hats. A soggy paper bag of clothes to be donated. And the butcher block of kitchen knives. She set that evil item on the center of the table and backed away cautiously.

There wasn't as much water to mop up down here, but Chelsea was eager to be done with it. Her hands were cold and sodden and her feet were like Popsicles on the damp floor. Thank goodness they hadn't upgraded the linoleum to wood yet. When she finally finished the minimum cleanup, her back ached and her feet felt numb. She went to wash her hands at the kitchen sink, but when she turned the knob no water came out.

Of course—it was on the same line as the upstairs bathroom. She plodded to the small bath under the stairs, grateful for the tiny stall shower here. She would call a plumber in the morning.

As she lathered up her hands, Annie let out a full-fledged wail. It had been three hours since she'd been fed.

"It never ends," Chelsea muttered as she opened the fridge. She downed a pint of milk without taking a breath, then lifted Annie into her arms. The couch swallowed them both into the nursing den. More like a cave. Chelsea pulled a throw over her frozen feet and unbuttoned her blouse. The sight of the baby nursing lulled her to sleep, but she roused herself to switch Annie to the other side. She dozed again, but Annie rousted her with a fierce shriek.

"What is it?" Chelsea asked.

Her only answer was another cry and a scrunched-up face that looked like she was being knifed in the belly. Colic, again.

Chelsea walked her around, patted her back, whispered sweet encouragements, but Annabelle kept wailing.

Desperate, Chelsea popped her into her stroller and took her out to the driveway for fresh air. The cover of the carport gave a feeling of security, and the night air felt crisp and dry.

There . . . that soothed her. Her cry sputtered to whimpers, then mewls, like a little lamb.

Go to sleep. Go to sleep. Chelsea repeated the mantra in her head as she pushed the stroller back and forth under the carport.

For once, it seemed to work.

Chelsea rolled the stroller up to the porch and put the brakes on. There was no way she was moving this baby right now. She grabbed the blanket from under the stroller and covered Annie up to the chin, then ran inside to pee.

Chapter 13

Amnio was a double-edged sword: a relief that you could learn so much about your baby before it was born, but frightening to consider that the news about the little being inside you might break your heart.

"That's it," the technician said. "You should hear your results in seven to ten days. Your genetic counselor will call you."

Emma propped herself up on her elbows to watch as the woman wiped gel from the mound of Emma's belly. "And you think it's a girl?"

"Looks that way to me, and I've been doing this for six years."

"A girl." She lay down again and laughed. "Jake is going to be thrilled." And she couldn't wait to tell Chelsea. A playmate for Annabelle! After all the worries, the long months when they had trouble conceiving, it was finally happening for them.

Out in the waiting room, Jake picked up on her good mood. "So it went well?"

"Yup." She slipped on her coat, unable to hold in the news. "It's a girl."

"A little Emma." He grinned. "Double trouble for me."

"And Annabelle is going to have a little cousin to boss around. Sort of the reverse of Chelsea and me."

"It's your bossy big-sister karma coming back to bite you."

She linked her arm through his as they waited for the elevator. "Chelsea's going to be pleased. Do you want to bring dinner over to her?"

"I'll drop you off and make a dinner run. She's probably eager for company with Leo gone all day."

As they went to the car, she told him the test results would take two weeks or so, but he was more focused on the idea of having a daughter.

"We should paint the baby's room pink. We'll get her a pink tricycle. A pink puppy. We'll play Pink for her."

In the passenger seat, Emma fastened the seat belt and rubbed her belly. "Do you hear that? Your father is a nutcase."

"But I love her." Jake palmed her tummy and spoke to the baby. "I'm celebrating your girl-ness."

Emma laughed. She put her hand over Jake's and turned to him. Something about his broad smile and sleepy eyes gave his face an openness; Jake was a clear lake, and she felt confident that she could see straight through to the bottom and everything there was pure and loving and good. Emma hoped their baby would have that same quality—a broad, friendly face that beamed with approval.

"You're going to make a great father."

The house was dark when Jake pulled up in front. Emma opened the door to the sounds of barking coming from the house next door, mixed with the awful shrieking of a small animal or child.

"Is that Annabelle?" The wails pierced the cold, dry air. Emma closed the car door and tried to filter out the yapping of the neighbor's rat dog.

"Where is she?" Jake leaped over the curb. "Are they out in the backyard?"

Since Emma had a key to the side door, they headed up the driveway that separated Chelsea and Leo's property from their obnoxious neighbor, Louise Pickler. The wailing grew louder as they approached the shadowed darkness under the carport.

"Chelsea?" Emma called tentatively. "Are you there?" She imagined her sister in a daze, dozing on the little bench.

But the only answer was the shriek from the stroller that Emma was just beginning to make out beside the brick steps.

"The baby is out here all alone." Jake paused to lean over the stroller. "Are you okay?" He patted the blanket tucked over the crying baby. "She sounds mad."

"Oh, poor baby!" Emma swooped down and lifted her from the stroller. "Are you cold and scared?" The baby felt stiff in her arms. Emma cuddled and cooed, trying to calm her. Annie's protests faded to a whimper as she pressed her face to Emma's chest, nuzzling for milk. "Where's your mommy?"

"That's what I'm wondering. I hope Chelsea's okay." Jake unlocked the door and held the storm door open for Emma and the baby.

Inside, the kitchen was dark but it smelled clean. Emma flicked the wall switch and the overhead light popped, sparked, and fizzled out. She held Annie close to her chest, ready to bolt out the door. "What the hell is going on here?"

"The light shorted out because it's wet." Chelsea's dead voice came from the darkness of the living room. "A valve broke upstairs and everything got flooded."

"Oh, honey. Are you okay?" Emma asked as a table lamp flicked on, revealing mops and buckets leaning against the kitchen counter, and Chelsea in her usual spot on the couch.

Jake blinked in the light, looking around the lampshade at Chelsea. "We found Annie outside in the cold. Did you forget her out there?"

"Annie? Oh. I must have left her out there." Chelsea rubbed her eyes, then pushed herself to the edge of the couch to twist around toward the changing table. "Is she all right?"

"She needs a diaper change." Under the blanket, the baby was soaked through.

Chelsea rubbed her eyes. "I don't think she was out there very long. It was just a few minutes."

With a diaper this wet and soiled, it had been more than a few minutes. Emma didn't want to upset Chelsea, but this was scary behavior. She didn't want to think of the terrible things that could have happened to Annabelle. And what if she and Jake hadn't stopped by?

"The important thing is that you're both okay." Jake kneeled behind the coffee table opposite Chelsea, his voice soothing. Emma loved the way he could calm a volatile situation. "I don't know what you used to mop up that water, but your kitchen sure smells clean."

"A little Murphy Oil Soap." Chelsea raked her dark hair back, and her pretty heart-shaped face revealed the shadows of exhaustion. "It was such a mess."

"Well, it looks pretty good now," Jake said, kindly ignoring the mops and buckets.

"And everyone smells better now," Emma said quietly, walking her fingers over Annabelle's tummy. A poem that their mom had made up popped into her head. "Elephant dad, wrinkled and gray, nudges his baby to greet the day. Elephant mom bats her eyes, telling her baby to reach for the sky."

Annie grinned, watching her with bright eyes.

Emma leaned close, breathing in her baby scent. "Such a sweet baby elephant."

"You two in the mood for some dinner?" Jake asked.

Before Chelsea could answer the doorbell rang.

"Hold that thought," Jake said, going to answer it.

Emma fastened the last snap on yellow fleece footie pajamas that made Annie resemble a little duckling.

"What's going on, officer?" asked Jake.

Emma's heart leaped in her chest. Sweeping Annie into her arms, she went toward the door.

"Someone reported an abandoned infant at this address." The officer seemed small under his bulky, dark winter coat and equipment. The radio clipped to his shoulder, the holstered gun and a nightstick hanging from his belt . . . he seemed so confrontational, standing there in the front vestibule. "Do you know anything about that?"

"There's only one infant at this address." Jake pointed to Annabelle. "And as you can see she's fine now. But she has been crying."

"And she was outside," added Emma. "Sometimes the fresh air calms them."

The officer nodded, obviously satisfied with the explanation. "I'm glad everything's okay."

"Who called?" Chelsea asked.

"One of your neighbors."

"Probably Louise Pickler," Chelsea said.

The cop didn't confirm or deny it as Jake led him to the door.

"I thought Pickler spent the winters down in the Carolinas," Emma said.

"Unfortunately, she rode her broom back early this year."

Emma was torn between hatred of that wicked Ms. Pickler with her yapping dog and concern that her sister would actually leave Annabelle out in the cold. It was in the thirties, and the temperature was dropping quickly. Chelsea could not risk leaving Annabelle outside anymore.

When Jake left to get some Thai food, Emma seized the opportunity to talk with her sister.

"I hope you don't think that I'm criticizing you, but it was pretty scary pulling up here and finding Annabelle crying outside. I hope you know that it's not okay to leave the baby in the cold."

In the pale light of the living room, Chelsea's eyes glistened like blue diamonds. Was she feverish, or were those simply tears? She cried so much these days.

"I know that. I wasn't planning to leave her out, and she was only out there for a little bit. The cold air seemed to soothe her. I stepped inside for a minute, just to pee, and then I just sort of collapsed."

"Next time, just make sure she's safely locked inside before you collapse."

Chelsea nodded as a sob slipped out. "I'm so bad at this. I'm a terrible mother, a failure, and no matter how I try, it never gets any better. And it won't get any better because I can't do this. I just can't."

Emma looked down at Annie, lying on her back on the floor, reaching up at the plastic toys dangling from the portable mobile over her head. *Please, don't listen to this, Annie-bananee,* Emma wanted to tell her. *Don't take any of it personally.*

"It's all so overwhelming. Just when I think I'm starting to gain control, something else falls out of place."

"It's been hard for you," Emma said. "But you're a good mother. Look at how determined you've stayed to breast-feed. That's so good for Annie, even though you're losing sleep for it." She sat beside her sister and rubbed her back. "Do you want me to stay tonight? If you want to pump, I can do one of the feedings for you."

Chelsea took a deep breath. "No, that's okay. I'll be fine."

Emma's conscience pushed her to argue, but she really didn't want to stay. They were having a baby girl, and she wanted to spend the night at home with her husband, celebrating in their quiet way.

"I need something to drink. Some milk or herb tea or something."

"Here's milk." She handed Chelsea a small container of milk from the fridge. "And I'll make tea for both of us." She put the kettle under the sink, but when she turned the faucet on, nothing happened. "No water?"

"I had to turn it off on this side of the house. You can fill it in the bathroom under the stairs."

Emma crossed the living room with the teapot. "Sort of like camping."

Chelsea started crying again. "You're always so positive. I can't even think good thoughts anymore."

"Aw, honey . . . you'll get your positive mojo back. Let's start with that visit to Dr. Chin on Wednesday. You did get a sitter. . . ."

"That high school girl is coming. I guess she's okay during the week when the boyfriend isn't around."

"Good. See, you did get something accomplished today. I would have watched Annie for you, but I have a faculty meeting Wednesday afternoon that I just can't miss." As she pulled the dead leaves from a houseplant in the kitchen window, an old childhood memory threaded through her mind. Mom had loved flowers and plants, and she had enjoyed teaching her daughters about pruning and watering and planting seasons.

"You know, I can't take Wednesday, but I can take off tomorrow. We can do something together." She knew the perfect place to help lift Chelsea's spirits. "We need to get you and Annie out of the house."

"Don't miss work for me," Chelsea said, staring down at the milk carton. "And I have to get a plumber here tomorrow."

"Schedule him in the afternoon. We'll be back by three. And I'm happy to miss work. I have vacation days I need to take before the end of the year." There was a tap on the door, and she opened it to find Jake smiling over two plastic bags.

"The green curry noodle smells great," he said.

"Yum. Thanks for doing that." Emma smiled, happy to have a plan. She fetched flatware and plates . . . then backtracked and dug paper plates out of Chelsea's pantry to save them from washing dishes in the little bathroom under the stairs. "I'll call for a sub. We're going on a field trip, and no excuses about being tired. I'll pick you and Annie up at ten."

The next morning Emma arrived at Chelsea's house to find a box of muffins sitting on the side porch under the carport. The index card taped to the box read: *GOOD NEIGHBORS HELP EACH OTHER.* Hmm.

She knocked three times, then keyed her way in. "Good morning." She dropped the muffins on the counter. "Looks like you got some homemade muffins from one of your neighbors." When there was no answer, she stepped to the bottom of the stairs and called up. "Chelsea?"

"Almost ready!" Chelsea called back.

"Take your time. I'm going to leave these muffins on the counter."

"Muffins? What kind?"

Emma dipped her finger in the frosting and took a taste. "Carrot with cream cheese frosting."

"Yum," Chelsea answered.

Annie's eyes seemed huge and round, framed by the fleece lining of her little hood as Chelsea carried her down the stairs.

"What an adorable snowsuit," Emma said.

"Isn't it cute? I'll save it for your baby. I'm sure Annie will be out of it by next winter."

Emma beamed. Next winter, they would have two babies in tow. Maybe they would do trips like this once or twice a week. "What time do you have to be back for the plumber?"

"Not coming until Thursday. It would have cost extra to get them here today."

"Thank God you have a second bathroom," Emma said.

Chelsea nodded. "Looks like I'll be camping out of the downstairs bathroom for a while."

On the way to the gardens, Chelsea was withdrawn and quiet, staring out the window with a bland expression. Emma hoped that her news would bring a spark of interest to her sister's eyes.

"I found out something exciting yesterday. We went for an amnio, and the technician told us she's positive we're having a girl. Another baby girl in our family."

"Is that good?" Chelsea's fingertips ran along the edge of the seat belt, as if searching for an encoded message there. "Is that what you want?"

"We want a healthy baby, but we're thrilled to know that it's a girl. And she'll be in the same grade as Annabelle. Just think about that. They can do dance class and Girl Scouts and soccer together."

"Sometimes I can't believe those days will ever come."

"They will, honey. You said it yourself. Next winter Annabelle will have outgrown her snowsuit."

Chelsea leaned back against the headrest and took a deep breath. "You're right. Time is marching on. I have to keep up."

When Emma turned through the gates to the New York Botanical Garden, Chelsea turned toward the window. "Is this the surprise?"

"Yup. I know the weather's crummy, but the conservatory is open, along with a few of the gardens."

"I was sort of hoping for a pedicure or massage," Chelsea said, and Emma smiled at the hint of the old, wry Chelsea.

"Wake up, sleepyhead," Emma said as she leaned into the backseat to unbuckle Annabelle. The baby's face remained calm and expressionless until Emma lifted her out into the stroller.

"She never sleeps through the transfer," Chelsea said tightly.

"But she's not crying. I think she's going to like this. There's a lot to see from down there."

The steel-and-glass dome of the Haupt Conservatory, a Victorian-style greenhouse, was a sight familiar to Emma and Chelsea. Their parents had brought them here frequently as kids, and when the girls were older Judith's volunteer work had lured them here for exhibitions and concerts. Although Emma never liked getting her hands dirty in flower boxes, she had been a sucker for the other projects—the papier-mâché flowers, the millions of ways you could decorate a planter. Chelsea had always been the one who liked to dig in to the soil, toss in mulch, and then skip along the trails like a fairy-tale character on a quest through the woods. Emma hoped that, coming here, Chelsea might reconnect with that sense of fun.

The conservatory was busier than Emma had expected. One school group was lined up in the lobby, another trailed their guide, who led them past green ferns for an eco-tour of the tropical rain forest entrance.

"Let's check out the orchid show," Emma said. "I think Annie will like the colors."

The orchid show had been designed to display the exotic

blossoms vertically, instead of just in flower beds, and the walls of bountiful blooms were breathtaking.

"Look at Annie," Emma said as they paused before a fat pillar wrapped with ribbons of purple and white orchids. "She's digging it."

There was such intelligence in the baby's eyes as she soaked in the colors and textures.

Emma picked her up and turned her so that she could face out. "Such a smart little girl," she cooed into Annie's ear. "I knew you would like the flowers."

A guard standing at the end of the lane smiled at Annabelle. "Her first orchids?"

Emma nodded. "And she loves them. But that's no surprise. Her grandmother used to work here. Our mom. She was a volunteer."

The guard beamed. "Then it runs in the family."

Chelsea's gaze was fixed on white orchids speckled with maroon. "Remember how Mom used to bring us here when we were kids?"

That's why we're here . . . to unlock those memories and feelings.

Their mother had been diagnosed with stage four cancer last March, and without treatment she had been gone before the year's end. Judith Maynard's decision to refuse painful treatment didn't sit well with Chelsea, who had thought she was giving up.

"Mom loved it here," Emma said. "Remember the children's garden? In my mind, spring was never official until we came here and walked through the daffodils and crocus."

"I used to love going off on the trails here," Chelsea said. "And at home, the best time of year was when it was time to plant flowers and turn the soil."

"You were always Mom's helper in the garden."

Chelsea's face puckered with pain. "Well, that's over now. She wanted it over."

The orange and white and yellow blooms became a blur of

color as Emma felt herself choking up. "Chelsea, she didn't want to die." But faced with either death or a round of painful treatment that wasn't going to save her life, Mom had made her choice.

"If she'd undergone the treatments, she would still be here," Chelsea insisted. "She would be here for me. She could have met her granddaughter. Now Annabelle will never know her . . . and I really need her."

"I miss her, too," Emma admitted, "but we can't be mad at her for dying. The treatment wouldn't have prolonged her life much. She was leaving us, and she had a right to choose to exit with speed and grace."

"She gave up." Chelsea sat down on a bench and folded her arms. "And I'll never forgive her for that. She left me here all alone with this baby that I don't feel any love for. It's her fault."

"Hold on a sec."

Chelsea watched glumly as Emma cradled Annabelle for a moment, then discreetly placed her in her stroller at the far end of the bench from Chelsea. Maybe it was an overreaction, but she didn't think Annie should hear things like that from her mother.

Emma perched tentatively beside her sister. "I know we don't talk about Mom's death, but you never had a chance to grieve. You became a mother before you had a chance to say good-bye to your own mother."

Chelsea's eyes were shiny with tears. "But I wanted this baby. Our little house and a little baby—that was all I ever wanted, and now . . ." She sobbed.

Emma reached her arms around her sister and squeezed her tight. Maybe it had been a mistake to bring her here today. She was no therapist.

"You've been through so much—a lifetime of pain and grief, all gummed into a few months. I know it seems hopeless right now, but that's one of the things about depression. It won't let the light in. Let's see what Dr. Chin has to say tomorrow, okay? You know I love you and I'll help you any way I can."

Chelsea sniffed. "But I hate my life."

"I know, honey." Emma tucked a strand of dark hair behind her sister's ear. "We're going to get to work on that, as soon as you see Dr. Chin."

Back at Chelsea's house, the neighbor, Louise Pickler, was out inspecting her frozen lawn as her cranky little dog wandered with no leash.

"It's the woman who ratted you out," Emma said as she pulled Chelsea's Subaru into the driveway. "Quick. Get the cheese."

Chelsea actually let out a laugh.

"Isn't there a law about keeping your dog on a leash?" Emma asked.

"Louise treats her dogs like family."

"And her family like dogs?" Emma added.

"Good one, Emma," Chelsea said as she pushed open the door.

The dog bolted over to them, and Emma stepped tentatively as it snapped at her ankles.

"ChiChi, back off," Chelsea ordered, opening the stroller. The dog growled as it tried to mouth the stroller wheels.

"Little beast," Emma muttered. She hoped to whisk Annie inside, but the neighbor was calling to Chelsea.

"Did you get a dog?" Louise accused Chelsea. The older woman stood at the edge of her lawn with her hands on her hips. "Tell me the truth, because someone's been shitting in my flower beds."

"It wasn't me," Chelsea said.

Emma bit her lips to hide a grin.

"I mean, no," Chelsea explained. "We don't have any animals. Just a baby."

"And that's enough." Louise marched over and leaned her gnarled face close to Annabelle. "Plenty of poopy diapers stinking up your house."

Horrified, Emma backed the stroller away. Chelsea was right: This woman was nuts. "Gotta go." She wheeled it up the driveway.

Chelsea unlocked the door and Emma hustled the baby inside.

"Lock the door, quick," Emma teased. "Before the Wicked Witch gets in."

"Really. I think ChiChi bit one of my toes off."

Emma laughed. "That woman is a lunatic!" she said, thinking that those muffins must have been from a different neighbor.

"Louise never liked us." As Emma got Annabelle out of her quilted romper, Chelsea told her that Louise had been tight with the woman who'd lived here before. "Leo is sure that the two of them had some sort of coven, practicing spells together."

"Don't witches do their rituals nude under the starlight?" Emma asked.

She and Chelsea looked toward the snow-covered yard beyond the back windows.

"Maybe a little backyard ritual?" Emma suggested, wriggling her eyebrows.

"We'd better get some good shades on the nursery windows," Chelsea said with a shot of her old sense of humor.

It was a relief to see that side of Chelsea, even if only for a moment. Maybe the medication was starting to work.

As Chelsea settled in to feed the baby, Emma felt the tug to get home. During the drive home she'd noticed some abdominal pain . . . not quite cramps. Was it something she ate? She and Chelsea had yogurts and a wrap from the little restaurant at the botanical garden. Was it just the food, not sitting right?

"I've got to get going," she said, turning on one of the living room lamps. "Anything you need before I go?"

Chelsea shook her head. "I'm fine."

No, you're not, Emma thought. *But tomorrow we're starting you on the path to recovery.*

She let herself out, locking the door behind her.

Worry plagued Emma as she drove home. Did the abdominal pain have something to do with her baby? She had miscarried once before, but it was a few weeks into the pregnancy.

It can't be a miscarriage. She was sixteen weeks now and having a baby girl. This was her paranoid imagination. She was going to be fine. Her baby was fine.

When Emma changed into her sweatpants, she saw the blood.

Oh, dear God . . .

She elevated her feet and called the doctor. "I think I need to be seen," she told the nurse practitioner. "Or maybe the emergency room . . . my husband will bring me in."

"Actually, the best thing you can do right now is just what you're doing," the nurse said. "Try to relax. Keep your feet up. It could be spotting, and that will pass."

"But there's so much blood! Can't you give me something to stop it? There must be something. . . ."

"No. I'm sorry, Mrs. Wyatt, but there's nothing anyone can do at this point. Check in with the doctor tomorrow morning. If you're still bleeding, he'll probably have you come in for a sonogram. If the fetus is nonviable, we'll schedule a D and C."

Nonviable. What a sickening word.

"A surgery? You would do that already?" Emma's voice cracked with emotion at the thought of the doctor's scalpel scraping away the last traces of the tiny life inside her. "How can it be over so . . . so quickly?"

"The truth is, between ten and twenty-five percent of all pregnancies end in miscarriage."

"But this is my second," Emma sobbed. "That's one hundred percent for me. It's not fair."

"Let's hope it's just spotting. For now, you need to rest. Call the doctor the first thing in the morning."

Emma hung up the phone, pulled the fleece blanket over her head, and let out a plaintive wail. It couldn't be over for her baby.

It couldn't be.

Chapter 14

"We spent most of the time in the orchid exhibit, which is really amazing. There are walls of flowers." As Chelsea recounted the outing, she moved through the kitchen, examining the ceiling in the late afternoon sunlight. No cracks, but a strange pucker and a gray ring around the naked bulbs. Maybe it would go away once it dried completely.

"And what did Annie think?" Leo asked.

"She seemed to like it. She was flirting shamelessly with the guard."

"Of course she was. Maybe we can go back this weekend."

"That'd be fun. How was your day?"

She filled a glass from the water pitcher in the fridge and drank it down as he talked. Lately she seemed to be thirsty all the time, a side effect of the medication. Did that mean it was working? Maybe. At moments like this she no longer felt the entire world crashing down on her head. She didn't feel like her old self, but she could hold her head up without that black space behind her eyes.

Still, she was tired from the trip to the garden . . . and hungry. It was too early for dinner, so she grabbed a fork and picked at one of the muffins while she talked with Leo. After they hung up, she decided to make the most of her good mood and get something accomplished. She pushed open the rolltop desk and called the Sounder helpline. When the recording told her it would be a twenty-minute wait, she opted for a callback.

Then she curled into her spot on the couch and switched on the television.

She awoke with a dry mouth and a fuzzy feeling in her head. The room was cold without the sunshine, and as she went to close the shades she saw the solitary streetlamp out front, its single cold eye reminding her that she was alone.

Alone.

How did this happen? She couldn't handle it.

She turned away and went to the kitchen, desperate for food. Had she eaten that burrito? Nothing in the fridge held appeal. The chicken or steak would have made a great meal, but she didn't have the time or energy to cook something. And the thought of cleaning pans in the bathroom sink was even less appealing.

She poured herself a tall glass of skim milk and dug into one of the muffins. The milk tasted like old paint, but the muffin was a treat. She dug into another one. Maybe this would tide her over until the morning.

Staring up at the ceiling, she imagined herself trying to coat the damaged ceiling with the chalky skim milk . . . like a wash on a canvas.

She would paint white on white on white, and that gray ring would still bleed through, like the spot on Lady Macbeth's hand.

A shiver passed up her spine. Was someone watching? She turned and spotted them . . . the kitchen knives. How did they get out on the table with those boots? If someone slid them too close to the edge, they would drop right down into Annie's little bucket seat.

Frightened, Chelsea went over and pulled out the longest knife—a carving knife with a serrated blade. Her heart thudded in her chest at the cold gleam of light on steel.

It was so sharp; it could cut a person to ribbons in seconds.

She had bought it when her cousin was selling knives to help pay off her student loans, but she always had worried about getting cut with it. What if it clattered from the holder and hit Annabelle? She imagined it swinging through the air, sinking into flesh.

No, no, no!

She shoved the rest of the muffin into her mouth, embraced the heavy butcher block knife holder, and marched it over to the closet. Leaning into the hanging coats, she pushed it toward the dark corner and let it drop like a fat stone in a pond.

The thump of it dropping seemed to rock the house, and Annabelle woke up whimpering.

"It's okay. Mommy's not going to hurt you." Her voice sounded desperate and hollow, as if she were shouting in a dream. Why were her palms sweating when it was so cold in here?

Slamming the closet door behind her, Chelsea leaned against the closet and prayed that no one would ever find those knives.

Please, please, please, let them go away.

She imagined the knives rising up and stabbing at the door. She felt a jolt behind her, and let out a cry. Just her imagination.

And Annie was shrieking. Did she know about the knives?

No . . . of course not. She was a baby. A hungry baby.

She scooped Annie out of her chair and her fingers touched something moist and slippery. Oh, she needed to be changed. Her heartbeat was a dull thud as she tossed Annie's pink flowered onesie to the side and tore off the swollen diaper. What a mess. The wipes seemed to flap away from her grip like white birds as she did her best to clean Annie up. With this weight on her head, she'd never get another onesie snapped up. A clean diaper and a yellow nightgown with a drawstring were the best she could do.

Annabelle screamed right up to the second when Chelsea pressed her nipple to the baby's round, yowling mouth.

Thankful for the quiet, Chelsea shifted low in the couch and rested her head against the pillow. The sensation of falling through space enveloped her, and she held tight to her baby, afraid of losing her in midflight.

The phone was relentless. "Hello?" she answered, her voice floating in the black space.

Sounder Health Care. There were more forms to fill out. Endless pages of boxes and fine print extended before her, a line that led through the living room and down the front lawn and up in the air on a silvery path to the moon. She wanted to get the forms right, but she was too tired to remember the numbers and dates that defined her little family.

Fill out the forms. That's your job now. Fill out a form, then another, and another . . . then ride them to the moon.

And fall back to earth to take care of your baby.

The bleating phone woke her, its face glowing in the dark living room. Emma's name and number flashed in the caller ID.

"Hello?" Her voice was a dry riverbed, cracked and dusty.

"Chelsea?" Emma's voice sounded childish, like a shrill girl on the playground. "I'm so scared. I might . . . I might be losing the baby."

"Huh?" How could Emma lose her baby when it wasn't even born yet?

"A miscarriage. I'm bleeding and . . . there's no way to stop it, if it's . . ." That giddy voice again, only this time Chelsea realized her sister was crying.

"Don't cry, Emma."

"But my baby . . ."

In a cloud of exhaustion, Chelsea wondered why Emma didn't feel incredible relief. She would be off the hook now.

"I want to be a mother, more than anything." The tremble in Emma's voice filtered through Chelsea. "It's all I can think about and—"

"Take my baby." Chelsea's voice was low and raspy. So thirsty. "Please, take my baby." It wasn't a gesture of generosity, just a heartfelt request. "Will you come get her now?"

The only answer was the noise of her sister sobbing.

Such a sad sound. Chelsea sank into the darkness, fading into a sad dream.

After a few minutes of sobbing, Emma said she had to go, that she would call tomorrow.

But when will you come to take the baby? Chelsea wondered after the call ended. And where was her baby?

She fumbled on the end table and finally found the lamp switch. Annabelle's bucket seat was empty, but the baby nestled into the crevice of the couch beside Chelsea.

"Not safe," Chelsea told herself. Annie could have smothered. She could have fallen. So many terrible things that could happen.

"Be more careful next time." The voice had all the patience and authority of Judith Maynard. Mom. "You should be here."

Annabelle whined, the light in her eyes. Feeding time again?

"All right, all right." Chelsea chugged from a bottle of water on the end table, then unbuttoned her shirt.

The milk machine. The great silencer.

When the baby was done, Chelsea was too tired to head upstairs.

Why bother?

"You can sleep here," she told Annabelle, strapping her into her bucket seat. Then she settled back on the couch, pulled the throw up to her chin, and slid into the shallow pool of exhausted sleep.

Chapter 15

Chelsea rolled over in bed and took a deep waking breath. What a wonderful feeling—to sleep, really sleep, and not be interrupted by Annie's shrieks. At last, her little girl had slept through the night.

She nudged her chin into the pillow, thinking about all the advice about how it got easier. Everyone told her three months was the point of grace, but Annabelle was fourteen weeks now, and since the day she was born her screams and voracious appetite had kept Chelsea in a state of exhaustion.

But not last night.

With a sigh, Chelsea checked the clock. It was still dark, six thirty a.m., and the flat, cold mattress on the other side reminded her that Leo was out of town. Boston.

She'd been so upset when he'd left . . . left her feeling alone and abandoned and helpless to handle the cute little baby that needed so much but still seemed like such a stranger. "A little alien," Leo had joked. "She even has the bald head and the big eyes, like those pictures of alien creatures."

Well, at least last night the cute little alien had let her sleep.

She stretched, becoming aware of her rock-hard breasts. Milk had leaked through her nightgown to the sheets. Time for a feeding.

Chelsea threw back the covers and braced herself for the cold floor. Well, at least Annie was cozy in a onesie and footie pajamas. Or was she? Chelsea seemed to remember Annie in bright yellow, the color of baby chicks. Or had she dreamed of her daughter as a baby chick? Shivering, Chelsea pulled on a robe and went downstairs to pee, sure that the baby would begin to cry as soon as she heard the movement. But the blessed quiet prevailed.

Finally, a good night's sleep and a moment of quiet. Maybe they were turning a corner.

She hurried up the stairs and into Annabelle's tiny nursery, actually looking forward to starting Annie's day. "Good morning, sunshine," she said, going to the crib.

The bare sheet with little pastel elephants stopped her. She touched the rail, staring. Where was Annabelle?

"Oh." Backtracking quickly in her mind, she wondered if she had let the baby sleep downstairs.

Right. She had left Annie in the bucket seat while she slept on the couch.

But she hadn't slept on the couch. . . . Had she left Annie downstairs alone when she came up to bed? Her memory of last night was hazy.

She barreled down the stairs. "Annie . . ."

The bucket seat sat across from the sofa. Empty.

The stroller wasn't parked in the chilly vestibule. "Annie, where are you?" With a rush of fear and horror, Chelsea saw that the side door was open—that was why it was so cold down here. The storm door was closed, but unlocked.

"Oh, Annie . . ." Her voice held a whimper. Had she left her baby out all night?

She crashed outside to see the stroller in the driveway, facing away from her.

"Annie!" she gasped, grappling to look inside the carriage.

It was empty except for two abandoned baby blankets. Empty! She flung out the blankets, digging for her daughter.

"Annie!" She ran to check the car parked at the front of the driveway. The door refused to budge—locked. The infant seat was strapped in, but there was no sign of her baby.

This can't be. She must be inside, somewhere. What did I do with her last night? Think. Think. Where did you leave her?

She raced back into the house and began to recheck every spot.

Upstairs she checked the queen-sized bed she and Leo shared. Her hands fished under the covers until she ripped them off, impatient to get to her baby.

She combed through Annie's crib, the couches, the kitchen and bathroom, dining room and then closets. Where, where, where could she be?

Where is my baby?

A panic gripped her, but she couldn't give up. She would find her baby . . . but she needed help. She grabbed the phone and stumbled on her way up the stairs, going to check the nursery one more time.

Yanking up the hem of her robe, she let the world stop for one moment to press the numbers. Nine. One. One.

PART 2

Chapter 16

While the police searched the house, Chelsea stumbled outside to check the stroller one more time. Empty, of course. Still, she tossed out the blankets one more time and searched the cargo area under the stroller. She ran her hands over the vinyl mesh seat as if her fingertips would come across a clue pointing to Annie.

Satisfied that there was nothing there, she stuffed the blankets back inside and wheeled the stroller over to the tile bench. She could have been taking Annie for a midnight walk.

I'll take you on thousands of late-night walks. I promise, if you'll just come home . . .

Her hand securely on the stroller, she sat down on the bench she had tiled with her own hands. Her fingers traced the heart-shaped tiles embedded in the armrest. She had found the bench at a reclamation center and tiled it with an eye toward the spring. Once the daffodils bloomed, Leo would move it to the backyard, where she could sit with Annie in the afternoons.

She had seen herself sitting there this summer with Annabelle, telling her daughter the names of all the trees and plants in their backyard, pointing out shapes in the clouds, walking her around in the grass. And next summer, they would run through the backyard sprinkler together, and maybe splash in a little wading pool.

Those were the good visions.

An odd sense of disbelief had overcome her with the arrival of the police. Cops exuded authority, something she needed desperately right now. They would take care of things. They would find Annie.

They were proof that she wasn't going crazy, and yet they confirmed that this wasn't just a terrible nightmare terrorizing her sleep.

Rocking the stroller back and forth, Chelsea stared into the flashing red and blue turret lights. Blue and silver, then a swarm of red that glowed like fire in the winter night. When she blurred her eyes the colors mixed and morphed into purple and violet.

Mesmerizing. Hypnotizing.

How did anyone ever look away from those lights? They held her captivated, spellbound, lifted above the pain and panic. Her mind slid back to a safer place, to a narrow Dutch Colonial in Yonkers, the house she'd grown up in.

It was a summer night, so hot and still you could hear scrawny girl legs stirring under the sheets as she and Emma tried to get comfortable in their twin beds. Chelsea was scraping the sweat from her eyebrows when the leaves outside their window suddenly danced with a light display that rivaled the Fourth of July display in the park.

"What's that?" Chelsea pulled the sheet to her chin, afraid of aliens.

"The cops." Emma seemed to cartwheel out of bed and over to the window, and eight-year-old Chelsea wasn't far behind her.

The flashing, rotating lights atop the police car splashed light over the trees and lawns and warm asphalt, washing everything in dense, dark light. The driver's side door opened and a cop got out and walked around the car.

Chelsea was at once riveted and frightened. "Why are the police here? We're not criminals."

Emma shushed her as a lady cop got out on the curb side and pulled the handle of the back door. The two girls watched, holding breath and focus, as their older sister stepped out of the police cruiser.

"Look! Melanie is the criminal!"

The police marched Melanie to the door and rang the bell, causing a stir in the house that didn't settle down for years, until Melanie graduated high school and proved herself worthy in Dad's eyes by getting into college.

Emma and Chelsea crept to the top of the stairs and pressed their faces between the balustrades to listen as the police explained that sixteen-year-old Melanie had been found at a beer party. The adult voices were calm as they discussed things that bored Chelsea. Mostly she wanted to know if Melanie had gone to jail, and why would she want to drink something that tasted so fizzy-fuzzy and sour.

Suddenly, everyone stood up and the police were leaving. The girls scurried upstairs, not wanting to be caught spying. As soon as Melanie was sent to her room, Chelsea and Emma couldn't resist peeking inside.

"Did you go to jail?" Chelsea asked.

Emma pushed the door open and stepped inside. "Are you grounded for life?"

Melanie kicked off her denim cutoffs and pulled on some boxers. "Do you mind? I'm going to bed."

"Don't be mean. You scared me." Chelsea went to her and wrapped her arms around her. "I thought the police were going to take you away for good."

Melanie hugged her back, then sprawled onto her bed. "Don't worry, bug. They were hard-asses until Daddy started talking."

"What did he say?" Emma asked.

"Whatever. He knows the right stuff to say. That's the thing. Daddy knows how to handle things. Not that I want to tangle with the cops again, believe me. But if it did happen, it's nice to have that safety net."

That night, Chelsea went to sleep soothed by a new pearl of wisdom.

Daddy would care of everything.

It was a truth that lasted for nearly two decades, until Mom got sick. But for so many years, Chelsea dropped off to sleep believing that her father could handle any problem that threatened his daughters.

Now I need you, Daddy. I need you to help my *daughter. Help me find her.*

Would he fly up from Florida to help her? Oh, but he couldn't fly in this storm.

Snow was falling beyond the carport, a whisper of white already beginning to coat the brown grass and gray pavement. Would it cover Annie's tracks? Of course, she couldn't walk, but there was the path of the person who had taken her. Maybe they would bring dogs to sniff her out. Dogs could sniff through snow, couldn't they? Or maybe the rising sun would melt the snow and the mystery and show them Annie, safe and sound at Emma's house or in Leo's arms.

So many possibilities. She couldn't give up hope.

And she had to keep tamping down the horrible possibility that the police would find her daughter shoved into an old laundry bag, dropped from the bedroom window, or pinned to the floor with that ghastly knife collection.

Killed by the hands of the mother who was supposed to love her.

Chapter 17

Snow glittered in the beams of her headlights as Detective Grace Santos drove to the address. During her five years in the Missing Persons Squad, she had investigated and recovered plenty of runaway teens as well as younger children involved in family abductions. Infant abductions were rare. In the past twenty-five years, there had been around two hundred cases nationwide. She had worked on an infant abduction at the hospital, a more common scenario these days, but an infant taken from her home in the middle of the night was a first for her. Most likely the baby was taken by a family member or caregiver. Sometimes a caregiver or parent claimed that the baby was abducted to cover up the child's death, either intentional or accidental. The good news was that the recovery rate for infants was extremely high. Thank God for that.

Every case had a life of its own. In the next few hours, her focus would be on building the web of family and friends that surrounded Annabelle Green.

While waiting at the traffic light, she shot a look at her cell phone for the names of the major players—the parents and the child, three-month-old Annabelle.

"Where did you go on a snowy night, baby Annabelle?"

Her first responsibility was to the missing child, and Grace whispered a heartfelt Hail Mary for the safe return of this baby. It was part of her routine when starting a case, and she believed that God heard every word and answered in His own way.

The house was cute, in a nice neighborhood. She turned off the engine, took out her iPhone, and copied the Maple Lane address onto a Web site that tracked registered sex offenders. The results gave her four addresses of men within a two-mile radius. She checked the map, taking in the four residences lit in red. The closest was about six blocks away. Something to check out, though these men were not likely suspects in this case. They didn't fit the profile of a typical infant abductor: a compulsive female, age twelve to fifty-three, married and living in the community.

As she got out of her car, she was surprised to see a woman sitting calmly by the side door, nudging a stroller. The red and blue lights from a cruiser's roof rack washed over the scene, casting a surreal glow over the woman framed by falling snow that glimmered at the fringes of the carport. Mid-twenties, brunette, and dressed in a robe, she sat on a bench, rocking that stroller as if it were an August morning.

The distraught mother?

"Did you find my baby?" Stress flashed in her pale eyes underlined by gray arcs.

Grace noted that her robe wasn't even belted. "I didn't find your baby, but it's freezing out here. Why don't we step inside?"

"But my baby likes the fresh air. See? She's quiet now." The young woman rose to check the stroller. Her face fell when she saw that it was empty. "My baby! Oh, she's missing." She pressed her hands to her face, suddenly remembering. "Do you think the police will find her?"

"Finding your child is our top priority. I'm Grace Santos, with the Missing Persons bureau. You're Chelsea Maynard?"

The woman nodded, her eyes round as quarters. "But my baby is named Annabelle Green. My husband has a different name."

"I've got that in my notes." This woman was on the edge, and Grace suspected the team of officers and dogs that would be arriving shortly to search would make things worse. "I think we should step inside and see how the officers are progressing." She put a hand on the fragile woman's shoulder and shepherded her in through the side door. The poor thing was barefoot and shivering under her robe, but Grace suspected that was more from shock than the cold.

Inside, the house was quaint; you could tell that a lot of care had gone into this home. The living room was cozy, with a fireplace covered in pretty white-and-blue tiles. There was a sour smell, which Grace quickly identified when she saw the soiled diapers on the floor by the changing table. The kitchen was a bit disheveled, with mops leaning against the kitchen counter, boots and hats set on the kitchen table, but then whose house looked like a spread from *Better Homes and Gardens*?

"Do you have some slippers you want to put on?" Grace suggested.

Obediently, Chelsea fished a pair of mules out of the mound of shoes on the table. She stepped into them, then stumbled into the living room and fell heavily onto the couch.

Grace leaned against the counter, taking in the kitchen. What was the reason for the buckets and mops? The counter was free of bread or fruit, though there was a gift box with two frosted cupcakes and a lot of crumbs. She picked up the note taped to the lid and read the message: *GOOD NEIGH-BORS HELP EACH OTHER.*

At the other end of the counter was a framed photo of a baby with a joyous, toothless grin. No doubt, Annabelle. One plastic bag held a cell phone, another a little pink-print baby outfit. Miklowski had probably bagged the clothing for the dogs to use to follow Annabelle's scent.

"I have to call my husband." The hand that reached for the telephone shook. Grace watched as the young woman pressed numbers, frowned, and started over, as if she couldn't get it right. Poor thing.

Grace went into the living room and sat beside her on the couch. "Chelsea, why don't you let me make the call?" She suspected that the patrol officers hadn't had a chance to notify the husband yet, and she did need to talk with him.

"It's just that the numbers keep slipping around." Chelsea poked at the phone again, then sighed. "I keep messing up."

Grace nodded, keeping her voice sympathetic. "Chelsea, are you on medication?"

"Just Nebula, from my doctor. For depression. But don't worry, I can still breast-feed the baby. It won't hurt her."

"That's good to know." She wondered if Nebula could make a person confused and disoriented.

Chelsea touched her chest gingerly. "I need to pump. And Annabelle . . . she must be hungry." Her eyes filled with tears. "Do you think they'll feed her? Whoever took her?"

"Most babies give a shout when they're hungry. Does your Annabelle have a healthy pair of lungs?"

Chelsea nodded, swiping at her eyes with one sleeve.

"I'm sure she'll let it be known that she's hungry. Why don't you let me put the call through for you? I'll tell him what's going on, then you two can talk."

Chelsea had to go to the directory of her cell phone to find her husband's number. "He should be here, but he had to go to Boston for work. Do you think he came home early and took Annabelle for a walk?"

"I would love to think that happened." Grace bit her lower lip. "But don't you think your husband would have told you he was home? And most parents don't walk their babies in the frosty cold before dawn."

"Of course not." Chelsea bit her lower lip, trying to hold back tears. "That was stupid. What was I thinking?"

"You're upset," Grace said. "Keep breathing. That's good." She punched in the number Chelsea showed her.

When the call went through, the man on the other end of the line sounded groggy. "Mr. Green, this is Grace Santos from the New Rochelle Missing Persons Squad." Grace always tried to put herself in the other person's shoes when handling a case like this; it was rough, but there was no easy way to pass on difficult news. She tried to give it to them straight. "I'm here with your wife, Chelsea, and we've begun a search for your daughter, Annabelle, who was reporting missing this morning."

Leo Green's reaction quickly shot from disbelief to fear to action.

"I'm coming home . . . the next flight," he said. "Who took her? Do you have any idea?"

"I was going to ask you the same thing," Grace said. In fact, she had a long list of questions for Leo Green. It would have helped to have a more stable person here to draw information from, and she would have liked to see the child's parents together to get a sense of their relationship. A large percentage of missing infants were taken by family members, often as a result of custody disputes.

"We're going to do everything we can to find your daughter." Grace gave Leo Green her contact information, wished him a safe flight, and handed the phone to his wife.

Grace listened as Chelsea cried, trying to piece the situation together for her husband. The young mother was distraught, not making much sense, and once again Grace felt for her. She thought of her own son at three months—a screamer. That baby boy shrieked through every dinner she and her husband attempted. Eventually she gave up on dinner; her husband gave up on their family.

Was Annabelle a crier? Grace wondered as a uniformed cop came down the stairs—Trent Miklowski. Outside, car doors were slamming. The search team was assembling. Grace motioned Miklowski into the kitchen, out of earshot of the young mother.

"What do we have?" she asked, leaning back against the kitchen counter.

"A fourteen-week-old infant goes missing in the middle of the night. Only child of Leo Green and Chelsea Maynard. The father is out of town. The mother says no one else lives in the house."

"Did you find anything when you searched the place?"

"Nothing unusual upstairs, except the mother tore a few

things apart looking for her. We've searched inside and out. Closets and cabinets, piles of laundry, inside appliances. Viloria searched outside with a flashlight. Nothing has been dug up in the yard and her car is clean. And we poked through the trash. Didn't want to do that while the mother was sitting outside, but she didn't seem to notice or care. There's no sign of a B and E, but the mother left the side door unlocked. Or at least she says it was unlocked when she woke up this morning. Maynard says her husband cleaned the house this weekend, so it's worth trying to take prints. We'll eliminate anyone who's been here since then."

"Good." Fingerprints were just one facet of a case, but if you didn't gather them immediately, you couldn't backtrack later.

"The kid was wearing something bright yellow," Miklowski went on, "but the color is the only thing that stands out in Mom's memory. She can't remember some of the details of last night, like what time she put the baby to bed or even if she put her down in her crib. Do you think she's on drugs or drinking or just plain crazy?"

Grace wanted to smack Miklowski. "When was the last time you gave birth to a child and stopped your life to take care of it twenty-four seven?" Grace asked.

He drew a hand back over his head. "Giving birth is no excuse for losing your kid, and look at this place. She could barely find this photo of the baby when I asked her for it. Didn't know the baby's weight. And do you see those dirty diapers over there?"

"I can't tell you the whereabouts of Annabelle Green, but I can tell you that woman in there is compromised, either by medication or shock or depression or a combination of those. Right now, with the father out of town, she's also our only resource in finding this child."

"Exactly. Do you want to take her down to the precinct?"

"I can talk to her here. Have you issued an Amber Alert yet?" Time was of the essence. It was critical that information about the missing baby got out right away.

"Sgt. Balfour is issuing the alert. Do you want to make the house a crime scene?"

She nodded. "It never hurts. We can always break it down later if it seems unwarranted."

"That's what Viloria said. I'll go tell her."

Grace went back to the living room, wishing she didn't have to badger this forlorn woman with a million questions. "Your husband sounded very upset. It must be a shock to wake up to a call like that."

Chelsea nodded.

"Chelsea, I'm sorry but I have to ask you some questions. Your answers might help us locate Annabelle." As she spoke, she took out her iPhone and went to the notepad function.

"So, you said you're legally married to the baby's father, Leo Green."

"Yes."

"And would you say you have a happy marriage?"

"Yes. Well, it's been strained since Annie's birth, which was so traumatic—worse than I could have imagined. But Leo's been wonderful. He cooks all our meals, and he's great with Annie."

"Any custody issues regarding Annie? Angry exes looking for child support?"

"No, nothing like that."

Grace had moved to the front windows, where half a dozen marked and unmarked cruisers were now parked in the street. "What's the last thing you remember last night?"

Chelsea bit her lips as she scraped back her dark hair. "Putting Annie in her bucket seat? Or maybe it was eating a muffin. I don't know." She paused, pressing a fist to her mouth. "How could I be so stupid to leave the side door unlocked?"

"Maybe you locked it and someone got in with a key."

"I think . . ." Chelsea's eyes narrowed. "I mean, I might have put her in the stroller outside to calm her down."

"Did you?"

"I don't know. I woke up in bed upstairs but I don't remember getting there." Her thin thread of calm unraveled and, once again, she began to cry.

Off to the side of the living room, Grace noticed Miklowski and his female partner, Viloria, descending the staircase. She nodded as they crossed through the living room and headed out the side door.

"I know this is upsetting, but I need your help. I need to know who has access to this house—anyone with a key."

"Leo and me. And my sister Emma. She helps with Annie, and she lives in New Rochelle, too. Oh, and I think my sister Melanie has one, too, but she lives down in central Jersey with four kids of her own. Her youngest is in the terrible twos. She can't get here that often."

Grace made notes, her fingers flying over the iPhone. "And who else watches Annabelle? Is she in day care?"

"No day care. But we've used a baby nurse named Helen Rosekind. She came through an agency. And there's also a teenage girl someone recommended. I just used her this week and . . ." Chelsea squeezed her eyes shut and sniffed. "She seems like a nice girl, but I was worried. One Saturday night when we came home, her boyfriend was here, and we told her that wasn't cool at all. They're both so goth. They might be harmless, but I felt really uncomfortable around him."

Grace got their names from Chelsea and typed: *Eleni Zika* and *boyfriend Krispy*. "Any other relatives in the area? Grandparents? Aunts, uncles?"

Chelsea shook her head. "Leo's family is up in Maine, and my dad lives in Florida now. He and Mom . . . they moved down there, but she's gone now. She died just a few days before Annabelle was born."

"Is there someone, friend or family, who could come lend you some support?"

Chelsea shook her head. "No one."

"What about your sister Emma? You said she lives close by."

"No. She's very upset. She . . ." Chelsea squinted. "Or maybe I dreamed that. I think she was crying on the phone last night, but I'm not sure."

Grace picked up the phone and handed it to Chelsea. "Let's give her a call. Something tells me she'll want to talk with you now."

Grace was right. When Chelsea told her sister what was happening, she promised to come right over.

Chelsea ended the call and looked toward the open side door. "Shouldn't we be out there? I want to help with the search."

"You need to be here for when we find her," Grace said, praying they would recover this woman's baby sooner rather than later. A pang of compassion hit her as she noticed the two stains on Chelsea's robe. "Do you have a pump?"

Chelsea squinted, then looked down. "Upstairs." She pushed off the sofa, then fumbled up the stairs, nearly tripping on her robe. Grace followed her up, just to be on the safe side.

In the hallway at the top of the stairs, the doors were open but yellow crime scene tape spanned each doorway.

"What's that?" Chelsea paused outside the master bedroom, horrified.

"Not a problem." Grace pulled the tape off and motioned her through.

"Hey!" Miklowski called from the stairs as Chelsea shut the door behind her. "What about the crime scene?"

"You already searched the bedroom," she said. "And have a heart. The woman needs to pump her breast milk."

His face soured and he went back downstairs, shaking his head.

Grace wasn't sure why she felt so protective of Chelsea Maynard, but clearly the woman was in crisis. That observation scared Grace, for more than one reason. First, the desperation in Chelsea's eyes was truly pathetic. That aside, there was the possibility that Chelsea Maynard had snapped and done something to shut her child up—a chilling but valid avenue that would have to be pursued. And, if Grace was truly honest, she had to admit that when she looked at Chelsea Maynard, she saw herself a dozen years ago.

Trying to put personal stuff out of her mind, she peered into the nursery, noting the appliqué elephants marching across the valance. The cheerful yellow walls were stenciled with the same elephants, and the lampshade on the dresser was decorated with a mother elephant nuzzling her baby close with her trunk.

It was one of those well-planned, perfect nurseries, missing just one thing. Annabelle Green.

Chapter 18

Throwing clothes and his travel kit into his luggage with one hand, Leo held his cell phone to his ear. "I'm trying to confirm that you have a Detective Grace Santos working for you."

"Can I ask what this is in reference to?" The desk officer at the New Rochelle precinct was polite, but Leo didn't have the patience for a mannerly conversation.

"I got a call from her, and I want to confirm that it's not some sort of hoax." After he'd thrown on his clothes and slapped water onto his face, Leo had realized that this was just the sort of thing Jennifer would stage. Rip your heart out, then call it all a joke.

"Yes, we do have a Grace Santos on duty. Detective Santos."

"Oh." Hope faded in his chest. "Can you confirm this phone number she gave me? Or . . . wait. Can you tell me if you've had a missing baby reported in New Rochelle? It would have come in early this morning."

There was silence on the line for a moment, then the cop asked, "Do you live on Maple Lane?"

"That's right. Twenty-two Maple Lane. Leo Green." He paused as the cop's silence gave him the answer. "This is real."

"I'm afraid so."

"All right. I have to get home. Thanks." He slid the cell phone into his pocket and put his dress shoes into his suitcase without even bagging them. In the bathroom he snatched up his shampoo and aftershave and tossed them into the trash can. He wouldn't take any liquids in his bags. Nothing to slow him down. He would carry his bag on the plane and speed home from the airport.

Downstairs in the lobby he asked the concierge to get him a cab to the airport right away.

"If you don't mind waiting a bit, I'd be happy to call a shuttle service we recommend," the woman said. "The service is excellent at half the price."

Leo thanked her but explained that there was no time for that. "It's a family emergency."

The phrase seemed so alien, and yet, for the first time in his life, he was in the thick of it. A true emergency . . . Annie was missing. It seemed impossible—insane!—but right now his house was probably crawling with cops and detectives contemplating the same question that baffled him. Who would steal a baby from her crib on a winter night in a suburb?

The cab smelled of cigarettes and old shoes. He sank into the seat, raked his short hair back, and tried to imagine what could have happened. He opened his wallet for the photo of Annie that they had taken at Sears. She hadn't been old enough to prop herself up yet, but the photographer had managed to capture that gummy smile. And the light in her eyes . . .

Those intelligent, curious eyes that followed him as he loaded the dishwasher or cooked up a batch of spaghetti sauce.

What could have happened to her? He knew Chelsea had been in a bad way, but she would never have lifted a hand to hurt their baby. She barely had the energy to lift a hand at all lately. No, Chelsea would never hurt Annabelle.

But who, then? Who the fuck took their daughter?

Why didn't you tell me you have a baby?

Jennifer.

A sick feeling hit him when his ex-wife came to mind. The messages that filled his voice mail were unsettling. *Why don't you ever call me? When can we get together? I want to meet your kid.*

He had thought he was rid of her, but no . . . now she was back in New Rochelle. Jennifer was a borderline personality—unreliable and self-centered—but would she stoop so low as to kidnap an infant? He couldn't imagine what she would do with an infant once she had it in her clutches.

Another thought that stopped him cold.

Oh, God, don't let anything happen to Annabelle. She wasn't even crawling yet. Where was she right now? He had to know. She was out there somewhere, maybe hungry, maybe cold, and here he was, hundreds of miles away, unable to help her. What kind of father was he?

Where was his Annabee?

He sank low in the backseat of the cab and began to cry.

Chapter 19

The fog was lifting.

The haze that had hung over her head through the night was draining away at last, and as her mind began to awaken, a few things solidified in her thoughts: She was a mess. She didn't care who knew it. And she didn't care if the police taped over everything in her house if it meant that they would find her baby.

Last night, she'd been worse than ever. Comatose. Unaware of her own actions. She didn't know why that would happen, when she'd been religiously taking her Nebula every day, but she couldn't let it happen again.

Images from this morning rushed through her mind. Stammering when the cop questioned her. Her garbled words and jumbled memory of last night. Had she really sat outside pretending to rock her missing baby in the cold? There'd been a frantic search for a photo of Annabelle when there was one hanging on the wall over the desk. She'd been mortified when the cop pointed it out while she was digging through old mail and insurance bills.

Chelsea zipped up the baggy old fleece jacket she'd been wearing since Annabelle was born, grabbed the bottle of breast milk, and held carefully to the railing as she went down the stairs. The detective was still in the kitchen, making notes on her iPhone.

She placed the bottle in the refrigerator, where it stood on the shelf, a lonely soldier. Annie would be drinking it before it went bad. Yes, she vowed. Yes, she would.

Closing the fridge, she wondered where the two cops had gone. "Have they given up?" Chelsea asked, her voice catching. "The police can't stop looking. She must be around here, somewhere."

"There are several search teams outside canvassing the neighborhood." Grace looked up from her iPhone when she spoke, and her dark brown eyes were reassuring. "We called in the canine squad, and they've been searching. Remember that outfit of Annabelle's you gave to Officer Miklowski?"

"That's right." He had taken the little pink-flowered romper, the last outfit she remembered stripping off Annabelle when she changed her. He had told her that it would help the dogs know her scent so that they could search for her. "I'm sorry. I've been in such a fog. I don't know what came over me last night. Maybe the flu."

"How are you feeling now?" Grace asked.

"Better. Like my thoughts have a connection to reality. Does that make sense?"

Grace nodded. "What you're going through, it can't be easy. Why don't you make yourself a cup of tea or some coffee?"

Something warm to drink sounded soothing, but when Chelsea turned on the faucet, she remembered about the leak. "I had to turn the water off on this line," she explained, telling the detective about the broken valve upstairs.

"Isn't that just how things go?" Grace said. "Bad enough you get a leak, but it has to happen when your husband is out of town."

Chelsea's fingers tightened around the handle of the kettle. This woman wasn't out to get her. In fact, the kindness in her voice made Chelsea mist over. "Would you like some tea?"

"That sounds great."

Chelsea went to the little bathroom to fill the teakettle. As she started the electric stove and went about straightening up the kitchen, Grace's words washed over her, brisk but reassuring. There was an Amber Alert out for Annabelle, so people everywhere would be on the lookout for her baby. Search teams were combing the neighborhood.

"They'll do an extensive grid search of the area," the detective told her as she removed boots and shoes from the table and tossed them back into the dry closet. "Right now they're going door-to-door, asking neighbors if they've seen anything."

Neighbors? A chill crept up Chelsea's spine as she thought of the caustic woman next door. "You need to talk to Louise Pickler," Chelsea said.

"On which side?" Grace made a note as Chelsea pointed toward Louise's house and recounted the relationship that had always been tinged with bitterness.

"She was cold to us when we moved in, but we thought that was just because Louise was close with the previous owner. While we were building the carport, Louise used to come out and measure to make sure we weren't violating the building codes and encroaching on her property. She warmed up to us when she noticed I was pregnant, but even that made me uncomfortable. There's something off about her."

"How's that?"

"She treats Annie like . . . like a pesky pet lizard. Louise says creepy things like how she's going to gobble Annie up. It sounds like she's going to roast her in the oven, like a turkey. And she always has some dire warning about keeping Annie out of the street, away from the germs breeding in malls, or safe from baby snatchers."

An image of Louise's stern eyes flashed before her. *"They like the blue-eyed, blond ones,"* Louise had said. *"You'd better keep an eye on her."*

A new panic bubbled inside Chelsea as she babbled on about Louise. "She's crazy. We've got to go next door and see if she has Annie."

"We'll check it out. I'll talk with her myself," Grace promised.

The shrill whistle of the kettle snapped Chelsea out of her panic. Yes, she had to keep moving. Straighten up . . . eat something. It wouldn't help Annabelle to have her mother fall apart. She took two mugs from the cabinet.

"So, then, I guess this Louise Pickler isn't the kind neighbor who gave you these cupcakes," Grace said, pointing to the last two cupcakes in the box.

"What?" Chelsea blinked. "Oh. Actually, no. Those are carrot muffins from my sister Emma."

"Really?" Grace picked up the card, attached to curled yellow ribbon. "And she left this card?"

Chelsea picked it up, then frowned when she saw the message about good neighbors. "I thought Emma baked them. She brought them over." She pushed her hair back behind one ear.

"And you ate some of them?"

Chelsea nodded. "Last night, I was so hungry but I didn't feel like making anything. I had a few in the evening, then woke up later and ate some more."

Grace's fingers closed on the yellow ribbon. "I wouldn't eat any more of them until you check with your sister."

"Do you think someone . . . someone tried to poison me? Maybe that's why I felt so foggy last night." Chelsea's hand shook as she removed the tea bag from her mug. "Oh, God, any poison would have gone to Annabelle in my breast milk."

Grace frowned. "It sounds a little farfetched. Let's see what your sister has to say about these muffins, okay?"

She sipped the tea, still too hot, but it helped brace her against the awful truth. "What if I hurt my baby?"

Although Grace didn't answer, the question floated uncomfortably in the air.

Cupping the hot mug, Chelsea leaned against the kitchen counter and squeezed her eyes shut and prayed to wake up from this nightmare.

Chapter 20

"How could Annie be missing?" Jake's voice was reassuring, even over the phone.

"I don't know." Emma turned onto Maple Lane, Chelsea's street. "But I'm worried. What if Chelsea left her outside again, and someone came by and snatched her?"

Jake heaved a weary sigh. He had been on the early train to the city when Chelsea first called. Now Emma imagined him walking down the Manhattan street to his West Side office, looking so handsome in his suit. Jake rarely wore a coat; he just didn't get cold.

She wished he could hold her now, warm her up. He was her rock.

"Are you okay to go over there?" he asked. "You should be resting."

"Chelsea needs me. I'm almost there."

"And Leo?"

"I imagine he's on his way back from Boston, but it'll take a few hours." She had to park two doors down, behind a police cruiser.

"What a wretched thing. Look, if they need volunteers to search, I'll take the next train home and join in. Just say the word."

"I'll keep you posted."

"And you take care of . . . of yourself."

Take care of our baby—that was what he'd been saying these past couple months. Emma unbuckled her seat belt and fanned her fingers out over her belly.

Are you still there, little baby? Not knowing was killing her. God help her, but she wanted to be done with this business with her sister and get over to her doctor's office. Maybe it would all be resolved by now; maybe a kind neighbor had found Annabelle outside in the driveway, given her cover, and returned her as soon as the sun came up.

A handful of cops were standing out on Chelsea's front lawn, their radios squawking, their words forming puffs of white in the cold air. Their expressions, heavy as lead, told her that they hadn't found Annie. One cop questioned Emma as she turned up the driveway, but when she identified herself as Chelsea's sister, he walked her up to the side door.

"Can you vouch for this one?" he called inside.

"Emma." Chelsea's face crumpled, that froggy expression her sister always got as a kid when she was about to cry. Emma went over to the table and leaned down to give her a hug.

"We'll take it from here. Thanks, officer," said a woman's voice.

"Honey, what happened?"

"I don't know," Chelsea said, a tremor in her voice.

Emma slid out of her arms and took a seat beside her. "When I called you last night . . . do you remember that?"

Chelsea nodded, her eyes shiny with tears.

"That was around nine, nine thirty, and Annie was with you, right?"

Chelsea scraped her hair back. "I wasn't sure what time you called, but I thought we talked on the phone. Yes, Annie was here. I . . . she was beside me on the couch or . . . maybe I was feeding her. Something like that."

"So the baby was still here when you called around nine thirty," the woman said. "That's helpful for our timeline."

When Emma looked over, the woman nodded. "I'm Grace

Santos, a detective with the Missing Persons Squad. And you're Emma Maynard?"

"Emma Wyatt."

The detective had warm brown eyes and shiny black hair in a stylish cut that curled under her chin. Emma would not have pegged her as a cop; there was an easy, nurturing vibe about her. "Thank you for coming over. Your sister really needs your support right now."

Emma nodded, wishing she could tell the woman that she needed support, too. She was so worried about her own tiny baby, but no one besides Jake seemed to understand what she was going through. "I want to help. I don't think Chelsea should be alone right now, but I have to head off for an appointment soon. Is Leo coming home?"

"On his way," Grace answered. "He was hoping to catch the next flight out of Boston."

"That's a relief. Leo will be able to help you more than I can." Emma pressed her palms flat on the table, as if it could keep her upright. "But what happened to Annabelle?" She turned to Chelsea, who seemed lost inside herself. "Did someone snatch her from out in the driveway?"

"I don't know." Chelsea's voice was quiet and dead. "I don't remember."

"But she does remember finding the side door unlocked," Grace offered.

"Chelsea." Emma put one hand on her sister's arm. "Did you leave her out in the driveway again?"

Grace Santos was looking at her iPhone. "She's done that before?"

"The other night . . . my husband and I found her out there," Emma told Grace. "Chelsea walks her out there sometimes. The fresh air soothes her."

"I know how it is with a colicky baby." Grace nodded. "You have to go with the things that calm them down, even if they are a little unconventional."

"Annabelle was crying when we found her, and soon after we got here the police arrived. They said there'd been a noise complaint. We figured it was from the obnoxious woman next door."

"Louise Pickler," Grace said. "I'll check on that. But I'd love to know about last night . . . whether someone keyed their way in or was Annabelle out in her stroller. What do you think, Chelsea? Has your memory gelled at all? Do you remember taking Annabelle outside last night?"

"I don't know."

"Just try and remember, honey, because it's so important." Emma knew her frustration was coming through, but she wasn't going to sit back and let Chelsea play dumb when Annabelle was in danger. Just yesterday, her niece had come down those stairs, bright-eyed and curious in her little snowsuit with the hood. She wanted that moment back. She wanted Annabelle back.

"It was a terrible night," Chelsea said. "I couldn't stay awake. When you called, I didn't even think I'd make it up the stairs to bed. Everything just came down on me and . . . I couldn't think clearly."

"I have a question for you, Emma," Grace said, shifting the focus. "Is there anyone you can think of who would have a reason to take Annabelle? Any relatives or friends? Caregivers?"

Emma shook her head. "I can't think of anyone, but that doesn't happen very often, does it? The random kidnapping of an infant?"

"It does not." Grace's eyes flickered over to Chelsea, as if testing the moment. "Infant kidnappings are rare, and when a baby is taken the odds are much better of finding that infant than of recovering an older child. Generally, pedophiles do not steal infants. They tend to take older children."

A whimper escaped Chelsea's throat, and Emma squeezed her hand.

"That's the good news, I guess," Grace said. "But when an infant disappears, the odds are that the baby has been killed by a caregiver, either accidentally or intentionally."

Emma's belly roiled as that fact sank in. Was Chelsea one of those statistics? Had she acted through one of the dark visions that had been playing out in her head these past weeks? She didn't want to believe that was possible of her sister, but then the woman sitting beside her at the table barely resembled the little sister who had believed she could conquer the world.

Tension was thick in the air. Neither Emma nor her sister dared tread on that tender spot.

"Maybe you can answer a question for me." Grace picked up a box on the counter and showed Emma. There were two muffins left. "Did you bake these for your sister?"

"No. They were from a neighbor. That's what the note said."

"But you brought them over yesterday," Chelsea said sharply. "I'm not imagining that."

"No, honey. I didn't make them. I just brought them inside. They were sitting on your porch, with that note. I figured you would know who they were from."

Chelsea raked her hair back. "You didn't make them for me?"

Emma shook her head. "I'm sorry, honey. I'm . . . I told you. I guess you didn't hear me."

"Okay, then." Grace put the lid on the box. She picked up the note by the yellow ribbon and dropped it into a bag. "This might sound crazy, but I'm going to take these last two muffins and have our lab do some analysis. Chelsea, you said you ate three or four of them, and you weren't feeling well. It's worth checking to see if they're laced with something."

"Who would do that to my sister?" Emma asked.

"It might be unfounded." Grace looked down at the box. "And in the end, maybe they're just two carrot muffins from a kind neighbor, right?"

Emma couldn't bear to look at her sister, thinking that she might have contributed to making Chelsea even more disoriented than she already was. *But I told her they were from a neighbor. I know I said it. Why didn't I just toss those damned muffins in the garbage?*

Chapter 21

Shrugging on her jacket, Grace headed out to the cluster of cops in the front yard, where Balfour was coordinating the search. She was glad to have a veteran like Mike Balfour in charge. With eighteen years of experience, he knew the routine but was open to changing it up if they got a lead, and he was a good boss who got the most out of his squad because he treated them with respect and humor.

Over the radio, someone was calling in addresses that had been canvassed. A cop made a note on his clipboard while Balfour listened in.

"How's it going, Mike?"

"I wish I had better news for you. Or any news." At six feet, Mike was a head taller than Grace. His short-cropped hair glimmered with silver, and his blue eyes could be stern. "If the child was older, I'd send a helicopter up to do an air search, but Annabelle Green isn't able to motor on her own yet."

"Yeah, at three months, she's not going anywhere on her own." Grace pulled her jacket closed against the pelting snowflakes. "I saw the dog out here. Any luck?"

"He caught the scent, but the trail ended three doors down, southwest. It's possible someone took the baby to a car that was parked there."

Grace shielded her eyes against the snow to check out the

houses in that direction. "How about the people who live there?"

"An older couple—retired." He flipped open his notebook. "Tina and James Wilkinson. Tina Wilkinson let us search their yard, but honestly, the dog just sat down at the curb there. The trail ends in the street."

"But he did lead you somewhere." Grace turned toward Chelsea's Subaru, which sat gathering snow in the driveway. Had it been moved during the night? If Chelsea had loaded her daughter into the car, dead or alive, it didn't seem likely that she would have parked three doors down and toted the child that far in the middle of the night.

Mike Balfour looked over at the car. "Yeah, I know. The first cops on the scene did a search. Miklowski says they didn't disturb any evidence, but I hate to impound the car at this point."

Grace nodded. She didn't think it was time to turn all their focus on Chelsea Maynard as a suspect. At least, not yet.

She studied Pickler's house, a cape similar to her neighbor's, only more rundown. White dripped down the brickwork from the shutters. The porch awning listed drunkenly to one side, and the windows were a dingy gray.

"Have you talked to Louise Pickler yet?" she asked Mike. "She's the neighbor on this side."

"No one is answering, and we don't see a car in the garage. But I can tell you, there's been some conflict between Pickler and our family here. On Monday night two officers were here after a report that a child was abandoned in the street. The complaint came from Pickler. The officers responded at nineteen thirty-two and found the child inside with the mother, Chelsea Maynard. I e-mailed you a copy of the police report."

"I'd like to talk with Louise Pickler," Grace said. "I'm going to call her information in to Chris, see if he can run a check on her as soon as he gets to the office." Chris Panteleoni was her partner on most cases.

"And I'll let you know as soon as she comes home . . . *if* she comes home." Mike's eyes narrowed as he stared up at

Pickler's house. "The house has that abandoned look. You can't tell from here, but there are a bunch of old flyers on the porch, and see how the walkway wasn't shoveled or trampled all winter?" Mike Balfour knew his stuff.

"Yeah, I'd say that house has seen better days. Let me know if you see any sign of Pickler."

"You're sticking around, then?"

"At least until the husband gets here. I want to get a full profile of the family."

Back inside the house, Grace was relieved to see Chelsea at the kitchen table eating eggs, toast, canned peaches, and cottage cheese. Emma had taken charge of the kitchen in that big-sister way, but the conversation between the two women was strained. Even after Grace stepped inside, they didn't acknowledge her or miss a beat.

"How can you be mad at me when I don't remember anything?" Chelsea stared at her plate, tracing invisible shapes with the tongs of her fork.

"I'm not mad. I'm worried about Annabelle, and you don't seem to get that we'd be able to find her much more quickly if you could just remember what you did with her."

"I told you, I don't remember." She dropped the fork and pressed her palms to her face. "But I do remember talking to you. Didn't I ask you to take her?" Chelsea's voice was dull and listless, almost disembodied. "I knew I couldn't handle her. I begged you to take her."

"I couldn't. Dammit, Chelsea, I'm spotting and I might be miscarrying. Do you remember that?"

Chelsea looked up tentatively. "Sort of. I'm sorry. So . . . what's going on?"

"I've got to get to the doctor this morning, and . . . You know what? Never mind about me. I wish I had helped you, okay? But I needed to rest and I thought you'd be okay. You've been feeling better. The Nebula has been working . . . at least until last night. You were joking around at the garden yesterday. I thought you'd be fine."

"Well, I wasn't." Chelsea got up from the table and cradled

her mug of herb tea in both hands. "It's time for my happy pill. Ha, ha."

Grace and Emma watched in silence as she went up the stairs, carefully holding on to the rail.

"Do you think she asked anyone else to take her baby?" Grace asked.

"She doesn't mean it that way. I've helped her out a few times. Stayed overnight, gave the baby a bottle so that she could sleep. Leo does it for her on weekends. I would have done it last night, but . . ." Emma's eyes filled with tears.

"Don't blame yourself. You have your own life, your teaching job. Third grade, right?"

"That's not it. I'm pregnant, after a hundred rounds of in vitro. I'm finally pregnant and . . . I'm afraid I'm miscarrying." She gasped for air, then sobbed. "The bleeding started last night."

"I'm sorry to hear that." Grace had overheard as much. "Can I get you something?"

Emma shook her head, swallowing hard. "I just have to go. My doctor will do a sonogram, just to see . . . to see if . . ."

Grace put a hand on Emma's arm. "I'll say a prayer for you and we'll hope for the best, right?"

Emma sniffed, tears streaking down her cheeks. "Thank you." She slipped her jacket on and went to the side door. "Tell Chelsea I'll call her later, okay? And you have my cell if you think of any other questions."

"Right. Take care."

So much pain in the world, Grace thought as the door closed behind Emma Wyatt. Sometimes it was a wonder that the human race kept on going.

Chapter 22

Worry was a ball of pain in her gut, a prickly pineapple that cut straight to the core when she pictured her baby's innocent face, those trusting eyes watching her as she nursed. The pain filled the void that Annabelle had left, and Chelsea braced herself, bargaining with the sense of order in the universe. If she endured the pain, then Annabelle would make it home. A pineapple in the belly in exchange for the safe return of her baby; she could do that.

She had wanted to help with the search, but the detective had insisted that she was better off staying here, helping her fill in the details of Annabelle's life. How many details could a person have after three months on this earth? Parents. Doctor. Sitters. Annie was too young for playmates in the sandbox at the park or creepy Scout leaders or boyfriends from the dark side. But Chelsea settled into her spot on the couch and answered every question she could find the answer to. She wanted to appear helpful. She wanted them to think she was a good mother. The big lie.

You're not a bad person. You're just tired. You're suffering from depression, that postpartum monster. The kind voice inside her tried to be warm and reassuring.

The cruel voice dug under her skin with questions that chilled her to the bone. *What did you do to your baby? Did you drop her down the stairs or push her out the window? Did*

*you silence her cries with a pillow, or were you under the spell
of one of those dark visions in which knives sail through the
air and babies fly from their mothers' arms like nightjars?*

Two of the cops stood talking with Grace, their big, dark
uniforms and guns and radios filling the kitchen with authority and a sense of safety. Cops from the crime scene unit had
come and gone, leaving a fine black powder smeared here and
there throughout the house. She couldn't imagine what they'd
done in Annie's room, and she couldn't bear to look.

She rubbed her fingertips, still tinged with ink that didn't
come clean. Grace had explained that they would rule out fingerprints of people who had reason to be here. Chelsea and Leo,
Emma, too. She didn't mind the stain of ink that remained in
her cuticles—a reminder that something was being done to
find Annie.

And Grace had told her that most infant abductors were
women.

A woman!

On the one hand it was reassuring that Annie was probably
not in the arms of some creepy man. But how could a woman
take another woman's child? *And what woman would steal
my baby?*

Grace was talking with the cops about the media, how they
could keep the reporters off the lawn, though the street was
fair game. Chelsea wondered what kind of a world it was
when a dozen people were paid to stand outside the home of
someone going through the worst ordeal of her life. Paid to
gather the scraps of sorrow and distress.

Their voices blurred to soothing white noise as Chelsea
stared at the fireplace, her gaze moving gently over the familiar
tiles on the facade. Delft tiles, from Holland. The hand-
painted white-and-blue tiles were installed years ago, then covered with fake brick, which Chelsea and Leo had removed
themselves. What a kick it had been to find these beautiful tiles
hidden away under the tacky brick facade. Chelsea and Leo
had lovingly restored the mantel, replacing two broken tiles
with originals shipped from the Netherlands.

The project had consumed them. They'd spent nights and weekends working on the project, chiseling away the soft mortar of the bogus brick, being careful not to damage the tiles underneath. Chelsea documented the project with photos and wrote an article for *Home Handyman* magazine. That was when Leo had dubbed her the DIY Girl, a nickname that had stuck at the office.

Through the long hours of tedious work, she and Leo talked about their growing family, their dreams, their baby girl. They had gotten the phone call that they were having a girl while working on the fireplace, and they had talked about the bobbing dresses and cute hats they'd dress her in. Birthday cakes with pink frosting and dance lessons. Girl Scouts and prom dresses. "What if she wants to be a cheerleader?" Leo asked. Chelsea responded that it wasn't in their genetics, though she had been on a cheering squad for a year in high school. "You, a cheerleader? This could change the nature of our relationship. Would you put one of those little skirts on for me some night?" She had tossed a sponge at him, laughing. Then she shared the demise of her short career. One night, while she was cheering on the sidelines, a nice couple asked her to get out of the way so that they could see the game. After that, she'd switched to the tennis team. "Well, I bet you had some kick-ass pom-poms," he teased, and they'd had a good laugh over it all.

Resting her chin on the armrest of the couch, she wondered if they would ever laugh again. Would they ever light another fire in their fireplace? She couldn't see it in their future. No trace of their former life would survive without Annie.

"You've been staring at that fireplace an awful long time," Grace said.

"We restored it ourselves." She told Grace about the ugly brick facade, the discovery of tiles from Europe.

"It's beautiful. I noticed it as soon as I came in."

"We tackled a few projects to make this house a home. The carport outside. Painting and carpeting. We replaced the kitchen backsplash in just one weekend. Leo and I worked hard, so hard to make a home for our baby. Our dream house . . . a dream life."

"You did a good job with it," Grace said.

"But a house can be a prison." Chelsea bit her lips. "That's what happened here. Once Annabelle was born, nothing worked out as we'd planned. I couldn't do anything right. I don't have the energy to get off the couch, much less take care of a baby. I don't feel the way I'm supposed to feel and . . . I've failed. I always prided myself on conquering challenges. They used to call me the 'DIY Girl.' I could do anything. I was so independent and capable. But not anymore."

"You have postpartum depression," Grace said. "I know it because I've been there. My son, Matt, he's almost a teen now, and I can't imagine this world without him. But twelve years ago, I came this close to killing us both, and back then people didn't have patience for anything beyond the baby blues. But I get it, Chelsea. It's very real, but it can be treated. You need help."

"I don't deserve help. I'm a terrible mother. What if I left the door unlocked? Or maybe I left my baby outside last night. I don't deserve to be here now. Annabelle should be here, and I should be the one out there." Out in the cold. The property of some stranger. Or worse . . . dead and already buried. She pictured Annie's little body frozen like a little doll. A doll left out in the cold. Why could she see that so vividly when she couldn't imagine her daughter squirming in her arms or reaching for her hair or nestled in her crib once again?

The prickly ball twirled inside her, cutting her to ribbons, and she closed her eyes and rode the pain. Her penance.

Chapter 23

Leo squirmed in the narrow seat of the jet, wishing against time, wanting to be home now. The thought of his ex-wife getting her mitts on Annie had festered inside him through the flight, and now that they were in their final descent, his fingers clenched into fists at the prospect of facing Jennifer.

Oh, he would gladly have a showdown with her.

He winced against the nauseating dip in altitude and thought about the list. He'd hit on the profile of a typical infant abductor when he'd done an online search while waiting at the airport. He'd just about memorized the bulleted list of traits.

The typical infant abductor was a female of childbearing age.

Check.

Compulsive, manipulative, deceptive. A liar.

Check. Check. Check. Check.

Lived in the community where the abduction took place.

Well, she did now.

Frequently indicated she had lost a baby or was unable to have one.

Check.

Leo pressed his eyes shut. *How could you do this to me, Jen? You've stepped over the line . . . way over the line.*

The second the wheels bounced on the runway, Leo fished his cell phone out of his pocket and fired it up. If someone complained, what could they do? Throw him off the plane?

His first call was to Jennifer, and as luck would have it, she answered.

"Well, look who's finally getting around to calling me back. I knew you'd come around once you got my message."

"Enough is enough, Jen." It was a strain to keep his voice low, his tone even. "Is this your idea of a bad joke?"

"It's no joke, sweetie. This is for real. I am really here in town and I am really going to stay, so you'd better get used to it."

He gritted his teeth, annoyed that she was beating around the bush. She always was a ball buster. "Stop playing games and—" He cut himself off, knowing that Jennifer would only play wilder if he pushed her. "You know what? Don't waste my time. I'm coming over there. Now."

"Are you really? That's great. I have to ask, what swung you to my team after all these years and months?"

In the background he heard a sound that rent his heart—a baby's cry.

"You have her! She's there with you. I hear her!" he shouted. An inappropriate voice level for the cabin of a commercial flight—he knew that—but he couldn't help himself.

He turned away from the woman beside him, who looked like she was about to drop her teeth, but everyone else was staring, too. The other passengers gawked, then the bell released them from their seats and their interest slipped away with the urgency to pop up and jockey their bags down and get off the plane.

"Excuse me?" Jennifer copped a pouty attitude. "What are you talking about?"

He pressed into the emptying aisle and yanked down his duffel bag with his free hand. "Don't try to pass this off as a cute attention-getting device. It's kidnapping!"

"What the hell are you talking about?"

"Annabelle. Bring her back right now."

"Calm down, and don't use that tone with me."

She was getting mad . . . and Jen was a terrible driver even sober in the sunshine. Besides, she probably didn't have a car seat. She probably didn't know a baby needed one. "No, wait! Stay right there and I'll come get her." He pulled out a pen to write on his hand. "What's your address?"

"Go to hell!" She cut the line.

He marched up the jetway, calling her again. She didn't pick up, and the call went to her voice mail. He shoved the phone into his pocket and started running.

Annie's cry rang through his mind, a haunting echo. He had to get to her.

Now.

By the time he got to his car in long-term parking, his pulse was thrumming and sweat ran down the center of his back, despite the cold. He thought about calling that detective and telling her that he knew who stole Annabelle, but he didn't want to take the time now.

He needed to see the cops in person, let them know how much of a threat Jennifer Green could be . . . let them know that he had heard Annie's distinctive cry.

He had heard it himself. Annabelle was with Jennifer—kidnapped by her!

Memories smacked Leo in the face as he tore out of the airport parking lot. Memories of horrible things Jennifer had done to him over the years. The time she went through his cell phone while he was sleeping and deleted the number of every female in his directory. The sexual harassment complaint she filed against him at Sparklet when he asked for a divorce. The time he broke up with her and she sent him a gift box with a tiny coffin and a condolence card that read: *I have AIDS.* Although it had turned out to be false, he had gotten tested and walked around in a sick state for weeks. "It was just a joke," she said. "What happened to your sense of humor?"

Jennifer was a lunatic, but he blamed himself for ever falling for her, for confusing obsession with love. He just hoped that his mistake hadn't jeopardized his baby girl. He floored it onto the interstate, hell-bent on getting home and finding his Annabee.

Chapter 24

"The next-door neighbor is back," Officer Viloria called from the open side door. Her hat was in her hand, and her long dark hair was pinned at the back of her head, regulation style. At five feet two, Angie Viloria was a petite cop, but Grace had learned that size wasn't always helpful in law enforcement. Strong negotiating skills could bring a big man to his knees if you did your job right.

"Thanks." Grace grabbed her jacket and hurried around the kitchen table. "I definitely want to catch her." Chelsea Maynard was upstairs pumping breast milk, trying to keep it going, hoping the supply would be needed.

"No rush," Viloria said. "This one has 'cop buff' written all over her. She's talking with Sgt. Balfour, and I don't think she's budging anytime soon."

"Let's see if we can work her fascination to our advantage," Grace said, following Angie Viloria out the door.

With the arrival of the media and their vans with satellite dishes snaking up into the snowy sky, a carnival atmosphere had overtaken the street. The cops had moved their cruiser acting as temporary headquarters up into the driveway, establishing the sidewalk as a line of demarcation that the reporters were not allowed to cross.

Grace fixed her gaze on the woman who seemed to soak up Mike's every word, as well as the gestures of the two cops behind him. Pickler struck Grace as a woman who'd gotten caught in a time warp back in the eighties. Long hair, too much makeup, and clothes from the original "Let's Get Physical" video. Olivia Newton-John plus twenty years and fifty pounds. The conversation was punctuated by barking from a rat-like dog that scurried around, sounding an alarm.

"A real honest-to-goodness kidnapping on Maple Lane?" Louise Pickler's fake eyelashes batted the floating snowflakes. "That's quite a scoop. Now cut it out, ChiChi." She snapped her fingers at the dog, who circled behind her, then continued barking.

Someone hadn't heard of the leash law.

Pickler shot a curious look over at the Maynard-Green house. "And right next door to me. Should I be scared, officer?" she asked Balfour.

"It always pays to be cautious," Balfour told her.

"Ms. Pickler?" Grace stepped into the conversation holding up her detective shield. "I'm Grace Santos, a detective with the Missing Persons Squad."

"A lady detective?" Pickler tapped a finger on the tin of Grace's shield, as if testing it. "Just like on TV."

Grace forced a smile. "I'm wondering if you have a minute to talk with us about anything you might have seen around your neighbor's house."

"Sure. I can tell you a thing or two about Chelsea and Leo. I spend most of the winter down in South Carolina, but I see plenty when I'm here."

"We heard you had a place down there," Balfour said. "It's nice. I bet you don't miss weather like this."

"That's for sure."

"We were beginning to worry that you wouldn't be back until the spring thaw," the sergeant added.

Grace bit back a smile. Balfour was good at shooting the bull, loosening people up.

"I got back Monday. This morning I was just at the gym. It's the morning routine for ChiChi and me." Pickler adjusted the terrycloth headband holding down her hair.

"Really?" Grace stepped away from the small dog dancing at her heels. "Do they have doggy daycare at this gym?"

"ChiChi likes the gym, but he stays in the van." The dog was yapping rapid-fire, and she leaned down to swoop him up. "He goes everywhere with Mommy, don't you?"

ChiChi just panted, his ears twitching nervously.

The dog thing was annoying, especially with Louise calling herself Mommy, but it fit part of the profile of an infant abductor. That desire to have a child, so strong that the abductor set up a "fake" family with the stolen child.

"Ms. Pickler, would you like to step inside out of the snow?" Grace asked, pointing toward the woman's house. She wouldn't mind having a look inside.

"Do you have a search warrant?" Pickler asked.

When Grace's brows shot up, Louise Pickler grinned. "I'm just giving you a hard time. But we can talk out here." Pickler's eyes snared Balfour and the other cops talking by the cruiser.

Viloria was right; she was a buff. "Okay. What kind of relationship would you say you have with your neighbors?"

"I've always been a big help to Chelsea and Leo. Young couples starting out, they don't know anything about when to take the trash out or how you have to protect the parking spot in front of your house. I filled them in, but really? They don't want to hear it."

"So you'd say you have a good relationship with Leo Green and Chelsea Maynard?"

"Let's just say a good fence is important. I never complain when they play their music in the backyard in the summer. I figure they don't know that it drifts right up to my window. And I happen to know that they'd been ripping things out. Taking apart my friend Gloria's house, brick by brick. But I don't say anything. And that baby—they got a screamer for sure. You know, I went to South Carolina early last year because I couldn't listen to that baby howl anymore. That voice . . ." She pointed to her house. "It went right into my bedroom window. Cut a hole in my head."

Balfour scratched his jaw. "I can see where that would bother you."

Grace frowned. Mike was too kind.

"Not that you can pick your child the way you do a dog, but that baby . . ." Pickler winced. "She's a crier. She woke up ChiChi and me the other night, howling like a wild animal. She was so loud, I looked out and saw that the baby was out in the street. That was just crazy. So I called and reported it."

"Ms. Pickler, where exactly was the stroller?" Grace asked.

"Right there, plain as day." She pointed to the Green-Maynard driveway, the area under the carport. Not the street, but still not a safe place to leave your baby alone at night.

"And last night?" Grace asked. "Was the baby out in the stroller, crying again?"

"I don't know. I picked up some earplugs from CVS, and they worked like a charm." Pickler was looking back at her own house now, watching as a small woman in a parka backed up from the sidewalk and brought a microphone up to her face.

"That's my lawn you're on!" Pickler shouted. Her dog barked and twitched, no doubt eager to leap from her arms and drag the offending reporter from the lawn.

The reporter sidled back onto the sidewalk with a friendly wave. "Sorry! Just looking for a good angle."

"They'll have to pay a fee if they want to put my house on television," Pickler muttered. She stroked the dog, glaring at the woman Grace recognized as Suki Dinh from News 4 New York. "Maybe they want to talk to me. I could be on television."

Grace felt the interview slipping away. "Ms. Pickler, did you notice anything unusual in the neighborhood last night? A strange car on the street? Someone walking after dark?"

"No . . ." Pickler's voice was distant, her focus shifted to the news crew. "Louise . . ." Grace stepped into the woman's line of vision. "I'm trying to find a little baby who's missing. I need you to concentrate. Do it for Annabelle Green."

Pickler rolled her eyes. "I can't tell you anything if I didn't see anything."

"Maybe if we went inside . . . just another few minutes of your time . . ."

"That would be an invasion of piracy," Pickler said sternly.

Balfour cleared his throat, and Grace bit the inside of her cheeks to keep a straight face.

"Yes, I know my rights, detective." She adjusted her sweatband and turned toward her lawn. "I wonder what my story would be worth to them."

Grace wanted to stop her, but what could she do?

"Just make sure the camera gets your good side," Balfour called after her.

"Mike . . ." Grace glared at him. "Don't encourage her."

"She's got nothing for us, Grace. And if she gets an interview, maybe she'll incriminate herself."

"We'll have to watch the noon report. Though I don't know why she's so excited to get on camera when she's so secretive about her house."

"You heard her. It's an invasion of piracy." Balfour looked over at the two-story cape, a mirror image of the Green-Maynard house. "But there's something weird in there. When you get up to the porch, there's a bad odor."

"Mildew? Mold?"

"Something foul. And when you got a stink like that this time of year, in the cold, you know it must be potent. Maybe she's a bad housekeeper. Maybe worse. If you're going for a look in there, I'd recommend you suit up first."

As they talked, a car moved down the center of the street, negotiating among the parked cruisers and news vans a little too fast for comfort. When the car stopped in the street in front of Annabelle Green's house, both Grace and Mike turned to watch.

"Who the hell is that?" Balfour asked.

The car bounced to a stop. The driver's door flew open and a dark-haired man in his twenties was out in a flash, running up the driveway.

"That's got to be Leo Green," Grace said. "The father."

Chapter 25

It was like some macabre festival. Getting past the cluster of cop cars and news crews in the street in front of his house was like trying to find street parking at Yankee Stadium on game night.

He sneered when a cop stopped him halfway up the driveway. "It's my baby you're looking for. I'm Leo Green."

"Okay, sir. Go on ahead."

Leo lunged under the carport and leaped up the steps. Inside, it was warm and disheveled and oddly quiet. He could see the back of Chelsea's head, and from the way she sat alone in her spot on the sofa, you would almost think it was any ordinary day.

Except for the circus outside and the fingerprint powder darkening kitchen surfaces.

"Chelsea . . ."

She sprang up, more alert than he'd expected. Her blue eyes glistened with tears.

"What happened?"

She shook her head. "I don't know. I fell asleep and . . . when I woke up she was gone, and I can't sort out the details in my head about whether I left her down here alone or put her in her crib or left her outside in the stroller. I can't remember and . . . she's gone." A tear streamed down her face, but her eyes remained locked on his, strong, determined, and frightened. "I'm so sorry. I can't believe I slept through it . . . whatever happened to her."

He closed the space between them and folded her into his arms. "It's not your fault. We're going to find her. Where is that detective? Detective Santos."

"Right here, Mr. Green."

He eased away from Chelsea to glance back at the side door, where a petite woman in a brown coat stood beside a cop.

The woman, a brunette with intense black eyes, introduced herself as Grace Santos. The cop, Sgt. Balfour, was in charge of the police investigation.

"They took fingerprints," Chelsea said breathlessly. "And they used dogs. They tried to sniff out a trail, to see where she is, but it didn't work."

"The canines were inconclusive," the detective said. "Since Annabelle is an infant, we're focusing on finding witnesses who might have seen something in this neighborhood last night. A vehicle or someone near your home. We're also examining the circle of people who have had contact with her. In most cases, children are snatched by someone they know, someone denied custody or visiting rights." Detective Santos suggested that they sit down to talk, but Leo couldn't.

"I think I know who took our daughter."

His words seemed to suck the air from the room.

"You do?" Chelsea's eyes burned with hope.

"My ex-wife, Jennifer Green." He turned away from Chelsea; he couldn't bear to see the accusation in her eyes. "She's moved back to Westchester, and she's been calling me. Persistent calls. I think she may have been stalking Chelsea and the baby."

The detective nodded. "How long were you married?"

"Less than a year."

"Did you have children together?"

"No, but she was pregnant once. She miscarried."

"And did the marriage end amicably?" Grace asked.

"We remained on okay terms, but I had to cut her off as much as I could. She's not stable," Leo said, then amended that. "She's fucking crazy, and when she sets her sights on something, she doesn't let go." He told the cops about some of Jennifer's antics over the past few years. "I've come this close to calling the cops on her a few times, but usually if I ignore her for long enough, she backs off."

"But we haven't heard from her for a long time," Chelsea said. "Not since she moved to Philadelphia."

"Actually, she's been calling my cell over the last few weeks."

"What?"

"I'm sorry, Chels. I didn't want to upset you with it, with everything that was going on, but she's been calling persistently. Mostly I ignored her. But when I got your call, Jennifer was the first person who came to mind."

The detective nodded. "It's good to trust your instincts."

"As soon as my flight landed, I called her and . . . here's the big tip-off: I could hear a baby crying in the background."

Chelsea gasped. "Was it Annie?"

"I think it was. Jennifer stole our baby."

Chelsea pressed a fist to her mouth. "She's just crazy enough to do something like that."

"Maybe Ms. Green has a baby of her own?" Sgt. Balfour suggested.

Leo shook his head. "She would have told me. That was Annabelle crying. I know her voice."

"Your ex-wife is a good lead." The detective's fingers were flying over her iPhone. "Jennifer Green, right? We'll check her out right away."

"I'm going with you," Leo said.

Grace looked at the sergeant. "Not a good idea."

"Mr. Green . . . can I call you Leo?" Balfour asked. "The investigation will move faster if you let the detectives do their job. I'll be here, coordinating the scene. You want to be here, for when your daughter is returned to you."

When your daughter is returned to you . . .

Leo would remain glued to the threshold if it meant seeing Annabelle one second sooner.

"We'll keep you apprised of important developments,"

Grace said. "Do you have contact information for Jennifer Green?"

Leo gave the detective her cell number, but he didn't know where she was living now. "She returned to her old job in sales for Sparklet, a phone company."

Santos nodded. "We'll find her." She tucked the iPhone into a wide pocket of her jacket. "I'd like to talk with you more, Leo, but in the interest of time, I'm going to track down your ex-wife right away."

"Good. Thank you."

As the two cops left, Leo and Chelsea stared at the side door.

"I hope it was Jennifer," Chelsea said. "She would do something like this to get your attention, but she wouldn't hurt Annabelle, would she? I mean, she's not that crazy."

Leo didn't answer, various possibilities weighed heavily on his shoulders. He didn't think Jennifer would hurt a child, but she had fooled him before. Yes, she had fooled everyone.

Chapter 26

Jennifer Green wasn't so easy to find.

"Where the hell are you living now?"

Grace sat in the back of the police van, the command center for the search, and tapped away at the keyboard, trying to get an address for the woman who'd recently moved back to Westchester.

In Grace's experience, the fastest way to find a person was through the Department of Motor Vehicles. She had served warrants to guys who had evaded the law for years, but finally gave themselves up by providing the DMV with a current address. A man could forgo voting in an election or getting a birthday card from his mother, but a driver's license was essential. Grace was convinced that it was part of the definition when you looked up *manhood* in the dictionary.

But Jennifer Green's New York State license was still current. She probably hadn't switched it over when she moved to Philly. The address, an apartment in Larchmont, was old. The computer told her someone else was currently residing there.

She did find out that Jennifer Green had no prior arrests. No children.

But Chris was on his way, and she had promised him a "hot lead." They could drop in on Ms. Green at Sparklet, her place of employment, but of course she wouldn't have the baby there.

The directory for Sparklet, Inc., listed Arturo Testani as human resource manager. Grace couldn't demand any information from them without a warrant, but maybe they would work with her. It was worth a call.

"Mr. Testani's office," answered a chipper male voice.

Grace determined that the boss wasn't in, but his assistant Robert was "happy to help." Maybe that was better. She played the detective card, hoping that Robert would be impressed.

He was.

"I'm investigating a case, and we're trying to get in touch with one of your employees. A Ms. Jennifer Green?"

"Shall I transfer you to her line?" Robert asked.

"Actually, I'm looking for her home address. I know you're not in the habit of giving out personal information on employees, but, well, this is a police investigation, and I was hoping that your company could help me."

"Mmm. I'm not sure." Robert paused. "May I get your name again?"

She spelled it out, then waited while he "checked on something."

"Here we go, detective." He gave her an address in Pelham, just west of New Rochelle. "I hope that helps with your investigation."

"I'm sure it will." Grace was already mapping out the route on her iPhone. "You're a gem, Robert. Thanks."

As soon as Grace closed the door of the unmarked unit, Chris Panteleoni turned to her with a childish grin. "Okay, what's my surprise?"

"Whatever happened to, 'Good morning, Grace? How'd the night shift go?' "

They had developed an easy banter in the three years they'd worked together in Missing Persons. Chris was single and ten years younger than Grace, and sometimes she thought of him as a kid brother.

"I know how the shift went," he said. "You caught a case,

and now we're going to work it twenty-four seven until we find this kid. So what's up?"

"Turn left at the light. I've got it all mapped out." She flashed the screen at him. "We're going to Pelham to check out Leo Green's ex-wife."

"Ex-wife? And the domestic revenge plot thickens." Chris kept his eyes on the road.

"It might pan out." She told him about the ex-wife's notorious stalking habits. How she'd moved back to town recently. How Leo Green had heard a baby crying in the background when he called her on the phone today.

"Really? That would be a first for me. I've heard of scorned significant others stealing cars. Jewelry. Lottery tickets. Even drugs. But a kid? Especially when it's not even your own."

"The point is, the pissed-off person wants the most painful revenge possible."

"True. But it's a lot of work to deal with a baby once you steal it."

"Agreed."

"The ex would make an interesting perp, but what's the mother like? For infants, a home abduction is rare, and when it does happen a lot of times it's the mother gone crazy that takes out her kids."

"Chelsea Maynard doesn't remember many details from last night. She could be faking, but I have a feeling she's legit. You saw my report on those muffins that went to the lab. She seemed groggy this morning. Dazed. I know that postpartum depression can do that to a woman, too, but as the morning went on she came out of it."

"Another postpartum depression defense?" He rolled his eyes.

"I oughtta smack you. PPD is for real."

"That would be harassment," he said.

"You need to get enlightened. Read a book. Or at least check it out on Web MD."

"I'm just saying, it can be really bad. There was that tragedy back in Port Jervis a few years ago. The mother drove a van into the Hudson River. Killed herself and her three kids."

"That was tragic, but I don't think Chelsea Maynard killed her baby—and it's not just because I'm a soft touch."

"But you can't rule her out as a suspect yet. Unless you found some evidence you forgot to mention."

"I haven't ruled her out." But Grace felt sorry for Chelsea. Aside from the early morning babbling, the woman made sense. She seemed depressed but stable. Grace's instincts told her that Maynard didn't kill her baby, but instincts did not hold up in court.

"I've got a little something for you," Chris said. "Something popped from all the names you've been sending my way all morning."

"Something came up in a background check?"

He nodded. "A real blast from the past, too. Charges against the neighbor, Louise Pickler. A case so old, it's not even in the database."

Intrigue made the hairs at the back of her neck tingle. "What kind of charges?"

"From family court. Turns out Pickler has a history of child abuse. I had to go way back, thirty-some years to when she lost custody of her two kids to the husband. This after the kids showed signs of physical abuse."

"And that was back in the day when the courts rarely separated kids from their mother."

"You met her, right? Did you get a sense of that? A woman who'd use her hands?"

Grace thought about the woman with the thick makeup and the yappy dog. "Self-absorbed, yes, but she's all about taking care of her dog. There's something dysfunctional about her. And she claims to have no love for baby Annabelle. The baby's screaming bothered her before she went south last November, and she made that complaint this week."

"Could it be she snatched the kid to shut it up?"

Grace frowned. "As in, kill the baby? Not likely, but possible."

"Or maybe the annoyance is all a show. Maybe she's trying to replace the family she lost thirty years ago."

"And she's got Annabelle holed up in her house next door?" Grace said, thinking out loud. "We need to get inside that woman's house."

"I'm on it. We're working on a search warrant, but right now the evidence pointing to Pickler is flimsy."

"Can we get it to Judge Provost?" He was usually pretty liberal.

"He's away on vacation. They're trying Costantini."

Grace groaned. "She's a tough nut. What else you got?"

"I went over the reports from the team canvassing the neighborhood. The other neighbors seem to like the Greens, or at least what they know of them. An older man who lives alone said that Chelsea and Leo have made great improvements to their house. That stretch of mini hedges out front was a barren mass of mud and weeds until they moved there. There's a family with three kids—Rosanne and Rick Brunner. A firefighter and a stay-at-home mom who's very active in the schools. She's heard the Green baby outside, too. Heard her crying from her stroller. She said her heart goes out to the young mother; her kids were colicky, too. And there's a family with five kids that's kind of interesting—name is Jarvis. Apparently, two of the kids aren't supposed to be in this country. Their father has custody back in Brazil. Mom's remarried and she snatched the kids, brought them here."

Grace winced. "A baby snatcher in the neighborhood. We'll be talking to her. Although the custody issue with Brazil, that sounds like more of an immigration issue."

"But you never know who your neighbors are."

"That's the thing. These days, so many people don't even know their neighbors," Grace said. "When I was a kid, we knew everyone on the block. All the kids played stickball together."

"Yeah, yeah. Back in the Bronx in the good old days."

"Yeah, I'm so old. Slow the horse down. This is the street."

Jennifer Green's new address was a condominium in a complex called Fresh Ponds, though the small fountain circulating green water in the front courtyard wasn't looking so fresh. Housing complexes like this were common; two-story garden apartments had been converted to condos during one of the mad housing crazes in the metro area.

Jennifer lived in a downstairs unit, and as Grace and Chris approached, they noticed an infant stroller sitting under the porch awning.

"Well, would you look at that." Chris gave it a slight push. "She's got wheels for the kid. That's planning ahead."

Grace pushed the doorbell for the second time, holding her detective shield up to the peephole. "It could belong to the upstairs tenant."

Just then an infant's wail tore from the apartment.

Chris tapped the stroller handle. "I'd say the owner of this vehicle lives downstairs."

When no one came to the door, Grace cleared her throat. "Ms. Green? Hello? Ms. Green, I'm Grace Santos and this is Detective Panteleoni. We're police, with Westchester County." Since they were dealing with a woman, they had decided that Grace would do most of the talking. The dynamic was less intimidating.

A moment later the door opened just a few inches, chain on, and a pale, round face appeared in the crack. "Is there a problem, officers?"

"Ms. Green? We're wondering if we might have a word with you."

The hazel eyes came close to the opening. "Show me your badges again?"

"And ID," Chris said approvingly as he held up the leather sleeve with his shield and ID card for her to see. "You're smart to ask for ID."

"Okay." The door closed, the chain clicked, and then it opened wide to an overweight young woman with a doughy face and shiny hair down to her waist. The baby's crying was louder with the door open, and Grace had to stifle the urge to shoot past this young woman and tend to the baby. "Is my sister in trouble? She's probably the Ms. Green you're looking for. Jennifer Green."

"And you are?"

"Kylie Swanson, Jennifer's sister. She's been staying here for the past few weeks. Just till she finds a place of her own. Is she in trouble?"

Grace dodged the question. "Ms. Swanson, do you mind if we come in?"

Kylie looked behind her, her face crimping. "It's kind of a mess, but okay. I have to get him or he'll never stop crying." The young woman turned away from the open door, and the two detectives followed her inside.

Chris shut the door behind them while Grace followed behind Kylie Swanson, who pulled her voluminous green shirt down in the back to cover her black stretch pants. Maternity pants. The weight wasn't so much overall fat as baby weight, all through the middle.

The baby was sprawled in a bassinet. Red-faced and shaped like a fireplug. Not so bald as Annabelle Green, this little one had a glaze of corn-silk hair—same shade as Kylie Swanson's.

"What a cutie." Grace smiled as Kylie cradled him in her arms. "Well, that stopped the crying. You have the magic touch. Do you have a lot of experience with babies?"

The young woman shook her head. "He's my first. And picking him up doesn't always settle him down. A lot of times he cries when he needs a diaper change." She patted his bottom. "Uh-oh. Like now." Kylie shifted him in her arms so that she could look into his eyes. "Did you do something again, little man?"

"What's his name?" Grace asked.

The baby's name was Conner, and he got a diaper change right then and there as Grace looked on. Yep, that confirmed it. It's a boy, Mr. Swanson.

"We're sorry to bother you, Kylie, but as I mentioned, we're looking for your sister. Do you happen to know where we could find her?"

"She should be at work. She's got a new job at Sparklet.

That's why she's staying here." She snapped a pair of red over-alls over Conner's bottom and picked him up. "She's got a sleeping bag in Conner's room, but most mornings when I come out here I find her asleep on the couch."

Grace peered into a bedroom with a double bed and moved on, pacing, as if she were taking an afternoon stroll. "Was she out on the couch this morning?"

"No, she was holed up in that sleeping bag."

Chris shot Grace a look, and she nodded. That would be an alibi for Jennifer Green.

"Conner fussed all through the night, so I was out here walking him in front of the TV. Thank God for the DVR."

"Really. What did you watch?"

Kylie's eyes flickered to life. "*Pretty Little Liars*. I love that show."

"Those girls are great, aren't they?" Grace peered into one of the bedrooms and saw an empty crib, a tangled sleeping bag, and a mound of clothes spilling out of a suitcase on the floor. "It's nice of you to put up your sister, you having a new baby and all."

"Yeah, it's not really working for any of us, but she was desperate. Her last job in Philadelphia didn't work out, and she hasn't found a place here yet. But she's been apartment hunting." Kylie pulled a cloth infant carrier over her neck and plunked the baby inside. He wiggled around until his brown eyes peered out at Grace. "Why do you want to talk to Jen again?"

"It's in regard to her ex-husband, Leo Green. I don't know if you've seen the news today, but his daughter was abducted last night. We're interviewing everyone the Greens know."

"Really?" Kylie's arms closed around the baby in the sling. "You mean, like, kidnapped?"

"That's right. But you say Jennifer was here last night?"

"Well, yeah. But that's really scary." Kylie rubbed Conner's head, soothing. "Is there a kidnapper targeting babies?"

"So far it seems to be an isolated case," Chris offered, the low timbre of his voice reassuring.

Kylie held her baby closer. "That's awful. Leo must be a wreck. But you think Jennifer is involved? I mean, that doesn't sound like her."

"As I said, we're checking every possibility." *And this one isn't panning out,* Grace thought as she moved toward the door.

"You can talk to Jen at work. She's in the office till five. But I don't think she'll know anything about Leo's baby." Swaying from one foot to another, Kylie patted her son's back. "My sister is crazy, but not that crazy. She wants Leo Green—not his baby."

Chapter 27

As Leo cleaned up downstairs, he imagined himself testifying against Jennifer. It probably wouldn't come to that—most cases settled out of court—but it felt good to catalog her evil deeds in his mind.

He was wiping the forensic unit's dust off the kitchen door frame when the house phone rang. Between their two cell phones and the landline, there'd been something ringing or chiming every five minutes. He'd been screening calls, not wanting to talk to reporters, but this time the caller ID said *Santos. Grace.* He snatched the phone. "Detective Santos, do you have Annie? Is she okay?" He imagined Annabelle in the back of a squad car, fussing in some cop's arms.

Annabelle . . .

"No, we haven't found her yet. We just left the condo where Jennifer Green is living, and your baby isn't there."

Leo paused in the little nook with the rolltop desk, where two corners of paper stuck out. He opened the lid, shoved them back into the mess of insurance invoices, and pushed it closed. "I was sure I heard her there."

"You probably heard a baby—Jennifer's nephew. Your ex-wife is staying with her sister, Kylie, until she can find her own place here, and it just so happens that the sister gave birth two months ago."

Disappointment buzzed around him, a swarm of determined

bees. It had to be Jennifer, who was infamous for the stunts she pulled to get attention.

"I was so sure."

"I know, and it was good thinking on your part, but the baby in the condo is definitely a boy, definitely not your Annabelle. And Jennifer Green has an alibi—her sister will vouch for her."

"Damn."

Chelsea came halfway down the stairs and poked her head out. "Is it Detective Santos?"

He nodded. "But they didn't find Annie. Jennifer didn't take her. The baby I heard belongs to Jen's sister."

The light drained from Chelsea's eyes. Leo turned away from her but he could feel her padding down the stairs, lingering, listening to his side of the conversation.

"Just the same," Santos went on, "my partner Chris is going to head over to Sparklet to interview Ms. Green. Never hurts to be thorough."

"But where does that leave us? Who took Annabelle?"

"We're pursuing other leads, primarily in your neighborhood. Infant abductors usually live in the community where the abduction took place."

Leo raked back his hair. "I read that somewhere." And if that was true, he should be out there looking for his daughter. Something clicked inside him, and a plan began to form. "I'm going to go looking for her. My friends have offered to help."

"Mr. Green . . . Leo, the police have been canvassing your neighborhood all day."

"I know, but there could be something or someone they missed. Someone who wasn't home. People have offered to help and I'm going to take them up on it instead of just holing up here and doing nothing."

The detective's sigh came through the line. "All right, Leo. Just promise me you'll talk to Sgt. Balfour and take his advice. We don't want any of your volunteers botching evidence or getting harmed in any way."

Leo sucked in a painful breath. "Got it."

"And please, stay away from Ms. Pickler."

"Louise?" Leo looked out the window at the gray cape next door. "What about her? Do you think she's a danger?"

"Are you talking about Louise Pickler?" Chelsea put the laptop on the coffee table and joined him. "Do they suspect her? I told Grace that she's always been weird about Annie."

He held up a hand so that he could hear Grace. "Is she a suspect?"

"Pickler lost custody of her children thirty years ago over claims of abuse. But so far we haven't been able to show enough probable cause to get a judge to sign a search warrant. Let me ask you, have you ever been inside her place?"

"No, never." Leo looked at Chelsea, whose blue eyes flashed, feverish for information. He held the phone aside and shared the information with her. "The cops are trying to get a warrant to search her house."

"The money pit?" Chelsea crossed her arms over her baggy hoodie. "That's got to be a nightmare inside."

Leo told the detective, "We've never been in the house, but I can tell you that the stench that wafts over on hot summer days would turn your stomach." He rubbed his bristly jaw, pausing as another question came to mind. "Do you really think she took Annabelle? I mean, we'll go crazy thinking that she's right next door."

"Oh, no, no." Chelsea shook her head as the possibility sank in. "It's toxic over there."

"Very often infant abductors live in the same community as the child," Grace said.

"I know that."

"You sound pretty well versed in this."

"I've been doing some online research."

Chelsea's cell phone was ringing on the kitchen counter, and Leo was relieved when she stepped away to grab it. "Detective Santos, let me ask you a question." He lowered his voice. "One article I read said that most of the time when an infant is missing, it's to cover up the fact that the baby was killed by the person taking care of her. That something happened, maybe an accident, maybe not." He realized that he was holding his breath, but he couldn't take the next step.

"That's not a question. I'm guessing you want to know if your wife is a suspect."

"She's a really, really good person inside. It's just . . . she's not herself right now."

"I wouldn't be doing my job if I didn't consider every possibility. Do I think Chelsea is guilty? No. But I can't rule out foul play just yet. My sole responsibility is to find your daughter, and I'll go where the path takes me."

He looked over at his wife, so childlike in her bulky sweatshirt with the hood up. One hand was shoved in her pocket, the other held the phone to her ear as she looked out the front door, waiting for the crowd of reporters to part and reveal their Annabelle.

"Okay. Just find Annie." He had to believe that everything else would fall into place.

He couldn't look Chelsea in the eye.

When his gaze slid her way, when he caught the tears shining in her eyes or heard her trying to talk through the events of the night to clarify things, there was a tug of pity. Sympathy.

He felt for her, but now that Jennifer had been vindicated, his world had shifted. There were too many unanswered questions between Chelsea and him.

Where did Chelsea leave Annie?

How could she sleep through a home invasion, an intruder whisking their baby away?

The best way to avoid thinking about Chelsea's role in all this was to put all his energy into the search for Annie. He started making calls. Although Leo wasn't particularly close with his brother-in-law, Jake took his call right away and agreed to leave work to help with the search. Without losing steam, Leo called his office and rounded up some more hands. The next call to *Home Handyman* put him through to Chelsea's former boss, Sasha Barton, who promised to rally the staff as well as her brothers to come to the neighborhood and help search for Annabelle.

Chelsea was on the house phone when he ended his call. He shot a look out the front window for Mike Balfour, the sergeant in charge. It would be good to expand the search, to check and double-check. Some people might respond better to the average Joe than cops knocking on their door.

He waved at Chelsea and pointed toward the front door. "I'm heading outside to start organizing this search."

"Wait." She waved back at him. "He's here now. Hold on." She held out the house phone to him. "It's Dr. Chin, the specialist. She wants to talk to you."

Earlier in the day, when Chelsea had called to cancel her appointment, Dr. Chin's assistant had promised that the doctor would call back. Chelsea had reacted well when Chin called, writing down some notes and asking questions. Watching her pace, he'd been struck by the normalness of it all.

Now, he primarily listened on the phone as the doctor inquired sympathetically about Annabelle.

"I was so sorry to hear about it. I can't imagine what you're going through now. I can't help you with that, but I can help your wife cope with postpartum depression," the doctor said. "For now, I'm calling a new prescription into your pharmacy. It's the same medication, Nebula, but we'll bump up the dosage. That's a grandma dose she's taking. Can you make sure that she gets it as soon as possible?"

"Okay." Leo could pick it up himself or no . . . he didn't want to leave Chelsea alone. Maybe Emma and Jake would swing by the pharmacy.

"The medication won't interfere with Chelsea's breast-feeding," Dr. Chin went on, "but I already spoke to her about cutting down on that and switching over to a bottle. She's been breast-feeding for more than three months, so the baby has gotten many of the benefits and immunities. Right now, it's crucial that your wife starts getting a good night's sleep. We need a healthy mom to keep the baby healthy."

"Right." Leo wished that they'd hooked up with Dr. Chin weeks ago. Just talking to her on the phone made him feel that she had the problem under control. If she'd been treating Chelsea when this happened, maybe it wouldn't have happened at all.

Maybe Chelsea would have been alert enough to stop the abduction.

Or maybe . . .

No, he didn't want to go there. He'd already let himself glom on to the horrific thought that had jabbed at his heart when he read the article about infant abductions online, and it felt disloyal, even cruel to think of it.

"Mr. Maynard? Are you still there?" Dr. Chin asked.

He bit back a smile. He didn't mind being called by Chelsea's last name. "I'm here."

"I know I'm sending a lot of information your way. I don't mean to overwhelm you. When things settle down, Chelsea can come into the office for a blood test. We need to check her hormones, thyroid levels, things like that. And we'll get her into therapy."

Therapy.

Leo swallowed, daunted by the expense of all this. Their savings were probably going to be used up to fix the plumbing in the house, but . . . Chelsea needed help. She'd been suffering for months. They had to do this.

As he hung up, he noticed that Chelsea had hung up, too, though she still stood mesmerized at the doorway. "Maybe you should sit, Chels."

"I'm done with sitting. Done with sitting and waiting and worrying."

"Same." The pain in his gut was unrelenting, but he would take it in stride if it meant getting their baby back.

"Maybe we should talk to those reporters." Chelsea spoke without turning away from the door. "I know we said we wouldn't, but if there's the tiniest chance it might help us find Annabelle . . ."

"But they have her photo. Detective Santos released it to the media hours ago. They've got their story. I don't know why they don't just leave us alone."

"A photograph isn't enough to grab viewers," she said. "And neither is an interview with Louise Pickler. They want to show viewers the crushing truth." She went to the little table that was now covered with sheets of photos of Annie.

Chelsea picked up one photo and held it out to him. Annabee in her pink print romper. She had a giant cartoon grin, emphasized by the light in her stern eyes.

Leo wanted to reach into the photo and whisk their baby away. He'd been the one to make her smile that day in the studio. She'd come to trust him and now . . . now her eyes wouldn't be able to find him anywhere. Would she worry? Panic? He didn't know if babies were evolved enough to panic. His instincts said yes, and that crushed him.

He didn't want her to suffer any more than she had to.

"Go out there, Leo. Show them these. Let them know that our hearts will be broken until she's back with us."

"Come with me," he said.

She shook her head. "I feel so guilty. Even if I didn't do anything wrong, I know what people must be thinking. I can't face that right now."

He chose two photos of Annabelle—one spirited, one angelic—and headed out the door into the cold. The yard wasn't large, but it seemed to take an eternity to walk along the pavers to the sidewalk where the reporters waited.

He shot a glance back at the cape behind him. Their dream house.

Not anymore.

Chapter 28

"It's like driving through a war zone," Emma said as Jake pulled to the side of Maple Lane to let a police vehicle pass. The street was clogged with police cars and television news vans and groups of people with nothing better to do than congregate on the street and try to get their face in the background of a thirty-second TV news spot.

Emma had seen more than her fair share of cops today. She and Jake had spent much of the past hour in the police precinct, where they'd been fingerprinted. The forensic squad had been able to lift a good number of prints from the house, and they needed to eliminate anyone who had been there in the past week. "When this is over, I'm swearing off cop shows for at least a year."

"Yeah, I know what you mean. But you don't have to mess with this. Are you sure you want to?" Jake asked. "I can drop you off at home and come back."

"I need to be here." Emma thought of the promise she'd made to her mother, who knew that Chelsea would reach her tipping point one day. "I need to make things right with Chelsea. Even if I just have a cup of tea with her while you guys go out searching, I think that will help."

"Just as long as you stay off your feet."

"I can do that."

"And what else did the doctor say?"

"Rest. Get plenty of sleep and avoid stress."

"And how are you supposed to do that last part with Annabelle missing?"

"Honey, sometimes you just have to have the serenity to accept the things you can't control."

"I'm not good at that serenity shit." He reached over and touched her knee. "Good thing I have you for that."

There was no place to park near the house, but Jake squeezed in between two cars at the end of the block.

"Might as well be parking in Manhattan," he muttered, putting his arm behind her back in that gentle way that husbands had with their pregnant wives.

Emma clutched the white paper bag from the pharmacy and leaned into her husband.

There was an odd mixture of excitement and boredom in the air as they passed through the clusters of people on the street. Jake stepped right up to the cop at the wooden barrier and said something. The cop moved the wooden sawhorse, and they hurried up the path, escaping shouted questions.

The stroller still sat beside the side door, its little green elephants marching over the seat. The words of the elephant poem crossed her mind, along with the memory of walking her fingers over Annabelle's little tummy while she recited it.

"Take a breath," Jake said beside her.

She nodded, sucking in the cold air. The last thing she wanted to do was wax emotional in front of her sister.

The side door was open, and light and noise spilled out from the storm door. What were all these people doing in Chelsea's kitchen?

"What's going on?" she asked Jake.

"They're here to help search."

She stepped into the warmth of the kitchen, scanning the faces. Her brother-in-law Andrew stood by the door, and they hugged. Of course, Mel had to stay home with the kids, but it was good of Andrew to make the drive from central Jersey.

That's what family is for, he always said.

Emma recognized Sasha, Chelsea's former boss, as well as

two other editors from the magazine. There were more than a dozen men and women, dark-skinned and light, Hispanic and Asian and black and mixed race. They shared a common goal: finding Annabelle.

Chelsea motioned her over and gave up her seat at the table. Emma shook her head, but Chelsea silently insisted, and with that gesture, the strain between them slid away.

Leo and one of the police officers were giving instructions on how they would break up into teams of two or three and cover designated areas.

"Since Annabelle Green is less than four months old, we are not really a search party," the cop told the group. "Your mission is primarily to build awareness and open channels of communication. We want people in the community to reach out to us right away if they see or hear anything out of the ordinary. Sometimes the most meaningless events prove to be major clues in solving a case."

With flashlights in hand, the people headed out the side door, leaving the two sisters behind.

"Do you want tea?" Chelsea offered. "The kettle is still hot."

When Emma started to get up, Chelsea waved her off.

"Sit. I need something to do and it's my turn to take care of you. Herbal or decaf?"

"Some chamomile would be great."

"I envy Leo getting out of this house." Chelsea set the steaming mug in front of Emma, then closed and locked the side door. "I wish there was something I could do . . . some activity that would bring us closer to finding Annie."

Facing the living room, Emma saw the empty bassinette and changing table. Someone had tidied up, stacking Annabelle's squishy blocks in her bucket seat. The room seemed lonely and neglected, like a flashing VACANCY sign. She felt a new surge of regret over the way she had snapped at her sister earlier.

"I almost forgot." Emma handed over the paper bag she'd been clutching. "I come bearing gifts."

Chelsea opened the bag and held the brown plastic container close. "My new Nebula prescription. Thanks. Now I'll be extra happy." She put it on the counter. "How are you feeling?"

"Fine. Relieved. Still hoping that everything's okay with the baby." She had given Chelsea the doctor's good news over the phone, walking that tightrope between not wanting to boast and not wanting to withhold information from her sister and best friend.

"Do the doctors have any sense of what caused it?"

"They're just saying it was spotting, but I'm nervous about going back to school. With a high-risk pregnancy, working might be too much for me. Jake and I talked about it, and since money's not an issue, he wants me to give notice."

"Just quit? Can't you get medical leave?"

"I probably could, but that seems greedy when I have no intention of going back to work after the baby is born. The medical benefits from the firm are really good. So, yeah, I might just quit."

"Don't you think you'll miss it?" Chelsea dipped the tea bag in her own mug. "I feel like I made a mistake giving up my job, but there's no going back."

"I'll miss my students. But I'm excited about changing things up. We're both excited about the baby, and we're thinking of some other changes, too. Jake got an offer to move to the firm's office in Chicago."

"What? When did that happen?"

"A few days ago." With all that was going on, Emma hadn't been planning to spill the beans, but she never could keep a secret from her sister.

"And . . . is he going to accept? Are you guys moving to Chicago?"

Emma laced her hands around the warm mug. "We're actually talking about it. It might be fun to live in a different place. I've heard great things about Chicago, and it would be an adventure for the two of us—for our little family."

"Wow." Chelsea hung her head.

"I'm sorry, honey. This is the last thing you need to hear right now."

"No, don't try to coddle me. I've been so out of it, so stuck in the black hole; I might not have heard it if you'd told me two weeks ago. I just want to be happy for you, but I can't pull together happy right now."

"There'll be time for that later."

"Good, because you deserve an adventure, Emma. You've put up with so much crap from me. I talked to Dr. Chin today, and she thinks that treatment will help me. I'm going to get better. I'm going to be a good mother for Annie. I really will."

The unspoken hope hung in the air: Annie's safe return.

Emma pushed her mug aside and reached for her sister's hand. "Honey, you already are a good mother. And with a little help, you're going to be a great one."

Chapter 29

When Leo returned from combing the neighborhood, he didn't offer much of a report, and Chelsea didn't press him. She hadn't expected much from the "search party," but sometimes just the act of doing something constructive made more sense than sitting around deconstructing mistakes you've made.

When the last of the volunteers left, Chelsea showed Leo what she and Emma had accomplished while he was gone: Internet research on infant abduction.

"I don't know why we didn't look online this morning," she told Leo. "My mind was still so fuzzy."

But not anymore. For the first time in months, Chelsea felt alert and sharp. Trauma had brought the world into focus for her, and as she sat sorting through Internet facts with Leo, she couldn't get information fast enough.

The accounts were riveting.

One Christmas Eve, a woman who claimed to be visiting her sister in a maternity ward befriended a mother who had just given birth. The visitor convinced her that she would keep an eye on the woman's baby while she took a shower. She promptly made off with the infant.

More than half of the infant abduction cases took place right in the mother's hospital room. In so many instances, a woman pretending to be a nurse snatched a baby from a hospital maternity ward and walked right out with it. Sometimes the baby was hidden in a purse or a gym bag; other times the woman just walked out with the baby in her arms, as if it were her own.

In one case the infant's grandmother abducted the baby from the hospital, convinced that her daughter was incapable of raising a child on her own. In another case, a woman solicited information from pregnant women, pretending to be looking for models for a maternity calendar.

Scrolling down on the computer, Leo read aloud the case of a new mom in Virginia who had narrowly missed having her child abducted by a woman posing as a hospital worker.

" 'Still tired from sleep-deprivation and delivery, new mom Marie Onish received a phone call in her hospital room saying that she had won a new mother luncheon. A few minutes later, Alice Butler appeared in her room with a bunch of balloons, saying that the lunch and free gifts were waiting for her in the hospital cafeteria. She was told to go downstairs, find the chair with the balloons on it, and she would be met by another hospital staffer. Onish was not suspicious when this staff person offered to watch her baby while she went downstairs to claim her prizes.' "

Leo paused. "Why would anyone go for that?"

But Chelsea understood the woman's confusion over who was who in the hospital. "When you're in a hospital, countless people come through your room—technicians, doctors, nurses, and aides. I remember being on painkillers and wondering what they were all doing in my room. I couldn't tell a doctor from an aide. Could you?"

"I remember your doctor, but I wasn't really paying attention to the staff. I was all about Annie."

"Exactly."

" 'When Onish got to the cafeteria,' " Leo continued reading, " 'she found a chair with a balloon attached, but no representative was there to greet her. She waited for a few minutes, then returned upstairs, where she found a jumble of staff personnel as well as police officers in the hall outside her room. The hospital's electronic security system had been triggered when Butler cut off the infant's ankle bracelet. Hospital staff found Butler headed down the hall with the baby, already dressed in street clothes. Butler was charged with felony abduction of a child.

" ' "I couldn't comprehend what was going on until the cop showed me my baby's ankle bracelet," Onish said. "That was when I started to cry." ' "

As Leo read on, Chelsea could see it all.

The empty steel-and-plastic cafeteria chair with balloons bobbing.

The strange clothes on the baby.

The towering charge nurse.

The ankle bracelet, snipped in a crisp cut.

But in this case, the thief had been caught before she got far.

"They caught her," Chelsea said aloud. "They snagged that deluded woman before she got too far. Why couldn't we be so lucky?"

"But they usually do catch abductors. It says here that most infants are safely recovered within a week."

"A week is a long time." Time had slowed. Moments stretched into painful memories and sickening plunges into guilt. "And what will happen to Annabelle while this stranger is taking care of her?"

"I know. It feels disgusting." Leo clicked to another screen. "In the profile, it says that most infant abductors prove themselves to be capable caretakers. Some of them even take child-care classes."

"What's the profile again?"

"Most of them are female, overweight, and either married or living with a partner." Leo scratched the stubble on his chin. "Who do we know that fits that profile? Just about every female friend of ours."

"Isn't it weird that they're overweight? Every woman I know thinks she's overweight, but some of them just say that because they're not model skinny. Emma and I have the baby weight. Sasha's in good shape, but she's always complaining that her booty's way too big. How about Jennifer?"

"I haven't seen her for at least a year."

"That's the safe answer."

"Louise Pickler could stand to lose a few."

"Really. Is that a beer belly or has she been expecting for the past few years?"

Leo rubbed his eyes and let out a groan. "It's funny but it's not."

"I know." Chelsea tugged the zipper of her hoodie up and down. "Emma and I read an article about one of the baby snatchers. She was so delusional, she wore a pillow to make everyone believe she was pregnant. She convinced her boyfriend that sex could hurt the baby, so they started sleeping in separate rooms. She even had him drive her to the gynecologist every week. They said she would walk in the entrance, go out the back, and take a cab home. These women jump through hoops to stage a ruse."

"And who do we know that could be faking a pregnancy?"

"The only pregnant woman I know is Emma."

Funny how that came right out. Emma wasn't delusional, but she did have the perfect setup. She and Jake could take the baby to Chicago and no one would ever know it wasn't theirs.

But Emma would never steal my baby. Even when I begged her to take it, she declined.

"A few months ago, it seemed like you were around pregnant women all the time," Leo said.

"That's true. The women in my prenatal swim class. All those women at the doctor's office. The new moms in the maternity ward . . ." Had one of those women been faking it? "What if someone used the class to find someone like me? To target me and my baby?"

"What a frightening and brilliant theory." Leo closed the laptop and moved to the couch. "We need to talk to Detective Santos about it." He squeezed in behind her and slipped his arms around her.

Chelsea rested against him, loving the support of his solid chest, his strong embrace. Often over the past few months she had longed for a quiet moment to cuddle with Leo this way; now it seemed like a hollow consolation prize.

"I'm sorry," he said. "I've been mad at you for not remembering. For letting someone come in here and take her. But I know that's not how it happened. I know it's not your fault."

"You have a right to be upset with me. I'm mad at myself. I keep wondering how I could have slept through it all. I mean, since Annie was born, I've been in a constant state of exhaustion, but I never failed to wake up when she was crying."

"That's true. You never slept through a feeding."

"Except for the times you gave her a bottle."

"That's different. You still woke up. You knew what was going on."

"Maybe I was drugged. I want to believe that there was something in those muffins."

"When will Detective Santos have the lab results back?" he asked.

"It can take a week, but she put a rush on it. Not that it matters. It won't get Annie back to us."

"But it will tell us more about the type of criminal mind we're dealing with."

Once again she concentrated on the details of last night, trying to sort through them as if they were trinkets in a cluttered drawer. Emma's phone call. The muffins. The overwhelming weariness. The decision to stay downstairs. The same coins of memory glimmered, taunting her against a backdrop of velvet darkness.

"I'm sorry, Chels." His chin nuzzled one ear. "I should have been here."

"You had the convention. You're trying to be the breadwinner and take care of Annie and me. It's a lot, Leo. I know that. Do you know my sister calls you St. Leo?"

"A smart girl, that Emma." Leo eased away for a moment to reach for the remote and turn on the television. "It's time for the eleven o'clock news. Let's see how they're covering our story."

He switched from one major network to the other, trying to catch each newscast's coverage of Annabelle's abduction.

Chelsea felt like she was watching someone else's life unfold. Had it been only this morning that she'd woken up in the predawn stillness and found the house empty?

The reporter introduced their story, and there was the photo of her daughter under the caption: *Kidnapped!* "They got the pictures on," she observed. The sight of that gummy grin let down her milk, and she shifted in Leo's arms, pulling the front of her hoodie away from her body.

"Annabee." Leo didn't take his eyes off the screen.

It was odd to be in the center of the storm and watch the winds blowing around you from a distant lens. When the report ended, she went upstairs to pump. As she showered in the downstairs bathroom, she remembered that the plumber was supposed to fix the valve tomorrow.

Tomorrow was miles away.

She slipped on her last clean nightgown and her robe, though sleep didn't seem like an option tonight.

Leo was still at the computer. "I talked to Grace Santos."

"Any news?" she asked as she labeled the breast milk and tucked it into the fridge.

"Nothing on her end. I told her your idea about maybe being targeted by someone you met in one of those pregnancy groups. She says it's worth exploring."

"I wonder if the YMCA still has a list of people registered for past classes." She went over to him. "Are you hacking into the Y's computers?" He had said he was going to clear up his e-mail, but when she looked over his shoulder, he was Googling a name from a list.

"What are you doing?"

"Checking out our pediatrician and neighbors."

"What do you think you'll find?"

"I don't know. Maybe one of them had a weird, overweight cousin who has promised a baby to her husband."

She leaned over him, massaging his shoulders.

"The pediatrician's office is a good idea, but there are so

many receptionists there, I can't get them straight." The image of a soft, doughy woman came to mind. Not in the pediatrician's office, but in Dr. Volmer's office. "There's a woman in the ob-gyn's office who made a huge fuss over Annabelle. Val something. I'll have to find out her last name."

Just then the doorbell rang.

Leo straightened with a jolt and went to the door. Chelsea belted her robe and held her breath. It had to be news about Annie.

It was their babysitter, Eleni Zika. She blinked in the porch light, her eyes as round and shiny as quarters.

"Oh . . . the appointment." Chelsea swallowed hard. "You got my text, right? About canceling this afternoon?"

"I did. I need to talk to you." Standing there, without the dark kohl under her eyes, without feathers hanging from her hair, without a ring through her nose, Eleni looked her age— just a teenage girl.

"Come in." Leo held the door for her.

Eleni stepped over the threshold, her black-polished fingers quivering. "I saw the news report online. I recognized your house in the picture. And then . . . then I got a call from this detective who said they needed me to come in for fingerprinting."

Was that why she was shaking? Because she thought she was a suspect?

"It's not what you think," Chelsea said. "They want to have your fingerprints on file to eliminate them, that's all. We know you were here this week; of course your fingerprints will be on things."

"It's not that." Eleni's hand trembled as she swiped at the tears that streaked down her cheeks. "I mean, I'm sorry about Annabelle. I'm really sorry. But I didn't know. I didn't think he would do anything. I really didn't believe it."

Leo looked down at her, tilting his head. "What are you talking about?"

"My boyfriend, Krispy. I heard him talking about how much he could make selling babies on the black market. I think he took Annabelle."

Chapter 30

Grace drove over to the house as soon as she got the call. "You go," Chris told her. "I'll keep plugging away here." She had e-mailed him the remainder of her list, and headed out.

It was late, but then she was planning to work through the night, or at least until she'd run checks on all the names on her list. She had already hooked up Matt to stay with the Larsens for the second night in a row. A double bonus, as far as he was concerned.

"You behave, okay?" she'd warned him. "No staying up late. It's a school night."

"I'm aware," he said, sounding far more mature than his twelve years. Until, in the next breath, he told Ethan Larsen that he'd just made a "bonehead move" on the computer game they were immersed in.

"And turn that off when Mrs. Larsen tells you to," Grace added.

"Mama-dish, you know I will."

He was a good boy, her Matt, but twelve going on thirteen was that age when things began to change for a kid. Adolescence was a tough time. Sometimes angelic children fell away to drugs or booze or violent rebellion. She'd seen a lot of that, tracking down teenage runaways. Grace didn't want to lose her son that way.

Sitting in Chelsea and Leo's living room, waiting while their babysitter composed herself, Grace wondered if Eleni Zika's parents felt connected to their daughter. Did they worry that her black fingernails and piercings and dark makeup were a sign of a deep unrest inside? Or were they confident that the goth look was a phase she would work through?

"Take a deep breath," Grace said gently. "I always forget to breathe when I'm crying."

The girl pressed a ball of tissues to her eyes and nodded.

Seated beside the girl on the sofa, Chelsea wound and unwound the belt of her robe around her fingers. Leo leaned against the rolltop desk, though he had the look of a tiger ready to pounce. Grace was glad they had called her when the girl showed up at their door.

"So give me the whole story, okay?" Grace cajoled the girl. "This is about your boyfriend?"

"His name is Krispy."

"Krispy? That's an unusual name."

"That's what everyone calls him. His real name is Armand Krispalian. He's Armenian."

"How old is Krispy?"

"Eighteen."

"And how long have you two been seeing each other?"

"Six months, off and on. He's a nice guy. He always makes me laugh. That's why, when he first started talking about selling the baby, I figured it was a joke."

"He talked about selling Annabelle Green?"

"Like I said, it was a joke. He was here with me one night when Annabelle was crying, and he said he didn't understand why anyone would want to adopt a screaming baby. He said there was big money in it, though. That a baby like Annabelle could bring in thousands of dollars."

Tension sizzled in the air, but Grace continued. "And did he ever suggest that you help him with this? Did he have a plan?"

"Not that I knew of. But he acted like it would be fun if we were a team. I could find the babies through my babysitting jobs, and he would get them sold. He said we'd make a great team. But after a while I got sick of the joke, and I guess I just tuned him out. But now . . . Annabelle is gone, and . . . when I heard about it, I thought of him. One day I heard him talking with one of his friends. He said it was about a business deal, and he kept asking how much he could make, what his cut would be . . . stuff like that."

"And you thought that was okay?" Leo Green was on his feet, wiping his palms on his jeans. "To make money on kidnapping a baby?"

"I'm sorry." Eleni stared down at her knees.

Grace held a hand up, willing Leo to calm down. "Have you spoken with him today?"

"I texted him, but he didn't answer. Krispy doesn't always get back to me right away."

"We'll find him." Grace got Krispy's address and phone number from Eleni. He didn't live far from here.

"But how did he get into our house without breaking in?" Chelsea asked. "That part doesn't make sense to me."

"He knows the house," Eleni said. "He's spent enough time around here to know what windows are left unlocked, stuff like that. I know this is going to sound really bad, but he's been arrested before. Graffiti and drinking in the park, small stuff like that."

"And you let this guy in our house?" Leo lashed out. "You let him near our baby?"

"I never thought he'd do something like this!" Eleni faced Grace, pleading her case. "He's not a bad guy."

"Sometimes good people make bad choices," Grace said.

Leo slid on his jacket. "You said Wembley Street, right?"

Grace blinked. "You're not thinking of going there now."

"I've got to find this guy."

"My partner and I will do that, and I think most people are more likely to open their door to the police at this time of night than some pissed-off stranger." She rose and touched Leo's shoulder. "I promise you, we'll get right on it."

"What if you can't find him?" Leo asked. "What if he's run off with her?"

"We've been doing this for a while, Leo. We'll track him down. But I don't want you to hang your hopes on this kid. There's a good chance he doesn't have Annabelle. It's unlikely that this kid is involved in an organized kidnapping ring. Drug dealing, yeah, I've seen that. But not stolen babies. Not organized by kids this age." Although she spoke the truth, Grace knew anything was possible. Still, her words had the calming effect she was looking for.

Oddly calming.

Because if Armand Krispalian didn't have Annabelle Green, who did?

Chris yawned as she slowed in front of Krispalians' house—a well-kept brick row house.

"Nice neighborhood," he said. "I guess baby smuggling pays well."

"Not funny." She cruised to the corner and pulled into a spot. "I have a feeling Krispy lives with his parents. And I'm even more skeptical about his involvement in Annabelle Green's disappearance."

Chris stepped out and closed the car door. "You believe the babysitter? Think Krispy is a good guy?"

"I suspect he's a little mama's boy who preys upon slightly overweight babysitters with low self-esteem. Beyond that, Krispalian doesn't fit the profile of our abductor." She walked up the driveway with Chris. "But I've been wrong before."

"Let's see if you're right on Krispy Kritter."

They held their detective shields and IDs out as they knocked, and it didn't take long until the door opened to reveal a man who was too old to be Krispy—dark brows, receding hairline, and creases under his dark eyes. He wore a red sweater with rectangular designer glasses.

"Police?" He looked out into the street behind them. "Is there something wrong here, officers?"

"Sir, we're sorry to bother you so late, but we're looking for Armand Krispalian," Grace said. "Does he live here?"

"Yes, he does, but he's not home. I'm his father, Ara." He

turned to someone inside. "It's the police looking for Armand. *Ayo*." Turning back to Grace, he ushered them in the door. "Come inside, then. The neighbors all want to know your business."

The heels of her shoes tapped on the tile floor of the vestibule, and though Grace got a view of a living room decorated in rich tones of red and gold, the room was dark, with the distant look of a shrine.

"Can I ask why you're looking for him?" the man asked.

"We think he might have some information about a missing child," Chris said.

"A child?" He slapped the air as if waving away a gnat. "My son wouldn't have anything to do with that." He called down the dim hall in a fluid, baroque language.

"Has your son been arrested before, Mr. Krispalian?" Grace asked, though she knew the answer; Chris had checked his arrest record before she picked him up at the office.

"He's been in some mischief in the past, but it was small stuff. Graffiti and what-not."

A woman in velour pants and a matching jacket appeared, and he introduced her as his wife, Nayda. Grace surveyed the woman as the man explained everything in their language. Nayda's dark hair was stylishly short, but one of her front teeth was turned around—an eye-catcher when she smiled.

"Mmm." Nayda frowned, her dark eyes sanguine. "You must be mistaken, officers. Armand would never be involved in such a thing. He's a good boy."

"But we would like to talk with him," Grace said. "Can you tell us where to find him?"

He looked at his wife, who shrugged. "He's out with his friends," she said. "I'm not sure where."

"Out past midnight on a school night, Mrs. Krispalian? Don't you worry about his grades?" Grace asked.

"He's eighteen. A man now." The father seemed offended by their question. "Besides, grades don't matter for Armand. He's going to work in our family business."

"What kind of business is that?" Chris asked.

"A chain of convenience stores." Ara mentioned a name Grace recognized.

"Really?" Grace nodded. "That's quite a business opportunity for such a young man."

"It's what our family does. He'll have his own store as soon as he turns twenty-one."

"Sounds like a sweet deal," Chris said. "We're sorry to bother you so late, but we really do need to speak with your son. Where would we find him right now? Where does he hang?"

The couple locked gazes, sharing a warning to keep mum.

The eyes: That was one language Grace could decipher.

"He's with his friends," Ara Krispalian said. "We don't know where. He's old enough to stand his own ground, you know? Make his own decisions."

"He's eighteen, right?" Grace faced Nayda. "I admire your ability to let go. My son, he's just twelve, and already I get a little misty thinking of the day when he's going to leave the house."

Nayda nodded, her face softening. "Our children leave our houses, but never our hearts."

"You know, that's a beautiful expression," Grace said. "I'd like to remember that, but I have a mind like a sieve." She looked around the vestibule. "Do you think you could write it down for me?"

"Of course." While Nayda disappeared down the hall, Chris asked Mr. Krispalian if he had any other children.

"Four daughters. All older. Armand is the baby."

"Here you go." Nayda handed Grace a folded slip of paper.

Without opening it, Grace thanked her and turned toward the door.

"Sorry to disturb you so late at night," Grace told them.

After a round of polite good-byes, Grace and Chris were stepping outside into the cold, making their way back to the car.

"What was all that about?" Chris asked as they walked to

Grace's car. "Of course he's in his mother's heart; he hasn't moved out of the house yet."

"It was a bonding moment." Grace unfolded the sheet of paper, her eyes adjusting to the light of the streetlamp. "A mother-to-mother thing. And, yeah, it worked."

"Say what?"

"She says we should look for him in the field house at the elementary school. The one by Kendall Park."

"Okay." Chris nodded, looking a little impressed. "The mother ship has spoken."

Kendall Park wasn't much more than a treed lot bisected by asphalt paths.

"His mother said to check the field house." Grace strained to look closer at the school grounds. A play structure, bike racks, a parking lot where bald security lights shined in pools on the blacktop. "Where the hell is that?"

The school, tucked into a suburban neighborhood, was probably a choice spot for delinquents to hang, being secluded and away from cars and pedestrian traffic.

"Let's take a look," Chris said.

Grace had Chris reach into the console for a flashlight. Her gun, as always, was securely holstered at her waist. She had never used it on anything besides the target at the range, and she hoped she would never have to.

But in dark, unfamiliar situations like this, she was glad to be working with a pistol and a partner.

The snow had stopped and the ground was frozen underfoot, but the cold cut through her as soon as she stepped out of the car. That was the way it went whenever she worked overtime; her resistance got worn down.

"It's cold out here," she said. "Not really party atmosphere."

"Do you remember what it's like to be eighteen?" Chris paused beside a tall tree, staring past the handball walls and swings. "All you need for a party is a can of beer." He pointed to the far end of the asphalt playground. "See over there? That looks like the field house."

They decided not to use the flashlight, not wanting to scare them off. Under the cover of darkness, they approached the small outbuilding. The smell of burnt marijuana mixed in the air with low voices.

"Sounds like our guys," Chris said as they approached.

The young men were huddled together on one side of the field house. They sat on the ground in a line, their backs against the stone building, probably using it to stay out of the wind.

No one reacted as Grace and Chris got close. At least they're not scrambling, Grace thought. She was in no mood to get into a chase.

"Hey, guys. Got a little party going on. What's in the cans?" Chris asked.

"Coke."

"Really? You're out here in the cold drinking soda, when you could do that in Mommy's basement?"

"What are you, a cop?" someone asked.

"As a matter of fact, we're detectives. So what are you really drinking?"

"Just a little beer, officer," one of the guys said. "We're not hurting anybody and we'll clean up when we go. We don't want any trouble."

Chris turned the flashlight on and panned over their faces.

Boys, Grace thought. Some of them weren't much older than Matt.

"Because you had the balls not to run, we're going to let you keep your beer, as long as you cooperate." Chris ran the flashlight beam over their faces again, though the details were masked by hoods and watch caps and baseball hats. "Which one of you is Krispy?"

Four of the guys turned toward the kid on one end.

The light shone on a thin kid in a plaid jacket with a navy hood over his head. "Looks like you're coming with us. Put your beer on the ground and step over here, Krispy."

"Aw, man," Krispy protested, though he placed the paper sack on the ground and rose. A whole head taller than Grace.

Grace held the flashlight as Chris had the kid step around the side of the field house, where he checked him for weapons.

"Am I under arrest?" Krispy asked. "Are you going to cuff me?"

"Not if you come willingly," Chris said. He introduced himself and Grace, and gave Krispy a chance to look over their IDs by the light of the flashlight. They didn't want to terrorize the kid.

"We need to talk with you down at the precinct," Grace said.

"For underage drinking?" Krispy asked. "That's bullshit."

"This is about something else," Chris said. "Are you going to man up and cooperate? We can all be nice about it, unless you want to be a hard-ass about it."

Krispy paused, weighing his options. Since he was over sixteen, they could take him in without parental consent, and Grace suspected that Krispy knew that.

"Yeah, whatever," Krispy muttered. "Let's go already."

Although Armand Krispalian behaved like a model prisoner on the way to the precinct, once they got him into an interrogation room, he clammed up.

In his dark brow and the lean line of his chin, Grace saw defiance and fear. She didn't blame him for either; she wouldn't want to be in his shoes, dragged away from the smoky cool of a party to be questioned by police under a buzzing fluorescent light.

"I don't know, Krispy." Grace didn't mask her concern. "You're still on probation, and we could write you up for underage drinking. But that would get you in a snag with your probation officer, wouldn't it?"

"Not to mention that aroma circling your friends out there at the field house," Chris said. "Smelled like weed to me. I guess we could also go back and bust up the whole party, write up all your friends."

Armand let his head drop back on his shoulders, a gesture of resignation. "What do you want to know?"

"Tell us about your new business venture, Armand," Grace said. "Your big moneymaker."

He groaned. "It's just about getting a couple of kids some beers, you know?"

Grace bit her lips together. This wasn't what they were looking for, but whatever. "Go on."

The kid cupped his face in his hands, his dark eyes round with worry. "What I want to know is, how did you find out? Did my father notice stuff missing?"

"Tell us your side of the story," Chris said.

"It's just a way to make some cash. I buy a few cases of beer from my father's store. I just scan it out under my father's register code, and I pay for it. That's all legit. Then I sell it to the guys at the park, only at a higher price since they're all underage."

"You're eighteen years old," Chris said. "You're underage, too."

He rolled his eyes. "When my old man was my age, eighteen used to be legal in New York."

"And this all works because you've got an inside connection with the family stores. At least for beer, right?"

Krispy shrugged. "Beer is enough. It gets you buzzed as good as anything else."

"And that's it?" Chris spread his arms wide. "You've got nothing else to tell us."

"You can't pin the weed on me, man. I'm not a drug dealer."

Chris leaned back in the seat and scrutinized the kid. "What can you tell us about selling babies on the black market?"

Krispy's brows came together and he grinned. "For real? I don't know what you're talking about."

"Your girlfriend does. We hear you were making noise about how you could make big money selling off the kids she babysits."

"Eleni said that?" He laughed. "That's crazy shit."

"You remember saying that?" Grace asked.

"Maybe. I dunno. It was a joke. I mentioned it when we saw it on the soaps she watches. Did she tell you that part? She's addicted to that one show. She lives in fear that it's going to be canceled like the rest of them."

"So you saw it on a soap?" Grace asked. "*Y & R?*"

"That one. She was all freaking out about Daisy's baby when we were watching the show, and I said there was good money in something like that."

"But you didn't ask her to help you kidnap a child?"

"Hell, no. Do people really do that shit?"

"Unfortunately, people abduct infants," Grace said. "That's why we're talking to you, Armand. What do you know about Annabelle Green?"

He rubbed his chin absently. "Who's she?"

"Name doesn't ring a bell?" Chris said. "You've met her, at least once."

Krispy shook his head. "I'm drawing blanks. It's one of the kids Eleni takes care of, right?" Something seemed to click, and he squinted up at Chris. "This baby . . . that's the reason you brought me in tonight, isn't it? It wasn't about selling beer at all." He raked his hands back through his dark hair and winced. "Shit."

Although Chris continued to press Armand Krispalian, Grace was convinced there was nothing more here than a spoiled kid looking to take some shortcuts. He was not involved in selling babies; he was still a baby himself.

She tuned out, beginning to prioritize the hours ahead. They would return to grass-roots detective work, checking backgrounds and interviewing the neighbors, the receptionist at the doctor's office, the photographer who took Annabelle's photo at a department store. The circles started small, then got wider as they began to look at each and every person who had touched Annabelle Green's life.

Chapter 31

In Chelsea's dream she was walking through an open-air market in an arid Middle Eastern city. Baghdad or Istanbul. Walls of ancient stone rose behind the market, hemming everyone into the square blooming with color and music like the plaintive wail of a baby. Men in turbans and women concealed by veils moved past her like dancers, and all the fruits and olives and carpets for sale were hidden behind flowing veils.

A man with a machete stood alert and ready to hack down the veil concealing anything she chose to buy, but she didn't want anything but Annabelle. He kept pointing the machete to a curtain and asking, "You want to buy?"

But she couldn't afford anything except her daughter, and if he slashed the curtain it might hurt the baby.

"You want?" he kept asking as she hurried from one curtain to another, shiny silks and satins in red and purple, pink and turquoise.

Suddenly, a wind rose from the earth, blowing the curtains so that she could have a look inside. She moved toward a pink curtain, certain that Annabelle was behind it. . . .

And she was pulled from sleep by the squeal of a baby.

What? Annabelle!

She sat up in bed, shaking in a panic, and realized that it was not her baby crying but the howling of the dog next door.

Louise's dog, ChiChi.

And where was Annabelle? The wound was still fresh, exacerbated when she saw the empty bassinette against the bedroom wall. Her breasts were heavy with milk for her baby.

She squeezed her eyes shut as a small whimper squeezed from her throat. The dream had been so vivid . . . she had been close to reaching out and touching Annabelle's smooth skin, pressing her nose into the creases in her little neck.

She wanted to tell Leo about the dream, but the bed beside her was empty. He had never made it upstairs. Didn't it mean something that she wanted to find their daughter? That she had refrained from choosing a curtain for fear that Annabelle would be cut by the machete?

For the second night in a row, she had escaped to sleep, although last night it was a restless daze. She had floated on the surface of sleep, unable to sink down into oblivion. A good mother probably wouldn't have slept at all, but then she'd given up all pretense of goodness.

She pushed the covers aside and let her feet drop to the carpeting. It was dark outside, but a pasty dawn pinched the sky.

After she pumped, she pulled on jeans and a sweatshirt and headed downstairs. When she poked her head out from the staircase, she saw Leo on the couch with the computer on his lap.

"Since you didn't wake me, I know nothing good happened," she said, coming down the stairs.

"You're right." Leo rubbed his eyes as he explained that the detectives had interviewed Krispy, but they didn't think he had any involvement with Annabelle's disappearance.

"Oh." She carried the bottle of breast milk into the kitchen to store it. Inside the fridge, more than a half dozen bottles were lined up and labeled, and as she added the new one she realized she would need to sterilize bottles soon. She needed her dishwasher working again, but then the plumber was supposed to come today.

How long did breast milk last? It had never been an issue before, as Leo enjoyed giving Annie bottles so much, the expressed milk had never sat in the fridge for long. She looked at the clock. Barely seven. She would wait until noon to pump again—every five hours, as Dr. Chin had suggested.

The kitchen was tidy now. Leo had straightened up, put away pots. He must have washed dishes by hand. She went into the bathroom to fill the coffeepot with water. When she peeked out of the kitchen again, Leo was dozing, the computer open in his lap. He must have been searching online for clues to find their baby.

She tiptoed past him, wanting to touch the bristled line of his jaw.

How she loved this man.

The smell of brewing coffee and the yapping dog next door made things seem almost normal again. She put bread in the toaster, but ChiChi's barking was growing frantic.

She went to the window, but she couldn't see anything from the angle of the kitchen. "What is the problem out there?" she murmured.

"Welcome home, ChiChi." Leo's eyes were still closed.

Chelsea brought him a cup of coffee. "Maybe I should call the police about that barking dog."

"Love your neighbor as yourself," he said. "I say it's only fair, after Louise called the cops on us for a crying baby."

"An abandoned baby," she corrected, sitting beside him on the couch.

"Sitting right outside the door at, like, seven o'clock at night. It's not a crime," he said. "This is not your fault. And just so you know, we're going to find our daughter."

Holding his hand, she felt a kernel of strength taking hold. Something had shifted inside her and she felt more steady, more like her old self. Maybe it was the medicine, maybe it was having two nights of sleep in a row, or maybe it was the sharp dagger of crisis prodding her along, but now she felt ready to stand and help search for her daughter.

"You're right." She squeezed Leo's hand. "We are going to find her, and she's going to be fine. She's okay, Leo. I can feel it. Our baby's okay. We just have to get to her." Her eyes filled with tears, but she swiped them away with her free hand.

"She's okay," he said.

"I know that Annie's all right. It's just that I know she needs us. I never really got that before but she needs her mom and dad. She's probably looking around for you, wanting the sound of your voice when you sing those silly songs. And she needs me to feed her. I hate to think of her missing that."

Leo pulled her hand close and kissed it. "I'm glad to have the old Chelsea back."

The old Chelsea, for better or worse. "I'm not sure you're going to want the old Chelsea when you hear what I have to say."

"Try me."

She thought of the dream again—the feeling that Annabelle was just inches away, within reach, if only she made the right choice. "This is going to sound crazy, but I'm going to say it and then maybe it'll help me get it out of my system and move on. Emma and Jake are talking about moving to Chicago. Like . . . soon."

He nodded. "Jake mentioned the job offer."

"The crazy part? It's a perfect setup if she really did have a miscarriage and took Annie. They could go and just raise her there, and no one would ever know."

Leo took a sip of coffee. "You're right. It's crazy, but probable. It fits the profile of most infant abductions. But this is your sister we're talking about."

"I know. It's not real but . . . I just had to give voice to it to disqualify it from reality."

"You know what?" He stared off, his eyes dark and tormented. "Right now it would be a relief to know that Annabelle was with Jake and Emma. Even if we never could see her again, just to know that she was safe—"

"Don't go making any deals with the devil," Chelsea said.

They were interrupted again by the sound of the yapping dog.

"Give me a break." Leo looked at the clock. "Isn't it time for the old witch to be at the gym?"

It had always been Ms. Pickler's schedule: out of here by

six a.m. But it was after seven and ChiChi was in the adjoining yard, barking up a storm.

Chelsea went to the door, but couldn't see anything. "You don't think maybe Louise got kidnapped last night?"

"Wishful thinking." Leo went upstairs to get a look from the bedroom.

Chelsea went into the living room and picked up one of Annabelle's squishy blocks with a big purple Eeyore etched on the side. She was thinking of Annie trying to mouth the block when a muffled curse came down the stairs.

"What the hell . . . ?"

"What is it?" she called up.

"Call Detective Santos," he shouted, appearing on the top landing. "Louise is out in her backyard, digging. I think she's burying something in the yard."

"Why would she be out this time of year, digging in . . ." The horrifying answer to her own question sent Chelsea scrambling for the phone.

Chapter 32

The buzzing sound drew Grace's gaze away from the birth certificate on the monitor. She pushed away from her desk, turned off the alarm, and put a call through to Matt. Long-distance parenting was never ideal, but with technology there were still ways to stay in touch. She usually made a point of giving him a wake-up call on mornings when she couldn't be with him, and Matt had enjoyed Skyping last summer when he'd gone on an extended trip with his father.

"Good morning," she said. "How'd everything go last night?"

"Good." He yawned. "Ethan's dad made spaghetti sauce with turkey."

"How was that?"

"Pretty good. You'd never guess it was different." Matt paused. "Mom? Did you go to sleep at all last night?"

"I dozed off for a while, but no, I didn't go home to bed."

"So you didn't find the baby yet?"

She spun her chair back toward her desk. "Not yet, but we will." She had to believe that was true, though there was no denying the discouragement she felt every time a new lead was snuffed out. The ex-wife, the sitter's boyfriend . . . they had seemed like strong suspects in the moment.

"Do you think you'll find the baby by this weekend?" Matt asked. "I mean, what'll I do if you have to work?"

"This is your weekend with your dad." For once, Steve's weekend had coincided with the demands on Grace's life.

"Oh, yeah."

"And Dad said to tell you he got the tickets." Often Matt had to be cajoled into spending time with his father, but Steve had told her Matt would be psyched about this weekend.

"What kind of tickets?"

"Hockey! Dad got the Rangers tickets. He said he would."

The joy in Matt's voice soothed Grace's worries for the weekend. Glancing at the photo of Matt on her desk, Grace remembered how he would twist and shriek in her arms.

Not a happy baby.

Those had been dark days . . . uneventful except for the anguish of trying to soothe the baby writhing in her arms, and the reminder in the mirror, in the mail, and in her empty bed that her life was over.

Twelve years ago, when Grace had suffered the same depression that Chelsea was going through, no one really had a name for it. It went untreated until it wound down on its own two years later. When the dust settled, Grace was a single parent, behind on her bills, and missing her husband, who had been driven away by her insanity. PPD had cost her a marriage, and despite the knowledge that it wasn't her fault, she still felt a twinge of guilt over alienating Steve when she went "all kinds of crazy."

Chelsea Maynard was fortunate that her husband seemed to be in it for the long haul.

She ended the call with Matt and turned back to the birth certificate on her monitor. It showed a child born—Anthony Zika—to Eleni Zika, a year ago. The mother's birth date showed that she'd been sixteen when the baby was born.

"I got you a decaf." Chris put a paper coffee cup on her desk. "I know that caffeine keeps you up all night. Oops . . . you were up all night."

"Thanks. And you got a call while you were gone. Jay Leno wants to know if you'll take the *Tonight Show*, since no one is as funny as you."

"Ouch. Stabbing humor at this sick hour of the morning." He nodded at the computer screen. "What you got?"

She told him about the birth certificate. "She was barely sixteen when she got pregnant—just a kid herself. No father listed."

"Do you think Krispy was the father?" Chris blinked. "Hold on. Did they sell that baby?"

She shook her head. "I found adoption records that match. A private adoption, straightforward and legal."

"Okay. Where does that leave us?"

Grace warmed her hands on the coffee cup. "I feel for Eleni, but I also wonder if the girl still longs for her baby. Does she regret giving him up for adoption? Would she be desperate enough to steal Annabelle to try and replace what she lost?"

"But we checked her pedigree. The girl lives at home . . . where is she keeping the baby?"

She shrugged. "I haven't gotten that far, and maybe it's a dead end. It's just another thing that's got to be checked out."

He nodded. "And the boyfriend, Krispy Kritter, he seemed clueless."

"Right. If Eleni Zika took Annabelle, I doubt Krispy was involved."

Just then her cell buzzed and she glanced at the caller ID. "Chelsea and Leo," she told Chris as she picked up the phone. "Good morning."

"Louise Pickler is digging a hole in her backyard," Chelsea said breathlessly. "A big hole. She won't talk to us and she won't let Leo come into the yard. She's got a box there that she . . . she's trying to bury something."

Grace winced. Judge Costantini wouldn't sign the search warrant, and now this. "Hold tight. We'll be right there."

"But you said the judge wouldn't sign the search warrant."

"Things have changed. The digging could be construed as suspicious behavior." Grace grabbed her jacket as Chris tossed his empty cup into the trash. Some judge wouldn't be happy about getting called out of bed, but they would get their warrant.

*   *   *

While Chris drove, Grace made the calls.

The first call was to her boss, Sgt. Bruce Hopkins, who understood the urgency. "We'll get two uniforms over to the Pickler residence," he said. "I gotta ask, this woman's digging now, with the ground frozen? She must be using a pickax." He was sending over someone from the canine unit to help with the search. Next Grace called the prosecutor's office to request the warrant be run by another judge in light of the new evidence. The assistant prosecutor wasn't sure of the outcome, but she promised to get the search warrant before a judge, "even if I have to drive it over to some judge's house with a latte." Grace knew that a verbal okay was enough to start searching.

They arrived to find Chelsea, Leo, and the uniforms standing in Louise Pickler's side yard. One cop kept watch while the other spoke to Louise over the wooden fence.

"Where's our warrant?" Chris asked as he cut the engine.

"Any minute. At least she's communicating with them." Grace got out of the car and flew across the lawn.

"She won't let anyone in," Chelsea said, tugging on the sleeves of her hoodie.

"Why isn't anyone breaking through the gate?" Leo demanded. "Any of us could hop over the fence. We need to stop her."

"Please." Grace held up her hands in an attempt to calm him.

"Don't you dare tamper with my property, Leo Green!" Louise shouted from the other side of the fence.

"What about the search warrant?" Chelsea asked.

"We don't have it yet," Grace told her. "We really need to try to deal with this, and I have to ask you to move back. Wait inside."

"Tell the persecuting attorney to back off!" Louise barked.

Leo was shaking his head, but Grace insisted. "Please. I know you want us to make progress here." She lowered her voice. "She's highly agitated."

Chelsea pressed the cuffs of her sweatshirt to her face, nodding. She touched her husband's arm and gave him a tug. Reluctantly, Leo backed off, too.

"I'm one of the good guys," Louise lamented. "One of the true American heroes, like George Washington and Elvis. I cannot tell a lie."

One of the cops cracked a grin, but he was turned away so that Pickler couldn't see.

"Ms. Pickler?" Grace called. "Louise? It's Detective Santos. We talked briefly yesterday." She leaned close to the fence, trying to peer through the narrow slits. "We would really appreciate it if you'd open the gate and come talk to us."

"Talk is cheap, and so are you," Pickler responded. "Where'd that cop go? The good-looking black dude in the uniform?"

So much for female bonding, Grace thought.

"I'm right here, ma'am." Jefferson stepped up to the fence again. "Like I said, we don't mean to inconvenience you, but it would help our investigation if you would let us come into your yard and look around."

That's it, Grace thought, impressed with the officer's approach.

"No, no, not gonna happen," Louise said in a singsong voice. "In fact, you shouldn't even be standing on my lawn. If you don't watch it, I'll call the FDA and the FCC."

Grace shot a look behind her at Chris, who grinned in a mixture of amusement and bewilderment. They'd dealt with emotionally disturbed persons, but it wasn't often that they came wrapped up in such a colorful facade.

Jefferson turned away from the fence and shrugged in defeat as Grace's phone buzzed. She answered, got the message from the prosecutor's office, and nodded.

"That's it. We got the warrant."

The two cops straightened and went to either side of the fence. Everyone knew the procedure: knock and announce. The police had to knock on the door and announce themselves. This often meant giving a resident time to pull on some clothes or get down the stairs in the dark. In a case when the police needed the element of surprise, like a drug bust in which the resident could be flushing evidence down the toilet, knock and announce could be suspended. But Ms. Pickler deserved a formal warning.

"Ms. Pickler?" Grace called, knocking on the gate with her knuckles. "The police have a warrant to search your home. It would be helpful if you would open the gate and cooperate with us."

Silence. Then, in a quiet voice, Louise said, "Go away."

"That's it. She's denying us entry." Chris gestured toward the door. "We can go in."

"Ms. Pickler," Jefferson said, "we're coming in."

The gate swung open, and behind it, Louise Pickler stood holding her shivering little dog. Her hands were red and chafed, her face solemn. "Do I get to sit in the police car?" she asked quietly.

Jefferson squinted at the woman, but Grace nodded. "Sure, you do. It's a lot warmer in there. I'll get you set up." She reached for Pickler, but the woman stepped toward Jefferson. "Uh-uh. I'm going with Fresh Prince."

As Louise Pickler headed toward the street with Jefferson, Grace followed Chris and the other patrolman into Pickler's backyard.

Even from the gate, the mound of dark dirt in the corner of the yard was obvious. Rich and dark as coffee grounds, it rose up at least a foot above the rest of the lawn.

Grace probed it with the toe of her boot. "Looks like potting soil, and it's not very well packed."

"Looks like she tried to dig in a few places, but couldn't break through the frozen ground," Connors said, circling a few spots in the lawn that were hacked bald, the dirt a silvery shade of gray.

Chris spotted tools by the back porch: a shovel, spade, hammer, and an ice pick.

"An ice pick." Chris shook his head. "I've never tried to dig with one of those. I guess she wasn't going to let the frozen earth stop her."

"So what do you think?" Connors stood staring at the dark mound of dirt. "Should we wait for forensics?"

"With an infant missing next door?" Grace went to the porch for tools. "Time is of the essence. If there's a baby under there, we need to get her out. Can you get some quick photos before I start brushing away at the dirt?"

Quickly, Chris and Connors both took pictures with their cell phones. Holding a spade, Grace squatted down beside the pile of dirt. How could she stick a shovel into the mound if Annabelle was truly in there? Thinking of the films she'd seen of archeologists on a dig, she tossed the spade aside and used her hands to wipe away the top layer of loose soil.

The soil was cold, but the chunks of black dirt were easily swept away.

The moldering smell grew more acrid as the soil flattened out beneath her hands. A flat surface. And suddenly she was brushing dirt from a cardboard box.

"There's a box." Her fingers plunged into the dirt to seize the edges and extract the box from the earth.

The odor was cloying now—more foul than just the smell of potting soil laced with fertilizer. The box had markings on it— a decorative pattern, like those boxes you purchase to store things in your closet.

Everyone watched as Grace laid it gently on the ground and removed the lid.

Nervous anticipation was thick in her throat, and the odor that hit her made her gag and turn away. But not before she recognized the stench of death and the remains of a small body in the box.

She had just dug up a shallow grave.

Chapter 33

"What's in the box?" Chelsea asked from down below. "Can you see?"

"Grace just picked it up and put it on the ground." From his perch atop the garbage can, Leo had a clear view over the fence into Louise Pickler's yard, but it was no substitute for being there.

"How big is the box, anyway?" Chelsea asked. "A jewelry box? A shoe box? Or bigger?"

"Bigger." The muscles in his chest clenched when he saw Grace open the box and turn away. "Shit." He jumped to the ground.

"What is it?" Chelsea asked.

"I don't know, but it's not good." He took her hand and tugged her along, running around the fence to the gate in Louise's yard.

The fresh grave was a horrible sight, surrounded by perplexed cops. Without a word Leo pushed his way into the circle of people and looked down into the box, at the small carcass dressed in a pink knitted sweater.

"Oh, my God!" Chelsea gasped. "The bones of a little baby."

The foul odor brought tears to his eyes, but the sight wasn't as bad as he expected.

"That's not Annabelle." Leo stared hard. "It can't be."

"What do you mean?" Grace asked.

Leo knew he was no expert, but he had been a bio major in college. "The decay of the carcass is way too advanced to be someone who was killed in the past thirty-six hours."

"He's right," Detective Panteleoni agreed. "This thing is rotted down to the bone already."

"And look at that skull." Beneath the rotting sinew, Leo could see that the jaw was elongated. "It's not human. It's a canine . . . a cat or a dog or a wolf."

"We'll send the bones for analysis," Grace said. "Just to be sure."

"Why would someone put a dog in a pink knit sweater?" Chris Panteleoni asked.

"You're talking about Louise Pickler," Chelsea pointed out. "She's always treated her dogs like humans."

At that moment Louise appeared at the open gate with Officer Jefferson. "My Coco!" Pickler rushed toward the open box. She knelt beside it reverently, as if she'd been given a chance to say one last word to a dying friend. "Mommy's baby girl."

Leo turned to his wife, who watched the scene intently.

"Coco died down in South Carolina," Chelsea told Leo quietly. "Did I tell you that? She must have hauled the dog's body up here to bury it in the yard."

"Ms. Pickler, are these the bones of a dog?" Detective Santos asked.

"My Coco. I came back to New York early when she died. I wanted to lay her to rest here in the yard she loved. And down in South Carolina, my sister Gwyn kept complaining of the bad smell, even though the box was wrapped tight in a garbage bag."

"Your sister had a point," Chris Panteleoni said. "Dead bodies smell, Ms. Pickler. Is that why your house has a bad odor?"

Pickler's mouth formed a pout that reminded Leo of a monkey's ass as she cuddled ChiChi close. "It's not so bad. You get used to it, and it's worth a little smell to have my loved ones close by."

"You mean there are more dogs buried in this yard?" Jefferson asked.

She nodded. "Some in the yard. A few of them are in the crawl space under the house. That's what I used to do when they died in the winter and the ground was too hard to dig up."

"A pet cemetery." Leo turned and marched out of the yard.

He'd had enough of crazy Louise and her canine dysfunctions.

He was done with the roller coaster of emotions involved in tracking down Annabelle's abductor. The breathless chase when someone revealed himself, only to slam into a dead end.

"Leo . . ." Chelsea caught up with him by their side door.

"I'm done with this."

"You're giving up on Annie, just like that?"

"Of course not. But I'm done with the cops and our neighbors and the doctors. Everyone claims to help, but no one is willing to stick his neck out."

"Grace has been trying to help."

"It's her job." Leo put his hands on her shoulders. "Look, I won't get in the way, and I'm not giving up. But there's got to be a better way to find the person who took our baby."

Chelsea locked her hands on his arms, her eyes unwavering. "If there is, we'll find it," she said. "Every time one of these leads falls short, I'm devastated, too. But part of me is relieved that crazy Louise didn't take our baby. I want to find our baby healthy and whole. She's out there, Leo. We just have to find her."

There was certainty and clarity in her blue eyes. Chelsea was on solid ground again, and in the nick of time. With everything crumbling around them, they needed to hold on to each other.

He breathed again. "You're right."

"Of course I am." She released his arms and leaned into

him. Her head fit into the crook of his neck, and her body felt soft against his chest. Once, that had been enough, but now they had a family. They had Annabelle.

"Leo?" someone called.

With a deep breath, Leo turned and saw Detective Panteleoni standing in the driveway.

The detective nodded. "Can I have a word?"

Chelsea breathed against him. "I'm going to make some breakfast for us."

He watched as she moved up the porch steps. It was good to have his best friend back.

"Your next-door neighbor is quite a character," Chris said. "I haven't seen a commotion like that since my days on patrol."

"Louise likes drama."

"And how's your wife doing?"

Leo looked toward the side door. "Better."

"Grace mentioned that she's suffering from PPD. That has to be hard."

"It's been a challenge, but she's starting to come around. When this is all over, she'll get the treatment she needs. Right now, the medication she's on is sort of a Band-Aid."

"That's good. I understand she wasn't really attached to Annabelle."

"That's not true. She loves Annie." Leo shoved his hands into his pants pockets. "Who told you that?"

"We've been talking to everyone we can find who knows you and your wife, Leo. That's what we do."

"I know, but who would say that?"

"Forget that. What I was wondering is, do you think she ever acted on the violent thoughts she was experiencing?"

Leo couldn't believe Chris Panteleoni would talk to him this way. "So that's where this is going?"

"I'm advocating for Annabelle here. Did your wife ever take it out on the baby? Even in small ways?"

"Chelsea would never do anything to hurt Annie."

"But she was neglectful," Chris pointed out. "That could have hurt your baby."

"She would never try to hurt our daughter."

"But it happens in these cases. I'm sure you've read the accounts of mothers who kill their babies—for whatever reason—then try to cover it up by calling it an abduction."

"Really, detective? You think she killed the baby and hid the body?"

"Wow, you really cut to the chase there." Chris shrugged. "Honestly? It happens. Sometimes women with PPD, they just snap."

"Not this one." Leo squared off, getting in Panteleoni's grill. "You're wrong about Chelsea. She loves Annabelle."

"I believe that," Chris said. "But sometimes love isn't enough."

As Chris crossed the lawn, Leo was left feeling like a fool. He wasn't even home when Annie disappeared; what the hell did he know about what had happened?

But then, he knew Chelsea. She would never hurt their baby.

But she was neglectful, Chris had said, and that part was true.

Inside the house, Chelsea was pouring coffee for her friend from the magazine, Sasha Barman. Sasha had helped with the search last night.

"I can't stay long today," Sasha told Chelsea. "I just wanted to check in on you. I hope you don't have the guilts just because of the way you've been feeling. A lot of new mothers get fed up and wish they could just return to their lives before the baby."

And that was exactly what Chelsea had wanted after Annabelle was born. She had missed her old life, her job, and her independence. She had been stuck on the couch, mired in depression. She had been glad to have Leo take their baby from her arms . . . but none of those elements could combine into a toxic molecule. Discontent and depression were not a sure-fire formula for a killer.

"You can't help the way you feel," Chelsea said quietly. "But I have a lot of regret. I wish I could turn back the clock a few days, go back and redo that night."

We all wish we could go back.

Facing away from the women while he poured himself another cup, Leo didn't know what to think anymore. He didn't want to play the "what if" game, casting his wife in scenarios colored with accusation. He didn't want to think anymore. Thoughts led to guilt and anger and fear for his daughter. If he was going to get through this, he would have to shut down the terrible thoughts and move ahead on autopilot.

Doubt was a swamp, and he couldn't afford to get stuck there right now.

He had to keep a clear head. That was what Annabelle needed.

Chapter 34

It was sad, having to force your way into someone's home when she valued her privacy. Sad, but unavoidable. As Chris pushed open the front door of Louise Pickler's house, Grace hoped that the woman wasn't watching from the back of the patrol car, tears streaking her face.

Although it was against police procedure, Louise had wanted to wait in the police cruiser. Even in her time of duress, the bling of the patrol car seemed to lift her spirits. Fortunately, Jefferson didn't mind.

"As long as we've got to be here, she can sit in there," the young cop had said, and Grace had taken him up on it.

"Are we going for a ride?" Louise asked hopefully as Grace opened the door for her.

Jefferson shifted his cap back. "Uh-uh. No rides."

"You're such a hard-ass," Louise said jovially as Grace closed the door.

Now, standing on the porch, Grace grew impatient as Chris struggled with the door.

"I'm not surprised," he said as he rocked the door to get it clear of debris behind it. "Looks like Ms. Pickler is a hoarder."

Seeing the stacks of old newspapers piled up to the ceiling and the layers of debris on the floor, Grace understood Louise's fear and shame. The woman was a packrat, but she knew it wasn't normal or healthy. It felt embarrassing to have strangers picking through the trash in her home.

Grace winced as cardboard and foil crunched underfoot. "I'm not going too far, Chris. With garbage like this, there's bound to be an infestation." Mice and rats. Roaches and silverfish. Sometimes even raccoons or squirrels.

"I guess we know why Louise wasn't having the neighbors over for cocktails," Chris said as he stepped carefully around a mound of plastic bins, jumbled clothes, and countless wrinkled plastic bags stuffed with cloth and papers.

A doll peeked out from one of them, her hair mangled. Grace could decipher buckets and a broom head, a torn lampshade and a radio with an open, empty battery cavity. There was a small plastic treasure chest, but no treasures here.

"Let's bring the canine unit in," Grace said. There was a trained dog to sniff for cadavers, and another that could search for Annabelle Green. Grace figured it was worth bringing them both in, just to be sure.

The search of the house would take hours. That was the thing with police work: One small part of an investigation could suck up an entire shift. Fortunately, Grace could do some searching on her iPhone. And it didn't hurt to be right outside Chelsea and Leo's house. There was a chance that a friend or neighbor they had forgotten to mention might drop in.

Already she'd seen Leo Green and a few friends from work head off to do a door-to-door search. It wouldn't hurt, and she understood that it felt better to keep busy. She had seen Chelsea's former boss, Sasha Barton, come and go. That Sasha had a real sense of style, stepping between small piles of dirty snow in those wedge heels that Grace avoided, sure she'd break an ankle on them. That long red coat would have screamed like a fire engine on anyone else, but Sasha swaggered to her car looking like a runway model. Last night, during the door-to-door search, Grace had learned that Sasha was from a big family and got her fill of kids through her nieces and nephews. Grace's take was that she was a good friend and not envious of Chelsea's baby. But that didn't necessarily hold true for the other employees at the magazine. Grace needed a list of the staff members who had seen Annabelle when Chelsea took her to the office the previous week. It was on her "to do" list.

While Chris worked with the canine unit, Grace sat in her car and tinkered. A detective from the precinct had sent her an e-mail saying that Eleni Zika and her mother, Maria, had stopped in at the precinct so that Eleni could be fingerprinted. The girl was being cooperative.

Grace had an e-mail from one of her friends who worked for the local school system. Dolly had sent her the most recent transcripts for Armand Krispalian and Eleni Zika. Armand had a three point two, with math and science being his strong suits. Ironic, that he did okay but his parents didn't really care. As for Eleni—poor kid—it looked like the events of the past year had taken their toll. Her GPA hovered dangerously on the brink of failure at one point nine. Of course, grades weren't everything, as Matt reminded her whenever he tanked on a test.

Grace called Eleni's home number and left a message for the girl's mother, Maria. It was worth talking with the mom. More information was always better. But unless some earthshattering development came along, Grace was ready to rule out Eleni and her boyfriend.

Next she called the lab. Crash, the technician, told her that he hoped to have the toxicology results by tomorrow. "Maybe late today if we're really lucky."

Grace didn't feel too lucky lately, not with baby Annabelle gone for more than twenty-four hours now. She thanked Crash, then shot off a prayer for the baby girl. Sometimes there weren't words in her mind, but only a flash of a message. *Emergency, God. Innocent baby. Loving parents. Make this right.*

Looking over her notes—mostly a list of names with bulleted items under them—she noticed that there were very few bullets under Helen Rosekind's name. Why had she and Chris had so much trouble finding any information on the baby nurse? Even law-abiding citizens left some paper trail. A driver's license or registered vehicle. A phone listing. A mortgage. Even an account with the local cable company.

But Helen Rosekind was a blank . . . as if she didn't exist. Chris had tossed it off, saying that she probably used her husband's name for everything. It was a good theory, but Grace was eager to learn more about the nurse. She called the agency that booked the baby nurses as sitters and identified herself. Megan, the young woman on the phone, was polite, but when Grace tried to get some background on Helen Rosekind, she was stuck on "no."

No information. No verification. No way.

"You would have to talk to my boss. In person. She says it's illegal to release personnel records."

"The rules change when it comes to a police investigation," Grace said.

"You would have to talk to her," Megan said.

"Can you put her on the phone?"

"I can make an appointment for you, if you want to come in."

Grace screwed up her face in annoyance. She'd bet a bottle of Dewar's that this Megan was young, drunk with the power of her first job, and checking her text messages while she was talking to Grace.

"Fine. Let's make an appointment then," Grace said, sick of being disregarded. "But if she can't see me this afternoon, she'll see me with a search warrant for your company records."

It was an idle threat, but it got her in that afternoon. She was just ending the call when she saw Emma Wyatt heading up the driveway, carrying two grocery bags. Grace would have waved, but she knew Emma couldn't see her behind the tinted glass of the car window. Her anonymity gave Grace an opportunity to blatantly study Chelsea's sister.

Taller and leaner than Chelsea, Emma had a certain grace and dignity that made her seem aloof at times. Her students probably looked up to her, Grace thought, as Emma tried to keep things positive and constructive. Grace could imagine these two sisters growing up together, the prim Emma trying to keep order while Chelsea turned cartwheels over her sister's rules.

As she passed by, Emma's baby bump was evident beneath her short jacket. Actually, her belly was more obvious today, but maybe she was dressing to show it off—and rightly so. Yesterday, Emma had been hit twice, with the fear of a miscarriage and the news that her niece was missing.

Emma was met by Chelsea in the driveway, and she took one of her bags and gave her a kiss on the cheek. As Chelsea held the door for Emma, Grace wondered how much she really knew about her sister.

Did she know about her penchant for theft? Emma had been found guilty of shoplifting three times. The last time, she had been hit with a stiff fine and extensive community service.

Fortunately for Emma, her problem seemed to be under control. Her last arrest was more than five years ago.

But Grace had stumbled on some other surprises when she checked out Emma Wyatt.

A sudden trip, and a major move, far from New York.

Emma and her husband were scheduled to fly to Chicago at the end of the week. Jake Wyatt's assistant at the law firm had the gift of gab, and she had been eager to answer all Grace's questions. The couple was flying to the Windy City to meet the partners and explore their real estate options. They were looking at making a move in a matter of weeks! Emma had already given notice at her school, and they weren't even going to wait to have the baby here. . . .

For a woman who'd almost miscarried, Emma seemed to be making some radical changes in her life. Had she shared the news about the move with her sister? In the course of an investigation, it was suspicious to see a key player leaving town, but then maybe it was truly a coincidence.

As the morning waned, activity picked up next door. A minivan with Jersey plates arrived, and a woman with dark hair pulled into a ponytail emerged and opened the door to three children—a toddler and two older preschoolers who looked like siblings. From the Jersey plates, Grace suspected it was the older sister, who had kids that age. The woman corralled the children up the driveway, all three of them toting toys—including a lizard almost as big as the toddler—and canvas bags. Cute kids.

Wanting to meet anyone new on the scene, Grace got out of the car. She'd find some excuse for intruding.

Snow had receded from the edges of the lawn, revealing sprigs of grass that seemed far too brown to ever recover. At times like this, it seemed that spring would never warm the earth.

Glancing past the handful of police personnel still congregating outside Pickler's house, she saw a short girl emerge from a small late-model Honda that had just parked in front of the Wilkinsons' house. It was the spot where the dogs had lost the trail of Annabelle's scent.

Grace slowed her pace along the sidewalk, watching as the girl came into view.

Eleni Zika.

Was that where she tended to park when she visited the Maynard-Green house?

She paused and waited as the girl approached. Eleni wore a hoodie and a black backpack sagged down over her butt. Such a tough look for a girl with a sweet, round face and a hairstyle that reminded Grace of Pippi Longstocking.

"Detective Santos . . . Chelsea told me that you don't think Krispy did it. But you didn't find Annabelle, did you?" Her tone was bleak, swollen with guilt. No kid that age should feel so bad.

"Not yet," Grace said. "But I'm surprised to see you here today. Shouldn't you be in school?"

"My mom called me in sick." Her face puckered. "I *am* sick. I feel so bad for Annabelle and Chelsea. And when I think that it might be my fault . . ." She folded her arms over her waist. "I really feel sick. Maybe it's cramps, I don't know."

"You know, sometimes I get sick with worry like that—especially with this job. I have to remind myself that I'm not helping anyone by letting stuff eat away at me. I can't help anyone if I'm home sick. Know what I mean?"

"I guess."

"Besides that, I don't think you have anything to feel guilty about. It's good that you went in to be fingerprinted. Thanks. That will help in our investigation, because we want to eliminate your prints from the ones found at the scene. Beyond that, we checked out you and Armand. Frankly, there was only one thing that raised some questions." Grace motioned her to the little tiled bench in the driveway. "It's kind of private. You want to sit for a minute?"

With a tentative scowl, Eleni sat down.

"It's about a birth certificate for Anthony Zika. You were listed as the mother. That was you, wasn't it?"

Eleni's dark eyes flooded. "It was a mistake . . . my mistake."

Grace handed her a small pack of tissues as her tears and words spilled freely. She'd been careless—one time—and she'd paid the price. The guy turned out to be "really sketch." She had been so embarrassed, so mortified about talking to her mother that she hadn't said anything. When her mother noticed, it was too late to consider an abortion.

"It still hurts. But I wasn't ready to be a mom."

"It's a big responsibility."

"I'm still not ready. When I see how worn down Chelsea is all the time . . . it's awful. Some days, when I go over there, she's not even wearing any makeup. I can't live that way. And if I got a crier like Annabelle, I'd tear my hair out."

"Just so you know, I think it's different when the baby is yours."

"That's even worse. You can't get away from it. I didn't mind walking Annabelle around the house because I knew I'd be able to hand the baby over and go back to my life."

"It sounds like you've learned a lot from the experience," Grace said. "Sometimes it's the really difficult situations that force us to grow up."

Eleni nodded. "What were the questions you had, anyway?"

"I think you've answered most of them." She looked at the door. "Should we head inside?"

"My makeup is all messed up."

"Here." Grace took a tissue from the pack and dabbed away the black smudges on the girl's face. "Such pretty eyes. Hard to see them with your bangs, but pretty."

Eleni looked toward the house. "You won't tell Chelsea, will you? I mean, about me having a baby? I don't want her to know. I feel so stupid about it."

"I don't have to tell her," Grace said. "But you might want to, someday down the road."

"After you find Annabelle?"

"Right." Grace held the storm door open, and Eleni sniffed, touched her hair, which was fashioned into a half dozen wild pigtails, and finally went in.

The scene inside the house reminded Grace of her own family gatherings in the Bronx. Emma was prone on the living room floor, dividing her time between building with LEGOs with one nephew and surviving a menacing grumble from the toddler's "die-sore!" Chelsea sat at the kitchen table, her oldest sister sitting beside her with an arm slung over her shoulders.

"How's it going next door?" Chelsea asked.

"We've still got the dogs searching," Grace said. "But it's clear that Louise Pickler is not the person we're looking for."

"I know that," Chelsea said quietly. "This is Grace Santos, the detective we've been working with."

The woman rose and leaned across the table to shake Grace's hand. "Melanie Okano. I'm the Peanut's sister."

"Mommy, she's not a peanut," said the little girl kneeling on a chair at the table and licking butter from a bagel.

"That's what we called her when she was your age," Melanie explained.

"And our sitter, Eleni," Chelsea said, studying the girl with a question in her eyes.

"I just wanted to come by and say I was sorry about everything." Eleni rolled the tissues into a ball. "I can't stop thinking about Annabelle."

Chelsea nodded.

"Have a seat, ladies." Melanie got up and pointed to chairs. "You want some bagels? And there's fruit salad." She put a large glass bowl of colorful pineapple chunks and raspberries on the table. "Emma brought a nice brunch for everyone, but we wouldn't let her cook the eggs since there's no running water yet. Too much to clean up."

"That looks delicious." Grace spooned some fruit into a cup, knowing that it was more gracious to share in something than to refuse.

Eleni perched on the edge of a chair and took half a bagel from the platter.

"There's coffee and tea and juice," Melanie offered.

"And butter," said the little girl at the table.

Grace had coffee and Eleni had juice. Emma entertained the two children in the living room while Melanie kept the conversation going in the kitchen. She managed to mix just the right amount of questions and commentary, humor and respect. There was something very likable about Melanie Okano, who teased the three children not to let on to their older sister that Mom had sneaked them off for a visit to Aunt Chelsea.

"Nora is going to be livid when she hears about this," Melanie explained. "But you can't just pull a seven-year-old out of school these days."

The doorbell rang and the children raced to the front door.

The conversation in the kitchen stopped as Emma spoke with the elderly man with thick glasses and a craggy face.

"Chelsea? It's for you," Emma said. "A neighbor." She had the man step inside.

Curious, Grace moved into the living room to listen in.

"I didn't mean to interrupt anything," the man said, scanning the children's faces and the women in the kitchen. He patted one of the children's heads. "You don't know me, but I'm your neighbor over that way, catty-corner across the street.

The house with the screened-in porch—that's me. Anyway, the name's Joseph Kellog."

"Please come in, Mr. Kellog," Melanie insisted, ushering him into the living room. "Can I get you some coffee?"

"That'd be nice, but I won't trouble you long."

He sat down and started telling Chelsea how concerned he was for Annabelle. "I've lived here forty years and never, *never* have I heard of something so terrible happening in this neighborhood."

No sooner had Mr. Kellog begun telling his tale of how he and his wife, may she rest in peace, had found their house here than the doorbell rang again, and a woman with long dark hair was invited in with her two toddler children. She wore a puffy ski parka with a colorful woven tote bag slung over one shoulder, which she was rooting around in.

"Is Chelsea here?"

Grace pointed her toward Chelsea, and she stepped over the toddler with the dinosaur to hand her a plastic container. "I brought you some black bean soup. I hope you like it."

"Thank you." Chelsea blinked and handed the soup off to Emma. "You live in the neighborhood. I know your face."

"I live in the next block that way, and I just wanted to bring you the soup. The little ones, their stroller is out front, but I didn't dare leave them in it after what happened." The woman squeezed Chelsea's wrist. "I'm so sorry! I just had to offer my help to you. Any help at all. You probably don't even know me. My name is Raquel."

Raquel Jarvis? Grace wondered. The woman with the two children who legally belonged with their father in Brazil?

"I've seen you at the park," Chelsea said. "I took Annabelle there a few times, but she's not old enough to play yet."

"Oh, yes, I've seen you there. I wasn't sure where you lived, but when I saw the news vans parked out front, I thought this was a good guess."

"You have older children, too, right?" Chelsea asked.

"Two in school." Raquel nodded. "Five altogether." She

leaned down to mediate between one of her children and Melanie's youngest. "Look at his lizard, Stephen. It's so scary."

"Thanks for coming," Chelsea said. She introduced Raquel to everyone else there. "I have to run upstairs. Mel thought it would be a good idea to set out all the photos we have of Annabelle." Just as she started up the first step, the doorbell rang again.

Grace was beginning to feel as if she were watching a fast-moving drama. The children in the group saved the atmosphere from sinking to the morose level of a wake, but every connection between people here seemed to be underlined by the knowledge that Annabelle was still missing, the feeling that there was something to be done elsewhere.

Through the window of the storm door she saw yet another woman, this one Grace's age with pale blond hair. She had no coat, but wore a colorful shirt with teddy bears on it—pediatric scrubs—along with a navy beret.

Chelsea pushed the door open. "Helen . . . come in."

"I can't stay," the woman said. "I just brought you these." She reached into a canvas sack and pulled out a clear plastic bag of apples. "A healthy snack."

"Thank you. That was so nice." She started to place the apples on an end table. "If you'll excuse me, I have to run upstairs," Chelsea said. She seemed to notice Grace standing beside her and introduced her to Helen Rosekind. "Our baby nurse."

As Chelsea excused herself and headed upstairs, Grace stepped in the path of Helen Rosekind.

"My partner and I have been trying to track you down." When the woman's brows rose, she added, "Not for anything bad. You have a pristine record."

"My husband and I lead very quiet lives," Helen said.

"It's part of our investigation. Would you mind answering a few questions?"

"I don't mind, but I'm pressed for time right now. I took an early lunch to come here, and I can't be away from work for long."

"When would be a good time?" Grace took out her cell phone. "And I don't think I have a contact number for you that works."

Embracing the bag of apples, Helen Rosekind gave her a phone number, then glanced over the living room. "Quite a crowd. I'm just going to drop these in the kitchen and I'll head off."

"We'll be in touch later today," Grace said as she saw Chris outside, taking the front steps two at a time.

The Canine Unit was finished, and they wanted everyone to assemble to discuss their findings.

"What's going on here?" Chris asked.

"Family and neighbors, showing their support." Grace leaned closer and lowered her voice. "Don't be obvious, but see the woman in the kitchen with the beret? That's Helen Rosekind."

He squinted. "The baby nurse?"

"I tried to talk with her, but she's in a hurry."

He nodded. "We'll try to catch her on the rebound."

Louise Pickler's house was cleared; there were no traces of Annabelle Green inside, no scent of cadavers. Although it was good to rule out the neighbor, Grace was beginning to get that antsy feeling that things were not falling into place. She wished there was a way to step up their investigation.

As they were wrapping up the search, a black sedan pulled up and parked in front of one of the police cruisers.

A government car, Grace could tell.

Two men in suits headed up the walk to Chelsea and Leo's house.

Grace split off from Pickler's house to intercept them.

"Hey, how's it going?" she asked casually.

"We're with the FBI. Are you on the Annabelle Green case?"

"I'm the lead detective," she said, introducing herself. She had expected to hear from the FBI today. They didn't always get involved with kidnappings, but when the missing person was a child of "tender years," twelve or under, they were known to assist smaller police departments.

The Federal Bureau of Investigation and the National Center for Missing and Exploited Children were helpful in child abductions for the records they had been keeping for more than twenty-five years. For a detective like Grace, those cases provided patterns and profiles that were valuable in solving a case.

"Gracie? Is that you?" One of the men smiled—a broad, warm smile.

She took in his hooded blue eyes, square jaw, and dimples. Recognition clicked. "Flannigan. I heard that you got out of NYPD fast, but I didn't know where you landed."

"And you . . . a detective in Missing Persons." Jimmy turned to the other agent. "Grace and I were in the police academy together. Same class in NYPD."

The other agent smiled. "Small world. I'm Pete Ricci . . . and you know Jimmy. We've been following the case the last twenty-four hours. What do you think you have here?"

"It's looking like a home invasion and an abduction. The mother slept through it. There's a possibility that she was drugged that night. We've got a food sample at the lab for analysis. The dogs led us a few doors down, so it's looking like someone took the baby to a car that was parked there."

Jimmy nodded toward the house next door. "What's going on there?"

"The neighbor has a history of child abuse." She told them how the bits of evidence had led to the search of Louise Pickler's home and yard.

"So you've ruled her out as a suspect?" Ricci asked.

"Yes, sir. We've ruled out a few people close to the child."

"What about the mother?" Jimmy asked.

"She's suffering from postpartum depression, but I don't think she harmed her daughter. My take is that Annabelle Green was targeted by a classic infant abductor, a woman who wants an infant to raise as her own."

Pete Ricci nodded. "How can we help?"

"We would love to utilize some of your resources, certainly your data banks. And sometimes there's just so much red tape we need to cut through to gain access to a person or some information that the FBI is able to snap up."

"That can be arranged," Pete said. "Get Jimmy here to help you with whatever you need. I already talked to Sgt. Hopkins about organizing a joint task force."

Grace could easily imagine Hopkins's reaction to that idea. Local police forces in the New York metro area were usually resistant to working with the FBI. Grace saw it as a competition, a territorial thing. "And what did he think of that?"

"He wants to give it another twenty-four. He thinks your department can handle it."

"We've got it in hand. That said, we still haven't recovered Annabelle Green."

"Use us if you need us," Jimmy said, handing her a card. "My cell's on there. I'm still a team player, Grace."

Grace wasn't sure how she felt about working closely with Jimmy again, after so many years, but the investigation would move more quickly with the FBI's resources. She pressed her thumb over the sharp corner of the card and tried to maintain her best poker face. "Thanks. I'm sure we'll be calling."

Chapter 35

Chelsea struggled not to become overwhelmed by the events of the morning . . . all the strained faces, eyes shiny with tears.

And the hands . . . the palsied hands of Mr. Kellog. The cold hands of Helen Rosekind, who came in the door without a coat. The hands that patted her back or squeezed her wrist. Hands that told her to hold on, be strong, keep it together . . .

As if she had a choice.

And then there were Sasha's hands, smooth and soft, the color of cocoa. Sasha had beautiful hands with long fingers and perfect nails because she went for a manicure every Thursday after work. It had been a joke among the magazine staff: How could someone who worked at *Home Handyman* magazine have such pampered hands?

Sasha didn't cook or clean. She had no intention of having a baby. Ever. "When you've got five siblings, you don't need to have a baby of your own to be fulfilled," she had told Chelsea time and again. "I have twelve nieces and nephews and that's more than enough kid time for me. I want my own place and my own stuff. Call me selfish, but at least I know how I feel about kids and I'm embracing it."

That morning, as she'd watched Sasha's hands move whenever she talked—the girl could conduct a symphony of conversation—she couldn't help but think of how things had been in

Sasha's home while she was growing up. Did her mother kiss each child good night, or did time feel too constricted to lavish it on gestures like that? Did Sasha share special secrets with her mom, like getting to stay up late and watch television in the big bed between Mom and Dad when she wasn't feeling well? What was Mrs. Barton's secret? She had managed to raise six children and push them from the nest to fly in the adult world. They had all grown up healthy and whole.

People did that all the time . . . and here she and Leo hadn't been able to manage just one child. Her life had seemed overloaded with burden since Annabelle was born, but now that she was gone, Chelsea didn't know what to do with herself. Any activity seemed selfish and futile when their little Annabelle was out there somewhere, at the mercy of someone else. Grace Santos kept reminding Chelsea that the typical infant abductor took excellent care of the baby she'd kidnapped. That was some comfort, though it was hard to get past the disturbing image of her baby's face pressed to a stranger's shoulder.

Mel and the kids had been a warm distraction. As usual, Emma had bolstered her with food and gentle words. The neighbors had stepped out of their comfort zones to show support. Annabelle's sitters, too. There were gifts—bagels and fruit, bean soup and apples.

A houseful of people who cared. She should be grateful.

But they were taking time away from thinking about Annie.

And the morning had all the trappings of an Irish wake, the tradition of acquaintances stopping in to offer condolences and casseroles after someone died.

The strain. Somber voices and throats thick with emotion.

She wished she'd had the nerve to tell them all that Annie hadn't died. She didn't really want visitors, but she'd been drowning in the details, distracted by the search next door and the need to keep on her medication, keep drinking milk and pumping, keep strong for Annabelle.

What a relief when the plumber arrived and people took that as a cue to go home. Mr. Kellog needed to walk his dog. Eleni needed to return her mother's car. People had dinners to prepare, houses to straighten up, children to put down for their naps. All around Chelsea life was moving on, spinning like the wheels of a car. But Chelsea felt her own wheels spinning in the air.

Going nowhere.

And she worried that she would never connect with the earth again.

She couldn't touch the truth inside her, and that was scary.

How could she not remember? She was there, right? Why couldn't she piece the details of that night together? The only things she could pull out of the void were a bright yellow outfit, a pig-out on muffins, and a disorienting phone call from her sister.

Some people thought it was a cover-up, a wild goose chase to distract from the fact that she'd killed her own baby.

Grace's partner was clearly in that court. Chelsea had formed an attachment to Grace, but the woman's partner was a different story. Detective Panteleoni watched her like an irate principal, as if he were just waiting to catch her doing something wrong.

When Helen Rosekind left, Chelsea saw Detective Panteleoni intercept her in the driveway and walk with her to her car. He'd been grilling her, interviewing and interrogating. Had he asked her about Chelsea's inclination to neglect her daughter?

Or maybe Helen was a suspect? She imagined Helen stealing off with Annabelle in her arms, but the image was incongruous. Helen Rosekind was supremely professional, all about changing diapers, tidying up, and making money. It was hard to imagine her doing anything that would threaten her professional license.

No . . . Detective Panteleoni is probably just collecting evidence against me, Chelsea thought.

Proof of all the ways she was a terrible mother.

Chapter 36

"Who do we have an appointment with?" Chris asked as he drove toward Larchmont, the location of the agency Helen Rosekind used to book her nursing services.

"The manager of the agency, Iris Cantor. She might be the owner, too. It sounds like a small operation."

"I'm telling you, that Nurse Rosekind isn't quite so rosy," Chris said. "When I tried to make small talk with her, she cut me off at the knees. Said she was in a hurry."

"I had the same experience with her," Grace said. "She's a cold fish."

"And get this . . . I walk her to her car, an old Honda Civic, and there's a child safety seat in the backseat. The backwards kind, for a little baby. I asked her if she had a kid, and she said no. So I asked her what the seat was for. She said that sometimes clients ask her to transport their baby to doctor's visits or outings, stuff like that. What do you think about that?"

Grace mulled it over. "It sounds reasonable. If she's a full-time baby nurse, I suppose she would need a way to safely transport the baby in an emergency."

"She's no fan of Chelsea Maynard. The woman tried to be discreet. Said she felt bad for the mother, but if you read between the lines, she's pointing a big fat finger at the baby's mother."

Grace frowned. Chris had been wanting to charge the mother

since this thing began. "What's Nurse Wretched saying about Chelsea?"

"Rosekind feels sorry for her, but she says Maynard is unstable. She wasn't able to handle the baby. I have to say, I think she's got a good point."

"That seems too simple to me."

"Sometimes it's that simple. And yeah, I think we should talk to the DA about charging her."

"Based on what the baby nurse thinks? What we really need is a break in the circle of people around Annabelle Green. I feel like we've been so busy chasing our tails that we're missing someone who is right in front of us. Like Raquel Jarvis—that Brazilian woman with the immigration issues. You know, I might get my friend at the FBI to see what he can find on her."

Chris winced. "The FBI? Do you really want to open that can of worms?"

"Jimmy is a good guy; he wouldn't step all over the investigation."

"He works for the FBI now."

"And we're coming up on forty-eight hours with Annabelle missing. We could use some help. I'm wondering if Jarvis is one of those women who has always longed for a big family. Maybe it was a simple impulse. She heard baby Annabelle howling out in the driveway and she picked her up. She took her home to warm up . . . took her inside . . . and then found it impossible to let go."

"Mmm . . . I still want to blame the mother."

"Mother hater."

"Actually, I worked through that in therapy." Chris grinned as he turned into a small parking lot of a four-story office building that seemed tired and dusty.

The RN agency was small—three employees and two shared offices—and Grace had been correct about Megan, whose eyes returned to the screen of her cell phone anytime she was not being addressed by the office manager.

Iris Cantor cut a nice appearance in a black pencil skirt and a polka-dot sweater set. She had them sit in the stern steel-and-navy-blue chairs in the waiting area, and instead of inviting them into the other office, she pulled up a chair for herself. Glancing into the next room, where a woman talked on the phone behind a pile of manila folders, Grace suspected there was no room to meet inside.

"So what's this all about?" Iris asked. "Megan said you're investigating one of our nurses?"

"Not exactly." Grace noticed that Megan didn't miss a beat texting at the mention of her name. "We're just looking for some background information on one of your nurses. Helen Rosekind."

"What kind of information?"

"A copy of her state license would be a start," Chris said. "We weren't able to verify that she's licensed to work in the state."

Iris twisted around toward the receptionist. "Megan, would you please pull Helen Rosekind's file for me?"

The young woman nodded. "Where would that be?"

"Under Rosekind in the personnel files." When Megan's face remained blank, she added, "Those black file cabinets inside."

While Megan went to fetch the file, Iris assured them that all their hires were background checked and fingerprinted. "And we make sure their certifications are up to date. That's the service we provide for our clients. When they book a sitter through us, they're paying extra, but they can rest assured that they're getting a licensed nurse with a clean record."

Megan returned with the file, looking proud as a squirrel who'd found an acorn she'd buried.

"Let's see." Iris leafed through the file. "Helen has worked for us for twelve years. Wow. She was here before I took over the agency. She gets excellent ratings from clients. I see a copy of her state nursing license here. Yes . . . everything seems to be in order."

Grace was skeptical. "The nursing license. What's the date on that?"

Iris pursed her lips. "Let's see. It's 2007."

"And in New York State, a nursing license has to be renewed every three years," Grace said. "Sounds like Helen Rosekind is behind on her renewal."

"You're right." The woman sighed. "She may have renewed it and forgot to update our files."

"I don't think so, since the Board of Nursing doesn't have her on their registry," Grace said.

"Doesn't someone in your office keep on top of certifications?" Chris asked.

"Absolutely." Iris called into the second office. "Tina? Do you want to come out here and tell us how you handle the certifications?"

Moving slowly, the woman circled the desk and paused in the doorway. "I don't do the certifications. That was always Sarah's job."

Iris rolled her eyes.

"Can we talk to Sarah?" Chris asked.

Iris shook her head. "She's been gone for at least six months." She twisted around to pin down the other two women. "Who's going to keep up with this?"

"I was supposed to be trained for it," Megan said, her wide eyes playing dramatic innocence. "But no one ever showed me how to do it."

"Ms. Cantor? Can we take a look at Helen Rosekind's records?"

Iris Cantor's reluctance to share information faded in the face of her agency's incompetence. She handed the file over.

Grace opened it and held it so that Chris could see.

The records were not what Grace had expected.

"According to this, Helen Rosekind is in her mid-sixties," Chris said.

"That must be a mistake." Grace pictured the woman in Chelsea's house. Her skin was smooth; no lines around the eyes. "The woman we met today isn't a day over forty."

"The records must be wrong."

"Nope. According to this, Rosekind passed her state nursing boards more than forty years ago. She can't be forty now, unless she was a high-achieving infant."

"Looks like Nurse Rosekind took a drink from the fountain of youth," Chris said. "Either that, or the woman we met today is not Helen Rosekind."

"Who did you meet today?" Iris asked.

Grace was busy copying information into her iPhone as Chris explained that they had thought they'd been speaking to Helen Rosekind, but it appeared that someone had been posing as her.

"You mean I've been scammed?" Iris asked.

"That's exactly what we're trying to find out," Chris said as they headed out the door.

"Do you have an address for Rosekind?" Chris asked as they got into his car.

"She gave the agency a PO box." They could get a subpoena, but that would take some time.

As Chris drove, Grace called the phone number Helen Rosekind had given her that morning. The call went through to electronic voice mail, saying that Clive Delgado was not available. "Wrong number," Grace said. She checked the file from the agency; the number the woman had given her was off by one digit.

"Now that's just rude. Did she think I wouldn't find the number from the agency?" she said, quickly dialing the correct number. This time she got a generic voice mail message.

"Let's go back to the precinct." Chris made a quick right on red. "We can try the reverse directories."

While Chris tried to track down Helen Rosekind's address using the databases in the office, Grace did a wider search of Helen Rosekind. When she went back past five years, she started getting some hits on the sixty-seven-year-old Rosekind. Married to Ira Rosekind. Her name came up in newspaper articles as a member of the board for a local children's hospital, along with the photo of a silver-haired woman with a benevolent smile.

When a black-and-white photo of a smiling woman with a fifties bob came up beside an obituary, Grace let out a gust of breath. "The real Helen Rosekind does not have a criminal past," she said, "but she doesn't have a future, either."

"What's that?" Chris asked.

"Her death certificate. Nurse Helen Rosekind is dead."

Chapter 37

It was like a scene from a cozy TV drama, with a fire lit in the living room and Leo cooking in the kitchen.

Anyone watching would never guess that they were missing their baby.

Chelsea dropped her book on the kitchen table and took a seat. She needed to be near Leo in the sweet smell of rolls baking in the oven, the warmth of pots on the stove. The pasta water started to boil over, and Leo adjusted the lid without missing a beat in his conversation.

"No, Dad, Chelsea didn't see anything." Leo wore his headset so he could cook hands-free. "She just didn't. She was asleep." He paced away from the stove, grabbed a bag of Italian cheeses from the fridge, and tossed a handful into the Florentine sauce.

He was making Chelsea's favorite dish—turkey meatballs with spinach in a white cheese sauce—and she hadn't even asked him for it. Ordinarily, the smells would have drawn her to the stove to sample the sauce, but food was just a staple now—a bitter pill to swallow. A way to stay healthy until Annabelle was back.

"Dad, I wasn't here and Chelsea was asleep. It just happened, and we're doing everything we can to work with the police to find Annabee."

Chelsea put her head down on her book, its cover smooth

and cool against her cheek. She could imagine Mitchell Green's rapid-fire questions, and she was glad she couldn't hear them. Similar questions still echoed through her mind, refusing to be silenced. Doubt was an oily sheen over her conscience, preventing any sense of peace from soaking in.

"Tell your dad I said hi," Chelsea said, lifting her head. Sometimes an interruption got her father-in-law off the path of interrogation. Thankfully, her own father had been quiet but supportive. He had offered to fly up from Florida, but with his bad hip, she couldn't imagine him hobbling onto a plane right now.

"Chelsea's right here. She says hello." Leo cocked an eyebrow at her and she made the signal for *cut*. "And I've got to get going, or I'll burn the sauce."

She looked down at the book, *Your Baby's First Year*. Before Annie's birth, she had read the entire thing through. Now, she'd checked in every few weeks to refresh her memory. Leo was fascinated by how Annie's behaviors matched the descriptions of development. "You're a textbook baby!" he always said when she squeezed his finger or followed him around the room with her eyes.

And now, Annie was coming up on four months. They would be able to try her on solid foods for the first time, since she had good head and neck control. At last, they could sit her in the high chair. Chelsea thought about bringing the chair out of the closet and setting it at the end of the table. Would that be a good omen—a positive step toward bringing her home—or a reminder of the terrible limbo they were all in?

"We're just about ready to plate it." Leo poured the pasta into a drainer and stepped back from the steam. Usually, he called, "Facial!" and they both laughed at the silliness of it. Someday, Annie would laugh along with them.

She would be back. Most stolen babies made it home safely . . . in the cases when they were stolen.

"What are you reading there?" Leo asked.

She lifted the cover of the book to show him and his brows sank down. "Do you think that's a good idea?"

"She's going to be four months soon. I want to know what she's doing."

Whether she's with us or not.

He turned back to the stove. "What does it say?"

"At four months the baby can try solid food. And one of the big milestones is communication. She'll begin to notice when people are around her, and she'll respond to their actions."

"She's already doing that," Leo said. "Do you remember last weekend when I had her on the kitchen counter in her bucket seat, and I was doing peekaboo?"

"You kept hiding behind the fry pan."

He nodded. "It cracked her up. She definitively gets it."

"And she smiled." That cherubic smile, her eyes lit with glee. At that moment Chelsea could see Annie's face so vividly. She could imagine the chubby folds of her arms and imagine her sweet scent.

Earlier, while the plumber had been working on the valve in the bathroom, Chelsea had gone into Annie's room and closed the door. The need for Annie had been like a physical craving, primal and pure.

In the closet, she had pulled the little hanging outfits together and pressed them to her face. The baby powder smell of Purex was sweet, but it wasn't Annie.

She had felt her way around the room, trying to find something that reminded her of Annie. A picture, a stuffed animal, the musical chime on the mobile over the crib.

How strange to know that these weren't Annabelle's things. Not really. It was a room designed for a baby, but the collection of books, the squishy blocks, and the white pine crib might have belonged to any infant.

In the end she had curled up in the corner on the snowy carpet they'd had cleaned in preparation for Annabelle starting to crawl. Huddled in a ball, she stared up at the green elephants marching across the wall.

Had Annie stared up at those elephants from her crib?

Did she know that elephant girls spent their entire lives in a tightly knit family?

"Elephant mom bats her eyes, telling her baby to reach for the sky."

Chelsea helped Leo with the dishes. As she stowed the meatballs and washed the pot in soapy water, she realized that it had been months since she had stood at the sink beside her husband.

"I've been so out of it," she said. "You've been doing all of this stuff since Annie was born. If I were you, I'd be annoyed with me."

"Nah. You had your issues." He dried the plastic sauce spoon and shoved it in the holder. "But I'm glad you're back."

The phone rang, and they both turned to check the caller ID. Grace Santos.

A knot twisted painfully in Chelsea's stomach as Leo nodded toward the phone. "Go ahead."

Her mouth was dry. "Grace, have you found her?"

"Not yet, but I did get the lab report back, and I know you and Leo will want to hear this. The muffins checked out fine, but the frosting was laced with a strong sedative."

"What?" When Leo turned to her, she pressed the speakerphone button. "I've got you on speaker, Grace. Leo is here."

"I was just saying that the baked goods left on your porch contained a sedative. A prescription sleep medication, and plenty of it."

"Really." Leo winced. "So someone planned this. Someone set Chelsea up."

"It appears that way."

Chelsea's throat grew tight as the truth set in. Someone had drugged her and then stolen her baby while she was asleep. She hadn't acted out one of her dark visions from the postpartum depression insanity.

"So it was the drugs . . . that's why I didn't hear the intruder. That's why I can't remember where I left Annie or how I got to bed."

"Memory loss can be a side effect of this type of drug. Dizziness, disorientation. Some people report sleepwalking, even episodes where they get in the car and drive without knowing how they got there."

Leo came up behind her and gently pulled her against him. "I guess the next question is, who would do this to Chelsea?"

"And what kind of person masterminds a kidnapping this way? I mean, what does it mean about our chances of finding Annie?"

"This type of planning is typical of an infant abductor," Grace said. "It helps to fill out the profile of our suspect. I just wish the fingerprints at the scene were more definitive. Right now there are some partial prints that we haven't been able to identify."

It wasn't really an answer to her question, but Chelsea was getting used to hearing the detective think out loud. Grace went on to mention something being off with Helen Rosekind's credentials. They were still investigating it, but had trouble reaching Helen. Leo passed on her contact number, and they ended the call.

"I will never eat another muffin again," Chelsea vowed.

"I'm glad Grace figured out why you couldn't remember that night," Leo said, "but this is really scary. What if you'd eaten all the muffins?"

"There's too much trauma going on now to play the 'what if' game."

"You're right." Leo's arms tightened around her, and she leaned into him, feeling loved and secure.

"What do you think she's doing now?" Chelsea asked. "I keep worrying that she's not being fed or changed."

"I know. I hope someone's talking to her . . . holding her. Or maybe not. Maybe it's better for her to get really annoyed with them. She has that angry face now, right? She should lay that on the kidnapper, with one of those shrieking wails that can take the paint off a wall."

Thoughts of the baby made her aware of the heaviness in her breasts. "I need to pump again."

"Okay, Chels." Leo placed a kiss on her cheek and his arms fell away.

Sitting on the bed upstairs, with the machine humming, she tried to relax at the thought of Annie's little laugh, which they'd be hearing more of, come the fourth month.

If we get you back, I'll make sure you laugh every day, Chelsea promised. *Things will be different.*

The ritual of expressing milk had become Chelsea's own vigil to draw her daughter back to her. If she kept producing milk, Annabelle would return. Those bottles lined up in the fridge, carefully labeled and dated, would not go to waste.

When she finished, she carefully labeled the bottle and carried it down to the kitchen to store it. Leo was putting away the dry pots as she leaned into the fridge and blinked.

The bottles were gone.

"Leo?" She shuddered as betrayal chilled her veins. "I had seven or eight bottles in here . . . what happened to them?"

Chapter 38

"Did you enjoy your time with your dad?" she asked. "You know I didn't want to leave you, but it's good for a baby to be with her daddy, too."

Annabelle twisted away from the voice, her face puckering. She was tired and hungry and the sweet voice wasn't helping either of those things. She whimpered, clawed at her chin, whimpered again.

"I know you're hungry." The woman pressed the nipple to her lips. "Drink up, little one. This is much better for you than the formula you've been getting."

Annabelle frowned when her lips were teased with the rubber nub. This wasn't good and familiar. It was too hard, attached to something even harder and colder.

"Come on." The voice was patient. "You must be hungry."

The baby attached her lips to the cold nub and began to suck.

"That's it." The woman wriggled into a different position, not so comfortable for the baby, who had to stretch her neck to get the bottle.

"Is it yummy? This is what you need."

Her face, at the end of the long shaft of the bottle, was familiar. Round eyes and a shiny nose the baby could almost reach out and grasp. She had lips, too, but the baby rarely saw them smiling like the big smile that sang to her each night. A low, rumbly voice that made her smile, too.

"And just so you know, I thought of everything. Those first two bottles? Poured them down the drain, just in case there was any trace of the sedative left." Her big eyes came close. "I can't have my baby girl getting anything that might hurt her."

Annabelle blinked. This was different, and she missed the warm, soft body she always melted into at feeding time.

"Drink up now, baby girl. It's mother's milk. Very good for you," she said as Annabelle looked at her sternly. "Probably the only good thing she ever gave you."

Chapter 39

"So, best case scenario, what is this old man going to tell us?" Chris asked as they waited for Ira Rosekind to appear in the reception area of the assisted living facility.

"All about Helen Rosekind." Grace smiled at an older woman who walked past at a good clip. "We know she's not the woman who was providing nursing services for Annabelle Green, but maybe there's a link between Rosekind and the woman operating under her nursing credentials. If the sitter is faking it, she must have gotten Rosekind's credentials somehow. Maybe they met. It's worth a shot."

"You know, we should have thought of the baby nurse earlier," Chris said. "That's part of the profile in a lot of infant abductions. They pose as medical personnel."

"You're right."

"A little late to be right. I have this weakness with doctors and nurses. I tend to trust them," Chris said, a wry look on his face as he watched a nurse in formfitting white pants push a wheelchair toward them.

The man in the chair was hunched over but alert, his eyes shining behind silver spectacles.

"This is Mr. Rosekind," the nurse said.

"Ira Rosekind. And I gotta say, I don't get visits from police detectives every day. Tongues are going to be wagging around here."

Grace was charmed by his begrudging smile. "Mr. Rosekind, thank you for seeing us. We have a few questions about your wife, Helen."

"May she rest in peace. Or are you here to tell me she faked her death and ran off to Tahiti with a younger man?"

Chris shot the man a grin. "Is that what you suspect?"

"Ach! No." Ira waved off the notion. "I was there when she passed. My Helen is gone. That's why I'm wondering why you're here." He cocked his head. "Why are you here?"

"We're trying to locate an infant who's been abducted," Grace said. No need to beat around the bush.

The old man squinted. "The Annabelle Green case? I saw that on television. That's a terrible thing. What does my Helen have to do with that?"

"It appears that the woman who's worked as a baby nurse for this nice couple has been posing as your wife," Grace explained.

"Is that right?" He shook his head. "I have to say, that part doesn't surprise me. Some shyster stole Helen's identity after she died. How's that for the bottom of the barrel? Stealing from the dead!"

"How'd you find out about it?" Chris asked.

"Some credit card companies had the nerve to send me the bills. They made threatening phone calls, too, but I didn't let them scare me. My daughter fixed it. She got a lawyer, who told the bill collectors to cease and desist."

"Do you know if an investigation was done?" Grace asked.

"We reported it to the police. Whatever they did with it, I couldn't tell you."

The pieces were falling into place. If the baby nurse went so far out of her way to forge her credentials, chances were that the identity theft was a building block for the bigger crime of kidnapping.

"Mr. Rosekind, you've been very helpful," Grace said as they began to wrap things up. "Just one more question. Your wife worked as a baby nurse for many years."

"That's right. Helen loved the little ones."

"Do you remember if she had any complaints from customers? Any lawsuits against her?"

"No, nothing." He shook his head. "Everyone loved Helen, and her reputation was impeccable. Did you know she was on the board of the Mount Oliver Children's Hospital?"

"I happened to read an article about that," Grace said. "Sounds like she was a lovely woman."

"She was. A good woman with a big heart," he said, staring off down the hall. "I still miss her."

"I'm glad Ira Rosekind refused to give in to the bill collectors," Grace told Chris as they crossed the parking lot. "It really pisses me off when people prey on the elderly."

"Next stop, the baby nurse's apartment?" Chris asked. He had found an address in Eastchester using a reverse phone directory.

"Let's hope that it's the right address and that she's home," Grace said.

Just as Grace buckled her seat belt, her cell phone rang. "Leo Green," she said, reading the display.

The man sounded frazzled. "Chelsea is freaking out, and I don't blame her. Since Annie disappeared, she's been pumping breast milk and storing it in the fridge. Now suddenly it's all gone."

"Gone . . ." Grace squinted. "You mean the bottles are gone from the fridge?"

"All of them. Someone took them. It must have been one of the people visiting today."

"And you weren't there for most of the time." Grace got out her iPhone. "Can I talk to Chelsea? I need to know exactly who came into your house today."

Chelsea came to the phone, and though her voice was a bit shaky, she made an effort to stay calm. Her first visitor was her friend Sasha Barton, but Chelsea added a bottle to the refrigerator long after Sasha left. Then came Emma and Melanie and Melanie's kids. Eleni Zika and Helen Rosekind. The two neighbors, Raquel Jarvis with her kids, and the older gentle-man . . . Chelsea took a deep breath, trying to remember his name.

"Kellog," Grace interrupted. "Like the cereal. That's how I remembered."

"Right. Joseph Kellog. And Leo and me, of course. You and Detective Panteleoni. Was there anyone else? There were just so many people coming and going."

"That's okay. You can call me if you remember any others, okay?"

"Wait—the plumber was here. He fixed the valve upstairs. His name was Mark . . . from Triple A Plumbing."

"Okay, we'll add him to the list." *It's going to be a woman,* Grace thought. *Probably someone you know.* The plumber was a dark horse, but Grace added the man's name.

"Do you think the person who stole the milk is giving it to Annie?" Chelsea asked.

"I'd say that's likely."

"I can't believe this. If that's not a gutsy move, coming in here and stealing right from under my nose."

Grace could feel the woman's panic. "Chelsea, I know this must be a torturous situation for you, but I think this is a good development. The abductor has revealed herself by taking that milk. It's got to be someone who was in your house today. That narrows it down to about half a dozen suspects."

"And my two sisters are on the list."

"I know." Grace frowned. "We have to consider every pos-sibility."

"We need to find Annabelle," Chelsea said. "Can't you bring them all in for questioning? Or . . . or go to their houses and do a search."

"There are a few constitutional amendments standing in the way of that."

"Find Annabelle, please."

"We will." Grace looked up and saw that they were cruising slowly down a block of small Dutch Colonials.

"It's six-two-five," Chris said.

"I have to go," Grace told Chelsea. "Hang in there. I'll call you later."

She studied the house, its two upper-story windows resembling brooding eyes. "Looks too small to be a rental."

"In this part of New York, people will sublet a closet."

Chris paused over by the garbage cans beside the front porch.

"What is it?" Grace asked.

He slid a folded carton out from between the house and a plastic can. "Two boxes for baby stuff. A car seat and . . ." He turned to read the side of the box in the dim light from the streetlamp. "A stroller."

Grace sighed. "I want to get real excited right now, but I don't want to assume anything."

"I'm reserving my happy dance for when we find the baby."

Grace noticed ice at the corners of the porch stairs. No one had bothered to properly shovel, but she hoped it would all be gone soon, melted in the spring thaw. She turned to the door as Chris leaped up the stairs. "Two doorbells," she said. "Which one?"

"We'll try them both." Chris pressed the buttons, and a buzz sounded nearby in the house.

Immediately, the cry of a baby rent the cool air. Grace felt her heart leap in her chest. Could it be?

The porch light went on, and a moment later the door was opened by a man wearing a Giants sweatshirt and jeans. The rattling cry of the baby was louder with the downstairs door open.

"Can I help you?" the man asked. He seemed to be in his late twenties, with olive skin and dark eyes that, Grace thought, were either tired or very sexy, depending on how you looked at it.

Grace and Chris identified themselves and showed the man their IDs. "Sorry to bother you, sir," Grace said, "but we're looking for Helen Rosekind."

He squinted. "Who?"

When she repeated the name, he shook his head. "I dunno. It could be the upstairs tenants."

Chris pointed toward the upper story. "They're named Rosekind?"

The man scratched his jaw. "I dunno. Kiki, what's the name of the people upstairs? Rosekind?"

"That's it," a woman's voice called out from the open door of the apartment. "It's rose-something."

The woman's voice was low, with a thick New York accent—not Helen Rosekind's voice.

"Hello in there? Do you mind?" Grace asked the man as she stepped into the vestibule.

A young African American woman emerged from the apartment, a tiny baby in her arms. The woman's short, thick hair was scraped back with a band, accenting her high cheekbones and amber eyes. The baby shared her warm brown complexion and wide nose.

"What a cutie," Grace said. "Sorry if we woke the baby."

Disappointment stabbed at Grace as she and Chris made small talk with the couple, Kiki and Alex Trevino, obviously the owners of the baby paraphernalia that belonged to the boxes outside. The Trevinos didn't know the upstairs tenants well; the woman and her husband had just moved in three months ago. He was a truck driver, gone for long periods of time.

"Do you know if she's a baby nurse?" Grace asked.

"We really don't see her much," the woman said. "She hardly ever leaves the apartment, and he's never home. Always doing a truck run. But I did see her wearing scrubs once or twice. I thought it was sort of like her pajamas, but she went off in her car that way."

"Is she home now?"

"I think so," Kiki said. "I heard the television."

Grace looked up the long flight of stairs. "You don't mind if we go up and knock upstairs?"

Alex shrugged. "You're the cops, right? You got E-ZPass."

No one answered the door of the upstairs apartment.

Grace knocked again, identifying herself as a police officer. She and Chris were both leaning against the wall, as if they would park here until they had a better idea, when the chain lock on the door rattled.

Grace blinked as the apartment door opened and Helen Rosekind stood there in a bathrobe.

"Mrs. Rosekind . . . or is that really your name?" Grace said carefully, studying the woman's face for signs of nervousness. She seemed calm, maybe a little annoyed.

"You are one hard woman to find," Chris said. "Do you mind if we come in for a few minutes?"

"Not now. My husband is sleeping."

"And he works shifts," Chris said. "A truck driver, right?"

"Yes. You've done your research."

"You don't make it easy," Chris said.

"I'm a private person," she said, stepping forward and pulling the door nearly closed behind her. "Is that a crime?"

Grace got a chance to see that the dining room was set up like an office, with a computer desk, a headset attached to the computer, and a file cabinet. Probably Helen's home office for her nine-to-five consulting job. There were boxes stacked by one wall, and the television was on, loud enough to be heard from the hallway.

"No crime in that," Grace said. "But identity theft? And practicing without a license? That can get you in hot water."

"What are you talking about? I'm Helen Rosekind."

"We checked at your agency. The license they have on file for you belonged to a woman in her sixties who is currently dead. She's the real Helen Rosekind. So who are you?"

"Don't tell me that." She rolled her eyes. "I don't know where they got that information, but I am not in my sixties, and I'm not dead."

"We can see that. But you have no license on record. So you've been practicing without a license."

"Of course I'm licensed, just not in the state of New York," she said. "Rosekind is my husband's name. That agency must have made a mistake, and it wouldn't be the first time. My nursing license is from Arizona."

"Arizona? So what brings you here?" Chris asked.

The woman held up a hand, as if she had no patience for small talk. "I'm not licensed as a nurse here, but infant care is the same from one state to the other. I make sure to tell all my clients, but so far no one has cared as long as I'm on time and capable of caring for their baby. Sometimes, young couples are so desperate to get out and so overwhelmed with child care, they don't process details like that."

"So if we do a search in the Arizona bureau of records, we'll find you there?"

"Under my maiden name. Sometimes I still use my maiden name. Hold on one second." She slipped back into the apartment, closing the door behind her. A moment later she reappeared with an Arizona driver's license issued to Helen Janet Walker.

"How long have you lived in the state of New York, Ms. Walker?" Grace asked.

Helen tightened the belt of her robe. "Three years."

"And you didn't get your driver's license switched over?"

"Why should I pay a fee for that? It's still valid."

Chris scratched his head. "You know you're not supposed to use two names. That's establishing an alias. And I still can't believe the employment agency let you go on the record as Helen Rosekind. That's irresponsible of both of you."

Helen seemed offended. "The agency will have to answer for itself. Besides, that work is just a part-time thing, and I'm an excellent nurse. I would never compromise patient care."

Grace suspected that, at the very least, the woman was taking the freelance money on the side, not declaring it in her taxes. But she would be sure to check out Helen J. Walker with the Arizona Board of Nursing and the Arizona DMV.

"How about your nine-to-five job?" Chris asked. "Do they fudge the records, too?"

"First of all, I'm an insurance consultant and I don't need

nursing certification for that job. And really, is this what you do? Is it standard practice for you to come to my door at eight thirty at night and interrogate me about my employment records?"

"You know why we're here." Grace's gaze locked on the woman's cold gray eyes. "We're trying to find Annabelle Green, Helen. We think you can help us."

Green folded her arms across her chest. "I don't know where Chelsea Maynard's baby is, but she's probably a lot better off away from that young lady. She's not mentally competent."

"That's not for us to decide," Grace said. "Bottom line? You've broken the law, plain and simple. Now I'd be willing to look the other way if you help us find this baby."

Helen squinted at Grace as if she were insane. "I can't help you," she said sternly. "And don't bother me again tonight. Anything else can wait until the morning."

With that, she opened the door and disappeared inside.

As the latch clicked shut, Grace wanted to argue that this could not wait, but she knew it would gain her no ground.

Helen J. Walker was cold as the ice on the corners of her doorstep.

Chapter 40

Chelsea already had her coat on when she handed Leo the car keys. "Get me out of here." There was a gray cast to her eyes, and even though her hair was pulled back harshly, the soft lines of her jaw were childlike and vulnerable.

He would have done anything to end her pain.

He took the keys and pulled his leather jacket from the hook. "Where are we going?"

"I don't care, as long as it's out of here. I can't spend another night waiting for her. I need to search or spy on the neighbors or something that feels productive."

He got that. Despite their quiet dinner, the gap between them and Annie seemed to be growing wider. Hope and panic were twisting into a tight braid of desperation. "Okay. Let's go."

They started in the neighborhood, their headlights scanning only the black asphalt as they cruised slowly, block by block. Chelsea stared out intently, her fingernails scratching at her cuticles as she searched for God knew what. A sign that something was amiss? An older woman pushing a stroller in the cold?

Leo knew the headlights trailing behind them were reporters. He had seen them looking out from the front seat of a van as he and Chelsea went to their car in the driveway. Two others had scurried from the sidewalk to a car, watching to see what Chelsea and Leo were doing.

When they had circled around eight blocks or so and returned to Maple Lane, Leo thought they might return home, but she grabbed his arm before they got to their house.

"Stop here. I've got to talk to these people—the Wilkinsons. The police think the person who stole Annie parked here."

"But the police have already talked with them."

"I know, but I haven't."

She was out of the car before Leo could even put it into park. He jogged up the sidewalk behind her, a little surprised that she had the nerve to ring a stranger's bell at night.

"Chels, we don't even know these people. They might not open their doors after dark."

"But they have to talk to us. We're their neighbors."

A light went on in the front room and the curtain shifted.

"Hello?" Chelsea called. "It's Chelsea Maynard and Leo Green. Your neighbors. Our baby Annabelle is missing."

The door opened. Light spilled out when a woman with short-cropped white hair pushed open the storm door. "What's going on?" she asked, her fingers worrying a string of pearls at her neck.

"We need to talk to you," Chelsea said. "The last place our baby was seen was in front of your house."

"That's why you were shouting?" Mrs. Wilkinson squinted, assessing Chelsea. "Well, I can't say that I blame you. Come in. Get out of that terrible cold."

In minutes, the Wilkinsons seemed like family—the good kind that shared comfort and concerns and tips on how to bet in the Giants' Sunday game. Tina Wilkinson made tea, and her husband, James, turned off the television in the little side den and came over to join them. They sat in the Wilkinsons' formal living area, a room so pristine Leo could see the tracks of the vacuum on the carpet, and talked about the neighborhood, the Wilkinsons' children, who were all grown with children of their own, and the terrible thing that had happened to Annie-bananee.

"The night she disappeared," Chelsea said, her voice ragged

with emotion, "do you remember hearing anyone? Or maybe you noticed a car parked in front of your house."

"It's not something we would notice, dear," Tina said. "We have one car and we park it in the garage. I never was one for those street wars over who owned parking spots."

"I wish we could help you," James said, his hand quivering as he reached for his teacup. "It's a terrible thing, this kidnapping. I never dreamed something like that would happen in our neighborhood."

Leo nodded in agreement. He had never imagined something this terrible could happen to him—not in his worst nightmares.

When they left the Wilkinsons', Leo suggested that they leave the car and walk home, but she tipped her head up to the starry sky and said no.

"We have another stop to make," she said, opening the passenger-side door. "I need to drop in on Emma and Jake."

He glanced at the clock on the dash. "This late? Why don't you just call her back?" Chelsea had been avoiding both her sisters' calls, feeling awkward and sick about the fact that her sisters were suspects as far as the police were concerned.

"I can't do this over the phone," Chelsea said. "Please? It won't take long."

"No problem." As they buckled their seat belts, he thought what a ruse that expression was. You say "No problem" when there are dozens of problems. Someone removes the floor from under you, and you fall through darkness for hours, shitting yourself over the moment when you'll smash and splatter on the ground.

"Sorry," they say.

And your only answer is, "No problem."

Chapter 41

"**Y**ou are kidding me." Emma's eyes opened wide with wonder and horror. "Someone stole your milk?" She tucked her legs under her as she settled into a sleek upholstered chair. "Today? While everyone was there?"

"Sometime this afternoon," Chelsea said, watching her sister carefully. She believed in Emma's innocence. She would vouch for Melanie, too. But right now she needed to move rationally, without prejudice. She figured she could help eliminate her sisters from the list, narrowing things down for the detectives.

"Did you tell the police?" Jake asked.

"As soon as Chelsea figured it out. They wanted a list of everyone who was in the house this afternoon."

"Someone must have cleared out the fridge when no one was looking," Chelsea said, watching her sister. Something about Emma had changed; her face was softer, her eyes were round as quarters, and she seemed relaxed. It was as if she had finally grown comfortable in her own skin.

"Did you see anyone rooting around in there?" Chelsea asked.

Emma shook her head. "I didn't notice, but I was in the living room most of the time. I spent hours on the floor with Sam and Lucy and Max."

"Who went into the kitchen?" Leo asked.

"Everyone was in the kitchen." Emma hugged a cheetah-print pillow to her chest. "We'd put out bagels and fruit salad, and people were getting coffee and tea."

"And it's not like you could hide the bottles in your pocket. How do you walk out with eight bottles of milk?"

"Stash them in a bag," Jake said. "Did anyone have a back-pack?"

Chelsea nodded. "Eleni carries one, but so does every teenager in New York."

"That nurse had a big tote bag," Emma said. "I remember how she whipped out that fruit for you."

"Helen Rosekind and her fruit," Chelsea said. "Nothing says you're fat like a gift of apples."

"Don't take it personally," Emma said. "I brought fruit salad."

In two big grocery bags, Chelsea thought. Had everyone come with some sort of baggage that could have been used to sneak the bottles out? Raquel Jarvis had that colorful woven satchel she'd used to carry the black bean soup. Melanie's kids had toy bags and mini-suitcases. Mr. Kellog was just about the only one who had come in empty-handed.

As discussion of that afternoon's visitors went on, Chelsea felt her resolve to confront her sister fading. What had seemed logical an hour ago now seemed petty in the warm light of Emma and Jake's living room. The idea of Emma and Jake taking Annabelle to Chicago and passing her off as their kid—that was plain lunacy. For one thing, Jake was a lawyer. He wouldn't jeopardize his career by being an accomplice to kid-napping.

There was also the logistical issue of keeping Annabelle from the rest of the family. It would be impossible.

But mostly, Emma was her sister, and despite all the hair pulling, taunting, and infuriating arguments in their past, there was the tough, steady bond of family between them.

When their conversation went to Jake's prospective job in Chicago, she was reminded that Emma and Jake had an early flight in the morning. She slipped away and ventured down the hall to the bathroom. After this, she and Leo would go home. It would be inconsiderate to keep Emma up after the scary episode she'd had earlier this week; she needed her sleep.

The floors had recently been redone in a warm, gleaming teak, and as Chelsea made her way down the hall, she felt that familiar hook of envy. With Jake's salary and bonuses from the firm, Emma could have just about anything she wanted. No waiting to remodel the house. No qualms about asking for diamond earrings for Christmas.

Inside the powder room, the granite counter gleamed. The flecks of garnet in its travertine veins matched the oil-rubbed bronze fixtures. Chelsea sighed as she lathered up her hands. Maybe she was just a tad jealous of Emma's nice things.

As she stepped out of the powder room, a soft light coming from the guest room caught her eye. The light cast an odd shadow on the shiny wood floor—the parallel lines of bars.

A baby's crib.

A sick curiosity pounded in her chest as her socks whispered along the hall floor.

She paused in the doorway, her blood gone to ice, her heart trembling in her chest.

The dark walnut crib was lit from behind by a soft nightlight, which cast the patterned shadows on the floor.

What was Emma doing with a crib so soon? She had told Chelsea that she was superstitious about those things; since the last miscarriage, she had refused to buy any baby products until her last six weeks of pregnancy.

There was something inside the crib—a small bundle of cloth the size of a baby.

A bundled-up infant.

My baby.

Oh, Emma, Emma, how could you keep her from me?

Holding her breath, Chelsea rushed forward and reached over the high wooden rail. Before she even touched the cloth, she knew it wasn't a living thing. The mound of cloth was only a baby blanket, folded and rolled.

Still, she snatched it up and unfurled it and pressed it to her face. It smelled of a synthetic fiber . . . not even laundered yet. There wasn't a hint of Annabelle's buttery skin. Not even the sweet scent of baby detergent.

The dim quiet of the room closed around her.

Empty. Just like Annie's crib.

The air leaked out of her lungs in a sad whimper as she began to take in the rest of the room. The bed had been removed. The taupe paint had been covered with a buttery shade of yellow. The upholstered chair was gone from the corner, and in its place stood a white chest of drawers, still covered in hazy plastic wrap.

Baby furniture.

Emma had started her nursery.

And I'm a fool to even be here.

How could she suspect her own sister, a person she'd slept beside for years, the girl who'd shown her how to pluck her eyebrows and told her the real deal about getting your period?

It was a reminder that she needed to get in to see Dr. Chin as soon as they found Annabelle. Medication wasn't enough. She needed some therapy—maybe a change in diet. Her pink pills were not enough; you couldn't erase depression with a chemical treatment. The panic of losing Annie has shocked her into a certain sobriety, but she wasn't out of the dark woods yet.

She balled up the blanket and shoved it back in the crib. She could imagine her sister rushing in with a rushed explanation of how she hadn't told anyone about the nursery, how she'd wanted to tell Chelsea but knew it would be insensitive in the face of what Chelsea was going through.

Right now she couldn't bear to hear that from Emma.

Sucking in the hurt and embarrassment, she headed down the hall to say good-bye.

Chapter 42

"Did you notice the boxes in Helen What's-her-name's dining room?" Grace asked Chris.

"I just got a quick look when she stepped out," he said, checking the rearview mirror. "What were they like? File boxes?"

"It could be. She works at home, and I could see a computer desk set up. But they might have been moving boxes." She clicked to play a voice mail as she stared out at the darkness beyond the car window. "I'd hate to have her slip away. That woman knows how to move around without leaving a paper trail."

"If we had more evidence, we could get a search warrant. Till then, we could just sit on her place."

"Right now surveillance seems like a waste of time, with other suspects out there." She brought up Eleni Zika's address in her iPhone. "Like Eleni Zika. Her mother left a message saying we can head over there for a chat."

"Okay," he said. "And I think we have a little time if Helen Walker is thinking about skipping out of town. People don't usually take off in their bathrobes."

"With our luck, Helen What's-her-name would be the first woman to drive a U-Haul cross-country in her pajamas."

"Hey, I'm supposed to be the sardonic one in this partnership."

"I just want all these people checked out now, and we're not going to be able to do it all tonight." Grace tucked a strand of hair behind one ear and pressed her head back against the passenger seat. "Sometimes I wish I could clone myself."

"Two Graces? That's a scary thought."

She pinged his shoulder.

"Ouch. And we're not the only game in town. You've got your boyfriend from the FBI working that Brazilian woman who stole the two kids from her ex."

"And it's a good thing. Didn't I tell you we could use their help?" She checked her messages; nothing from Jimmy. "And he's not my boyfriend. He's a married man. At least, he was when we were in the police academy."

"You were married back then, too. Things change. I'm sure it didn't work out for him. Cops make lousy mates."

"So cynical."

"That's my job. I'm the bad cop, you're the good one. Got it?"

Grace grinned as she shook her head. Panteleoni could be such a pain in the ass, but she liked working with him. The guy had no filters, but at least you knew where you stood with him.

Eleni Zika lived with her mother, Maria, in a five-story building not far from Greenwood Lake. It was a nice neighborhood with good schools and plenty of trees, but this building showed signs of age, with brick that needed painting and casement windows that were hanging on by a pinch of putty.

"I'd like to make this quick," Grace told Chris as they rode the small elevator up to the third floor.

"No argument here." He checked his watch. "You need to get home tonight?"

She shook her head. "Matt is at his friend's house again. But I want to start checking Helen Walker's records in Arizona. Something about that doesn't sit right with me. And there's the Jarvis family. We should have followed up on them earlier."

"No worries. Your buddy from the FBI is all over that," Chris teased as she rang the bell for apartment 3-H.

Maria Zika was small like her daughter, but rounder, with a hard set to her jaw and a clipped, precision haircut that emphasized her eyes. She invited them in, but didn't ask them to sit on the green velveteen couch or loveseat. Normally, Grace would have pushed for something more personal, but tonight she was tired and antsy to keep the investigation moving at a good pace.

The flat-screen TV was on *Dancing with the Stars,* and when Maria picked up the remote, someone called from the kitchen.

"Leave it on," came the voice. "I need to see this."

Grace shifted to see beyond the half wall. Eleni made eye contact, then looked down at her notebook on the table.

"She's doing homework," Maria said, turning the volume down with the remote. "They give them so much these days."

Grace nodded, glad for the common ground. "I have a twelve-year-old, and he's already doing things in algebra that make my head spin."

"Twelve is a nice age." Maria looked toward the kitchen, her dark eyes pinched with worry. "You know where they are when they leave the house."

"Mrs. Zika, we're sorry to bother you," Grace said, "but as you know, we're trying to locate a missing child. A baby that your daughter has been babysitting."

"I know that." She dropped the remote onto the sofa. "And I know she told you about the things Armand said." She lowered her voice. "That boy is a bad influence. Irresponsible and spoiled. His whole life is being handed to him, while my daughter has to learn to make a living. I don't want her to see him. No more, that's what I said. But she doesn't listen."

"You don't trust him," Chris said. "I can understand why. But do you trust your daughter?"

"I've always taught her to do the right thing. Does she sneak around with that boy? Maybe. Would she steal somebody's baby to make money? No. Never. Not my Eleni." Suddenly, her eyes filled with tears, and she hurriedly swiped them away.

Grace and Chris waited, listening against the strains of a tango.

"If you saw her when she had to give her baby up . . . after she held him, just for a minute. . . ." She took a jagged breath and swallowed hard. "To have a baby torn from your arms . . . it's not something any woman should have to bear. She doesn't talk about it, but I know it's still with her . . . in here." She bumped one fist against her chest. "That pain will always be there."

"I hear what you're saying," Grace said. "But the saving grace of pain and memory are that they both fade with time. They may never go away, but it does get easier."

Maria Zika swiped at her eyes again and nodded. "I hope you're right. It's not easy for a girl her age to come back from what she's been through. But if you think she had anything to do with taking that little Annabelle, you're wrong. She would never do that to someone else because she knows how it feels." She thumped her chest again. "She knows it in here."

"So now we're down to Helen Rosekind and Raquel Jarvis," Chris said as they pulled away from the Greenwood Lake apartments.

"That's exactly what I was thinking. But what about Chelsea's sisters?"

Chris rubbed his knuckles against the stubble on his jaw. "Nah. They seem like decent people, pretty well adjusted. I don't think either of them is our perp."

"Agreed." For Grace, the two sisters hadn't really been strong suspects. Yeah, there was a possible scenario with Emma Wyatt leaving town, but it lacked teeth. A stolen baby was not easy to pass off in a functional family, which the Maynard sisters seemed to be.

Grace had a message to call Jimmy Flannigan. "I hope he's got a break for us," she told Chris.

"Sure. Let the FBI guys breeze in and crack our case with one phone call."

Ignoring him, she called Jimmy's cell.

"Pete and I just left the Jarvises a few minutes ago," he said. "As far as we could see, they check out. Totally cooperative. Raquel and the husband showed us papers they filed with the authorities in Brazil. It looks like the father there is going to release custody. He's agreed to it in writing, but it'll take a while for all the paperwork to catch up. You know how that is. I have a call in with a friend at the State Department to see if they can verify it."

"Did you see any signs of an infant being around?"

"Not at all. We found some baby stuff in the basement, but it hadn't been used for a while. I have to say, they were really open to anything we wanted to do. We even checked the refrigerator for those missing bottles."

"That was nice of them, but they have something at stake. They don't want those kids taken away."

"True. Raquel Jarvis already lost them once. For that reason, she was very sympathetic to Chelsea Maynard's position."

"Good point." She stared out the window but could only see her own reflection against the dark glass. "Thanks, Jimmy. I appreciate the help. Sorry to keep you away from your family."

"Mmm. Not a factor. I've been on my own for a few years now."

"Really." Grace scratched the back of her neck, keeping her face toward the window so Chris couldn't see. "Same. But I've got a wonderful son. Almost thirteen."

"He must keep you busy. But I'm glad we reconnected. We should grab coffee sometime. Is there anything else I can do for you right now?"

She told him about the records that needed to be checked in Arizona. "I can get on it in the morning, but I'm thinking you might have access to their databases right now."

"Let me see what I can do," he said. "I'll let you know the minute I have something."

As soon as she ended the call, she knew Chris would have some clever comment.

"So you got your boyfriend to do the dirty work so that you could go home and get some sleep? It's a good thing you never played me like a fiddle."

"He's not my boyfriend, and I'm not going home. We're going back to the office."

"Only to get your car. You said it yourself. You're not going to reach anyone in a state office in Arizona at this time of night."

"I don't want to stop. Not till we have Annabelle Green safe in hand."

"To be continued," Chris said. "We've run every lead we have at the moment. I say we close our eyes for a few hours and reconvene in the morning."

Grace hated to admit it, but Chris was right.

"And he may not be your boyfriend yet," Chris added, "but he will be. He wants to get together, right?"

"Did you hear him on my phone?"

"No, but I know how guys are. Did he mention going for coffee?"

"Shut up and drive."

"He did!" Chris laughed. "God, I am good."

Grace got off the Hutch at the exit for home, but instead of turning left toward their town house she made a right toward the Larsens. It was almost ten o'clock, but she knew Alicia Larsen wouldn't mind, and she craved seeing her son.

It took only ten minutes to get Matt into the car, his stuff stowed in the backseat. "Mrs. Larsen said I could stay another night." There was disappointment in his voice.

"I thought it would be necessary, but I'm done for the night, and I wanted to see your smiling face." She turned to him, not at all ruffled by his pouting. "I missed you, buddy."

"We were just getting ready for bed."

"So you're not missing anything, and you can walk to school in the morning. Your usual routine." They lived just three blocks from the middle school, and Matt had insisted on walking on his own this year. Even on rainy days, when she offered to drive him, he told her that he was "one hundred percent waterproof."

Once inside the house, Grace stole a hug from him, telling him that she'd missed him and that she hoped to be finished with this case soon. After he brushed his teeth, he came to say good night.

"It's good to be home, Mom," he admitted. "I like sleeping in my own bed."

Grace had to restrain herself from tucking him in; he insisted he was too old for that now. But after she showered and changed into sweats, she peeked into his room. Matt was asleep, his body a soft crescent under the comforter.

Quietly, she moved a Frisbee and a half-built LEGO creature from the beanbag chair and sank down into it. With her feet on the floor and her hands cupped under her head as a pillow, she watched her boy sleeping.

Soon, Chelsea and Leo would be able to sleep, knowing their child was safe. They were getting closer to Annabelle—she could feel it.

When she closed her eyes, Annabelle's face filled the scope of her mind—those stern blue eyes and baby jowls. That gummy smile.

Hang on, little one. We're coming to get you.

Chapter 43

Another morning without Annie . . .
Day Three.

"Every day on this medication, I feel like I'm getting just a little bit better, gaining some ground," Chelsea told Leo.

"That's great, Chels."

"The downside is, as the dark void fades from behind my eyes, I'm beginning to see what a rotten mother I've been."

He looked up from the dishwasher. "You were never rotten. Just distracted. In pain. Distant. But not rotten."

She pulled her hands into the sleeves of Leo's oversized sweater. "Still . . . I wasn't here for Annabelle. I feel so guilty. It's like God decided I wasn't a fit mother, and He moved her to someone better."

"God doesn't do social service placements," Leo told her. "And stop beating yourself up. You're Annie's mother, and you love her. She's a lucky kid to have you. And you're working on your problem, dealing with the PPD. Things will get better for everyone, all around, once she's back."

Once Annie gets back.

As soon as they find her.

They talked about it as if it were a given, mostly because they weren't able to deal with the alternative.

* * *

With Leo at the store buying new baby bottles, Chelsea meandered through the house, feeling like a stranger in her own home.

The sunken spot on the sofa screamed of the hours wasted there when she could have been soothing her baby.

Annie's empty bucket seat taunted her. *How many times did you stash me in here, too tired or grouchy to walk me around when I was crying?*

And the changing table, sanitized and flat as a runway now. No pack of wipes left open, no balled-up diapers left behind. *Can't you sleep three hours without a diaper change?* she used to lament to Annie. *What will it take to make you stop crying?*

The crying had stopped. The silence crushed her.

Through the living room blinds, Chelsea saw that news vans were still parked out on the street. What were they holding on for?

Video of the crying mother? So far, whenever she went out front, she had been careful to keep her face covered with sunglasses and a hooded jacket.

Should she go on camera and plead for the safe return of their daughter? She would do it in a heartbeat if she thought it would help, but the detectives did not advise it. "There's been no ransom," Grace had pointed out. "Infant abductors aren't motivated by money; they want a baby."

Or maybe they thought they'd spin a story out of a break in the case. That might interest viewers, but the detectives weren't feeding them any information. Grace didn't want the kidnapper to know if they were getting closer to her.

She watched a man hoist a heavy camera onto his shoulder, shooting footage of a woman in a parka at the edge of their lawn. Turning away from the blinds, Chelsea imagined the news crews filming everyone who had crossed the line of reporters and entered the house yesterday afternoon. The media would be buzzing once they found out that the person who had kidnapped Annie was one of those visitors.

She imagined them running old footage from yesterday.

Would it be Eleni, so young and tormented?

Or Raquel Jarvis, exotic and strikingly beautiful?

Or Helen Rosekind, aloof but efficient, with all her ducks in a row?

Chelsea was convinced that the person who had stolen her milk had Annabelle, and she thought it was a damned good assumption. Why else would someone take breast milk, right under her nose?

Taking a seat at the rolltop desk, she grabbed a pen and started to jot down her memories of yesterday's late morning. At first she'd been sitting in the kitchen with Sasha, then with Melanie while Emma played with the kids in the living room. But after that, Chelsea has spent most of her time in the living room. That's what a person did when a half dozen guests unexpectedly dropped by.

She circled her sparse notes and doodled tiny stars around the circle. Grace Santos was on her way, and although Chelsea had hoped to have something for her, she simply had not kept an eye on the refrigerator yesterday.

In front of her, the Sounder bills were neatly clipped into three stacks. Before Annie had been taken from them, Chelsea had been starting to get them organized. She didn't have the patience to go through these invoices with the rep today, but now would be a good time to get that preapproval for her visit with Dr. Chin.

It was a positive thing, a step in the right direction, so she called the helpline. With the speakerphone on, she was free to fidget, buffing the fixtures at the kitchen sink, dusting the fireplace mantel and the balustrades of the staircase. Nervous cleaning.

A few minutes later there was a tap on the side door, and Chelsea opened it to Grace.

"Come in." She tossed her dust rag under the sink and wiped her hands on her jeans. "I'm on hold with my insurance company, but I can't hang up. They're so hard to reach and I'm number two in the queue, and—"

"No problem." Grace nodded toward the speakerphone. "We can talk over it."

"I hate that annoying music they play." Chelsea adjusted the volume. "Do they really think anyone likes that?" For the first time she noticed lines radiating from the outer edges of Grace's eyes. Was there bad news? "What's happening?"

"To cut to the chase, we're closing in on Helen Rosekind, your baby nurse. Her credentials are questionable—we're not even sure she's a licensed nurse—and it appears that she's living under a stolen identity."

"But she came from an agency. They said she was a licensed nurse." Chelsea gripped the sides of the kitchen counter behind her as the shock faded and pieces fell into place. "But she's a nurse, and . . . and a lot of infant abductors pose as medical personnel, right?"

"That's true."

"Did you arrest her? Did you find her? Is Annie with her?"

"Chris is on his way over to stake out her place. We're doing some background checks, but it's not happening as fast as I would like. Right now, we don't have enough evidence to get a search warrant."

"But what about Annie?" Chelsea nibbled on a cuticle. "Isn't she the priority?"

"We have to operate within the law."

"I don't care about the law. We have to save my baby!"

"Chelsea, listen to me. Helen Rosekind—or whatever her name is—she's not going anywhere. We're watching her. And if she has Annabelle, we have every reason to believe she's taking very good care of her. Let's do this right, for Annabelle's sake."

"I can't wait anymore." Chelsea pressed her hands to the sides of her face. "Annie needs us, now."

The phone announced that her personal representative was coming on the line.

"Not now . . ." Chelsea crossed the room to disconnect the phone, but Grace waved her off.

"Finish your call." She held up an iPhone. "I have some messages to check."

As Chelsea reached the phone, the rep was on the line.

"This is Janet, your Sounder rep," the voice said brightly. "How can I help you?"

"I just want to know how I can get approval for therapy," Chelsea said. She would keep the phone call short.

"I'm happy to help you with that. Can I have the name and Social of the insured?"

Chelsea plucked an insurance invoice from the rolltop desk and read off all the information Janet needed. She hated this routine of going through every little bit of information with each call, but Janet said it was required.

"You were asking about therapy," the rep said. "Did your doctor recommend it?"

"Yes . . . for postpartum depression."

"I don't see a referral from Dr. Volmer."

"I had a consultation with a specialist—out of plan," Chelsea said. "She wants me to have therapy. I'm suffering from postpartum depression."

"You went out of plan? Then the therapy won't be covered."

"You're kidding me."

"That's Sounder's policy," the rep said. "But you should be okay without the therapy. The depression won't hang on much longer with Annabelle gone."

Janet's voice was a stab through the heart.

Chelsea tossed the invoice onto the stack. "How did you know that?"

"I'm sorry. It's on the national news, of course."

"So . . . wait. You're saying I don't need help because someone kidnapped my child?"

"In a way, you already got the help you needed." The rep's voice was deadly calm. "You were fantasizing about killing your baby, Ms. Maynard. You put her out in the cold in a flimsy yellow nightgown. What kind of a mother does that?"

"I . . . I don't remember doing that. I was drugged."

"You didn't want your baby, Ms. Maynard. Now she's with someone who wants her."

A second later, Grace was by her side, plucking a pen from the cubby in the desk.

The yellow outfit was NOT in any of the news reports. It's not public knowledge.

Chelsea's blood chilled.

Grace was right. The police had decided it was best to keep some of the details private and . . . Chelsea and Leo hadn't shared them with anyone.

OMG! Chelsea wrote: *How could she know that?*

Keep talking, Grace wrote, obviously baffled. *Tell her you want the baby back.*

"I know I was a wreck," Chelsea said. "I said some terrible things, but I'm starting to feel better and I need my baby. I want her back."

"Have you considered that maybe she's better off without you?" Janet asked.

"I made mistakes," Chelsea admitted as Grace wrote: *Who is she?*

Quickly, Chelsea put her pen to the notepad below Grace's scrawl.

Janet Walker, Sounder Health Care.

She studied Grace's face for a clue as to what was going on. How could this woman on the other end of the phone be connected to her baby?

How did Janet Walker know these things?

But all the information the woman needed was laid out on her computer monitor: Annabelle's address. Chelsea's medical history. A line-by-line version of their lives.

Janet Walker had used that information and now . . .

She knew about the yellow nightgown.

Janet Walker knew about her Annabelle, damn her.

Chelsea longed to grab her by the neck and start shaking the truth out of her. But for now, she would stay connected, keep her talking. Anything to get closer to Annabelle.

Chapter 44

When Chelsea first took the call, Grace had been distracted by the message on her own phone. Jimmy had sent her confirmation that Helen Janet Walker did not have a valid license to drive or work as a nurse in the state of Arizona. Not giving up there, Jimmy had thrown the net wider, but so far no hits on that search.

Her instincts shouted that the baby nurse had Annabelle Green; she hoped a judge would agree with her and sign a search warrant.

She had forwarded Jimmy's e-mail to Chris and their boss, Bruce Hopkins, who would move on the warrant. Grace was just about to thank Jimmy when she noticed Chelsea growing tense with her phone conversation.

The insurance rep was a bit of a psycho; her demeanor was invasive, to say the least. But something about her stopped Grace in her tracks.

Then she made the crack about PPD . . . and the yellow nightgown.

When Chelsea told her the rep was named Janet Walker, Grace was stunned.

Helen Janet Walker.

Of course! The woman needed a way to access information about pregnant women—delivery dates, health status, addresses—and working as a representative for a health insurance company gave her total access to that information.

Keep her on the phone, Grace wrote on the pad. *KEEP TALKING!!!*

She dashed out the door and ran to her car, ignoring the curious reporters who shouted out to her.

"Detective! What's going on?"

"Do you have a break in the case? Have you found Annabelle Green?"

As she steered toward the Rosekind place, she got Chris on the line. "The baby nurse is the one . . . she has to be. I hope Annabelle is with her. Are you there yet?"

"Been here for about ten minutes."

"I'm on my way. Rosekind must have the baby, or else she knows where Annie is," she said. "She was probably sleeping when we went there last night."

"I'll make sure no one leaves the building, and I'll call a boss."

"I already sent Jimmy's evidence to Sgt. Hopkins. I hope he can get us a search warrant."

"You want some uniforms?" he asked.

"Definitely. We could use extra hands and eyes."

Grace turned on the dashboard light and floored it on the Hutch, her heart racing as she sifted through details.

Yes . . . she had seen the office setup, the headset and boxes, and Helen had said she worked for an insurance company. That had to be how she found Chelsea and Leo—and any other pregnant couples she might have considered stealing from. Right now she was working on Chelsea and Leo's claims.

She had sneered at Chelsea, reminding her of the dark fantasies of postpartum depression. Of course, she knew Chelsea's medical history, and she'd been using it against her.

Had Helen/Janet dropped off the tainted muffins? But how could she have known that Leo would be out of town?

Still, there were so many unanswered questions.

What if the baby was inside with "Janet Walker"? Grace worried about a potential hostage situation. Could the baby have been there last night? Tucked into the bedroom? Maybe that was the reason that Helen wouldn't allow them to step inside.

At the moment, Annabelle was their first priority. They had to focus on safe entry and safe recovery of Annabelle Green. If Chelsea was able to keep Janet on the line, police staff would be able to surround the house and eventually coax the baby from her abductors.

When Grace pulled up, Chris was standing outside his car, looking up at the house with two uniformed officers. She was relieved to see that one of them was Mike Balfour. With a sergeant on the scene, they could make a move.

She scrambled out of the car and joined them. "Sarge. You got here fast."

"This missing baby has been on my mind all week. Since that neighbor was a dead end, I've been listening for this dispatch," Mike said. "You think the kid is inside?"

"I do." She gave him a quick update on the case.

"Okay." The sergeant glanced up at the house. "Second-story apartment, and you spoke with the woman yesterday, right?"

"Last night," Chris said. "And we evacuated the first-floor tenants before you got here—just in case."

"Good." Balfour scratched the center of his forehead with a thumb, as if preparing for the sign of the cross. It reminded Grace to send up a prayer of her own.

"Let's get someone on the back, just so no one squirts out a window or back door," the sergeant said. "As soon as we get the warrant, we'll go and announce ourselves and see if she comes out to talk with us. If we can get in to search, I see no trouble with her handing over the baby. In cases like these, abductors are not usually violent."

Grace opened her jacket to adjust her gun belt. "Not usually, but anything is possible."

"Right. Never let your guard down. We stay strategically safe," Balfour said as another unit pulled up.

Within ten minutes there was a call saying the judge had

signed the search warrant. Grace put her hand on her gun. She prayed that this was the end of their search for Annabelle.

Two cops were sent to cover the backyard, while Grace and Chris climbed the stairs, Balfour and Viloria behind them.

As she took her position on the side of the door, Grace listened for any sound of the baby, but it was too quiet. No fussing or crying. Damn.

"Mrs. Rosekind?" Chris knocked, then pressed the doorbell. "Helen Rosekind? It's the police. Please open the door and come talk with us."

Grace could hear footsteps behind the door. "Come back later. I'm busy with work."

"Helen," Grace said, "we need to talk with you, and we're not going away. We have a warrant to search your apartment."

The lock clicked, and the door swung in. Helen stood just inside the door, her eyes wary.

We're halfway there, Grace thought. Worries about a hostage standoff began to fade. A typical infant abductor didn't like confrontations, and she didn't want to hurt the baby.

Helen's solid, steady demeanor had fled and in its place was a flicker of fear. "I'll talk with you, but you can't come in. I have confidential insurance records inside, and it's my job to keep them secure."

"Don't worry about your paperwork, ma'am." Sgt. Balfour's tone was reassuring. "We're trying to locate a missing infant. What can you tell us about Annabelle Green?"

Helen folded her arms across her chest. "She's a very sweet baby. I can tell you that her mother wasn't able to take care of her," she said with a hint of her former confidence.

"Is that right?" Balfour moved closer, his hand pressing on the door. "How well did you know Chelsea Maynard?"

"She and her husband hired me as a nurse to care for their baby." Helen suddenly realized that the sergeant was pressing into the apartment. In a sudden panic, she pushed the door. "No, you can't come in here. I need to secure my files."

Balfour's hand stopped the door from closing, and he gave it a hard shove, knocking the woman off balance.

"No! I told you, this is not a good time," Helen insisted.

"This is the only time," Grace said as she and Chris moved into the apartment.

"They can't do that!" Helen complained to the sergeant.

Grace ignored the woman's objections, knowing Balfour and Viloria would do their best to restrain her.

She moved through the rooms in a flash.

The office set up in a corner of the living room was just as she'd remembered it, with a computer and a file cabinet and stacks of boxes.

In the kitchen, the kettle was just beginning to boil. Grace ignored it, disappointed that there was no infant seat, no outward sign of Annabelle in the tidy room.

The bedroom was the jackpot.

The breath caught in Grace's throat when she spotted a crib beside the double bed.

"That's it." She rushed forward to reach down into the ravine between the bars, but the crib was empty.

A changing pad was spread out on the floor. A box of wipes was open. The Diaper Genie sat at the ready. All signs indicated that a baby had been here recently.

"Where's the baby?" Chris asked.

"Good question." When Grace swung around, the little alcove in the corner caught her eye. The small nook was just big enough for a dressing table. But the wall above it was the showpiece—certainly Helen's pride and joy. It had been behind Grace when she entered the room, but now the photographs of newborn babies, each blown up to fill a full page, drew her close.

"Look at these babies." There were six of them, newborn infants with sleepy eyes and pinched faces. Each photograph had a handmade caption taped beside it.

"Conner, Bayside, Queens," Chris read. "Hayley from Long Island. Joseph and . . ." He pointed to a photo on the right. "Here she is: Annabelle, New Rochelle."

All these photos . . . Grace's mind swam with the possibilities.

"They're all from this area. We'd know if these kids were missing."

"So maybe they're safe at home with their parents," Chris said. "But they were all candidates to be abducted."

"And Annabelle just happened to be the unlucky one. I'll bet a little digging will show that Helen has worked with these families—either as a baby nurse or as an insurance rep. I don't know how she got the photos, but this woman has had a plan for a long time." She turned away from the shrine to babies and opened the closet door. "The question is, where is Annabelle?"

"I've got a feeling Rosekind can tell us," Chris said.

They faced her in the hall.

"Tell us where the baby is," Chris demanded.

"We know you abducted Annabelle Green." Grace didn't filter disdain from her voice. "Where is she?"

"I don't know anything about Annabelle Green." Helen's arms were crossed, her eyes dark beads of annoyance. "But if you don't get out of my home right now, I'm going to sue you all."

"Remember what I said, Helen?" Mike's gentle tone held a hint of warning. "We have a warrant."

"You have a crib that's been used recently. We found a half-used bottle of prescription sedatives in the medicine cabinet. Did you mix the other half into those muffins you left for Chelsea Maynard?"

"I don't know what you're talking about."

"How about these baby bottles, Mrs. Rosekind?" Angie Viloria appeared in the kitchen door. "There are half a dozen baby bottles in the fridge that match the ones stolen from Annabelle Green's home."

Something dark slid into Helen's eyes. A wicked slice of delusion. "Those are for my baby." She looked from Angie to Grace, eliciting sympathy. "You know how it is. Sometimes I have to pump breast milk for Lily."

"Your baby . . ." Grace stared at the woman, wondering

how they'd gotten to Crazy Town. "Helen." If that's your name. "You need to tell us where the baby is. Now."

The malice flew from her eyes, and suddenly Helen seemed pathetic once again. "I don't know what you're talking about."

"Let's take a ride to the precinct," Sgt. Balfour said. "Some-times, in a different environment, things seem clearer."

Viloria snapped handcuffs on Helen Rosekind, and Chris and Grace taped off the apartment, setting up a crime scene. The forensic unit would sweep through here this morning; it would take a little longer for the IT unit to start sorting through files and data on Helen's computer.

Grace watched from the bedroom window as Viloria and Balfour put Helen Rosekind into the backseat of their patrol car.

"Where did she leave the baby?" Grace asked as Chris searched through dresser drawers. "I wouldn't be so worried if I didn't see a glimmer of crazy in her eyes. Along with her weird answers."

"I know what you mean. Lights on upstairs but nobody home."

Grace called Chelsea Maynard; the woman had been left hanging, and though she didn't have the best news, they were getting closer.

"Helen Rosekind was more than your nurse," she told Chelsea. "She works for Sounder Health Care. She's also Janet Walker."

"Helen is Janet? That's . . . that's crazy."

"We're at her place now, taking her in for further question-ing." Grace bounded down the stairs, leaving the rest of the apartment for the more thorough forensic team. "We found your breast milk, as well as photos of Annabelle and other in-fants from the metro area. It looks like a baby has been here recently, but Annabelle is not here now."

"And she won't tell you where Annie is?"

"She says she doesn't know." As Grace descended the porch, she scanned the crowd gathering around the police cars pulled up at odd angles in front of the house. Moms were there with their kids. A few neighborhood walkers. A handful of older folks. So far, mostly neighbors.

A man wheeling a stroller cut through the crowd, a strong sense of urgency in his movements. He maneuvered around an elderly couple and came over to the cops.

"Hold on," Grace told Chelsea.

"Hey, what's going on?" The man was tall—probably six feet—with a gut that hadn't seen much exercise. He pointed up to the house. "That's my apartment. My fiancée is in there."

One look at the baby in the carriage, and Grace knew.

Chris's brows shot up. "Is it? Is it her?"

Grace nodded. "It is." She had memorized those steely blue eyes, that double chin . . . even the shape of her head under her pink hat.

She lifted the phone. "Chelsea? We've found her. Annabelle is here and she's safe."

"Oh, dear God. Leo . . . Leo, they found her!" Chelsea's gasp for air dissolved into rapid-fire questions. "She's okay? You're sure? Where are you? Is she awake? Where did you find her?"

"She's safe now." Grace gave her the address and reminded her to drive safely. "She needs her parents to be in one piece."

She put her phone away, bent down beside the stroller, and drank in the sight of Annabelle Green. The baby's cheeks were bright with color, probably from the cold, but her stern eyes were alert and observant as Grace smiled.

"Look at you, calm as could be. We've been looking all over for you."

Annabelle's mouth curved, imitating Grace's smile. She seemed to be well cared for, clean and warm. She wore a cute pink beanie on her head and a little quilted jacket zipped up to her double chin.

"So you're Ralph Rosekind?" Chris asked.

"What? No. Ralph Amicci. We're not married, but we're getting married soon."

Getting married soon. Grace wondered if Helen has used the baby as a means of getting Ralph Amicci to marry her.

"And what's the name of the woman you're marrying?" Chris asked.

"Janet Rosekind."

"Figures." Chris shook his head. "Yet another new name combination. She just can't keep it simple."

"Why are all the cop cars here?" The man's irritation was mounting. "What's this about?"

"We're police detectives," Chris said. "And your girlfriend is under arrest for the abduction of the baby you've been pushing in the stroller—Annabelle Green."

"Come on, Annabelle." Grace unbuckled the strap and lifted the baby out.

"Her name is Lily, and what the hell are you doing?" Amicci demanded.

"I'm recovering a child that was kidnapped earlier this week." Grace rested the baby on her shoulder and moved away from the irate man.

"What the hell? She's our baby. My girlfriend gave birth last month."

"Yeah?" Chris asked. "Were you there for the birth?"

"I was out west, on my route. I drive a truck."

"Let me tell you something about babies, Mr. Amicci." Grace rubbed Annabelle's back, instinctively resting the baby on her hip. "This child is nearly three months old. See how she's holding her head up on her own? And even her size. Most newborns are only eight or nine pounds. This baby is not a newborn."

"I'm telling you what I know, and I know that you've got my daughter, Lily, in your arms, detective. What you're doing is wrong. You can't just come in and take a man's daughter away."

"She's not your daughter," Chris said flatly, "and if you don't calm down, we're going to have to take you in cuffs, too."

"I don't care if you arrest me. I'm coming down to the station to file a complaint. Where's Janet? She'll straighten everything out."

"She's in the back of the patrol car." Chris went over and opened the rear door. "But I don't think she's going to give you the answers you want."

"Janet!" Amicci bent over, one hand on the roof of the cruiser. "What the hell? These cops say Lily isn't ours."

Janet—formerly Helen—blinked into the pale winter sunlight, then switched to indignant mode. "This is all a mistake. She's mine."

"Don't fall for that," Chris told Ralph. "Your girlfriend picked this baby from a group of infants she's worked with. Haven't you seen the baby shrine on the bedroom wall? Annabelle's photo is up there."

"Those are kids that Janet has helped. She makes sure their families get the insurance coverage they need."

"Ya think?" Grace wondered if the big guy could really be so naïve.

"They're marks," Chris said. "I'd say your fiancée has been watching these kids since they were born, trying to figure out which would be the best infant to swoop in on and steal."

Ralph Amicci shot a look at his fiancée. "Tell him, Janet. Tell him the truth."

"The truth is that Chelsea Maynard is a raving lunatic. An incompetent mother. When I heard she was thinking of killing her baby, I knew what I had to do. Annabelle is better off with us."

"What's with everyone calling her Annabelle?" Amicci sputtered. "You said you named her Lily."

"Your girlfriend has a thing about changing names," Chris said.

Ralph went to the curb and bent down to get in her line of vision. "You were pregnant all those months. If this baby belongs to someone else, what happened to our baby?"

"Of course Lily is ours." And there was that scary shift again, madness slipping into her eyes. "Don't worry, Ralph.

This will all be straightened out. When the truth comes out, everyone will know that I did the right thing for my baby."

"For *our* baby, right?" There was such earnestness in Ralph's tone, Grace felt bad about the heartache in store for him.

The baby gave a little squeak in her ear, and Grace felt her squirm. Growing restless. She patted the back of Annabelle's little quilted jacket and paced with her, moving out of earshot of the suspect.

All for the best.

Helen-Janet-what's-her-name would be off the streets, and this little bundle of joy would be safe and sound, back with her parents.

Thank you, God.

Grace looked down at the little girl in her arms, seeing Chelsea's eyes and Leo around the mouth. "This has been a good day," she told her. "A very good day."

Chapter 45

Chelsea spotted them as soon as she bolted out of the car. They sat in the open bay of an ambulance, Grace holding Annabelle in her lap while the paramedics checked her out.

"There she is." Chelsea grabbed Leo's arm as her eyes misted over.

Their baby.

"Hey, Annie-bananee," Leo called when they were a few yards away, and just like that Annie turned her head toward his voice. Her blue eyes took them in. She really saw them. She recognized them.

And she smiled.

Chelsea pressed her lips together to keep from crying as she approached slowly, not wanting to scare Annie after a few days away, days of possible trauma.

But Leo—earnest, gregarious Leo launched into a joke and messed up her hair and held her in the air with a rant that made Annie laugh. He chattered on, telling Annie the whole story as he took Grace's place on the back of the ambulance. He snuggled her against him, face out, as she always insisted.

"Yeah, I remember," he said. "You always need to see the world. I know that about you, Annabee."

Chelsea sat beside them, drinking in the details of her daughter's features.

A mother's inventory.

Her steely eyes were bright and alert. Her downy hair swirled over her pale, delicate skull. Chelsea took in her rosebud lips, her shiny nose, and those irresistible double chins that reminded Chelsea of an old grandfather.

She lifted Annabelle's hand to kiss it, and noticed the perfection of her tiny fingernails, the delicate curve of her fingers, the whorls of her fingertips and lines of her palm that made Annabelle unlike anyone else on the planet.

It was as if she were seeing Annabelle for the first time. She had been cheated out of a glorious first look when Annie had been born. The hours of surgery and the weeks of recovery had removed her from her newborn daughter.

But not anymore. She could see Annie clearly, and she was coming to this as a whole person now. Time and medication and sleep had accelerated her healing, and she was hopeful that therapy would help her deal with it for the long haul. The dark side was still there, lingering at the edges, but it was a different world when you could keep depression on the other side of the fence.

She turned Annie's hand around and planted a kiss in her palm. "Hold on to that," she said quietly, and she and Leo both smiled when Annie squeezed her hand into a fist.

Chelsea let her head rest on his shoulder as her hand outlined Annabelle's chubby shoulder. She would relearn every inch of her daughter with a thousand baths and diaper changes. It would no longer be baby jail, because she knew the way out. She would have her occasional nights out and even her work again. This time she would get help and figure out how to maintain some balance.

"How does our little girl check out, Doc?" Leo asked the paramedic who had given them some space.

"I'm not a doctor, but her heart and lungs sound good. You might want to bring her in to get checked out by her regular pediatrician, but this little girl doesn't need to go to the hospital."

"Good," Leo said. "Because we want to take you home." He stood up. "Let me just tell the detectives that we're going."

As he handed Annabelle over, Chelsea's breath caught in her

throat at the wonder of it all. Her arms knew how to wrap her baby securely; her lips traced the smooth shell of Annie's ear. "Are you a miracle in my arms?" she whispered to her sweet-smelling baby.

Annie did not respond, but Chelsea knew the answer. She had known all along.

Epilogue

Annabelle's baptism day was on a Sunday in May, one of those breaks in the weather that leaned heavily toward summer and drove everyone to dig out their shorts and flip-flops and hope that fair weather was here to stay.

Soon after they got home from church, Chelsea changed her little girl out of the fancy white dress that all of Melanie's babies had worn. These days Annabelle was a busy little baby with a social life that included rolling around, and creeping to explore new horizons.

"Was that white dress too confining for you?" Chelsea asked Annie as she pulled stretchy pants on over her big diaper butt. "Don't be a slave to fashion anymore. Now you can go out and dig in the garden, right?" She picked Annie up to take her downstairs, and held her at her shoulder for a minute, charmed by the way Annie tangled her fingers in her hair. At seven months, Annabelle didn't have total command of her hands, but she had recently begun raking them through Chelsea's hair, a gesture that melted her heart.

In the backyard, everyone seemed relieved to be outside in the sunshine. The fence was lined by the white blossoms of pear trees on Louise's side, and red, yellow, and orange tulips on this side. Leo and Chelsea had planted the bulbs while in nesting mode last fall, and Annie liked the vivid blooms so much she always headed that way when she was in the yard.

Leo, Jake, and Mel's husband, Andrew, were manning the grill, but Leo couldn't resist sneaking away for a minute to come tickle Annie and make her laugh.

He had a gift for that—the laughter and song. Sometimes Annie cooed along with his crazy songs. It was the cutest thing, hearing them sing together.

"There's the guest of honor," Emma called from the picnic table, where she sat sipping ice water under a picture hat.

"Love the hat." Chelsea sat beside her sister, letting her squirming daughter put her feet on the ground. "It's very Greta Garbo."

"It's old-fashioned sunscreen," Emma said. "I'm trying to avoid the chemicals, just to be safe."

"You're so good." Chelsea leaned toward her sister with a smile. "I was just thinking what a relief it is that Jake turned down that job in Chicago. We would have missed you guys so much."

"Really. You can only do so much Skyping."

Chelsea propped Annie up in her lap and discovered the clod of grass in her fist. "Are you helping Mommy weed again?" she teased, plucking the clump from her fingers. "This one's a natural gardener, like Mom. I think we have some trips to the Botanical Garden in our future."

"The foliage in autumn . . . and the lights at Christmastime!" Emma pressed a hand to her mouth. "We can go, the four of us. Sometimes I still can't believe I'm going to be a mom soon. I've read all the books and taken classes, but I know I'll still make mistakes."

"We all do," Chelsea said. "Remember how I had to have that designer changing table, and how I had everything set up just so before Annie was born? Take it from me, perfection does not go hand in hand with parenting. But you find your new normal. And you probably won't be taking a trip to the dark side the way I did."

Emma sighed. "I sure hope not. But if it happens, at least now we know what to do."

"And I can hook you up with an awesome therapist," Chelsea teased.

Just then Nora came running over. Sam trailed behind her toting his large dinosaur. "Aunt Chelsea, can I follow Annabelle around?"

"Sure. I think she's raring to go." Chelsea set her daughter down and watched as her niece followed alongside her. "Don't let her take you over to the tulips. She likes to smash the flowers."

"Oh, Annie." Nora bent over to face Annie. "Have you been smashing the flowers?"

"Mash da fwawahs," Sam said with an amused grin.

Chelsea smiled back at him. Whenever she was around Melanie's kids, she wanted to have more. "Pretty funny, huh?"

"No mashing da fwawahs!" he announced as he followed the girls across the lawn.

"Guys, here's the watermelon, all cut up." Melanie came through the gate carrying a big bowl. "Come and get it before the gnats do."

As neighbors and friends began to arrive, Chelsea went inside to feed Annie. She was settling into the couch when Grace Santos arrived with an adorable teenage boy.

"This is my son, Matthew," Grace said.

Chelsea was impressed by the dark-eyed boy who shook her hand. "The guys are playing Nerf football out back," she told him. "And there's plenty of food and a cooler full of drinks."

"Okay. Mom, can I have soda?"

"You can have one. I'll be out in a few minutes," Grace said as he headed out the side door.

"What a nice boy."

"He's a good kid. Though when I look back to when he was a baby, I think it's a miracle that he and I are both still here. I suffered through some terrible visions, thinking of ways to end my pain. Back then, postpartum depression wasn't on everyone's radar. Some people still didn't believe it was real. A lot of doctors weren't aware of it."

"Some doctors still aren't aware of it. My doctor kept saying I just had the baby blues." Chelsea shivered at the memory
of those days. As if Annie could feel her discomfort, she
squirmed in her arms. "I know, pumpkin. Bad memories all
around." She shifted the baby to the other breast.

"Annie seems to be thriving now," Grace said.

"She's doing well. We all are. After what we went through
with Annie, Leo and I have gotten better at not sweating the
details. I'm taking it one day at a time, getting help when I
need it. And Leo—he was carrying this family for a long time.
He's glad to have me back in the land of the living. Sometimes
I worry about the depression returning if we have another
baby, and I really want Annie to have a sibling."

"I think worry is every parent's middle name." Grace leaned
back against the couch, looking more relaxed than Chelsea
had ever seen her. "We worry about them when they're little.
We worry when they can leave the house on their own. I don't
know if the worry ever ends."

"You're such a Yoda." When Grace laughed, Chelsea added,
"Really, you're so wise, Grace. You had faith in me when I didn't
believe in myself. I have to thank you for that. I think those
first cops on the scene wanted to arrest me when Annabelle
disappeared, and I was such a basket case, I probably would
have incriminated myself, babbling on. But you knew what
was going on. You knew I was in distress."

"I just read people well." Grace shrugged. "It's my job."

"Speaking of that, what's the latest in the case?"

"They're still in the exploratory phase, taking depositions,
but the psychologist has been making some headway with
Walker."

Helen Janet Walker had been charged with kidnapping in
the second degree, a crime with a sentence of up to twenty-five
years in jail.

"Did you figure out which job came first—the baby nurse
gig or the insurance rep?"

"It was Sounder Health Care. She worked for the company
for five years, and during that time, she had a baby with her

former husband, Kevin Walker. Janet was an examiner, approving insurance claims, when her baby died in his crib—SIDS, apparently. The psychologist learned that it became difficult for her to process claims for families with newborns. But after a while, she turned it around, thinking that, with all these people having babies, she was bound to find some couple who didn't want theirs. When the opening came up for the New York area hotline rep, she jumped on it, knowing it would narrow her cases down to a specific area."

"So calculating."

"That's the thing. She saw herself as a savior. She was only going to save a baby who wasn't wanted."

Chelsea looked down into Annie's sleepy gaze. *But you were wanted. You are wanted and loved.*

"When the plan didn't seem to be coming together fast enough, she thought of the baby nurse thing. She got the idea when she saw Helen Rosekind's obituary in the news. Somehow she convinced the agency she was legit, and then she sent flyers to the families she had marked through Sounder Health Care."

"Conniving and surprisingly smart," Chelsea said. "She was probably a great employee for Sounder."

"Yeah, they loved her . . . until this broke. Now the company is trying to build safeguards into the system so that no employee has total access to customer accounts."

"Did you know the president of the company called us to apologize?" Chelsea had felt uncomfortable talking with him. "I told him that I just wanted my claims processed. After that they turned things around in forty-eight hours."

"It shows you; it can be done."

"What about the boyfriend?" Chelsea vaguely remembered a large, gangly man arguing with the police the day they'd found Annie. A truck driver, she'd heard.

"We dropped all charges against Ralph Amicci. It seems that Walker had him duped, too. That probably sounds crazy, but it happens sometimes in these cases, and it was easier for Walker to pull the wool over his eyes since he was away for extended periods of time, hauling loads cross-country. For nine months, he really believed she was pregnant, and once she had the baby, he was proud of her, thinking she was so brave to have that baby while he was gone and not complain one bit."

Chelsea shook her head. "It's scary to think of the Janet Walkers walking around on this planet."

"The good news is, they're in the minority," Grace said.

She shifted the sleeping baby to her lap. "Well, I'm sorry that Janet Walker lost a child, but that woman is loony tunes to think she can replace him with someone else's baby."

"Your deposition was important to the case—yours and Leo's. The DA will probably have you testify if it goes to court."

"That would probably be good for me," Chelsea said. "If nothing else, it might help more people understand what postpartum depression is really about."

"Thank you." Grace rose. "You and Leo, you guys are good people."

Chelsea smiled. "Back at you. But I don't think your partner liked me so much."

"Yeah, well, he just doesn't understand women. You coming out?"

"In a minute. Go, grab some food. Leo is very proud of his flank steak." She watched Grace head out, then buttoned up her blouse, thinking how lucky they'd been to have Grace Santos working on Annie's case.

Getting up from the couch with Annie in her arms required some abdominal strength now. "You're getting big, sweetie." She placed Annie in her bucket seat, strapped her in, and carried her over to the kitchen windowsill. From here, she had a clear view of the backyard.

Leo and Jake were doing another round on the grill. The kidnapping had bonded the two men who'd once just tolerated each other at family gatherings. Raquel Jarvis, now a good friend to Chelsea and Emma, had arrived with her family: her husband, a philosophical high school teacher; two exotic, dark-eyed boys who resembled their distant father; and three towheaded little ones who adored their older siblings.

Louise Pickler lingered near the gate with her dogs—three of them now. The two new corgis were her pride and joy; "They're the same dogs the Queen of England has." Louise had Mr. Kellog's ear, probably telling him how she was applying to be on the *Hoarders* TV show.

Tina and James Wilkinson sat on the swing, obviously entertained by the younger ones, who were acting out some prehistoric battle scenario with Sam's dinosaur action figures and Max's Nerf gun. Matt Santos was playing monkey in the middle with some of the older kids. Grace sat down between Emma and Melanie, and the three of them laughed, their joy ringing through the neighborhood like a bright bell.

In a minute, Chelsea would carry her napping baby out to join them.

For now, she stroked the back of Annie's hand, observing the baked beans dribbled on the counter, the mud tracks across the kitchen floor. The half-sliced onion left on the cutting board with a ghastly sharp knife. The dirty roasting pan and tongs in the kitchen sink.

What a mess.

But it was her family's mess, haphazard and far from perfect. Things like that, human things, they were what made a house a home. A work in progress. A home for Leo and Chelsea and Annabelle Green.

**Please turn the page
for a special Q&A
with Rosalind Noonan.**

A Conversation with Rosalind Noonan

It's been said that the plot of All She Ever Wanted *was "ripped from the headlines." Did a particular kidnapping spark the idea for the novel?*

The novel wasn't modeled after any particular case. For me, the story began with a woman suffering from postpartum depression. I thought about the stress in her life, the lack of energy, the guilt over not appreciating the baby that she'd wanted for so many years. This book was well under way—nearly completed—when Lisa Irwin was abducted in October 2011. Although my story is fiction, I admit that its resemblance to this real infant abduction is eerie. I was about to turn the manuscript in to my editor in April 2012 when Kala Marie Golden was killed, her child stolen from her in a clinic parking lot. Writing about infant abduction has made me more aware of cases reported in the news. Although it is not a widespread crime, I think the randomness of many of these abductions is frightening for mothers everywhere.

The details of Chelsea's suffering come through poignantly. What's your experience with postpartum depression?

When my first child was born, I remember holding her and crying and wondering why I wasn't happier when I looked into her beautiful blue eyes. After carrying this baby for nine months, I felt like I didn't know her. I was holding a stranger. And alienation was not something I expected to feel toward my newborn. I think I was experiencing the "baby blues," a short-term reaction to childbirth. The bad feelings faded after the first week, and I nearly forgot about the episode. Looking back, I think my reaction was a fraction of the suffering that some new mothers go through when they suffer from PPD.

A few years later, when another mom at nursery school drop-off started talking about her serious battle with postpartum depression, I thought she was exaggerating. In her deep depression she had dropped her baby onto the hardwood floor. "She just slipped out of my arms," Evelyn told us. An ambulance was called and her husband confronted her with an angry question: "What's wrong with you?" When the doctors told Evelyn and her husband that it was PPD, they were both skeptical. The whole notion of a mother not mothering her child seemed to defy nature. Some of the other moms thought it was a made-up disease. They chalked it up to Evelyn's flare for the dramatic. I wasn't sure what to think, but I was glad that Evelyn had gotten help.

Not long after Evelyn's episode, Marie Osmond went public with her struggle with postpartum depression. Women I spoke with were shocked that a celebrity like Marie Osmond, with personal wealth, fame, and resources, was so depressed that she sat on the floor of her closet and cried. Ms. Osmond is very generous with the details of her experience in *Behind the Smile: My Journey out of Postpartum Depression*. Reading it, I really felt her pain as well as her indomitable spunk. She was determined to find her way back to happiness. A few years later, in 2005, Brooke Shields shared her experience with crippling depression in *Down Came the Rain*. Her smart analysis of the way happiness slipped away and the fight to get it back shows the many facets of depression.

I am grateful that these high-profile women shared their difficult experiences. Despite the research and statistics on the very real, very treatable, very common problem of PPD, too many people dismiss it as either a myth or a temporary setback of motherhood. But when Marie and Brooke spoke up, people listened. And women got it. They recognized their own pain and were finally able to give it a name. Validation, understanding, sound advice. I think the turn of the century also proved to be a turning point for postpartum depression.

For your research, did you interview women who suffered from postpartum depression?

It seemed invasive to target people that way, especially when there were so many cases that had been published. However, whenever I talked about what I was working on, various friends and acquaintances came forward to share their experiences.

One friend admitted that she fired her full-time nanny because she didn't want to pay someone else to raise her child. Within a week she was struggling to get out of bed, missing her executive position in the city where people waited on her for decisions. The monotony and isolation of taking care of an infant hammered away at her psyche.

One mom at a lacrosse game recalled being caught in a deep depression when her baby was born. Listening to her, I recalled the image of her sitting with her baby on a bench at school years earlier, her face red, her eyes unfocused, as a woman beside her spoke encouragingly. I didn't know her back then, but I remember thinking what a stern mother she was. That critic inside me was brutal. Now I'm so ashamed to have passed judgment without having a clue about what had been going on.

My friend Beth spoke up recently while we were having lunch and I mentioned that the protagonist of my new book suffered from postpartum depression.

"What's that?" someone asked.

"It's when you stand on a bridge with your baby in your arms and watch her slip away and fall," Beth said, "and you see her hitting every pillar and rock on the way down."

That got everyone's attention. Without drama or reservation, Beth articulated the dark fantasies that had overcome her when she'd been a new mother.

She's been through so much, I thought, *but now she's owning it.* Beth worked through her PPD long ago, but the passage of time has not softened the memory. I admire her candor and strength.

The big thing with PPD is to get help, to reach out to family, friends, or your doctor. I hope that any woman who sees herself in Chelsea's suffering will know that help is nearby.

Your last few books have included characters in law enforcement, and the detectives from the Missing Persons Squad, Grace Santos and Chris Panteleoni, play significant roles in the second half of All She Ever Wanted. *Do you have an affinity for this profession?*

You caught me. My husband has worked in law enforcement for more than twenty years, much of it with the New York City Police Department, and it seems very natural to write about that world having an in-house expert. My characters are influenced by the place they live. *In a Heartbeat*'s Detective Greg Cody came from the NYPD but was adjusting to a different tempo of policing in Upstate New York. The NYPD is woven through the Sullivan family in *The Daughter She Used to Be*. And Sheriff Cooper Locklear grew up in North Carolina's Outer Banks, served in the military, and returned to keep the peace at home in "Carolina Summer" (in the *Beach Season* anthology). Currently, I have no plans for a law enforcement character in my next book, which is in the planning stages, but you never know who might sneak in.

You take a shot at the health insurance industry in this book. Is Chelsea's annoyance based on personal experience?

Absolutely. I consider myself to be fairly astute at keeping records and tracking things, but there are not enough hours in the day to chase the insurance claims that go awry for ridiculous reasons. Although I suppose I should consider myself to be fortunate to have health insurance coverage, it's very frustrating when 90 percent of most procedures aren't covered—and this after I chase paperwork or wait on the "helpline" for a rep who refuses to speak with me because I am not the policy holder. Recently, I was denied reimbursement for services, with the insurer stating that our policy did not exist. Really?

After all these years? It was like learning about a breakup from a greeting card. Fortunately, the representative I spoke with on that occasion was kind and helpful. But the situation is a worry for families everywhere. At times like that, I look to the sky and ponder moving to France. Imagine excellent health care for a minimal price. Wouldn't that be nice?

ALL SHE EVER WANTED

Rosalind Noonan

ABOUT THIS GUIDE

The suggested questions are included
to enhance your group's reading
of Rosalind Noonan's
All She Ever Wanted.

DISCUSSION QUESTIONS

1. Why do you think the novel begins with episodes from Chelsea's childhood? What insight do these "lifesaving" events add to her background?

2. Chelsea feels like a failure as a mother. "How did other mothers do it? She wanted to ask them, to shout a question out to the new mothers of the world, a plea for them to share their answers, reveal their secrets." What qualities does our society value in a mother? Does the image of a good mother match the reality?

3. Jennifer Green's determination to get back into her ex-husband's life is a force to be reckoned with. Have you ever known a person with Jennifer's single-minded resolve?

4. Chelsea still regrets not being present for her mother's last hours in the hospital. She "was convinced that a person on the threshold to the next world could still sense the presence of loved ones around them." In a sense, Chelsea is also lingering on a threshold to another world. Who is it that gets through to her and convinces her that she needs help?

5. Have you ever made a mistake because you were suffering from depression or exhaustion? Missed a turn on the road or put the car keys in the refrigerator? Share your story.

6. In what ways does Chelsea's memory of her mother influence her relationship with Annabelle?

7. How does Leo relate to his daughter? His sister-in-law Emma? How does his relationship with Jake Wyatt change by the end of the book?

8. Should Leo have gone to Boston for the convention? What were his alternatives?

9. In what ways do Grace Santos's personal philosophies influence the police investigation? Do you think things would have been handled differently if the lead investigator had been a man? Do you think Grace is too easy on Chelsea?

10. Why did the author choose to make Chelsea an editor for a home fix-it magazine? How does this color her view of the world?

11. Is Louise Pickler a tragic figure, a comic character, or both? What are some of her unusual habits?

12. How does the abduction of Annabelle Green affect the neighborhood?

13. How would you describe Grace Santos's approach toward people? Do you think her demeanor is productive to an investigation, or does it slow things down?

14. Chelsea and Emma recall a nursery rhyme about an elephant family, a beloved poem from their childhood. Do you have any traditions, songs, or rhymes that have been passed down through your family?